COLOR ME
CRAZY

COLOR ME
CRAZY

Carol Pavliska

Entangled Publishing, LLC
2614 South Timberline Road
Suite 109
Fort Collins, CO 80525
Visit our website at www.entangledpublishing.com.

Select Contemporary is an imprint of Entangled Publishing, LLC.

Edited by Karen Grove and Jessica Snyder
Cover design by Letitia Hasser
Cover art from Fotolia

Manufactured in the United States of America

First Edition May 2015

To my sister, Janet, the queen of romance novels. Look what I did!
And to the men in my life: Jeff, who still melts my heart with a strum on his old Martin acoustic or the black Les Paul, and my father, who would like the world to know he raised me better than this.

Chapter One

"I'm not interested in shagging your friends, Addie, so don't worry," Julian said, pretending not to notice his sister's nervous tics. He also pretended not to notice the clouds of green and blue mist floating in the air around them. It wasn't cool to look at things other people couldn't see. For one thing, it made them uncomfortable. For another, it labeled him a freak. Though he had to admit, "freak" was easier to say than "synesthete."

They walked down the cracked and uneven sidewalk. It was dusk, a humid San Antonio evening, and the sounds Julian saw as swirling colors took on the shimmering quality he associated with a sweltering Texas summer. His long-sleeved shirt was already soaked through. He unbuttoned the cuffs and rolled them above his wrists, exposing the beginnings of the dark tattoos that snaked up the lengths of his forearms. He should have worn a T-shirt, especially with Addie's insistence on walking in this heat, but a night at Slammers warranted a vintage sixties Van Heusen dress shirt—green and gold stripes—untucked to look casual.

Glancing across the street, he spotted the first dealer of the evening. And the dealer spotted him. The twitchy kid raised his eyebrows. *Interested?*

Julian lowered his gaze to his black Tony Lama boots and focused on putting one foot in front of the other. Addie marched along at his side, seemingly unaware of the young men on the corners slapping palms and hanging out. She didn't notice the cars slowing to let passengers off, only to cruise the block and pick them up farther down the street. Julian's nerves, however, sizzled with electrical currents from all the activity. He reached in his pocket for the comfort of his guitar picks.

"I'm not worried about you shagging my friends," Addie said. "They're hardly your type."

"Of course," he agreed, suppressing a grin. *They're probably pretentious, stuffy snobs.*

"Don't take that the wrong way. It's the truth," she added.

Unlike Julian's, Addie's clipped British accent hadn't been softened by her years in the States. While Julian was a natural chameleon and could adopt a convincing Texas drawl whenever he wanted, Addie's accent was sharp and pronounced. The southern men she encountered thought they were being scolded by her attempts at light conversation. Texas women, however, were another story. Julian's accent charmed the pants right off them.

A kid with his jeans halfway to his knees slunk out of an alley and squinted in their direction. He started to retreat, but then his eyes met Julian's, and he hesitated for a second.

Keep walking, brother—I'm not buying.

Julian breathed a sigh of relief as the kid disappeared back into the shadows.

It sucked that Addie walked this old neighborhood alone. Her dye studio, which also served as her flat, was in a revitalized area. But the line separating upscale and renovated from rough and unsafe was blurry. You had to be careful where you stepped, and Addie didn't always pay attention. He needed to have a talk with her about it, but she didn't accept helpful suggestions very well. She sure as hell could dole them out, though.

He looked one block ahead. That's all it would take before the grimy windows of the pawnshops and taquerias, with their advertisements of musical instruments, jewelry, and *barbacoa*, gave way to the restaurants, bars, and live music venues of Southtown. Already, the blues and greens of the perky rhythm of the *conjunto* squeeze-boxes, accented by the chest-rattling bass beats from cruising lowriders, were morphing into the reds and maroons of the bustling strip nearby.

"So," Julian said as he grabbed Addie's arm to steer her clear of a wino. "Tell me about these friends of yours and why I won't be interested in shagging them."

"Real breasts," she replied.

"Come again?"

"Real breasts. They've got them."

"Hey, I've got nothing against natural breasts. They're just usually not attached to women I'm attracted to, is all." That wasn't true, but getting Addie worked up was a habit.

"Real breasts are not *attached* to women, Juli," Addie said.

Julian cringed. "Please stop calling me that."

He hadn't been mistaken for a girl in thirty years, but Addie clung stubbornly to the nickname she'd used when he was a rosy-cheeked baby with dark curls and long eyelashes.

"And in addition to unaltered bodies," Addie continued, as if he hadn't spoken, "they're intelligent, so that's another deterrent for you. Sherry's a curator at a museum downtown, and Cleo is about to resume teaching at a local college."

"The smart ones are troublesome. Thank God they tend to avoid me."

Addie rolled her eyes. "There you go, then. No worries."

What were these new friends of his sister like? Addie was hard on friends in the same ways she was hard on brothers: overbearing and judgmental with a tendency to hover. One needed a high tolerance for henpecking and meddling to go the distance with Addie.

Soon they were jockeying for position among the throng of sweaty people milling about Slammers's outdoor patio. More people than usual were crammed into the small space due to the lure of a popular local band. Julian scanned the crowd with Addie, though he didn't know who they were looking for.

The band was fucking tight, which was a relief. Bad music was painful. Sloppy riffs and out-of-tune instruments produced a visceral mess in his mind—colors that blended together into a sludge that settled in the pit of his stomach.

"Oh!" Addie said, pointing at the tiny space a few drunks had turned into an impromptu dance floor. "There they are."

Expecting to see a couple of awkward librarian types bouncing around, Julian's eyes almost popped out of his head at the sight of a tall, striking brunette doing a bump and grind with two guys. She looked up and waved at Addie, who waved back with enthusiasm.

The definitely not a librarian continued shaking it like the rent was due, and a sensual maroon pulse tugged at Julian's abdomen...and lower. Maybe shagging wasn't out of the question this evening, after all. "Is that the birthday girl?"

"No, that's Sherry. Cleo is right there behind her. See?"

The tall brunette moved over to reveal a commotion, the center of which was a redheaded whirling dervish in a pair of ridiculous gangbanger jeans at least four sizes too large. *Birthday Girl* was written across the front of her black T-shirt in rhinestones. She was either having a horrible fit or suffering from an inexplicable lack of rhythm. Her dance partners were laughing at her expense. Under the circumstances, he had no choice but to hit the sorry excuse for a dance floor and offer his assistance. He wasn't the kind of man to ignore a damsel in distress, even if she did seem to be enjoying herself.

•••

Cleo forced one eye open and looked around. Thanks to the blackout curtains, there wasn't much to see except a rogue ray of sunshine streaking through the room. She opened the other eye and considered sitting up. Her bladder was full, no doubt the reason she was awake in the first place. With a huge exhalation that could peel paint off walls, she kicked the covers aside and went for it.

The room spun and her head pounded as she bravely swung her feet over the side of the bed, seeking the floor with a tentative toe. Standing up was a momentous occasion. She felt like Heidi.

"Look, Grandfather," she said to the pile of clothes on the armchair. "I can walk."

Grabbing her phone off the nightstand, she began the short hangover shuffle toward the bathroom. An unfortunate glimpse in the mirror revealed insane hair, smeared mascara, and an Aerosmith T-shirt on backward. Because having a shirt *not* on backward would have lent entirely too much class to the scene. *Oh, Jose Cuervo, you are such a bastard.*

She grabbed her toothbrush and pulled up last night's photos on her phone, looking through squinted eyes to lessen the shock of whatever was about to pop up. She'd hoped to turn over a new leaf on her thirtieth birthday, but there she was in the first picture, brilliantly balancing a lime wedge on her nose. She sighed, set the phone down, and turned on the water.

Fresh from the shower, she towel dried her hair and

frowned. Her parents were hosting a birthday dinner for her tonight. She'd have to tell them she hadn't gotten her teaching job back. It would be one more disappointment.

As if she needed confirmation of her many disappointments, her eyes lit on the small stack of *Rock 'n' Spin* magazines sitting on her old cedar chest. The six issues represented her short-lived career at the famous music and entertainment publication. She hadn't the slightest idea what to do with them. Burn them? Frame them? Rip them to shreds? For now, she'd settle for putting them out of sight. Into the cedar chest they'd go.

It was some kind of irony that the monstrous chunk of furniture was romantically referred to as a hope chest. She'd received it on her twelfth birthday, a traditional southern gift from her traditional southern mother. She'd asked for an electric guitar. "Don't be ridiculous, dear," her mother had replied before filling the chest with what she considered a respectable trousseau.

Cleo ignored the bone china resting on top of the heirloom monogrammed napkins and looked down at the huge stack of *Rock 'n' Spin* issues she'd saved since she was fifteen. Eddie Vedder and the rest of Pearl Jam stared up at her. She dropped the latest six issues on top of Eddie and shut the lid, watching John Mayer and his sleepy eyes disappear with a set of Oneida stainless and an embroidered linen tablecloth folded neatly at his feet.

Coffee. She needed coffee. She inhaled the rich and promising aroma wafting out of her kitchen. Wait a minute… she hadn't made any coffee.

Frantically, she racked her brain. Only certain parts of the evening were retrievable from the old memory banks, but she definitely remembered hot, sweaty dancing and a guy with a British accent. Oh, boy. She swallowed hard. She'd met Addie's brother.

She followed her nose, sneaking down the short hallway on her tiptoes. Would he be in her kitchen in his underwear? Would he be in her kitchen *without* his underwear? With a deep breath, Cleo peeked around the corner.

The kitchen was empty. As was her trusty French press. The coffeemaker in the corner, however, steamed away with vigor, and there was a note taped to it. *You're welcome.* The flowing script was Addie's.

Cleo melted into the countertop with relief. She vaguely remembered Addie driving her home last night, the two of them singing along with Depeche Mode while a heavily tattooed party pooper groaned and muttered in the backseat.

At some point in the evening, Addie's brother had turned from a charmer into a grouch. And Cleo had the uncomfortable feeling she'd had something to do with it.

She poured a cup of coffee and glanced around the tiny boxed-in room. She missed her old apartment in Southtown. It had been small, and the ancient plumbing had ensured a refreshingly cold shower every morning, but it had oozed character from every nook and cranny. This unimaginative one-bedroom unit in a sprawling urban complex was all she could currently afford. Actually, it was more than she could afford. The not-so-friendly reminder about the back rent she owed stared up at her from the counter. Her stomach churned.

Just as she set the mug down, her phone chirped with a text: DON'T PANIC. WE'VE GOT YOUR CAR, REMEMBER? WE'LL POP BY AROUND NOON.

She looked out the window. Sure enough, her Honda Fit was missing. Her palm smacked against her forehead. Of course Addie had her car. How else would she have driven home? She and her brother had walked to Slammers.

Grabbing the phone, Cleo zipped through the frames, stopping when she came to a picture of Addie's brother. His dark hair was wavy and shoulder length. Thick eyelashes framed chocolate eyes that turned up at the corners, like his sister's. But that was where the resemblance ended. It was inconceivable that prim and proper Addie could have a brother so deliciously wicked. Thank God he lived on another continent. She didn't need to get tangled up with anybody's brother, wicked or otherwise, especially now that she'd met Josh, who was delightfully stable and thrillingly normal, two attributes she was determined to appreciate.

She opened the refrigerator and considered breakfast. A half-eaten fajita taco stared up at her, unearthing the memory of the post-bar sojourn through the Taco Cabana drive-through. Addie's brother had self-righteously lectured her about the evils of eating meat. *Oh dear God, he was a holier-than-thou vegan.*

The half-eaten taco did not tempt her in the slightest, and she shut the refrigerator, frowning a little as she remembered how grabby he'd been on the dance floor. In fact, she hadn't been felt up so thoroughly since her junior prom and… *Oh, boy.* That brought it all back. He'd made a brazen grab at her ass during a slow rock ballad, the final song of the evening. She'd pushed him away and then, for good measure, had punished him with a pinch through his shirt, twisting his nipple.

A familiar heat rose in her cheeks. Why hadn't she just slapped him like a normal person? Why was she so freakishly bizarre when drunk? And how in the world was she supposed to have known his nipple was pierced? She winced at the memory of his unmanly squeal. No wonder he was pissed.

She deleted every picture until all evidence of birthday debauchery was destroyed. Then she glanced at the text again.

DON'T PANIC. WE'VE GOT YOUR CAR, REMEMBER? WE'LL POP BY AROUND NOON.

Two things immediately stood out as alarming. The first was the word "we." The second was the word "noon." She had five minutes.

She bolted to her closet and spun in circles. Everything was wrinkled or dirty. She dug hastily through a basket—not even a clean bra to support the troops! Oh, what the hell. He might not even come, and if he did, she wasn't going to be taken in by sexy bedroom eyes or drool-worthy tattoos. For the first time in her life, she would repel trouble instead of sucking it toward her at warp speed. She stepped out of the closet, ran her fingers through her curly, damp hair, and went to the kitchen to wait by the window. Barefoot, no makeup, and a Rudy's BBQ T-shirt, complete with stains. If the wounded warrior from their dance floor battle showed up, he was about to see her in her natural habitat, with her natural hair and her natural, unsupported boobs—the trifecta of trouble repellent.

•••

Julian winced beneath his dark shades. Fucking sun. He was going straight home as soon as he could. He needed one of two things: complete silence or a wailing guitar. Silence would get rid of the swirling colors that bled together in his head until his mind floated in a sea of pea soup. Playing guitar wouldn't get rid of the colors, but it would force them to stay where they belonged, separated into a candy-coated rainbow of flavor, which he much preferred to pea soup.

The colors were only a problem if he was stressed or, like today, exhausted. He'd been in no condition to drive after Slammers and had spent an uncomfortable night on Addie's couch. She'd insisted he follow her to the redhead's flat so he could take her back home. He'd considered arguing, but his curiosity as to what kind of shape the woman would be in had won out in the end. He hoped she was worse off than he was. Drunk or not, there was no excuse for the humiliation—and pain—she'd dealt out on the dance floor.

"She's on the third floor," Addie said.

Julian let out a groan. The only thing worse than climbing stairs would be sitting in the sweltering car, so he took a deep breath and prepared to summit.

"You can do it," Addie said, clucking her tongue. "Serves you right, anyway. And when we get inside, do you think you might avoid the groping and such? I'd hate to see you get yourself into another, er…pinch."

"Very clever." He ran a hand across his chest to see if his nipple still smarted. He winced. It sure as hell did.

All he'd done was brush her ass with his fingers. He'd been aiming for the small of her back, but he'd overshot. It wasn't even intentional. So what if his hand lingered a moment or two? He closed his eyes, recalling the opening strains of "November Rain" and the way the music had surrounded him like a cloak of crushed purple velvet. Cleo's curvy body had pressed against his, and he'd had a completely innocent and involuntary physiological reaction. She'd felt it—goddamn, she'd rubbed against it—right before his hand made the unfortunate venture south.

He narrowed his eyes at the stairs leading to her flat. Maybe there was an apology waiting up there.

"Come along," Addie chirped. Confident that he'd snap to and follow orders, she marched off without so much as a glance over her shoulder.

He'd already taken a step to follow, but at her bossy tone he stopped and reached his arms over his head for a nice, long stretch. A light breeze brushed his stomach as his T-shirt rode up. He'd found it at Addie's, and she'd sworn it was hers, but what would she be doing with a Sex Pistols T-shirt? It had to be his, even though he rarely wore the T-shirts in his huge collection. It was clean, so he'd put it on, dismayed that Addie had shrunk it. His shirt from the previous evening wasn't exactly fresh. In fact, thanks to his overzealous dance partner, it had a tiny bloodstain on it.

He let Addie get to the second landing before sprinting across the parking lot to catch up. Breathless from the effort, he stopped at her side and bent over, gasping. Stupid move under the circumstances. He rubbed his temples, hoping his head wouldn't explode.

"You know," Addie said, "you really shouldn't drink like you did last night."

"I was fine," Julian said. He'd been pretty plastered. "And it's not your problem, anyway. Butt out." He straightened, squared his shoulders, and exhaled. Running a hand through his hair, he subtly sniffed an armpit. Not too bad. Still smelled like soap. He'd refused his sister's Sensual Secrets deodorant.

Addie snorted.

"What now?" he said.

"Going to try again, are we?"

"Try what? It's not like I'm even attracted to her." At least not now that he was sober.

"You should reconsider the type of women you *are* attracted to. Maybe if you were to get to know some strong, intelligent women—"

"Addie," he said, through clenched teeth, "I'm quite happy with my life just as it is."

"You are not," she said.

"Focus on your own lack of happiness, would you?"

A secretive smile formed on her lips. "I have."

Julian eyed his sister. "What is that supposed to mean?"

She turned her face away, but not before he'd seen the blush. *What the—*

The door jerked open, and there stood the redhead, satisfyingly disheveled. Her damp hair stuck out in every direction, and she hadn't a spot of makeup on her freckled face. A mess in every sense of the word. So why was she looking at him as if she were the queen and he the hired help?

"Addie!" she said, giving his sister a vigorous hug. At the sound of her silvery voice, Julian experienced the same odd phenomenon he had last night—pale orange bubbles popped gently along the edges of his peripheral vision. He was used to living his life inside a psychedelic kaleidoscope, but the redhead had just added another dimension.

He received a less enthusiastic welcome from his effervescent hostess. "Well," she said. "Here you are again." As though he were a stray dog who kept turning up.

He scowled. "Too hot to wait in the car."

She gazed at him with a critical eye. Her lashes were pale, but long and thick. One eyebrow raised, a dainty red arch that seemed to say, *Oh, really?* She stepped back and extended her arm toward the interior of the flat. "Won't you bring yourself, your lovely sister, and your bloodshot eyes into my humble abode?"

The two stepped in. And even though he wasn't feeling charitable, he said, "You don't look the worse for wear, Big Red."

"Really? I feel awful. You?"

"I'm perfectly fine, thanks for asking."

"Oh. Well, you looked better last night," she said. "Of course, you know what they say. The girls all get prettier at closing time."

Was she really insinuating that last night's advances—and she *had* made advances—were the result of dim lighting? And worse, was she really quoting a Mickey Gilley song? The slow burn of irritation spread through him. The woman literally made him see red.

He didn't usually respond so foolishly to what might only be good-natured ribbing, but he was inexplicably rattled, as if he were a monkey in a cage that had been given a good jiggle.

Wanting to get rid of the smirk tugging at the left corner

of Cleo's upper lip, Julian gave her a quick and intentional once-over. "That's most definitely true," he replied. "At closing time, guys make overtures they often regret the next morning."

The hint of a smirk disappeared, and the other eyebrow rose to match the first. Then they both dived down to form a vicious scowl. She looked like a teakettle just before it whistled. Slamming the door behind her, she said, "At closing time, some people become desperate gropers." Her eyes dusted over him. "And yet somehow they manage to appear even more pathetic the next morning by showing up stubbly and wearing a girl's shirt."

"This is not a girl's shirt. This is *my* Sex Pistols shirt."

"Well, the cap sleeves look cute on you." She smiled sweetly.

What the hell were cap sleeves? Unable to resist, he glanced at his shoulders. The sleeves did look a bit funny.

"Told you so, Juli," Addie said, with the singsong smugness she'd used throughout their childhood. *Perfect timing with the fucking nickname.* Because cap sleeves were not quite emasculating enough.

"Juli. Good grief, that's it," Cleo said. "Sorry. For the life of me, I couldn't remember your name. I just knew it was something effeminate."

"It's Julian Wheaton, and there's nothing effeminate about me," he growled, standing taller and trying to look… well…as manly as possible in a girl's shirt.

The redhead glanced at his sleeves and cleared her throat. The corner of Addie's mouth curled up, causing a dimple to appear out of nowhere.

This situation was annoying as hell and hadn't gone at all according to his plan, which had been to whip off his sunglasses and cook Lava Locks with a smoldering stare, even though nobody wearing a stained T-shirt and some sort of horrible men's trunks deserved one. In no part of his plan was he supposed to be wearing women's clothing while suffering the scrutiny of an unimpressed, pint-size bundle of bravado.

He lifted his eyes toward hers and did what he did best: a perfected sexy glance, followed by a boyish gaze through the lashes. Her full bottom lip jutted out in annoyance, which pleased him immensely. He looked lower, in order to make the obligatory pause at the breasts. Okay, more than a pause. White T-shirt. No bra. Very nice.

He was gratified by a furious blush.

She crossed her arms over her chest. "I, um, probably owe you an apology for this or that, you know," she said, glancing in the general direction of his right nipple. "I mean, nothing actually *ripped out*, did it?"

She looked pale, and her eyes had turned into green saucers.

"Nice place," he said, ignoring her inquiry. It was, in fact, a horrid little flat.

"I hate it," Cleo mumbled.

"Well, maybe after you've been here awhile you can doll it up," he suggested.

"Can we continue this pleasant exchange over lunch?" Addie asked. "I'm hungry."

"I'm not," Cleo said, plopping down on a chair. "And I have tons of laundry to do today. He doesn't want to hear the continuing saga of my pathetic life, anyway."

She was right. He didn't. "Okay, let's go, then," he said, turning toward the door. "Come on, Addie."

Was it his imagination, or did the green-eyed monster look disappointed? He headed for the door with a smile.

"Wait," she called. "How about the Cove?"

He stopped and turned. The Cove held the unusual distinction of serving as both a restaurant and a Laundromat. In fact, it also had a car wash. The red eyebrows were back up, inviting and hopeful.

"Well," he said, looking pointedly at her breasts as she stood there wearing her own dirty laundry, "since Addie's hungry, and you're obviously out of bras, the Cove is a perfect suggestion."

He was rewarded by another flaming blush.

Chapter Two

Julian struggled down a flight of stairs, burdened by two huge garbage bags of dirty clothes. "I'll toss the other two bags over the balcony," the little laundrophobe called down, leaving a trail of tangerine bubbles in the air.

"There's more?" How could one person collect that much laundry? Laundry wasn't hard. Whites on Monday, colors on Wednesday, towels on Friday. Routines made the world go around.

"I hate doing laundry," she said. A huge black bag fell from above his head and landed with a padded thud in the parking lot below. Shit. Did she have any clothes left at all? That explained the outfit she'd changed into. Sporting some sort of crocheted hippie halter dress — still no bra — and a pair of worn cowboy boots, the woman was wearing the dregs of her closet.

He paused on the steps as she caught up. He had to admit the ugly green dress clung snugly in all the right places. As he appreciated that fact, he lost his grip on one of the bags. Leaning over to get a better hold on it, he looked up to see

Cleo's purse headed straight for his face. He just had time to think, *oh, crap,* before the bag smacked right into his mouth and nose. Pain exploded across his face and spread throughout the rest of his head in a scarlet shock wave. He lost his balance—had he been hit by a purse or a ton of bricks?

He was spared the indignity of a complete backward somersault, instead suffering the cartoonish bouncing on his ass down five steps before landing with his head smashed into the iron railing. For good measure, the bag of laundry landed on his midsection, bursting open and ejecting its contents. Something lavender and silky floated down dreamily before landing on top of his head. Cleo scrambled down the stairs, throwing herself onto him with a look of complete horror.

"You're bleeding!"

"I am?" he wheezed. The air had been knocked out of him. He reached behind his head, expecting to feel something warm and sticky, but his hair was completely dry.

"No, your nose."

"Ah. Your twenty-ton butt-ugly purse. What the bloody hell do you have in that thing?"

"Rolls of quarters." Her nose wrinkled as if he were a bit of distasteful road kill. "Dang, I don't do blood very well. I need to sit down."

She plopped on her ass and began fanning herself with her hands.

"I'm all right, thanks," Julian said. "Mild to moderate concussion and a broken face is all."

Shit. She looked pale and shaky. He sat up, dropping items of clothing here and there on the landing.

"Do this," he said, gingerly pushing on the back of her head to get it between her knees. He grabbed an article of lingerie and held it to his bloody nose.

Another black bag emerged from above. Addie peered over the top and spotted the catastrophe on the landing.

"Oh my God," she cried, dropping the bag and bounding down the stairs. "Cleo, are you okay?"

"Don't mind me," Julian said. "I'm just bleeding."

"Still?" Cleo's voice sounded muffled, having forced its way through her arms, which were snugly wrapped around her knees.

"Whatever happened?" Addie asked. "Did the two of you fall down the stairs?"

"Just the one of us. She pushed me, actually."

"I did not," Cleo said. She lifted her head and eyed him through the wild mess of auburn chaos. "Not intentionally, anyway. And are you seriously sniffing my underwear?" She grimaced in revulsion.

"What?" He yanked the item away from his face. "No, I was just—"

"*Bleeding?* You were just bleeding on my underwear?"

That was exactly what he'd been doing. He hoisted himself up by the railing and offered a hand. "We're not aborting this mission," he insisted. He held what he now realized were a pair of pink panties with the tips of his fingers. "I'm still hungry, and your laundry is dirtier than ever."

Cleo's brows drew together as she accepted his hand. He yanked a little too hard, and she barreled right into his chest, setting him off balance. For a brief, horrible moment, he teetered on the edge of the step. Cleo gasped—her face a comical distortion of disbelief—and grabbed for him. Luckily, she missed, and Julian caught himself by the railing. When his heart rate returned to normal, he hoisted up the bag as if nothing had happened.

"Whew!" Cleo said. "That was close. You're a bit accident-prone, aren't you?"

Surely she wasn't serious. Was she? Julian extended his hand toward the stairs. "Ladies first."

Addie patted his cheek. "What a gentleman."

"Just afraid to turn my back," he said. "Cleo seems determined to kill me."

•••

Cleo and Addie walked with Julian toward an ugly old brown car—one of those half-car, half-pickup contraptions. Even in a girl's shirt, Julian was all man. The silly T-shirt showed off more of his arms than what he'd worn last night, and she loved every inch. *Stop being a sucker for tattoos. Tattoos start with* T, *just like trouble.* At least her repellent was working. The attraction didn't seem to be a two-way street.

Julian casually tossed the bags into the hideous vehicle's open bed. "We'll take my car," he said. "All the bags will fit in the back."

She was confused. "Unless you rented that from Clunkers 'R' Us, I assume it's yours?"

"Clunker? Are you kidding me? This is a classic El Camino. It's been refurbished to perfection, I'll have you know. And yes, it's mine. Why else would I be driving it?"

Someone was sensitive about his car. "How did you get it here?"

"I drove it. I'd have pushed it, but it's just so hot, you see."

"You're not visiting from England?"

"Why would you think that? I have a loft downtown. Not too far from Addie's place." He hesitated, then realization dawned on his face. "I guess she hasn't talked about me much."

No, she hadn't. Of course, Cleo didn't talk about her brother, either. He was the family's golden boy, and she'd grown up floundering in his overachieving shadow.

Julian opened the passenger side door. "I embarrass Addie," he stage-whispered.

"You do not," Addie said. "You just never came up. It's not like I know how many siblings Cleo has."

Cleo gulped down a guilty knot. "I have a brother, too," she admitted. "He's perfect in every way, an orthopedic surgeon in Portland." *And I'm an unemployed thirty-year-old with a hangover.*

"Well," Julian said, "Addie's brother is far from perfect, and he's been nothing but trouble." He held the passenger door open and extended a hand toward the leather bench seat.

"Stop being so pathetic," Addie snapped.

"I wasn't bragging about my brother when I said he was perfect," Cleo said. "And I'm the sibling who's been nothing but trouble in our family."

Julian gave her a sympathetic nod. "Hurry up, hop in. Addie's too gangly to sit in the middle. Hope you don't mind straddling a stick." He winked.

She climbed in, and Addie followed. Julian slammed the door, a little too hard. *Great,* Cleo thought, as she awkwardly attempted to get one leg over the long-handled shifter in a dress. *This is going to be fun.*

Julian came around and slid into the driver's seat. "It's only second and fourth that'll give you any trouble," he said, with an intentional glance at the stick between her knees.

He turned the key and brought the old car roaring to life. "Oh, and reverse, of course. But I'll do my best to remain a gentleman during the shifting." The mischievous smile he produced was cute but not convincing.

With hardly a glance in the rearview mirror, he threw the car into reverse, and they shot out of the parking space. Cleo's stomach flip-flopped, and she put a hand on her tummy to settle it.

"You okay?" Julian asked, raising an eyebrow.

A cleansing breath in through the mouth, out through the nose. She could do this. "Yeah. But do you think we could take it easy? I don't like roller coasters even when I'm not hungover."

Julian made a little sound in his throat that wasn't quite a snort. Then he shifted smoothly into first, and Cleo's stomach didn't protest in the slightest. Another equally smooth shift into second landed the stick back between her legs—she stared straight ahead—and they pulled out onto the highway that ran in front of her apartment complex. Julian skipped third and went directly to fourth, forcing her to open her knees even farther—hard to ignore, so she pushed herself as far against the back of the seat as she could, and the car rumbled down the road.

Brake lights ahead. "Fucking hell," Julian said. "Road works."

Coming to a stop in the unending line of cars, trucks, and SUVs, Julian reached down and flipped on the old-fashioned radio, spinning the dial to find a station. Then they sat there, waiting for their turn to inch up. Even though Julian appeared practiced at driving a stick, they lurched along, with him riding the clutch, and Cleo's stomach began to complain with rolling waves of nausea.

All the while, Julian's leg rubbed against hers, his arm repeatedly bumped her breast, and the corner of his mouth curled up each time he shifted. He was either clumsy or her repellent was wearing off. She scooted over until she was thigh to thigh with Addie, but Julian immediately filled the space, radiating heat. He smelled good, like soap. She took in a deep breath through her nose—she was a sucker for a guy who smelled good—but her stomach still threatened mutiny. She'd broken out into a light sweat.

"Does this thing have air-conditioning?" she asked.

"Sometimes," Julian answered. He pushed a button and held his hand in front of a vent. "But not today. Sorry, love."

"Are you feeling worse?" Addie asked.

Cleo shut her eyes and nodded. She was afraid to open

her mouth and speak.

"Oh, dear. Julian, do you have some water in here?"

"Nope, no water. But there's an empty bag beneath your feet if she's going to toss."

"She's not going to do that."

"Actually," Cleo said, sinking lower into the seat in a wave of misery. "I might."

"Shit, Addie, grab the fucking bag!" Julian shifted into second, inadvertently slamming his elbow into Cleo's diaphragm.

Oomph. Cleo crumpled over.

"Sorry," Julian said. "Holy fuck, Addie, what are you doing?"

"I can't find the bag," she said. "But here, use this—"

Before Addie could thrust the dirty towel she'd located on the floorboard in front of Cleo's face, Cleo threw up the morning's cup of coffee all over Julian's arm.

"Fuck," he yelled. He took his hand off the gearshift as his foot slid off the clutch, stalling the car. Impatient honks came from the line behind them while Cleo did her best to finish emptying the contents of her stomach into the towel. When she was done, Addie dabbed at her face with the other side of it.

"Get my arm, would you, Addie? Jesus."

Addie used the dry corner to wipe off Julian's arm while he restarted the car. He edged across several lanes to take the nearest exit, and Cleo rested her head against his shoulder, not caring at all about the frustrated sigh he let out in response. Her head pounded and her stomach still gurgled, but mostly, she could barely look at Julian. She hadn't exactly been trying to turn him on—quite the opposite—but throwing up on him was a bit extreme.

Addie fanned her face with a piece of paper. "How are you feeling?"

"Just swell."

Julian glanced down at her and laughed.

"What's so funny?" Cleo asked with a frown.

"I use that towel to check my oil."

"So?"

"So look at my arm."

She looked at his grease-streaked arm.

"You should see your face," he said. Then he laughed some more.

"Stop it. I'm trying to be sorry for throwing up on you."

He was still laughing as they pulled into the parking lot of the Cove. "You know, I knew it from the moment I first saw you."

"Knew what?"

"That you were eventually going to vomit on me. You just had that look about you."

"Happens a lot, does it? You must attract a classy crowd."

"Says the girl with vomit breath."

She lifted her head off his shoulder, not really enthused with the idea of lunch. Julian exited the car and held out his hand. She took in the tattoos on his forearm, following to where they disappeared into his shirt. Detailed and morbid — flames and skulls with ghostly, frightening faces.

"Is this Hell?" she asked, longing to trace the inked images with her fingertips.

"No, Big Red, it's just a hangover," he answered. "Come on, now. Go wash your face."

Lunch was miserable, and Cleo sat through it with a simmering tummy and a boiling head. But the view was nice. Julian sat across from her, eating a juicy portobello mushroom sandwich.

"Are you going to eat your fries?" he asked.

Normally, she loved the sweet potato fries at the Cove, but her stomach turned at the mere thought. She was about to offer them to him when a burly Hispanic guy walked up to their table. Julian pushed his chair back and stood.

"Rooster!" he said. "How have you been, brother?" The two men clasped hands, then launched into a grizzly bear hug. Rooster had an impressive braid hanging down his back. It stopped just above his leather belt, which was tooled with the words "El Gallo."

"When are you gonna come jam with us?" Rooster asked, releasing Julian. "We've been missing you and that skanky guitar."

Wonderful. Julian was a guitarist. Cleo mentally hit the panic button. The words "musician" and "guitarist" were screaming red flags. She'd vowed to stay away from musicians, and she intended to run like hell at the first available opportunity, no matter how good this one smelled.

After a minute or two, Rooster went on his way, and Julian sat back down, casually tossing the hair out of his eyes. *Red flag.* He leaned back in his chair, balancing it on the back legs, and stretched. The stupid shirt rode up to reveal a taut, ripped stomach. *Red flag.* He caught her looking and grinned.

"You play guitar?" she asked. It was a casual question, not a curious one. Just making conversation.

"A little. And I write songs."

Of course he did. Her heart fluttered slightly, but she got a grip before it started full-blown hammering. There were lots of horrible songs floating around. Julian probably wrote that kind. Nothing to get excited about.

Addie cleared her throat and dabbed at the corners of her mouth with a napkin. "Cleo, how is Josh?"

Whew. Hearing Josh's name was like an ice-cold bucket of water hitting a sizzling fire. "He's fine. I'm seeing him tonight."

Josh was part of the Pinocchio Plan, a quest to find Cleo a real boy. Sherry's voice filled her head: "*You'll never have an adult relationship as long as you're stuck with puppy-love crushes on musicians, Cleo."*

Sherry was right. Since her preteen years spent pining away for *Rock 'n' Spin* centerfolds, Cleo had been a sucker for musicians. But no more. Her days of chasing idiots with guitars were behind her. Josh had no musical talent that she knew of, no tattoos, no pierced nipples, and no red flags.

"What's that face for?" Julian asked.

"What face?" She hadn't made a face.

"You grimaced."

"I did not." Had she? Because Josh was a delightful person. A great guy. Awesome, actually. And he did not play guitar—he played golf—which was possibly way cooler. Cleo took a huge gulp of iced tea. "Josh is a lawyer at my dad's firm. We've gone out three times."

"Three times?" Julian let out a low whistle. "That's perseverance. He's either in love or a total masochist."

"Julian," Addie scolded. "Behave."

"He's not bothering me, Addie," Cleo said. He was infuriating her. And turning her on. *Musicians are bad, musicians are bad, musicians are bad…*

"What are you doing now?" Julian asked.

"Huh?"

"Your lips were moving."

Addie cleared her throat again. "So, Josh is going to meet your mum tonight, right?"

Cleo snapped out of it. Josh *was* going to meet her mother at the birthday dinner tonight, and she was going to love him. "That's right."

"I'm sure the lawyer's quite smitten with Big Red here," Julian said. "Who wouldn't be? I just couldn't handle another round of her myself. That could be the blood loss or the concussion talking, though."

Cleo glanced at the time. She had at least another thirty minutes before her clothes were dry. "So," she said, pushing her untouched plate out of the way, "are you in a band, or what?"

"Or what," he replied.

"He used to be in a band," Addie said. "But he's not anymore." She gave Cleo a stern look.

So this was why Addie hadn't mentioned a brother. The Pinocchio Plan.

Julian stuffed a handful of sweet potato fries in his mouth and tossed out a mischievous grin. She closed her eyes. *He is not a real boy.*

"He owns a recording studio," Addie said. "It's a small setup for local acts. Mostly, he gets high school kids with garage bands or small-time Tejano groups."

"They're not all small-timers," he said, wiping his greasy fingers on a napkin. "But I like helping out the kids. It's cool. And sometimes I get to sit in on sessions."

"He's a session musician," Addie insisted. "Nothing more."

"Wow, way to stroke my ego," Julian said before turning his dreamy bedroom eyes back to Cleo. "But she's right. Except I also play backup, so sometimes I'm out performing."

Performing. She imagined Julian on the stage, guitar hung low against his hips. A drop of condensation slid down the side of her iced tea glass. *Julian shirtless, drenched in sweat, wailing on a Fender…*

"Anyway, it's hard to balance running a studio with the demands of being available for backup," Julian continued. "What about you?"

"Huh? Oh, I'm not in a band."

He laughed. "What a surprise. So, what do you do?"

The question slammed her back to reality. "I'm currently between jobs."

"But you're going to start teaching English lit again, right?" Addie asked.

Cleo sighed and began shredding the napkin she'd balled up in her hand. This was not what she wanted to talk about. "I didn't get my old job back," she admitted. "I'm totally screwed."

"I thought it was a sure thing," Addie said. "What are you going to do?"

"I have no idea. I've pissed away all my savings waiting for the end of the semester and the contract reviews. I was sure they'd take me back."

"Tell me," Julian said. "Was it the drinking?"

"Shut up," Addie snapped. "I'm sure it's budget cuts or something like that. Right, Cleo?"

Or maybe it was because I left the tenure track to chase after some rocker like a teenage groupie.

"Probably," she replied meekly. She took a sip of iced tea and forced it down past the lump in her throat.

Chapter Three

Julian stared at the shelves of bed linens. After dropping off Cleo and her mounds of laundry at home, Addie had dragged him around town on errands. He hoped this was the last one, as the fluorescent lighting of the home superstore was excruciating. The lights fluctuating at sixty hertz per second produced a disgusting vomit-green haze he couldn't clear. His head, whether from the stubborn hangover or the injury he'd sustained when Calamity Cleo had thrown him down a flight of stairs before puking on him, was pounding.

He sighed as a happy young couple almost bowled him over with a squeaky cart full of kitchen gadgets and big, fluffy towels. If they were like most married couples he'd known, they'd be fighting over who got to keep the bloody blender in just a few years. They disappeared into the aisle with window shades and curtains, and an image of Cleo's sparse, ugly flat popped into his head. It could use some curtains.

Oh, well. She wasn't going to be in that flat much longer. Not with the eviction notice they'd discovered taped to her door upon returning from lunch.

"Julian," Addie scolded. "Did you hear me?"

No, he hadn't heard her. How could anybody hear anything over the buzzing of the fluorescent tubes?

"What?"

"I like that purple comforter on top. Can you reach it?"

Christ. Of course it would be the one on top. He sighed and pulled his hands out of his pockets, away from the guitar picks that had been calming his nerves. Reaching his arms up, he stood on his toes and stretched out his fingers. The tip of his right index finger brushed the corner of a plastic zippered bag. All he had to do was crook it and give it a yank...

"Not that one!"

He jerked, causing an avalanche of Bed-in-a-Bags to shower down upon him.

"Fuck!" he shouted, as bag after bag bounced off his head in a painful flurry of browns, blacks, and grays—his warning colors. As the last bag came careening down, he turned on his sister. "Goddammit, you sound like a cat when you screech at me like that." He took a mighty kick at a paisley-print queen-size sheet set and missed. For the second time that day, he landed on his ass.

"Fucking hell!"

Two women poked their heads in the aisle, saw him sitting there, and scurried off in the opposite direction.

"Julian, calm down," Addie pleaded.

"Hey," a guy said from the end of the aisle. "You mind? I've got my kids in here."

"Sorry," Addie said.

Several people stood at the end of the aisle, staring at them. Julian supposed that seeing a grown man, fallen on his ass and cursing like Courtney Love at a custody hearing, was more entertainment than people were used to getting at Bed Bath & Beyond.

"Let's leave before they kick us out," Addie said. She

turned for the exit and ran smack into a tall man with a big frown and a little security badge. "We were just leaving."

"Good idea," he responded.

"Um, shall we pick this up first?" Julian asked. The heat of the moment had passed, and as usual, he felt stupid and ashamed. He picked up the nearest bag and looked at it. "See here, Addie. This is the one you wanted, isn't it?"

"We'll get this cleaned up," the security guard said, yanking the bag from Julian's hands. "You folks can head on out the door."

Addie didn't need to be told twice and took off without offering to help him up. Well, fine. He hoisted himself to his feet and strolled after her, refusing to rush.

Addie didn't stop until they reached the car. "Why do you always have to ruin everything?" she asked. "Why can't we go to the store and buy a comforter like normal people? Why is everything such a ridiculously dramatic affair when you're involved?"

"I told you hours ago I needed to go home. As usual, you ignored me. And now you have the nerve to be angry with me over something I have no control over."

"Oh, please," she said. "You don't want control. You like playing with a different set of rules just because you're—"

"Just because I'm what?"

Addie sighed, turned around, and yanked on the El Camino's door handle. It was locked, and she smacked it in frustration. "Listen. I'm sorry, okay? I didn't realize you'd reached meltdown status."

That was a stupid thing to say. Meltdown status was reached when it was fucking reached, and that was all there was to it. There'd been plenty of warnings, which he'd been giving since before she'd dragged him through the fabric store, the bookstore, the coffee shop, and the dry cleaner's.

He balled his hands into fists and pressed them against his

eyes. "I told you I needed to go home. I'm too tired to keep things where they belong."

Although he was far from being the only person on the planet with synesthesia, he did seem to be the only one who needed to keep the colors separated. It was like trying to keep your peas from touching your carrots every waking moment of the day.

"I think you said earlier that you *wanted* to go home, which is different from *needing* to go home."

"I'm sorry I embarrassed you, okay?" He kept his fists pressed against his eyes and watched the colors parade across the backs of his eyelids. "Let's just get out of here."

He'd been embarrassing his sister in one form or another since the day he was born. He'd ruined countless childhood holidays and had caused her to be the butt of jokes in school. He'd chased off numerous friends, boyfriends, and acquaintances. And yet, when she spoke next, her voice was full of tenderness.

He hated it.

"Juli, I'm sorry."

She was sorry? He pushed his clenched fists harder into his eyes. He shouldn't do that. He should pull them away and open his eyes. But he wasn't ready to let the world back in yet. In fact, some faint buzzing began. It might be a good idea to check out entirely. That was another weird thing other synesthetes didn't seem to do.

Addie's cool, slender fingers pried his fists away, and he forced himself to look at her. Her brows were drawn, weary with concern. She must be so tired of him. *He* was tired of him.

He put his arms around her. She was his half sister, but because their mother lacked every maternal instinct known to man, she'd acted as mum as well.

"Can you drive?" she asked.

He took a deep breath and gave her a squeeze. "Of

course." She'd kept him from sliding over the edge. Again.

He let her go and opened the door. The familiar click of the El Camino's door handle and the squeak of the seat were welcome sounds. He sank into the car with a sigh and breathed in the familiar fusion of old, hot leather, Juicy Fruit gum, and man sweat. Once Addie climbed in, he turned the key, and the El Camino rumbled awake—the color of deep amber.

Addie cleared her throat. "Don't kill me, but we need to make one more stop."

"I can't drive in the fetal position."

She rubbed his shoulder. "You're fine now, and you'll barely have to slow down. I left my scarf in Cleo's car. It's on our way home."

"Her flat's on the other side of town. And besides, I've had enough drama for today. I can't stand those pathetic puppy dog eyes again." *No matter how pretty they are.*

He'd been forced to listen to over an hour of tears as the redhead pondered her impending homelessness. When he'd finally snapped and offered her a fistful of money, she'd smacked his arm and shrieked, "I don't need money, you idiot."

When he'd pointed out that she most definitely seemed to need money, why else wouldn't she be paying her rent, she'd replied, "I need to grow up."

Then there had been more crying and commiserating. He had almost died from the female hysteria. Women.

"We don't have to go across town," Addie said. "She's at her parents' house in Terrell Hills, probably suffering through dinner and working up the nerve to tell them about the eviction. I'll run in while you stay in the car."

She was bloody right he was staying in the car. "I'm sure her family will help her," he pointed out.

"That will be a last resort, believe me. Only if she feels

she's hit rock bottom."

Julian laughed. "As you well know, hitting rock bottom is my specialty. She's nowhere near the bottom just because of an eviction notice. Not unless she has nowhere to go and ends up living on the streets, which seems unlikely." He swallowed. *Been there, done that.*

He pulled out of the parking lot and accelerated toward the expressway. He was in control of himself again, thanks to Addie's soothing touch and the powerful vibrations of the El Camino's Turbo-jet V8, to which he felt solidly connected. He shifted into fourth—the amber engine noise deepened to a comforting gold—and merged into the fast lane.

...

Cleo sat on the silk brocade couch and listened to Josh and her father discussing sports. Dinner was over. All she had to do now was choke down some cake, then she could escape. Luckily, her mom was so enamored with Josh that she wasn't too tuned in to Cleo's mood. *Evicted.* Her first priority was going to be the avoidance of moving home. She'd stay with a friend—hell, she'd hit the local homeless shelter—but she was not moving in with the folks.

"Are you boys going to talk basketball all night?" her mother asked. "It's Cleo's birthday. Let's talk about something else."

"Sophie," Josh said as his wineglass was refilled, "I think tonight's pork tenderloin was the best I've ever tasted. I can't wait for dessert. I don't know why Clark isn't a butterball."

"Why, thank you, Josh." Her mom nodded with an unmistakable expression of approval, as if Cleo was the farmer who'd brought the prized pig to the fair. If she had a blue ribbon, she'd stick it on Josh's forehead.

Cleo drained her extra-large glass of cab and smacked it

down on the granite coffee table, earning a laser look from her mother. "Pardon me," she said, appreciating the nice buzz humming over the remnants of her hangover.

"In the kitchen, Cleo," her mom said. "Help me make some coffee."

Cleo rose obediently and followed. She was about to get an earful, but at least she wasn't going to get the *What were you thinking?* speech in regard to her date. Every time she looked at Josh, with his clipped blond hair and his crisply pressed clothes, all she heard was *Winner! Winner! Winner!*

Her mother spun on her heel as soon as they made it through the kitchen's swinging door. "Cleo, what were you thinking?"

The kitchen door swung shut and bumped her on the ass. "What was I thinking about *what*?"

"Your outfit. What on earth are you wearing? You look like a flower child. What did Josh say when he saw you in that?"

"It's a sarong, Mom. A one-of-a-kind, 100-percent silk, hand-dyed, super-expensive sarong. And come to think of it, Josh didn't say anything." She frowned and leaned against the counter.

Sophie's face relaxed, and the eyebrow that had disappeared into her bangs came back down to a more reasonable position. "Well, it does bring out your eyes. You just pick the strangest things, dear."

"I didn't pick it," Cleo said smugly. "Addie dyed it for me."

It was a swirling ocean of green, indigo, and deep purple. It fell to mid-thigh, so she'd paired it with dark, skinny jeans and some purple suede boots she'd found on sale. She'd left her hair loose to bounce on her bare shoulders.

"Oh?" Sophie perked up. "She's the most delightful girl. I adore her accent. And yes, now I can see it. That top is exquisite. I should have recognized Addie's work."

"Right." Cleo watched her mother get the silver coffee service ready. "Actually, Addie should be dropping by any minute now. She texted that she left her scarf in my car."

"She can stay for cake," Sophie said. "Get down an extra plate, dear."

Cleo walked into the formal dining room, rolled her eyes at the ostentatious cherubs floating across the domed ceiling, and removed a china plate from the sideboard.

"Make that *two* extra plates. Your brother's in town for a medical conference. He said he'd try to stop by."

Ben was in town? "Why didn't anybody tell me? Have you seen him?"

Her mother refused to make eye contact. "No, we haven't seen him." She busied herself polishing an invisible spot on a sugar spoon.

"Well, we need three extra plates then, don't we?" Cleo asked.

"No. Just two." Sophie began humming as she always did when she intended to end a conversation.

"But isn't Ben bringing—"

"Don't start, Cleo."

"Mom—"

"Your father and I thought that with Josh here for the first time, we didn't need any complications. Ben understands."

There was no way that her brother understood their mother's refusal to let him bring Marcus, nor her desire to wait out what she referred to as his "gay phase." As if on cue, her phone vibrated in her back pocket. She pulled it out and looked at the text.

TELL MOM I CAN'T MAKE IT. SORRY, KIDDO—HAVE A HAPPY BIRTHDAY.

Cleo sighed. "Promise me you won't kill the messenger," she began.

She was saved by the doorbell. "That must be Addie,"

her mother said. She rushed off to open the door, thereby escaping the conversation. Cleo sighed and followed her mother to the front door.

After the hugging and greeting, Sophie started the begging. "Oh, no, you have to stay," she said to Addie. "Just for a few minutes."

Inspired by the distraction Addie provided, Cleo joined in. "Yes, stay for cake, Addie. Pretty please?"

"Speaking of pretty"—Addie winked at her—"Juli's in the car. I really need to be going."

Cleo looked at the door. He was in the car? And he wasn't coming in? Well, fine. She didn't want to see him again, anyway. Much.

"Well, invite her in, too," Sophie said. "There's enough cake to go around."

Addie laughed. "Juli is my brother. Julian."

"Oh my goodness. I didn't realize. Go and get him, dear. I won't take no for an answer."

"Well, he wasn't feeling well earlier," Addie said.

Sophie stared at Addie with a frozen smile on her face. It was the face she wore to show she expected her orders to be followed—no questions asked. Cleo was unfortunately familiar with the *see how patient I'm being with you* expression.

"I'll go see if he'd like to come in," Addie said.

The night was getting interesting. Even Sophie wouldn't be able to remain focused on Cleo's shortcomings while a tattooed British man dropped f-bombs all over the chintz chairs.

As soon as Addie was out of earshot, Sophie clapped her hands. "I didn't know Addie had a brother. I'm sure he's absolutely charming. Have you met him, Cleo?"

"I barfed on him earlier today."

Her mom let out an exasperated sigh and waved her hand.

"No, really," Cleo said. "I did."

Josh walked up. "Did what?"

"Nothing, dear," Sophie said.

Cleo grabbed the wineglass out of Josh's hand and drained it. Then she stared at the door and waited for the show to begin.

The main event walked through the door—obviously reticent—dragging his feet and hesitating in the foyer. The Sex Pistols T-shirt had ridden up to reveal a couple of inches of sculpted abdomen, and Addie reached over and yanked it down. Cleo's traitorous body sparked to life like a lit fuse. A warm wave of desire bloomed between her legs and worked its way up to her tingly scalp before zipping back down to the tips of her toes. She stifled a shudder.

"This is my brother, Julian Wheaton," Addie said.

As if someone flipped his on switch, Julian ran a hand through his shiny, dark waves and gave a shy grin.

Josh instinctively placed an arm around Cleo's waist.

"Hello," Julian said. Sophie's gaze traveled up his tattooed arms to his face, where the grin had turned into a dazzling smile. Cleo smirked. There was no way her mom would be charmed by that cheesy act.

"Where are my manners? Come in and have a seat, won't you? I'm Sophie Compton."

There was a warble in Sophie's voice, which sounded at least two octaves higher than usual, and Cleo cringed in embarrassment over her mother's extended hand. She obviously expected Julian to kiss it.

Without missing a beat, Julian did just that. He administered a simmering gaze and brushed his lips across Sophie's knuckles. It would have been hysterical had her mom not been smiling like an idiot and fluttering her eyelashes.

"Nice to meet you, Mrs. Compton," Julian said. The accent came on thicker than Cleo remembered. Good grief.

"Please, call me Sophie."

"Sophie," Julian said, gently releasing her mother's hand in order to shake her father's.

"Hello, son. Nice to meet you." Clark grinned, clearly amused by his wife's response to whatever pheromones Julian was oozing.

Next up was Josh, who wasn't nearly as impressed by Julian's sex appeal. His grip on Cleo's waist tightened, as if she were a slippery little fish who might be eaten by the big, bad shark. "This is Josh," she mumbled.

Julian's eyebrow lifted. "Why is it that I see no outward signs of injury or mutilation?" He winked and gingerly rubbed the top of his slightly swollen nose. Then he held out his hand, forcing Josh to let go of her in order to shake it.

He held everyone's rapt attention as he leaned over to kiss Cleo on the cheek. "That looks gorgeous on you. Did Addie make it?"

She wanted to roll her eyes, but she was flattered and they wouldn't budge. "Yes, she did," she said instead. "Thank you."

"It's like Stravinsky's 'Rite of Spring,'" he said, continuing to stare.

"Pardon?"

"The beginning of Act One, where the girl dances herself to death as a pagan sacrifice. But I'm talking about the orchestral arrangement, of course." He stepped back a little, as if to get a better view. "The tonality and dissonance look just like these swirling colors…"

Addie cleared her throat, and Julian looked around the room. "Sorry," he mumbled.

"No, don't stop," Cleo said. "I don't know what you said, but it was lovely."

Julian stared at the floor, seemingly preoccupied with the toe of his black boot. A few awkward seconds passed before Sophie piped up. "Well, well, well. Everyone have a seat. Cleo and I will bring out the cake."

Cleo didn't relish the idea of more mother-daughter bonding time in the kitchen. "Come give us a hand, Julian."

Julian raised his eyebrows—so did Josh, for that matter—but then followed them into the kitchen under the officious guise of a three-man cake siege. Once through the door, Sophie began a scattershot of questions.

"How long will you be in town, Julian?"

"I live here."

"Oh! I didn't know. I just assumed…"

"Apparently, it's a well-guarded secret," he said.

"And what do you do?"

Cleo sighed and shook her head. Her mom could be charmed by Julian and still lack the ability to imagine him in any type of gainful employment. On cue, Sophie glanced at his arms, in case he didn't get the crux of the question.

Julian smiled. "I'm a musician."

"Oh, I see," Sophie said, as if that explained it. Then she looked at the cabinets behind Julian's head. "Be a darling and get that cake platter down for me."

Julian reached for the platter on top of the cabinets, raising that pesky shirt again. *Oh, boy. Tattoos down his back, too.* Sophie cleared her throat.

"And what type of instrument do you play?"

"He owns a recording studio, Mom," Cleo said. The conversation needed to head in another direction.

"And I play guitar," Julian said.

"Oh, dear," Sophie said, stepping to the refrigerator to retrieve a white bakery box.

Cleo rolled her eyes. "Mom—"

"Does my occupation present a problem?" Julian asked, leaning casually against the counter.

"Compton girls have a weakness, that's all," Sophie said.

"Mother."

"For handsome guitarists," she continued, patting Julian's

cheek and scooting him away from the cutlery drawer. She placed the cake on the counter with a suspicious glance at Cleo. "I wonder if Josh plays an instrument?" Subtlety was not one of her mother's virtues.

"Is this what I think it is?" Cleo asked, opening the cake box. *Let's move along now.*

"It's *tres leches* cake from Mi Tierra," her mother said. She looked at Julian and smiled. "It's Cleo's favorite."

Cleo couldn't resist sticking a finger in the rich, creamy frosting and bringing it to her mouth. The light whipped topping melted in a puddle of milky sweetness on her tongue. She closed her eyes and shivered in delight, then took one more swipe at the cake. "Oh my God," she moaned. "So sinful."

"Goodness, Cleo," Sophie said. "Behave yourself."

"I don't have to. It's my birthday."

"You're being crude in front of our guest. Keep your fingers out of the cake and out of your mouth."

Julian did, in fact, look a tad uncomfortable. He was staring at her mouth, and his cheeks were flushed. His tongue darted out and licked his lips, almost as if he were thinking *she* was a delicious *tres leches* cake.

Sophie snapped him out of it. "Where did you receive your education, dear?"

"What?" Julian said.

The woman wouldn't quit. "Mother, most musicians are self—"

"I have a degree in composition from the Royal Academy of Music," Julian replied, glancing in the box. He stuck his finger in the frosting and held it up in front of Cleo's face. "I'm just a few credit hours short of a music performance degree, as well."

Well, now. Cleo hadn't expected that. Like her mother, she'd drawn some incorrect conclusions about Julian Wheaton.

Did Julian know the icing wasn't vegan? Apparently not, because he stuck his finger in his mouth and closed his eyes. "Mmm," he groaned.

Heat rose in Cleo's cheeks. Surely she hadn't looked as orgasmic when she'd done it? *Twice?*

"I didn't know they taught guitar at conservatories," Sophie said with a slight frown. Clearly, she didn't like all the finger licking and moaning going on in the suddenly too small kitchen.

"Sure they do. But I studied violin." Julian had a spot of frosting on his knuckle and licked it clean.

"What in the world is that in your tongue?" Sophie asked.

"A silver barbell," Julian said. He swallowed and then stuck his tongue back out for Sophie's inspection. She surprised Cleo by getting right up close and peering curiously into Julian's mouth.

"Why would you do something like that?" she asked.

Julian pulled his tongue back in. "Women say it enhances certain—"

"Oh God," Cleo said. She did not care to experience her mother's reaction to whatever skilled feats of oral heroism Julian thought he could perform with his tongue. "Julian, grab that stack of napkins, would you?"

"You take the napkins, Cleo," her mother said. "I need Julian to pop this cork." She handed him a dripping bottle from the silver ice bucket. "It's too bad you didn't complete your second degree, dear."

"You mean the performance degree? It's not too bad at all," he said, twisting the wire on the top of the bottle. "I was fourteen and quite done with the fuckers there, anyway."

Pop!

Her mom's mouth formed a perfect *O*, and Cleo was grateful the cork didn't land in it.

"You were only fourteen?" Sophie exclaimed when she'd

recovered. "Bless your heart. That's impressive. Come on, you can pour the bubbly."

Now it was Cleo's turn to be stunned. "Your mouth is open, sweetheart," her mother said as she followed Julian through the door. "It's unattractive."

•••

Julian demolished a piece of cake, making Cleo's mum deliriously happy. "It's good, isn't it?" she said, cutting another piece. "Have another."

"I really shouldn't, Sophie," he said. "I'm vegan."

"Goodness, don't be silly. There's no meat in it." She delivered the large chunk onto his plate.

"Mom, it has cream."

Julian shook his head at Cleo. He wasn't *that* big of a stickler, and besides, he didn't want to hurt Sophie's feelings. Also, the cake gave him something to do with his mouth while the other men talked about things in which he had no interest.

"Are you going to hit the charity golf tournament at the club, Clark?" Josh asked.

"I might take a stab at it," Cleo's father responded. Then he looked at Julian. "Do you play?"

"No, sir, I don't." Nothing bored him more than sports, in general, and golf, in particular.

"So, what sports do you like?" Josh asked.

Julian wiped his mouth and pretended to ponder an answer. "None," he said.

"None?" Josh repeated with an air of incredulity. "What about when you were a kid?"

"I suffered from a condition. Made it hard to play sports." He took a sip of water and then crammed another big piece of cake into his mouth—hoping the conversation would move quickly to another topic.

"Like asthma or something?"

What a dick. "Or something."

"I had asthma as a kid," Cleo's dad piped in. "That's why I play golf. Everyone knows it's not a real sport." He winked at Julian.

"Now, wait a minute there, Clark," Josh protested.

Addie cleared her throat, and Julian had the dreadful feeling she was about to defend his lack of athletic prowess. "Julian was in a music conservatory when most kids were kicking balls around," she said. "He was a musical prodigy."

He groaned, and Clark smiled at him. It was hard not to like Cleo's dad. He was cheerful and sharp, and even though his hair was thinning and gray, he was a ginger through and through, ruddy complexion and all. Luckily, Cleo got her ivory skin and delicate features from her mum.

Sophie reached over and patted Julian's hand. "He's a violinist," she said.

"Well, I play guitar now."

"No kidding," Clark said. Julian narrowed his eyes—maybe the old guy was being sarcastic.

Clark wiped his mouth and pushed his chair back. "Come with me, son."

"Oh God. Here we go," Cleo said.

Julian followed Cleo's old man into his den, where he pulled down a battered case from a closet. Inside was an old Martin beauty. Julian ached to touch it, and he let out a low whistle. "What is that? A 1910? Or maybe '08?"

Clark's eyes lit up as he recognized a fellow enthusiast. "It's a 1910. I'd offer to let you play it, but it needs to be restrung." He held up his hands. They displayed the classic signs of advanced arthritis. "I don't have the strength to string it anymore, much less play it."

Josh came into the room. "Hey," he said. "That looks old. What's it worth?"

The two guitarists gawked at him. "You mean in *money*?" Julian said.

"Well, yeah."

Julian shook his head and peered into the case. There was a pick and a pack of strings. "How about I put some new strings on for you, Clark? It won't take me long."

Clark rubbed his hands together in glee. "Only if you promise to play her when you're done."

Just what Julian was hoping to hear. "You've got a deal." He ran his hands up and down the instrument's neck, caressing it like a lover, then rested it on his lap and opened the pack of strings.

"Come on," Clark said to Josh. "Let's go have a cup of coffee and leave the two of them alone." Cleo had a cool old man.

A few minutes later, the new strings were on. Julian sat in front of Clark with the guitar resting comfortably in his lap. "What did you like to play?"

"I doubt you're familiar with my kind of music," Clark said.

"Try me."

"Okay. You ever hear of a fellow named Doc Watson?"

Julian smiled. "I might have." In fact, he'd been lucky enough to play with Doc once. But he didn't want to brag about it. Instead, he flat-picked "Beaumont Rag," relishing the stunned expression on Clark's face. Clark began tapping his foot and slapping his hand against his knee. Before Julian knew it, a sweet tenor voice rang out, blue and clear, like a lake sparkling in the sun.

This day hadn't been so terrible, after all. Julian was actually enjoying himself when the door to the study flew open.

"Clark," Sophie shrieked, interrupting their jam session. "Talk some sense into your daughter."

The women filed into the room in various states of distress. "What the heck's the matter?" Clark asked.

"For one thing, she's been evicted from her apartment."

The lawyer boyfriend slipped in quietly—a bit shell-shocked, if Julian had to guess. Addie wrung her hands together. Her eyes met Julian's and then quickly flitted away. Hmm. His sister looked guilty as hell. It didn't take a genius to figure out who had let the eviction bomb slip. She was at his side in an instant. "Just go along," she pleaded. "And don't be mad at me."

"Why would I be mad at you?" he whispered.

"Cleo," Sophie said. "Julian's a nice young man. And I'm sure he has a fine recording studio." She paused and looked at Julian with a pained smile. "But it makes no sense whatsoever for you to work there, much less move in."

What? Julian vigorously shook his head. Surely he'd heard wrong.

"It makes perfect sense. He needs a manager, and I need a job," Cleo said. "He has a manager's flat at the studio, and I need a place to stay."

Julian glared at Addie. "Manager's flat?"

"You know," she whispered. "Where I stayed while my place was being renovated?"

"You mean the spare room in my loft? Are you daft?"

"Wait a minute," Clark said. "What about the college?"

"I didn't get my job back," Cleo said. She crossed her arms defiantly and tapped her foot.

Clark rubbed a gnarly hand over his face. "Well…"

"What did you think was going to happen when you uprooted and followed that man to New York like some sort of stalker?" Sophie asked.

"Mother."

"You invited a stalker to move in with me?" Julian whispered to Addie.

Things disintegrated quickly. Julian only understood every other word as Cleo and her mum stood face-to-face with their hands on their hips, gums flapping and heads bouncing like pecking chickens.

"Now, now, girls," Clark said, his voice soothing. They stopped talking momentarily. "Cleo, I think it makes sense to stay with us while you get back on your feet. You haven't even looked into that job I heard about at the prep school. I know you're overqualified, but it's a start in the right direction."

Relief washed over Julian like a cleansing turquoise shower. Clark was clearly the voice of reason. But then Sophie had to open her mouth again.

"I mean, really, dear. You made one huge mistake already. Do you want to make another?" She glanced at Julian apologetically.

That might have been okay, but then the jock weighed in. "There's an obvious choice here, Cleo. You can either get a professional position at a prep school with a benefits package and a future, or you can work for this guy." He jerked his thumb in Julian's direction and did not sound at all apologetic.

Cleo, the little darling, puffed out her perfect chest and had the heart to look offended on his behalf. Before he knew it, he was talking. "The studio pays well, and she's perfect for the job. And," he added with a sneer at Josh, "I've been told I have a nice *benefits package*."

He was immediately covered in redhead. "Oh, Julian! Thank you."

The icy panic over what he'd just done thawed beneath the gratifying heat of Josh's glare and Cleo's soft tits pushing into his chest. He looked at Addie, who did everything she could to look elsewhere and awkwardly patted Cleo on the back. What the bloody hell had just happened?

Chapter Four

Cleo pulled into the gated lot as Julian had instructed. She squinted through her dirty windshield at the redbrick building. Was this it? She quickly checked the address again—hoping she had it right—because this place was freaking adorable.

It was the right place—201 Gonzalez Street! Oh, and there was Julian's El Camino, parked beneath the branches of a pecan tree overhanging the fence.

Cleo climbed out of her little Honda and gazed up at the three-story structure Julian called his studio and loft. Clearly a historic building, it could have been lifted right off a western movie set. A wraparound balcony hugged the second story, and a suspiciously nonfunctioning fire escape snaked up one side. Cleo shielded her eyes against the sun with her hand and looked at the windows. Which one belonged to the manager's flat?

A horn honked, and she jumped two feet in the air. It was Sherry pulling into the lot in the rented U-Haul. Her eyes widened as she took in the building, then she gave Cleo a thumbs-up and parked. Cleo yanked the big door open and reached in to help Sherry out. "Isn't it awesome?"

"Our boy's got some dough. The rent is astronomical in this tourist district."

"Oh, he's not paying rent," Cleo said, as Sherry hopped out of the truck. "Addie says he owns this building."

Sherry's eyebrows went up, and she slammed the door closed with her hip. "He's a hot, rich musician? And you're moving in with him? Cleo, we'd been making such progress. And now you're right back where you started."

That wasn't true. "No, I'm not. This thing with me and Guitar Boy, it's strictly business. I've got Josh, remember? And the job won't last long, anyway. I have no idea what to do in a recording studio."

Sherry rolled her eyes and waved her off. "It better last long enough to find another job. Let's get your stuff inside."

They opened the back of the truck and gazed upon Cleo's life in boxes. "God, I hope all this fits."

She'd already downsized significantly when she'd moved to New York. Surely the manager's flat in this decent-sized building wasn't any smaller than her New York efficiency, no matter what Addie said. Just in case, Cleo had already looked into a storage unit rental.

The sound of tires on gravel drew their attention. Addie pulled in next to the moving truck. "Sorry I'm late," she said, climbing out of her car.

Cleo held out her arms, and Addie gave her a quick hug. "We haven't seen much of you since my birthday."

"Yeah," added Sherry. "And that was two weeks ago. What have you been up to?"

"Oh, just lots of work," Addie said. She brushed invisible lint off her shirt and glanced around the parking lot—eyes flitting about but never landing directly on Cleo's. She and Sherry exchanged a brief glance. They'd have to dig up the dirt later. Addie obviously wasn't offering anything up at present.

"Well," said Sherry, tossing a curtain of shiny dark hair over her shoulder, "what are we all standing around out here for? I want to see this joint."

"He's done a lot of work to it," Addie said, locking her door with a chirp. "It really is a beautiful building."

Cleo and Sherry followed Addie down the sidewalk. *Conjunto* music from Sunset Station across the street floated festively on the air, but Cleo checked her enthusiasm. This was a short-term gig. She was only sticking around until she could find a real job. Because this was not a real job. And Julian was not a real boy.

Addie paused at the big double doors nestled into the corner of the building. Shaded by the balcony, the entrance was cool and comfortable, and the sidewalk and steps were clean and freshly swept. A neon sign lit up the window: SOUNDBOX STUDIO.

Addie bypassed the doorbell and opened the lid on a discreet keypad. She entered a code and turned the handle on the door. "After you," she said, extending an arm.

The big door closed behind them, and the outside world disappeared. It was so quiet—like a museum or a library— that Cleo whispered. "Wow. Look at this place."

The brick walls were adorned with autographed photos and posters of the bands who'd recorded here. Concert promotion posters, audition notices, and job opportunities covered the supportive columns in the center of the room.

Cleo and Sherry walked quietly around, taking in everything. A small anteroom sat off to the side, and Cleo poked her head in the door. A couple of ratty futons were pushed against the wall next to a small kitchenette.

"Is this my apartment?" she asked. The futons would have to go. She could probably squeeze her love seat in, but where the hell would she stick her bed?

"Goodness, no," said Addie. "Your flat doesn't have a

kitchen."

Cleo spun around. "I don't have a kitchen? Are you kidding me?"

"Julian's going to take care of that straight away. No worries. Anyway, that's just a lounge for musicians. Sometimes they need a comfortable place to take a break, especially if they're recording all night."

"Oh. So where *is* my apartment?"

"It's upstairs," Addie answered.

Cleo automatically looked at the ceiling. Didn't Julian live upstairs?

"You can peek in at the studio, if you want," Addie said, flipping a light switch. A window to the right lit up, revealing a room filled with Persian rugs, plump cushions, and overstuffed chairs. Guitars and percussion-type instruments rested in stands or on tables, and some were mounted on the walls. In the back was another small window. It was dark—must be the actual recording room where the equipment was. A stinging dart of panic pierced Cleo's armor of optimism. What was she doing here? Had she ever made a decision in her life when she wasn't drunk?

Addie moved past the recording studio to the back of the room. "Let's go upstairs." She pushed a button on an intercom to the right of a narrow door.

Julian's tinny voice came through the speaker. "It's unlocked."

Addie opened the door and led the way up narrow, steep stairs. Dim wall sconces did little to light the way, and Cleo grasped the wooden handrails. Julian stood at the top, appearing in silhouette with light pouring in from behind. His hair was a wild tangle of waves and a guitar hung on his back. A laser show would have been a nice touch.

He waved. "Howdy, girls," he said, allowing the rock star facade to go up in an anticlimactic puff of smoke.

Thank goodness.

...

Julian beamed as Cleo soaked everything in. He couldn't help it. Even though he did not want anyone living in it with him, he'd worked hard at fixing up the loft, and she seemed to appreciate it. The hardwood floors were polished to a gleam, and nothing was out of place. Tidy, just as he liked it.

A Steinway baby grand piano sat off to the left, its lid open and sheet music resting on the bench. The pages tugged at him. He'd been writing all morning—orange notes mostly—to distract himself from worrying about his newly acquired employee. *And roommate.*

He suddenly remembered his hair. When he wrote music, he tousled it like a madman. He must look like he'd licked his finger and stuck it in an electrical socket. He ran his fingers through his hair while he led the women past the couch, which held three guitars: a red Fender Stratocaster, a white Gibson Les Paul, and a Martin acoustic. He had over a hundred guitars, but those three were his workhorses. "Watch out for cords," he warned, kicking one out of the way. Amps were everywhere, and their relaxing buzz bathed the place in a golden hue.

Cleo's eyebrows shot up, clearly appreciating the hammered tin tiles on the ceiling. "Original?" she asked.

People rarely noticed the ceiling, even though he had painstakingly cleaned and painted each tile. "Yes," he said. "I have more in storage, because I tore out most of the third floor—only my bedroom is up there now. Don't know what I'll do with them but can't bear to part with them just yet."

Cleo put her finger on her chin, as if she were actually considering what to do with the tiles. "They'd make a great backsplash in a kitchen or bath."

"That's actually one of the projects I'm considering," Julian said.

"Oh, wow," Sherry said. "Do you guys know what just happened?"

"No, what?"

"I got bored."

Cleo laughed and elbowed Julian in the ribs. "Sherry was an art history major. Talk about boring."

"Hey, there's lots of sex in art," Sherry said. "Right, Addie?"

Addie stood quietly by the window, gazing out. "Right," she said, clearly distracted. That was the first word she'd said since coming up the stairs. Something was up.

"Ooh," Cleo said, tilting her head back. "So much natural lighting through those windows." Her deep red curls trailed down her back toward the swell of her ass, which was encased in a ridiculous patchwork skirt of crazy colors—like a jazz saxophone riff. A treasure of a Flogging Molly T-shirt topped off the ensemble. It was a shame she hadn't taken proper care of it. The logo was cracked and peeling.

"I hate artificial lighting," he said. It was a bit of an understatement. He could fucking *hear* artificial lighting.

Sherry had wandered over to the stairs, which were hidden in a polished oak cylinder jutting out of the brick-and-mortar wall. "What is this?"

"It's an enclosed spiral staircase. Addie can tell you about it. She's the one who found it while on holiday in Spain."

It was one of Addie's favorite stories—one of her greatest finds—and she never tired of telling how she'd rescued the staircase from destruction and the huge headache involved in getting it to the States. Julian waited for her to pick up the thread, but she remained silent, staring out the window. "Addie?"

She looked up at the sound of her name, but her eyes

were glazed and distant.

"Julian says there's a story with the staircase," Sherry prodded.

"Huh? Oh, yes. It was in an old cathedral they were tearing down," Addie said. Then she went back to staring out the window.

Okay, this thing with Addie was getting weird. He caught a furtive glance dart between Sherry and Cleo—apparently, they didn't know what the fuck was going on, either.

"Moving on to the kitchen," he said. "Your flat doesn't have one yet, so make yourself at home in mine." He tried to smile, but it severely pained him.

"And where is my flat?" Cleo asked, gazing around the loft.

Julian pointed to a door to the left of his refrigerator. "In there." He swallowed. "And I'm warning you. It's not very impressive."

"Oh," Cleo said weakly, "I don't need much. As long as my folks aren't in there, I'm good to go."

"I doubt they'd fit," he said. "Now, normally, you'd enter through your own door that comes off the parking lot. There's a set of stairs that lead straight to your flat." *In other words, don't traipse through my place to get to yours.*

He walked over and threw the door open with a flourish. "Ta-da!"

Cleo walked in first, followed by Sherry. They both stopped just inside the doorway. "Oh, Cleo," Sherry said. "This totally sucks."

Julian's skin prickled over the insult. Cleo stood in the doorway, gawking at the single room with a tiny alcove off to the side. The walls were brick, covered over with cement and mortar that was peeling off in chunks. The wood floors needed refinishing. No kitchen, as he'd already pointed out. His face grew hot with embarrassment.

Cleo inhaled deeply and clapped her hands over her mouth. Her green eyes were huge with shock, the eyebrows arched to the point of ridiculousness. He swore her hair was blushing. At the first smart-assed remark, he'd bloody well remind her that beggars could not be choosers.

He braced for it, but she made no sound other than a tiny squeak. He doubted that happened often. "Listen," he said. "If this doesn't suit you, you can damn well—"

She broke out into a huge grin, and her face lit up like fireworks. Fizzy orange bubbles floated to the ceiling and popped. Julian's nose tickled, as if he might sneeze, and his stomach fluttered a bit in a possible prelude to a laugh or, God forbid, a giggle. He hoped she'd speak before he did any one of those things or possibly all three.

"I love it."

"You do?"

"What's not to love? Just *look* at it."

"I am looking at it," Sherry said. "Are you joking?"

"It's absolutely perfect." Cleo sighed. "I mean, it's small. Don't get me wrong. But look at all the character." She ran over to the window and peered at the fire escape. "I've been living in a sterile, white-walled box with the formaldehyde smell of a FEMA trailer. This is great."

This wasn't what Julian had expected at all. He pointed to a low archway that led to the alcove. "That's where Addie slept when she stayed here before," he said. "There's a curtain rod up there. She hung some silky things from it and made a bedroom of sorts."

"I left them in the closet," Addie shouted from the other room.

Cleo ran to the closet and pulled out bolts of sheer purple organza. "Perfect," she said.

Julian turned the knob on a small door in the corner. "This is the water closet."

Cleo squealed as if she were on a silly game show. "I have a water closet!"

"You do know what that is, don't you?" he asked. The toilet was pushed right up next to the sink. A miniscule shower commandeered the corner, and you could only get to it by sucking in your gut and slipping past the sink.

"It's hilarious," Cleo said. She turned to face him, grinning. "I can brush my teeth, shower, and pee all at the same time."

"Thanks for the mental image," Sherry said.

Julian laughed in spite of himself.

A couple of hours later, they were finished bringing Cleo's things in. She would have to put some of it in storage, but she didn't seem to mind. She bounced around, opening boxes and rattling on about what to put where.

"I mean, why do I need more than two towels, anyway, right?" she asked nobody in particular. "How many can I use at one time? And I have a washer and dryer now, so no need to go to the Laundromat."

That sounded a bit too cozy. "Actually, *I* have a washer and dryer," he said. "You don't even have a kitchen."

"Oh. Well, I'll need more than two towels, then."

The idea of Cleo hoarding dirty towels in black trash bags to be hauled down the stairs made his blood run cold. "Just kidding," he said. "Of course you can use my washer and dryer."

First the kitchen, now the washer and dryer. What was next?

...

Cleo lay in her bed, which fit perfectly in the cozy alcove. Her muscles ached from carrying boxes and furniture upstairs, and she was exhausted. But sleep wouldn't come, even though she'd counted hammered tin ceiling tiles. There were seventy-two.

Tomorrow was Monday, and Julian hadn't said anything about what time to report to work. She doubted he'd rise at the crack of dawn and head to the studio. But should she? And what would she do when she got there?

Josh had come by earlier, taken a look around, and suggested she move in with him. What nerve. As if she'd move in with someone she'd only had a few dates with. *Better to move in with someone you just met in a club while drunk.*

A toilet flushed upstairs, and the ceiling creaked above her head as Julian walked across the floor to his bed, which was apparently right smack above her own. It squeaked as he climbed in. Holy cow, they might as well have bunk beds. Was the ceiling made out of rice paper?

She rolled over, aware of every sound she made. Hopefully, she wouldn't break out into hog-like snoring the moment she fell asleep. Had Julian heard everything Josh said earlier? Because he hadn't been charitable.

As she pondered what she had come to think of as the Josh Situation, a soulful electric wail floated down. Every exhausted muscle in her body responded by becoming blissfully heavy and melting into the mattress. Whatever Julian was playing, it was better than a massage. Her eyelids fluttered and then shut. Soon she struggled to finish a thought. *He's not a real boy, he's not a real boy…*

Something startled her awake. The air felt thick and heavy, overly warm. Maybe she'd just gotten hot and stuffy. The small window unit probably wasn't powerful enough to reach the alcove.

She jumped at a loud *bang!* Someone pounded on the door at the bottom of the stairs that led to the parking lot.

Had Josh come back? She tossed the covers off and padded across the room to peer down the stairs at the metal door. "Who is it?" she shouted. No answer. She went down the first two steps, then froze when the person banged again.

"Who is it?" she yelled a little louder.

Silence. She reached up and yanked the string that turned on a single lightbulb. It swung back and forth, lighting up the narrow passage with undulating shadows in true slasher film style.

She tiptoed down, and just as she reached the bottom step, whoever it was hit the door again. *Hard.* It shook from the force, and Cleo hightailed it back up the stairs, squealing the whole way. As she reached the top, a terrible thought occurred to her. What if she hadn't remembered to lock the door when she'd walked Josh out? She sure as heck wasn't going back down to check. Instead, she ran across the room to the door that led to Julian's loft.

She didn't bother knocking—just turned the knob and… it was locked. He had locked his door! Did he think she would sneak in there and steal something? Momentarily distracted by his gall, she almost forgot she was about to be killed and dismembered. Then the ax murderer banged on her door again.

"Julian!" She smacked the door with her open palm. "Help!"

No response. She grabbed her phone and called him.

"Whatzit?" he slurred.

"Somebody's trying to get into my apartment—"

"Addie?" All traces of sleepiness disappeared. "I'll be right there. Call nine-one-one!"

"No, it's Cleo." After a long, awkward pause, she added, "Compton."

"Jesus. You scared the shit out of me," he said.

"Someone's banging on my door!"

"Listen, love, old buildings make a lot of strange noises. This one never shuts up. You'll get used to it."

"No, really—"

"It's the wind. Have you looked outside? That tropical storm pushed its way through from the Gulf. We have some high winds, and your hollow metal door is popping in and out. I can hear it from here. It does that, okay? Now go to sleep. You've had a big day."

There was no need to speak as if he were soothing a silly little girl. She looked out the window. Leaves from the pecan tree swirled about the parking lot, traffic lights swung back and forth, and the loose pane of glass vibrated beneath her fingers from the force of the wind.

He was right, and she sighed into the phone. "Sorry for waking you."

"It's okay. My bedroom is right over yours, and I heard the banging. I mistook it for something else, even though it was more forceful than I'd expect from your boyfriend. I guess he's gone? Or is he cowering beneath the bed?"

He hung up before she could respond.

Settling back into her mattress, Cleo watched the shadows play across the wall and listened to the turmoil outside. A huge boom shook the room. She sat up and fumbled with the lamp on her nightstand. No electricity.

She had a storm phobia. When she was a child, Hurricane Gilbert hit the coast, spawning storms and tornados all across south Texas. One of those storms had forced the limb of a chinaberry tree through her bedroom window in the middle of the night. She hadn't been physically injured, but it had left her traumatized. Everyone who knew her knew she didn't suffer storms well.

Something smashed hard against the window, and the phone was to her ear before she knew what she was doing. She chewed her nails until she was treated to a very annoyed,

"What?"

"The electricity is out. Did you know that?"

She swallowed during the pause.

"No. I was asleep. Thanks for informing me. I'm hanging up now."

"Julian?"

Shit. He'd hung up.

Well, he was the landlord. He had to deal with this. She had no intention of going without electricity for the rest of the night. It didn't matter that there was really nothing he could do about it. She called him back.

"Fuck," was all he said.

"I'm sorry to bother you, but it's getting hot in here."

"I'll call God for you in the morning. I'd call him now, but it would be bloody inconsiderate of me since he's probably trying to sleep."

"I'm scared," she whispered.

"What?"

"I'm scared of storms."

A loud exhalation invaded her ear. "Are you kidding me?"

"I wish I was. This is embarrassing, believe me."

"I'm not sure what you'd like me to do about it."

"Would you consider sleeping on my couch?" It was more of a love seat. But the thought of him curled up on it made her feel safe.

"Why would I do that? I've got a nice, comfy bed. Be a big girl and go to sleep now, would you? Daddy will see you in the morning."

He hung up. Cleo crawled out of bed and away from the window. Good grief, she was thirty years old. At what point, exactly, would she grow up? Normally, she could pull it together enough to avoid dissolving into a toddler-style fit, but this building was so old and...*shuddery*.

She sat on her love seat—no way was she crawling into bed in front of that window—and decided to ride out the storm like an adult.

Her phone rang.

"What?" she answered.

"If you're truly frightened you can crawl in bed with me. We'll add it to the nonexistent list of employee benefits."

"I don't think sharing a bed is a suitable solution, and you know it. I don't see why you can't just come down here. My couch is fine."

"Are you seriously worried that I'm going to roll over and accidentally fuck you?"

She gasped. And yes, that was exactly what she was worried about.

"Forget it. And I couldn't get up there even if I wanted to, seeing as how you've locked the door." She followed it up with a silent *asshole*.

"Suit yourself. And, by the way, the door locks from your side."

She hung up and settled in with new resolve, hugging a pillow to her chest. The door banged, the wind howled, the window rattled, and a flash of lightning illuminated the old pecan tree in the yard. A branch scraped loudly against the window, and she was back at Julian's door.

•••

Julian felt his way down the hallway to the bathroom. He automatically flipped the light switch before realizing the futility of it. The toilet was a few steps away; he found it easily and lined himself up for a whiz.

The redhead was a hysterical moron. He was glad she hadn't taken him up on the offer of his bed. The last thing he needed was to lie awake with her curvy body next to his all night.

He finished up and headed back to his bedroom. Lightning lit up the hallway like a nightclub dance floor, and the unmistakable form of a woman appeared out of nowhere. She began to scream. And because adrenaline was a strange chemical, he screamed, too.

"Jesus Christ, Big Red. Are you trying to give me a heart attack?"

"Julian?"

"Who else would I be? What are you doing up here?"

She stepped toward him with her arms outstretched like a zombie. Her fingertips met his bare chest, and she yanked them to her sides as if he were a sizzling-hot poker. "Can I take you up on your offer?" she asked.

The darkness prevented him from seeing her face, but the outline of her curls trembled. He fought a stupid urge to wrap his arms around her. "I thought you were afraid of accidental sex."

"I'm more afraid of the storm."

He wasn't. With a sigh of resignation, he stepped around her. "C'mon."

She stayed on his heels until they hit the doorway to his bedroom. She hesitated before following him to the bed, where she stood awkwardly at the side while he climbed in. He lay down, but she didn't budge.

"You're creeping me out," he said, patting the pillow next to him. "I've seen this movie, and I don't like how it ends."

"Nice," she said, finally getting in bed. "Bring up something like that right now."

"I'm the one who should be scared," he said. "Now lie down and shut up."

She did. And with much fanfare and pillow fluffing.

Julian rolled over, facing away from her. The bed shook constantly as the silly woman jumped at every sound. Julian clung to the side. How long could the night possibly last? He breathed loud and regular in an effort to feign sleep, but she stirred fitfully and cleared her throat in obvious attempts at waking him.

"You know, this building is almost a hundred years old. It's withstood a lot of weather," he finally said.

"It's probably all crumbly and barely holding itself together." She flopped over on her side. "We shouldn't even be on the top story like this. We're going to get whisked away like Dorothy in *The Wizard of Oz*." He sensed those red eyebrows knitting together. "I wish you had just come downstairs and slept in my apartment like I asked you to."

"Are you kidding? We'd be squished like cucumbers in a sandwich when the whole thing fell down."

She made a snorting noise, and he tried to think of something to take her mind off the storm. He thought of one thing, but it was a horribly bad idea. "So," he said. "Why'd you run off to New York?"

"Do you know Lou Michaels?"

"Lou Michaels?"

"Yeah. Of End Times."

"He's an iconic guitarist in one of the world's most famous bands. I don't exactly live under a rock, love."

"Yeah, well, I kind of had this obsession with him. Actually, I kind of had this obsession with rock stars in general, but with him in particular."

She really was a stalker. "Tell me he doesn't have a restraining order against you."

"Of course not. Although I admit it was a long infatuation. I fell for him when I was fifteen years old and he was on the cover of *Rock 'n' Spin*. I was insanely crazy for him."

"Wow." Julian yawned. Her and about half the female population. "He owns *Rock 'n' Spin* now, you know."

"Yeah, I know. Anyway, when we were seventeen, Sherry

and I got all dressed up for an End Times concert. We pushed our way to the front of the stage, hoping to get noticed."

"Like groupies?"

"Kind of," she whispered, as if they weren't alone in bed together during a typhoon and might be overheard.

He rolled over so he could hear better, seeing as how they were now whispering and things had become interesting. "Are you telling me that you and Sherry got dolled up like hookers to get the attention of Lou Michaels?"

"We weren't dolled up like hookers, good grief. It was more of a punk slut look."

A clap of thunder stifled his laugh. Thinking about Big Red in fishnets and heavy black eyeliner cracked him up, but it also had his dick standing at attention, and he really didn't need that right now. "And?" he asked, because he couldn't resist.

"I got noticed."

"I bet you did," he muttered.

"I was whisked backstage, where it was hectic and crowded, and I didn't even realize Sherry wasn't with me. Before I knew it, I was on a bus headed for the hotel."

"Go on," he urged.

"I don't know if you've ever been to one of those post-concert parties," she said, "but believe me, it's everything you've heard times ten. I was terrified."

He knew exactly what went on at post-concert parties. "Did you meet Lou?"

"Lou never showed up. It was mostly the backup band and roadies."

Bloody hell. The road crew and backup musicians were not the guys you wanted to party with. Overworked, underpaid, and unappreciated made for some truly bad behavior on the road. She was lucky if she escaped with her fishnets intact.

The idea of Cleo being mishandled by those rough, brawly

guys was unsettling. "Then what happened?"

"A guy from the opening act took care of me."

"Took care of you how?"

She giggled in the dark, and he loved the sight of it—orange sparklers on the Fourth of July. "By calling me a cab and waiting in the lobby with me. Do you remember that band Slice?"

His already tense stomach lurched as a tide of panic rolled through him. He forced his jaw to unclench in order to ask casually, "It was somebody from Slice?"

"The singer. What was his name?"

"Mitch Landrum," he spat.

"Right. Mitch. He was there, and he saw right through me. I'm sure I was lit up like a bonfire. Don't know if you've noticed, but I have a tendency to blush. Anyway, he protected me and made sure I got out of there safely. Such a nice guy. I wonder what he's doing now."

Julian put his fists up to his eyes. What were the fucking odds?

"Hey, have I bored you to sleep?"

"No, I'm awake." Utterly, completely, and infuriatingly awake. And the redhead kept talking.

"I never quit carrying the torch for Lou, so when End Times came to town last year, I — "

"Donned fishnets again?"

"No! I went with our student editor to snag an interview. I was the faculty sponsor for the campus newspaper. Anyway, we were able to sit down with Lou. He and I hit it off, and a couple of months later, a job opened up at *Rock 'n' Spin*. In the throes of a pre-midlife crisis, I left my teaching position in the naive hopes of fulfilling two teenage dreams."

"Two? Besides Lou, who else were you hoping to fuck?"

A hand came out of nowhere and smacked him on top of his head. "My dream was to interview rock stars like a real writer. But I ended up being the world's oldest and most overqualified coffee girl instead. That worked out about like you'd expect, and I returned home in humiliation. Now I'm in bed with my boss, so things aren't really looking up."

Her auburn curls fanned across the pillow. He'd love to run his fingers through them, but he turned over instead, reaching beneath his own pillow in the hopes of locating a guitar pick or two. He found one and began knuckle-rolling it through his fingers.

"Did you and Lou ever hook up?" he asked, lowering his voice to sound sincere and save her pride.

"That's another story for another storm."

Poor darling. Lou had probably passed her in the hall, bumped into her hand, and she hadn't washed it since.

The skies opened up, and hail began pounding the roof, showering the room in a mesmerizing deluge of glowing blue streamers.

A warm behind scooted up next to his, and he rather liked the feel of it.

. . .

The next morning, Cleo woke with a start, as if she'd heard gunshots or a bloodcurdling scream, which of course, she hadn't. She sat up in bed, lifting her hair out of her eyes. Where the holy hell was she?

An unfamiliar room, that's where. In an unfamiliar bed. Lying next to a...guitar. She sighed and flopped back against the pillow. She was in Julian's bed. Dang, but that hadn't taken long. Sex or no sex, she'd already plowed through some boundaries.

Shit, what time was it? The sun was up, but not *too* up. It was maybe seven. Julian was probably in the bathroom or eating breakfast.

She rolled out of bed and crept out to the hall. The bathroom was empty, and after taking advantage of that, she headed for the stairs, combing her hair with her fingers and wiping the dried drool off her cheek. *That must have been pretty.* She tiptoed down and paused at the bottom to take a deep breath, then power walked into the room with her chin held high—looking as professional as one could in Hello Kitty pajama pants.

And it was all for nothing, because the kitchen was empty. So was the rest of the loft. She followed her nose to the coffee and found the mugs on her first try. *Bingo!* No tacky World's Best Guitarist mugs, either. Julian had a full set of matching grown-up artisan stoneware.

She opened the refrigerator and frowned. No half-and-half. *Damn vegan.* She found a carton of almond milk, watered down her coffee with it, and took the first glorious sip. Her tummy growled mightily, and she realized she was in the awkward position of having no food of her own. She eased the fridge door open—*sleeping with the boss and stealing his food all within the first twenty-four hours*—to see what she could find.

Heavy footsteps bounded up the stairs from the studio, as if someone took them two at a time. She didn't even have a chance to shut the door before Julian burst into the loft, shirtless and drenched in sweat. He'd been running, obviously. Which meant bad guys were after him with machetes or, worse, he was a regular morning runner. A vegan runner—she narrowed her eyes—with a *man bun*. Holy cow, the only way he could be more of a cliché was if he lived in Austin.

He performed some truly obnoxious stretching, and Cleo took advantage by practicing tattoo appreciation. Tribal Aztec designs on both pecs, complemented by pierced nipples (thank God they were both still there), and a musical score across a very toned lower abdomen. No point in asking where he kept the doughnuts hidden. She took a sip of coffee, swallowed, and then cleared her throat. Loudly.

Julian looked up. Blankly.

"Don't tell me I'm going to have to introduce myself after we've slept together," Cleo said.

"I'm sure it wouldn't be the first time," Julian said with a wink and a *caught you looking* grin. Cleo hid behind another gulp of coffee, and her stomach created a timely diversion with a strategic growl.

"Help yourself to anything in the refrigerator or pantry," Julian said, yanking his man bun loose. "I've got to hit the shower—meeting in twenty minutes."

"Do you have actual edible things? And what meeting? Should I attend?"

Julian breezed past her, headed to the stairs. "Yes, don't worry about it, and no."

Okay, so not super chatty after a run. "Well, what do I do today?"

He paused at the stairs and shrugged. "Whatever you want, I guess."

Two hours later, Cleo was showered, dressed, and fairly unpacked. Also, untethered. She floated around from one spot to the other, adrift in her new life and so-called job.

Julian was still in a meeting down in the studio, where she hadn't even ventured, while she was apparently expected to settle into being a fully kept woman. The whole situation reeked of New York and Lou Michaels, and she didn't like it. She pulled her hair back, tucked her pink blouse with the Peter Pan collar into the best invention since sliced bread—dressy yoga pants in steel gray—and headed for the studio.

• • •

Julian tapped his pencil on the table while his lawyer, Neil, gabbed on the phone. This was taking longer than it should, and he had a million things to do. He reached over and grabbed a bottle of water from the lounge's mini-fridge, holding it up to Neil with raised eyebrows. Neil shook his head and mouthed *no, thanks*, so Julian unscrewed the cap and chugged half the bottle. There were only two left. He'd have to restock the fridge before the scheduled band showed up to record tonight. That was if the bloody technician ever arrived. He was an hour late. If the bass feed didn't get fixed today, Julian would have to reschedule the band.

On top of all that, the orange notes running through his mind tugged at him like a small, annoying child. If only he could get to his piano…

"Sorry about that," Neil said, putting his phone on the table. They were in the lounge because every square inch of the desk in the studio's foyer was covered. At first glance, it looked a mess. But Julian had a system. Rows of sticky notes in decreasing order of urgency. Mail to be dealt with, mail to be recycled, mail to be filed. To-do lists and contact information. He couldn't move any of it because if even one thing were amiss, the entire system fell apart.

"Now where were we?" Neil asked.

"Carlos's royalty payout," Julian said.

A door slammed. The studio's front door was locked—people had to be buzzed in. A little jolt shot through him—a bright orange one—because either they had an intruder, or Cleo had come down to the studio.

"Is somebody here?" Neil asked.

"No. Well, yes. It's just my—" God. What was she again?

"Studio manager." Orange bubbles floated in with Cleo's voice. She smiled at Julian and walked right up to Neil, hand extended. "Hi. I'm Cleo Compton."

Neil took her hand and glanced at Julian. Great. What was she doing down here? At least she was wearing real pants—Julian looked closely—or something fairly close to real pants, anyway.

"Cleo, this is Neil Martinez. You might want to jerk your hand back. He's a lawyer."

Cleo's smile intensified. "I love lawyers!"

Neil laughed. "I'm not used to enthusiasm where my job is concerned."

Julian rolled his eyes. "She dates a lawyer. She's like a lawyer groupie."

Cleo laughed, but it sounded wrong. It looked wrong, too. No orange bubbles, just bursts of mist. It sounded—and looked—insincere. He'd been kidding. Was she insulted?

"I'm just teasing, of course," he said. Lame.

"I know." She looked around the room, wringing her hands together.

"Do you need something?" he asked.

Cleo frowned at him. "No. Do *you* need something?"

Julian crossed his arms and leaned back in his chair. "Nope."

Neil had returned to his laptop screen, which displayed Carlos Tejada's recording contract.

"You know this kid should have an agent looking out for him, right, Julian?"

"That's the last thing he needs, believe me," Julian said, watching Cleo out of the corner of his eye. "It would just be one more person taking a bite out of him. You shore this up and send it back to the label. If they don't take it, I've got another plan in mind."

Cleo stepped away and opened the nearest cabinet, then scribbled in a spiral notebook. What the fuck was she doing?

"How many acts are you managing for free now?" Neil asked.

Julian downed the last of his water and tossed the bottle in the recycling bin by the door. "I don't manage acts. You know that."

Neil pushed his glasses up on his nose and typed in a few numbers. "Right. You just pay me to negotiate contracts for people for no reason at all."

Cleo stopped scribbling, but she didn't look up. Nosy woman.

"It's not for no reason at all. It's just not for profit. Are we almost done?"

Neil shuffled some papers. "I'll be out of your way as soon as possible."

"Don't be silly," Cleo said. "Nobody's in anybody's way."

"That's not entirely true," Julian said, under his breath.

Cleo noisily scrounged through all the cabinets, the closet, and the mini-fridge.

"What are you doing?" Julian asked. He didn't like people riffling through his shit.

"Making a list," she said. "We need to restock the lounge."

"No, we don't," Julian said. "But put water on the list."

"Already did."

She put her notebook down and began yanking pieces of paper off the overburdened bulletin board. Julian had been meaning to do that himself—most of the flyers and notices were outdated. She probably couldn't ruin anything, so he tried to focus on Neil, but Cleo hummed while she worked— juicy tangerine notes that increased his desire to sit down at the piano—and he found it hard to concentrate.

In under a minute, the bulletin board was practically bare. Three notices were left, one of which he'd been looking for. Cleo tossed the excess paper into the recycling bin and, without so much as a nod in Julian's direction, headed into the foyer, straight for his desk. "Excuse me, Neil," Julian said, jumping up. Couldn't let her get near the desk.

He was too slow, and Cleo reached the desk just as the phone rang.

"Soundbox Studio. How may I help you?" Bubbles, bubbles, bubbles… They floated to the ceiling, and a few popped in his stomach.

"Cleo," he whispered. "Give me the phone."

Cleo put her hand up and glared at him. He took a step back. She had actually *given him the hand.* "I'm sorry, Eddie. Why are you calling?"

"Give me the phone," Julian hissed. Eddie was the technician. The little shit was going to try to reschedule, and Julian needed him here today.

Cleo frowned at Julian and dodged his grab for the phone. Then, while she listened to Eddie, she scanned the desk, eyes darting back and forth until she settled on the open schedule.

"No," she said. "We're not rescheduling. We have a band coming in tonight." She snatched up a business card—messing up the entire perfectly aligned row sorted by color first, and alphabetically second. "If you're not here in thirty minutes I'm calling Pete's Pipes and Plugs."

Julian put his hands over his face as Cleo continued threatening the recording equipment technician with calling a plumber.

"Dang right you will," Cleo said. "And we'll expect a 10 percent discount for the stress and inconvenience." She hung up.

Wait…it worked? "He's coming?" Julian asked.

"Of course he is," Cleo said. "Let's see, what else do we have going on here?" She fingered the sticky notes and business cards, sorting them *not by color.* Julian's vision began to blur as she mucked it all up.

"What are you doing?"

"Organizing. This is a mess."

"No, it's not a mess. It's a system." And he knew how to work it. He was probably the most organized person in the world.

"Well, I don't like it. And why on earth is everything written down on *paper*?"

She said "paper" like it was dirty word. What else was he supposed to write things down on? He reached in his pockets to grab his picks. Otherwise he would grab everything out of Cleo's hands and begin lining them up perfectly. According to color.

Neil came into the room, carrying his briefcase and laptop. "We're all done," he said. Julian reached out for a handshake but realized too late that Neil offered his hand to Cleo. Julian's was left hanging like a lonely matzo ball.

"I'll email a copy of the revised contract." Neil said.

"Okay, that would be—"

"When can we expect it?" Cleo asked.

Really? Did she even know what the contract was for? For all she knew, it was for Pete's Pipes and Plugs.

"How does two weeks sound?" Neil asked.

Cleo raised an eyebrow. "How about one?"

"You got it." He waved at Julian. "Later, kid."

Seriously? Julian abandoned his picks to run both hands through his hair. He was losing control of things, but it felt… *fine.*

Cleo sat and turned on the computer. Strands of hair had sprung free from her ponytail and curled around her face. She tapped her fingers on the desk while waiting for the machine to boot up. "I'm going to get you all set up. Don't worry."

He pulled up a chair to see what she'd do next. She turned her green eyes on him. "Oh. You're dismissed."

"Dismissed? Are you kidding?"

"No." She waved her hand in a shooing motion. "You're in my personal space. Go make music or something."

There was nothing he wanted to do more, but he put it aside. "Would you like to learn a little about recording?"

Chapter Five

The daily recording lessons on the mixing board were fun. Three weeks ago, Cleo had been intimidated by it all, but with Julian's help, she'd become more comfortable and was having a blast with the levers and knobs. She'd never get to record anyone—Soundbox used engineers for that—but she'd learned some basics. Guitar Boy was a surprisingly good teacher. And he loved his studio.

Cleo had worked extra hard over the past few weeks. She'd overseen a website launch because the idiot hadn't even had one, had written marketing literature—he didn't have any of that, either—and was in the process of updating the billing system because the current one consisted of Julian telling the bands how much they owed as they walked out saying they'd pay him later.

She was enjoying herself. And she was mingling with more artists than she ever had at *Rock 'n' Spin*. Maybe they weren't famous, but they were interesting and talented.

This was beginning to feel like a real job and not just something to do while waiting for plan B to materialize out of thin air.

Julian sat next to her. He put his hand over hers and pushed a lever up. "Did you know you poke your tongue out when you're enthralled with something?" he asked.

If she didn't know better, she'd think he was flirting.

"I don't poke my tongue out, and stop staring at my face."

"What would you have me stare at instead?"

Okay. He was flirting. And she didn't dignify it with a response. "Can we go over clipping again? Or how to reduce the system gain?"

Julian uncrossed his arms and slid off the stool. "What do you say we go grab some lunch? You're starting to ask questions for an engineer to answer. You've exhausted me."

"Poor baby. I know you're not used to working hard."

That was a lie. He was an incredibly hard worker. Devoted to helping the artists who came to the studio, he often played on their albums, and not just guitar, either. He was wicked with a set of drumsticks, and he pounded the piano like a pro. He produced new arrangements on the fly, made subtle suggestions that yielded huge results, and she suspected he could out-engineer the engineers.

She stole a sideways glance at him. His hair stuck out like Einstein's. Must have been writing music earlier. His concert T-shirt—Better Than Ezra—had creased sleeves, as if he'd ironed it. Tousled hair, vintage T-shirts. A relaxed exterior disguised an inner control freak. His right hand tirelessly worked the guitar picks he kept in his pocket, making soft clicking sounds.

"Let's go grab a taco before the lunch crowd," he said. "I'm hungry."

"The Morones Brothers are coming by at two o'clock. Did you forget?" The look on his face told her he had. Honestly, how had he ever managed without her?

"We'll eat lunch here then," he said, nodding toward the

stairs that led to the loft. "By the way, don't let them scare you. They're pussycats."

Cleo waved her hand as if she weren't worried, even though she was. "No problem. I used to teach at a community college."

The Morones Brothers were a Latino hip-hop group who'd recorded their demo at Soundbox. They had a reputation for being bad *vatos*. But that wasn't what concerned Cleo. She gulped at the memory of her self-assured response of *Sure!* when Julian had asked her to interview the trio and write an article. Julian's longtime friend Manny Bloom had promised to publish it in *Upbeat*, a local arts and events rag that barely stayed afloat. It was hardly a *Rock 'n' Spin* assignment. But still, what if it ended up being a steaming pile of bullshit? She didn't want to let anyone down.

Julian grinned and followed her to the staircase. "You keep going over all the questions you've prepared, and mumbling to yourself, and doing that thing you do with your knuckles. You're an annoying little fucker when you're nervous."

Cleo stopped on the second step and turned around to protest being referred to as an annoying little fucker. Julian bumped into her, then took a step back. They were nose to nose. Perfect kissing height.

"Josh doesn't find me annoying."

"That's because he's too self-absorbed."

Josh wasn't self-absorbed, he was just busy with important things like contracts and golf and avoiding words like "fucker." And he still managed to make time for her. At least weekly. Or every other week, anyway. Busy, mature people ran busy, mature lives.

She spun back and marched up the stairs, pushing the door open at the top. The loft was, as usual, pristine, orderly, and humming with the buzz of the amplifiers plugged into every outlet. Four guitars rested on the couch, lined up like perfect soldiers. She headed for the kitchen. "Sorry I annoy you. You have no annoying habits at all, of course."

She touched his red Stratocaster as she passed, intentionally moving it a couple of inches to the left. Julian came right along behind her and straightened it.

"No annoying habits at all," he said. There was a smile in his voice, and she grinned in response.

Cleo began pulling out salad fixings, because ham and cheese for a sandwich would result in a vegan diatribe for which she currently had no patience. "You want kale?" she asked, knowing that of course he wanted kale. Vegans always wanted kale.

"I can do that," Julian said, grabbing the greens away and pointing at a bar stool. "Stop acting like the fucking maid."

He couldn't do anything nice without making a girl feel like it was all her fault.

"Thanks for trusting me to do this interview."

"You can write, right?" he asked. "Not that anybody is going to read it."

"Of course I can write. And if not, I make a killer cup of coffee."

"So far, I've seen evidence of neither."

That was true. By the time she got up in the mornings, he'd already made coffee. And because she could smell it from her apartment, she didn't see the point of brewing her own.

Julian quickly prepared a salad and set it in front of her, along with a bowl of strawberries. "Don't be nervous," he said quietly. "You'll do fine. More than fine, probably, just like you've done everything else."

He patted her hand, and the contact sizzled, causing her heart to pound. Good grief. That should have stopped by now.

"Dressing's in the fridge. I'm going upstairs for a few minutes."

"You're not going to eat?" she asked. "You said you were

hungry."

"Changed my mind."

He loped casually toward the stairs, but Cleo had the distinct impression he was trying not to run.

...

Julian tingled all over. His vision was clouded with colors that weren't even associated with sounds. A guitar would help.

Cleo was killing him. It was time to power through the outer edges of lust and get to the eye of the storm. In other words, to where reality set in and her endless faults irritated him instead of turning him on.

She had moved in under the guise of working until she could get back on her feet. Nobody had come out and said that, but it was the unspoken understanding. Instead, she was working her sweet little ass off and doing a bang-up job. And if that weren't bad enough, he fucking liked her. And he didn't want to like her.

He sat on the bed and reached for his faithful Fender. Predictably, it was already plugged into an amp. He liked predictable. He ordered his life around it. And now Cleo had muddied it all up by barging into his life—and his heart—uninvited.

That had only happened once before, and it had been disastrous.

He ran his fingers over the tattoos on his forearm, feeling the small scars beneath the ink. If only everything in his past was as easy to hide.

He leaned back against the headboard, letting the weight of the guitar settle into his lap. If he was patient, a song would come.

At first, it was a single turquoise note, but he quickly teased a rainbow out of it. A few sexy thoughts of Cleo were teased up as well, and he settled the guitar lower on his hips. His head sank back as a melodic strain poured through him. The instrument moaned in ecstasy as he bent a note up, coaxing, enticing, and sweet-talking a candy-apple wail out of it before bringing it down with a shudder.

With Cleo in mind, he tickled the strings and stroked the neck, caressing a deep, mellow tone from somewhere inside the guitar's polished wood. He raised his hips and built a crescendo, bringing the guitar to a fucking scream. *He'd like to make Cleo scream...*

"Knock, knock. Julian?"

With a pathetic flat wail, he tossed the guitar aside and hastily sat up.

"Excuse me," Cleo said, exploding into a scarlet blush. "I'm sorry..."

"I was just playing guitar," he stammered. *Not wanking off.*

"The Morones Brothers are here. Um, take your time, though," Cleo said. Then she fled as if a swarm of bees was on her heels.

Julian cringed and closed his eyes. He allowed exactly ten seconds of utter humiliation, then got up and gathered his wits. As he headed for the door, his phone buzzed with a text. He looked at it and smiled. He could practically hear the overdone Texas drawl of one of his favorite female pastimes.

HEY, Y'ALL—BOOTY CALL! I'LL BE IN TOWN TOMORROW IF YOU FEEL LIKE WRINKLIN' SOME SHEETS.

This was exactly what he needed—to wrinkle some sheets with a woman who didn't frazzle him. With a woman who, unlike Cleo, had somewhere to go the next morning.

Chapter Six

Cleo lay in bed, keeping a wary eye on the ceiling fan. The creaking thing rocked back and forth, whirring and humming, its blades squeaking in time with the box spring upstairs. She couldn't believe it had taken this long for the headboard to start hitting the wall—no part of Julian suggested a life of celibacy—but it sucked that she had to listen to it.

She flopped over and sighed. Her pillow was flat, so she fluffed it. With her fist. It was also hot in the room, so she kicked her covers off. Her feet became tangled, so she went to war, kicking and shoving and grunting until she had them in a wad of a mess that she kicked to the floor. There now. That was better.

She lay back down and closed her eyes. *Creak, creak, creak…whir, whir, whir…bang, bang, bang.* It was hard to relax while imagining the gruesome details of being chopped to bits by a ceiling fan. Or while imagining Julian on top of her, making her moan like that obnoxious woman—whoever she was—upstairs.

Something that felt like plaster hit her face. She swatted

it away. The entire ceiling would come down if they didn't finish soon. Finally the squeaking and whirring became faster, and the woman's moans turned into a frenzied chorus of, "Oh God, oh God, oh God…Julian!"

"*Oh God, oh God, oh God…Julian!*" Cleo mimicked in her best whiny voice, the one she could do while sticking her tongue out. Then it was quiet. Blissfully, awesomely, peacefully quiet. Her ceiling fan settled down to its usual death rattle, and she retrieved her bed linens from the floor. Now she could finally get some sleep. It was five in the morning. What kind of people had sex at five in the morning?

She turned over, pulled the covers up, and relaxed into her pillow. But then she heard something. She held her breath to hear it better. Giggling. Great. And creaking floorboards. It was Julian's footsteps…*one, two, three, four, five—pause— one, two, three, four, five*. He'd walked to the guitar stand and back. More giggles. More squeaking bedsprings. The rhythm of conversation.

Cleo put her pillow over her head. One simply *must* get some sleep, after all.

She closed her eyes. Were they still talking? She lifted the pillow—didn't hear anything, so she held her breath and waited…sure enough. They were still talking! Were they just going to *blab, blab, blab* until the sun came up? How was a girl to get any sleep?

Finally, the slow, familiar wail of Julian's guitar rang out. It was his lullaby song, the one he played almost every night. Only it wasn't doing its job. Instead of being lulled into sleep, Cleo was edgy, irritable, and…*horny*.

She dragged her hands across the sheet, pressing her palms into the textured pattern of the mattress, digging her nails in slowly. What would it feel like to run her hands all over Julian's back? She closed her eyes. The strains of music entered her room through the ceiling, and their ghostly, melodious fingertips brushed her skin, leaving trails of gooseflesh. A long note ached with passion as Julian milked it for vibrato. It shook Cleo to the core, and in her mind she saw his face—eyes closed, lips parted, brows drawn in an excruciating mix of pain and pleasure—his sex face.

She swirled in an erotic whirlwind, stirred by Julian. If only she could seamlessly transfer those feelings to Josh.

Josh. She wasn't trying to string him along. He was a great guy, a handsome guy, an almost perfect guy. But her tiny obsession with Julian—yes, she admitted it—was getting in the way. Why couldn't she get past musicians? What was it about them that turned her into a spineless, quivering mess?

But she wasn't spineless around Julian. She was competent and strong and…a quivering mess.

The Strut and Putt Gala at Josh's country club was tomorrow evening, looming like prom night. All the big decisions had been made: shoes, dress, hair. But what about the big one? Would she put out or not? It should be a no-brainer. Especially after what she'd listened to all night.

Her mind followed one train of thought—*guitars and tattoos*—to the next—*tuxedos and ball gowns*—until it finally veered off into the murky world of dreams.

She woke up a couple of hours later, feeling hungover from both the quantity and quality of the sleep she'd snagged. What she needed more than anything was coffee. And while she owned a perfectly good French press, normally she had coffee with Julian. In his kitchen and with his organic, free-trade coffee she couldn't afford but had come to appreciate.

She listened to the sounds from the other side of the wall—pipes groaning, cabinet doors slamming, teakettle whistling. Wait a minute, a teakettle? Julian might be British, but she'd never seen him drink tea. He drank coffee in the mornings. Cleo narrowed her eyes. *He was still entertaining his guest.* She smacked her empty mug against the palm of her hand. Crossed and uncrossed her legs, knocking off an armadillo slipper in the process. Her phone buzzed with a text: YOU UP? WANT COFFEE?

Oh, she was definitely up. And she wanted coffee. But— she bounced her foot up and down—was he really inviting her to have it with his morning-after buddy?

She texted back. ISN'T THREE A CROWD?

She was already standing, though.

I'M INVITING YOU FOR COFFEE. NOT A THREE-WAY.

Cleo ran a hand through her hair, retrieved her errant armadillo slipper, and opened the door. Julian stood near the stove, shirtless. He was pierced, inked, and ripped as hell. The familiar sight got her juices flowing more effectively than a triple shot of espresso. She forced her eyes up to his face.

"Good morning, sunshine," he said. "Did you sleep well?"

There was enough sauciness in his tone to indicate he knew darn well how she'd slept. "You should call an exterminator," she said. "I think we have rats."

Movement caught her eye, but it was no rat. A small blond head peeped around Julian's shoulder.

"Hello, there," the head said.

"Oh," Cleo said. "I'm sorry. I didn't see you." She did her best to smile.

The woman came around to stand beside Julian, and he casually slipped an arm across her slim shoulders. She was vaguely familiar—tiny, like a delicate pixie, and drop-dead gorgeous. She was older than she looked, though. The neck and eyes did not match the perky boobs. She'd had some star-quality work done, for sure.

"Cleo, this is Sylvie Sandstone," Julian said.

No freaking way. What the heck was a legendary country

music star doing in Julian's kitchen? While wearing something black and lacy?

The country crooner smiled graciously. "Nice to meet you," she said.

"Holy cow," Cleo gasped. "Nice to meet you, too. I'm Cleo. I manage the studio. And I live here. Well, not here, as in this very spot. I live there." She pointed to the open door next to the refrigerator, which looked seriously inadequate as a boundary. "We just work together."

She heard herself talking, but she didn't know how to apply the emergency brake. "We have a professional relationship and nothing more."

She slapped her hand over her mouth. Why had she said that? Julian choked on his coffee, dribbling it onto his bare chest. And she did *not* want to lick it off. Much.

"Yes, she's right," Julian said. "It's strictly professional around here, as you can probably tell from the way she flounces about in a ratty bathrobe and anteater slippers."

"I don't flounce." She glanced down at her bathrobe. Dust bunnies clung to its hem, but it wasn't ratty. "And these are armadillos," she said, sticking a foot out. "If you were a real Texan and not some Stevie Ray wannabe with a weird accent, you'd know that."

Sylvie gave a yelp of approval and offered up a fist bump. "I like this girl," she said. And even though Cleo was seething with something that could not possibly be jealousy, she liked Sylvie right back. They bumped fists hard enough to slosh tea out of Sylvie's cup.

"Oh, sorry," Cleo said.

"She's too enthusiastic for her own good," Julian said, grabbing a dish towel. "About everything."

Sylvie laughed, and Julian gently dabbed the cloth at her substantial bosom. Good grief. Cleo had unintentionally set that up for him. Why couldn't the tea have spilled on *her* instead of Sylvie?

With the excessive dabbing finally concluded, Sylvie headed for the stairs. "I need to get dressed and head on out. Gotta be in Dallas tonight."

Cleo and Julian stood silently as Sylvie sashayed off, her lacy black robe barely covering her ass. As soon as she was out of earshot, Cleo turned to Julian. "Oh my God. You're a boy toy."

He looked aghast. "I'm quite certain she loves me for my mind, Big Red."

Cleo rolled her eyes and headed for the coffeepot. "Right."

"And I'm hardly a boy."

"To her you are. I mean, how old is she?"

"A gentleman never asks a woman her age. Of course, I'm no gentleman, and I happen to know she's fifty-two."

Cleo's mouth dropped. She doubted she'd attract any toys at fifty-two that wouldn't require batteries. "She's twenty years older than you."

"Stop exaggerating, it's only nineteen. And she has an awesome body, which she knows how to use." He raised an eyebrow and lowered his voice. "Sometimes, when she's done with me, I get a cookie."

Cleo took a sip of coffee. "How do you know her?"

"There's cream in the fridge, if you want some."

Cleo gasped. "You bought her *cream*?"

Julian had the good grace to lower his eyes, properly chagrined.

"You must have really needed to get laid," Cleo said, opening the refrigerator.

There it was. *Holy namaste*, the boy had bought 100 percent organic, full-fat, anti-antibiotic, cruelty free, pasture-grazed cream! She yanked the carton out like a crack addict. The seal was unbroken—the bitch hadn't even used it. Cleo poured a healthy amount into her coffee and took a huge sip.

Heaven.

"It's so weird how the bodily fluids of bovines excite you," Julian said. "Anyway, I played on one of Sylvie's albums. That's how we met."

"Love at first sight?"

"What can I say?" Julian waggled his eyebrows like Groucho Marx. "She liked my instrument."

Cleo rolled her eyes until it actually caused pain.

"Lucky for you," Julian continued, "we've been friends ever since."

"No kidding. When Sylvie's here I get animal products." She took another sip.

"You can buy your own cream whenever you want, you're just too cheap. But that's not what I'm talking about. She's agreed to an interview."

Cleo set her mug down. "With me?"

"Who else?"

This was way better than free cream. Cleo grabbed Julian's hands, pulling him in for a hug. She jumped up and down while he stood as motionless as a tree stump.

"Settle down," he said. "You're going to come out of your anteaters."

Gosh, he was cute with his little grin, looking so ridiculously pleased with himself. She stood on her toes and kissed him on the cheek. His face went blank for a moment, but then he smiled and returned the hug with a squeeze so big, Cleo's armadillos left the floor.

Julian's nipple rings pressed into her breasts through the thin fabric of her robe. Every nerve in her body stopped what it was doing and paid attention. Julian's did, too, and she got a healthy salute. He let go immediately and took a giant step back. But she'd felt it, and he knew it.

Good thing she was a woman. There were no telltale signs of her arousal. None whatsoever. Unless, of course, her cheeks were as hot as they felt, or her pupils were dilated like saucers.

"Right," Julian said. "Okay, then." He crammed his hand into his pocket, which Cleo knew was full of picks. "I'm going to the studio to lay down a track," he said.

You do that, Guitar Boy. See if it helps.

• • •

Well, this was awkward.

Josh sat on Julian's couch as if he were impaled on a large cylindrical object, right up his ass. It could be the awful tuxedo he was wearing, but more likely, he wasn't thrilled about Cleo asking him to wait in Julian's loft while she got ready for the stupid gala. Julian wasn't thrilled, either, but at least he knew how to be polite.

"Seen any good films lately?" he asked.

Josh tore his eyes away from Cleo's door and looked at Julian as if he had just now noticed him. "I don't really have a lot of time for movies right now," Josh said. "I'm trying to make partner and…well, you wouldn't understand. Let's just say we can't all sit around playing with guitars and watching movies."

Right. *Trying to make partner by dating the boss's daughter.* "Can I get you something to drink? You look nervous."

Josh tugged at his collar. Julian didn't blame him—it was at least a half size too small. "No, I'm fine. So tell me, have you seen what she's wearing tonight?"

Julian stifled a grin. Maybe it wasn't the collar that was making Josh sweat. "I haven't seen anything, but I did hear the girls talking earlier. Something about a pink and white polka-dot mermaid dress. Sherry referred to it as a prom dress explosion. Or maybe it was implosion. Sorry, I can't remember exactly."

Josh went from bright pink to very pale.

It was all true. Julian had overheard the girls discussing a polka-dot mermaid dress. They hadn't bought it, but Josh didn't need to know that. And besides, Cleo could have very well bought something even worse.

"I wonder if mermaid dresses have clamshells?"

"What?" Josh said. His eyes were ridiculously round.

"You know," Julian said. "Clamshells." He cupped his hands over his chest.

"Oh, God," Josh said.

Julian wished Cleo would, in fact, emerge in a polka-dot mermaid costume. It was time to put Josh to the test. Just how badly did he want to make partner? And why couldn't Cleo see what he was up to?

The door opened, and Josh bolted off the couch. Was he going to make a run for it? No. He wasn't running. He was frozen in his tracks, eyebrows raised, mouth agape. Curiosity got the better of Julian, and he turned to see what their little princess wore—

She did not wear a prom dress. She wore a very grown-up black lace evening gown that hugged every inch. And the inches formed a perfect, old-school hourglass figure. She should take off those horrible hippie dresses and yoga pants more often—let those curves out to play. Julian's fingers moved automatically, like they did when he thought of a song and needed a guitar. Only he was *not* thinking about music, and what he needed…well, his romp with Sylvie obviously hadn't scratched that itch completely.

"Well?" Cleo said. "Do I look okay?"

"Perfect!" Josh said. He grinned from ear to ear and his voice—usually a hunter green—sounded almost aqua. The fucker was so relieved he was changing colors.

Cleo turned her eyes on Julian. For about three seconds, he literally couldn't breathe. She raised her eyebrows in question.

"You look beautiful," Julian said. He'd wanted his voice to sound strong and sincere—gray, like slate—but it came out breathy, an embarrassing, wispy silver.

Heat rose in his cheeks. Maybe Cleo couldn't see sounds, but she could sure as hell hear them. And his voice sounded… *hungry*. She tilted her head and gazed through her lashes. The girl could work it.

Josh seemed oblivious, probably because he was still awash in relief. "Black lace was a good choice," he said, as if he were critiquing the red carpet. "A lot of the other ladies will be in black lace, too."

Cleo's mouth turned down a little at that. "Oh. Maybe I should have bought the polka-dot one."

Julian grinned. "You would look lovely in anything," he said.

Cleo's smile came back, full force. "Thanks. What do you guys think of my hair?"

She turned around slowly. A river of lava spilled down her *very bare* back. The front of the dress covered everything, but the back covered very little. "Take a good, long look," Cleo said. "Because I'm never straightening it again."

"Very nice," Josh said. "And some things are worth the effort."

Cleo spun back around with a faltering smile. Julian waited for the dick to follow the statement up by saying something about lovely curls, but he just clapped his hands and said, "Ready to go?"

"I'll follow you out," Julian said. "I'm going to the club to hear a band."

Josh laughed. "For a minute there, I thought you meant the country club."

"No, don't worry," Julian said, grabbing his keys. "No riffraff in the country club tonight."

Cleo lifted the hem of her dress to head down the stairs, and Julian recognized the toes of her black biker boots. Maybe there would be a little riffraff at the country club, after all.

Chapter Seven

Julian looked around the depressing, shabby offices of *Upbeat* and waited for Manny to get out of the bathroom. He took the liberty of sitting in his friend's nasty throne of ripped vinyl, propping his feet up on the cluttered desk. He leaned back, and the springs squeaked out an alarm that made its way through the small battered door in the corner of the room.

"Get outta my chair."

Julian glanced at the door. "Yeah, okay. Sure." He leaned back and rocked in earnest. He loved fucking with Manny, and it was so bloody easy.

The toilet flushed.

Julian yanked his feet off the desk and leaned over to grab an issue of *Upbeat* off the stack on the corner. The ugly mugs of the Morones Brothers glared up at him from the cover, and a bizarre sense of pride surged through him. He opened the magazine to the proper page and began reading.

Not surprisingly, Cleo had done a bang-up job.

Manny emerged from the bathroom, lighting a cigarette. He nodded in Julian's general direction. "Move."

Without taking his eyes off the article, Julian stood. The chair squeaked as Manny slid in and leaned back. "Your girl delivered, pal."

She really had. The Morones boys hadn't made it easy for her. They'd shown up with shaved heads and wearing stupid gangbanger outfits. Cleo had arched those eyebrows, indicating she recognized posers when she saw them, and before the Morones Brothers knew it, they were calling her ma'am and politely answering questions quicker than you could roll an enchilada.

Manny Bloom was ecstatic. His old rag had finally managed to run a real story instead of its usual sad array of upcoming calendar events.

"Where's the redhead?" Manny asked.

"Late, as usual," Julian mumbled, still scanning the article. "She's going to go insane over the monthly feature. She's going to hug you. Consider yourself warned."

"Yeah?" Manny blew a cloud of smoke out of his mouth, and Julian wrinkled his nose. Manny ran a hand over his bald, shiny head. "I think I can handle a hug or two from your girl. I just hope she doesn't like the feel of my Manny meat so much she dumps you." He made a thrusting gesture with his hips that was meant to be obscene but was closer to hilarious.

"She's not my girl, but try to keep your meat in your pants, anyway." He grinned and nodded at Manny's tired slacks, stained and spotted with cigarette burns. "Nice pants, by the way."

"Right? They look like yours. Who knew I was a fashion plate?"

Julian smirked and adjusted his gray and black indie mod hipsters. "I got mine last month from an expensive vintage dealer in L.A. I'm guessing you got yours at JCPenney back in 1962?"

"It was 1963, asshole. And hey, if she flips over the monthly column, I wonder what she's going to do when I tell her about the Sylvie Sandstone article."

"What about it? You're running it, right?"

"Nope. I sold it to *Country Times*. She hit the big leagues with that one."

Julian dropped the magazine into Manny's lap. Holy shit. She was going to flip. *Country Times* was country music's equivalent to *Rock 'n' Spin*.

"So, Julian, if you're not banging this chick, how come you're helping her out, huh? You like this woman or something?"

"Or something."

Manny raised his bushy eyebrows, and Julian pretended to ignore him. He wasn't going to spill his guts. What would he even say? Manny took the hint and changed the subject. "The Up and Coming segments are going to be great, but there's something that would be even better."

"Forget about it, Manny."

"Come on, man! How about a nice, juicy article that starts with, 'Whatever happened to Slice?' Mitch Landrum lives in Austin now. I bet he'd be game for an interview."

A shiver traveled up and down Julian's spine at the mention of Mitch's name. It was true that Mitch was in Austin—so fucking close—but Julian had been lucky enough to never run into him. "I hear he's in a band with a bunch of middle-aged freaks playing pool halls and bar mitzvahs. He'd probably appreciate the publicity. But being your has-been of the week doesn't hold any appeal for me, so fuck off. Stop bringing that Slice shit up every time I see you."

"You're hardly a has-been, brother. And I hear the Roustabouts are tight. Austin loves them, and it seems they're having a good enough time. Maybe you and Mitch should bury the hatchet, huh? I mean, how long's it been?"

Not long enough. Suddenly, Julian didn't feel like sticking

around. An urge to escape came over him. He needed to do it before Cleo showed up and Manny helped her connect the dots in his convoluted life story. She'd figure it out on her own, but he'd prefer she not do it today.

"I have to head out now. I just came by for a few of these." He grabbed a stack of the magazines off the table.

"Hey, wait a minute—"

"Tell Cleo I'll see her later. And keep my has-been status to yourself." He turned and left Manny stuttering in his wake.

By the time he hit the hot sidewalk, he was at odds and didn't know where he wanted to go. The heat melted the traffic sounds from the nearby freeway into pea soup. He grabbed the handle of the El Camino's door and jerked his hand away, cursing. Welcome to south Texas's sorry-ass excuse for autumn. Using the tail of his shirt, he pulled the handle up again and yanked the door open. A belch of hot air ambushed him. He threw the stack of magazines onto the seat and slid into the oven next to them.

"Julian!"

Orange bubbles poured in through the window. Julian looked up to see a pair of perfect breasts in a horrid ruffled blouse.

"Hello, Cleo."

She leaned in, replacing the view that caused serious shifting in the layout of his trousers with one that caused serious shifting in his heart. He smiled at her sweaty face, cheeks pink from the heat and framed by damp and curling ringlets of red hair. She was grinning and out of breath.

"I was running to catch you," she wheezed. "Why are you leaving?"

"Where did you park, genius? There are spots all in front of this building."

"I know. But I can't parallel park worth a crap. I had to go into that garage by the mall."

Julian looked about. With the exception of his car, there were no other cars on the street. Your average blind man could parallel park a double-decker bus anywhere within the block. "The list of things at which you're inept just keeps growing. It's impressive."

"Thanks," she said with a grin. "Where are you going?"

"I have someplace to be. I'll see you later."

Her lips did something adorable that he thought might be a pout. "Oh. Well, okay. How did the article look?"

"It was all right." He palmed her forehead and pushed her head out of his window. Then he drove off, leaving her to her own devices with Manny Bloom.

He didn't have a destination in mind, but a street sign reminded him he was close to Addie's place. He might as well stop by and share Cleo's good news.

Addie had been mysteriously absent ever since Cleo arrived on the scene. It was as if his sister had hired a babysitter for him and gone on holiday. One left turn at the next block brought him to her neighborhood. He drove slowly down the narrow street. It was lined with parked cars on both sides—some up on blocks—and he remained alert for children, dogs, or chickens, all of which had darted out in front of him on previous occasions. He drove with his window down, soaking up the sounds and colors of the neighborhood. Many of the homes and apartments didn't have air-conditioning, and music and conversation poured through their windows. The bright, festive colors of a fiesta danced before his eyes.

Addie's turquoise door came into view. He looked for a spot to squeeze into and found one right behind a black Lexus. What the holy fuck was a black Lexus doing in this neighborhood? He pulled in, frowning. Across the street, Addie's ever-vigilant neighbor, Senora Lopez—the woman had to be close to a hundred years old—sat on her front porch, fanning herself with a magazine. She wore the same two things she always wore: a scowl and a faded housecoat. She was the neighborhood watch, so surely, she'd noticed the Lexus.

"*Hola,*" Julian yelled as he climbed out of his car. He lifted his hand in a wave, and Senora Lopez nodded slightly, with no change of expression. Maybe her cataracts were getting the best of her, because she didn't seem at all concerned with the Lexus. It wasn't pimped out, but Julian drew a conclusion anyway. *Drug dealer.*

The fiesta colors disappeared as a tremor of nerves washed over him. He looked up and down the street. Where was the brazen asshole? Middle of the fucking day, and in close proximity to his sister and Senora Lopez's great-grandsons, who would be home from school any minute.

He reached his hand into his pocket and clicked his picks together. There had been a string of home invasions in the next block. Why did Addie insist on living here and giving him one more thing to worry about?

He navigated the cracked, weed-riddled sidewalk to her front door and knocked loudly. The familiar chemicals of her dye studio—a tapestry of metallic hues—wafted under the door. The curtain in the window moved, and he waited patiently for the door to open. When it didn't, he knocked again, louder. He reached into his pocket and found the picks. Why wasn't she answering the door? Or even shouting *just a minute*? What if someone was in there with her, not letting her speak? The surface of his skin erupted in pins and needles, and then he pounded on the door, creating a ruckus that traveled up and down the street—and his spine—in red waves of alarm. "Addie," he yelled. "Open up!"

Someone tapped on his shoulder, and he spun, hand clenched in a fist, picks pressed against his palm. Senora Lopez stared stoically at him, concern etched in her ancient forehead. "*Mijo*, it's okay," she said. "Your *hermana* is fine.

Her *novio* is in there."

"Her *novio*?"

"*Sí.*"

"Addie doesn't have a boyfriend."

Senora Lopez gave him a look that suggested she knew better. The door behind him swung open, and he spun back around. A tall man stood in Addie's doorway. Julian's heart jumped to his throat. Addie *never* had men over. And this one looked vaguely familiar.

"Whoa now, settle down there, cowboy."

That voice—an amber rumble with piss-yellow edges—was unmistakable. What the bloody hell was Mitch Landrum doing in his sister's flat?

The shocking blue eyes were the same, although Mitch had obviously spent the past twelve years etching laugh lines into his formerly pale and ashen face, which was now a healthy tan. There was barely any resemblance to the angst-ridden young man Mitch had been when he'd fronted Slice. The dark and brooding expression had been replaced by a buoyant and cheerful countenance, and it looked fucking ludicrous.

Mitch's eyes were on guard but twinkling. The motherfucker was practically smirking. Without thinking, Julian punched him—right in the face—and picks flew as if he'd struck a piñata.

Mitch went down, writhing, groaning, and holding a hand to his bloody nose. The asshole needed to get up so Julian could hit him again. He gave him a little prod with his foot, and Senora Lopez mistook it for a kick and exploded in a fit of Spanish, no doubt a scathing annihilation of his character. She even swatted him with her magazine, and it kind of hurt.

"Ouch! Stop that. This guy is"—he searched his limited vocabulary of Spanish curse words—"a *pendejo.*"

The old woman gasped and reached into the pocket of her housecoat. He flinched, but she didn't pull out a paddle for his ass or a bar of soap for his mouth. It was a handkerchief for Mitch's bleeding nose.

Where the fuck was Addie? The bathroom door at the back of the flat creaked open, and her dark head peeked out. Her mouth gulped like a goldfish out of water as she took in the scene.

"Addie—"

"Julian, what have you done?" She ran out in nothing but a towel and joined Senora Lopez in fawning over Mitch.

"What is Mitch Landrum doing in your flat?"

Mitch had the audacity to look him in the eye with a smirk that answered the question—*I've been doing Addie.*

"Good to see you again, punk. As you can see, I've met your sister."

•••

Cleo was walking on air, or rather, driving on air. She'd already been by her parents' house to brag, and even her mom had seemed pleased. Her dad had been downright proud. *An article in a national magazine! A local monthly feature!*

She pulled up to a stoplight and looked at her phone. Had she missed a call from Julian? She'd texted him a million times, but he still hadn't responded. She was dying to talk to him. She longed for that stoic British look, the one that said he'd known she could do it all along. The look that made her feel as if she *could* do anything.

The Morones Brothers had landed a producer, and tomorrow they were all going out to dinner. Now they'd have even more to celebrate. The light changed, and her phone rang. Julian always did that—called or texted just as she was thinking about him. She hit the phone button on her steering wheel—*hands free, San Antonio*—"Guess what?" she blurted.

There was a quiet pause. "Hello? Is this Soundbox

Studio?"

The studio's calls were forwarded to Cleo's phone. In her excitement, she hadn't even looked to see who called.

"Sorry," she said. "You've got the right number. What can I do for you?"

"This is Cory. I'm calling to let Julian know about a release party. This is the only number I have. Is it the best way to get in touch with him?"

"A release party?"

"For our new album. Julian played on it."

Cory must be with one of the local bands that recorded at Soundbox.

"Details, Cory. I need details."

He laughed. "Well, I'm not certain of all the details. It's just my job to show up. But let's see, there will be people. There will be food, some kind of L.A. crap only the record label executives can stomach."

"You mean Los Angeles?"

"Yes. We love Julian, but not enough to bring the party to him. He's going to have to drag his ass to us. But even he will need an invitation to get in, and we don't have his address."

This wasn't the band next door. "What band are you with again?"

"Dead Ringer. This is Cory Maxwell with Dead Ringer."

"Are you for real?" She pulled into a convenience store parking lot so she wouldn't crash the car. "Julian knows you guys? He played on your album? Oh my God, you're Cory!"

"And you're enthusiastic. I love that about you."

She blushed. "I'm usually very cool," she stammered. "This is probably the first time I've ever not been cool."

A hearty laugh filled her ear. "I'm flattered."

"You should be. Can you send an autographed picture with that invitation? I swear I won't sell it on eBay."

"How about I send you an invitation to the release party

and you can get something signed in person?" Was he flirting with her? She managed to give him the mailing address for Soundbox, then hung up with a squeal. This had been a spectacular day.

Back at the loft, Cleo shouted Julian's name and took the stairs two at a time. He couldn't hear her over his guitar, but she shouted anyway. A screeching wail from his bright red Stratocaster met her as she burst through the door.

"Julian, I just talked to—"

The note ceased as if cut by sharp scissors. Cleo cleared her throat. The tension was thick, but why? The only sound came from an amp buzzing at his feet.

"So, guess who called?" she said.

With no warning, Julian exploded into a blur of motion and kicked the amp, jerking it free of his guitar. It careened across the room, narrowly missing Cleo.

"Dammit, girl," he yelled. "You can't barge in here while I'm playing. What the fuck is wrong with you?"

Cleo's pulse pounded in her head. She took a small step back toward the door. Was Julian joking? The veins bulging in his neck, trembling hands, and clenched jaw said no. Cleo would probably do well to quietly retreat down the stairs she'd just clambered up. But her pounding pulse had turned from fright to rage.

"What's wrong with *me*?" she shouted. "How about what's wrong with *you*?"

Julian smacked his hands over his ears and shut his eyes.

"Very mature." She walked over and yanked his hands away. "You can damn well take it if you can dish it out, buddy. Don't you *ever* yell at me like that. *Comprende*?"

No *comprende*. He stood there with his hands at his sides,

eyes squeezed shut, swaying. "Open your eyes and look at me," she said.

He didn't. Holy cow.

"Hey," she said, instinctively lowering her voice to a whisper. "You okay?"

No response. She timidly touched his cheek, and the contact severed the invisible strings holding him up. He dropped to the floor, landing in a heap with his guitar in his lap. He lowered his head to his hands, rocking back and forth.

The tension fizzled out of the room, replaced by a still and suffocating blanket of silence. "Julian?"

He rocked faster.

What should she do? Turn out the light and leave? Call an ambulance? She was in over her head. Her phone buzzed with a text, and she snatched it in irritation. Oh, it was Addie!

HAVE YOU SEEN JULIAN? HE ISN'T ANSWERING HIS PHONE.

Cleo hit call. This required voice to voice.

Addie answered almost immediately. "What's he done?"

"Um, he's acting weird." She glanced at him. "Rocking and stuff. I don't know what happened. I just walked in and — "

Addie sighed in her ear. "He'll be fine. Make everything quiet, give him some space, and he'll pull out of it."

"What the hell is wrong with him?"

Addie laughed, but it was bitter. "I don't even know where to start. Basically, he's upset because I have a boyfriend."

Cleo frowned. It made no sense. "I don't understand. And really? You have a boyfriend?" Wow. She'd love to dig deeper into that, but not while Julian was doing whatever it was he was doing.

"Listen, I don't really know how to say this, but I'm done," Addie said. "He's all yours."

"Addie — "

"I can't, okay? He gave me an ultimatum. And I didn't choose him." She hung up.

Cleo stared at the phone in her hand. Apparently, Julian and Addie had synchronized their timing in going off their rockers. She lowered herself to the floor next to Julian, because somebody had to help him, even if it was just to sit with him. She gingerly lifted a few strands of hair out of his face.

He stopped rocking, hesitated for a moment, then leaned over and buried his face in her neck. She wrapped her arms around him as he curled up and leaned into her, warm and heavy. He was shirtless, and his skin was hot and slick with sweat. His warm breath tickled her neck as he settled in completely, almost knocking her over with his weight. Letting go of his guitar, he wrapped his arms around her waist. A soft moan escaped his lips as his breath brushed the sensitive skin beneath her ear.

This was not a good time to get turned on. It was a freaking weird and disastrous time to get turned on. But it was happening all the same.

Cleo shifted her weight, and the guitar slid off Julian's lap, landing on the floor with a heavy thud. It broke the spell, and he yanked his head up, startled.

"Cleo?" he rasped.

"Hello," she said stupidly. "Are you okay?"

He let go and straightened himself up. His eyes flitted about the room before finally settling back on hers. "Oh, fuck. I'm so sorry."

He ran his hands over his face and through his hair, leaving it sticking out in all directions. "How long was that?" he asked.

"How long was what?"

"How long was…this?" He pointed at himself. "I mean, has it just been a few minutes, then?"

"Yes. I, um, interrupted you while you were playing."

He stood shakily, held out his hand, and pulled her up.

She waited for an explanation. And an apology would be nice, too. But all he said was, "I really need to play right now. Would you excuse me?"

"Are you serious?"

"Quite." He retrieved his amp from the other side of the room where he'd kicked it, plugged himself back in, and began to play.

This was total, unadulterated bullshit. Was she supposed to act as if nothing had happened? Because she could. She *would* do that. She'd go strictly professional on his ass. If he wanted to talk to her, he could email her. In fact, she'd email him. That's how she'd tell him about Cory Maxwell. She'd send a professional correspondence about the Dead Ringer party, and he could go, or not, and it wasn't any concern of hers.

She stomped down the stairs to the studio foyer to compose a message for His Crazy Highness.

Subject: Dead Ringer Release Party

Dear Julian,

I spoke briefly with Cory Maxwell. He requested your address in order to send you an invitation to a release party in Los Angeles. You can expect the invitation within a couple of weeks.

Cleo Compton

She hit the send key and tapped her fingers on the desk. A few seconds later, she composed a second message.

Subject: Cory Maxwell

Dear Julian,

I am also invited to attend the release party. I might see
you there.

Cleo Compton

She hit the send key. It was satisfying, but not satisfying
enough. The occasion called for one more.

Subject: Cancellation of Dinner

Dear Julian,

I am just letting you know that I will be unavailable
tomorrow evening for dinner, on account of you being
an asshole.

Cleo Compton

She officiously hit send. It felt wonderful, warm and
delicious and generally delightful…for about a minute.

So much for her foray into professionalism. She began
typing away, attempting to gain access to his account so she
could delete the last message. She'd been in it before— what
was his password? *Major Strat? Minor Strut?* She wasted
twenty minutes trying variations of those words, typing them
in uppercase, lowercase, and every way in between. No luck.
Just as she'd typed STUPIDDUMBASS, the front door
buzzed.

Dang. She was supposed to have an early dinner with
Josh. With all the excitement of the afternoon, not to mention
the recent scene from *One Flew Over the Cuckoo's Nest*, she'd
completely forgotten.

She buzzed him in. A wave of humid heat poured through
the door with him, but Josh looked cool and crisp. He always
did.

"Hey, there," she said, trying not to act surprised. He

pulled her out from behind the desk and delivered a kiss. It was chaste, but the look in his eyes was anything but.

She'd given in after the Strut and Putt Gala. It had been a wonderful night; Josh was entertaining, attentive, and looked mighty handsome in a tux. They'd gone back to his place after the party, a nice cottage in Alamo Heights, and skinny-dipped in the rock pool. Later, there'd been candles, flowers, and satin sheets. It was over-the-top romantic, and the sex should have been good. Josh had done all the right things. But in the end, it just hadn't worked. Not for her, anyway.

She'd considered ending it tonight. But now she wasn't so sure. Did she want to throw away the possibility of a mature relationship because she couldn't let go of a teenage-style obsession with what was shaping up to be a seriously loony musician? Josh might not set her heart on fire, but he hadn't kicked an amp at her, either. And he was *real*.

Maybe passion didn't have to wash over you like a rhythm-driven bass beat. Maybe it could sneak up on you, like a pretty background melody.

"Are you ready to go?" he asked.

"Absolutely." She grabbed her purse and off she went, her body in one direction and her traitorous heart in another.

Chapter Eight

Julian woke to a buzzing sound. Was it external? Or was it the internal buzzing he often heard in his head? He lay still, waiting for his consciousness to settle back into its usual, upright position.

Soon, he knew three things. He was lying on the couch in his loft, the dusty light beam coming in through the west window indicated it was late afternoon, and the buzzing was his phone. External, then. Good.

He ignored the phone. What had he been doing before zoning out? His guitar leaned up against the armrest of the couch, so he'd been playing. Cleo had come in and…bloody hell. He'd scared the shit out of her before going completely mental, as he was prone to do. Jesus, he needed to apologize, but how? *Sorry, I failed to mention I'm a freak.*

His mouth was dry, so he hauled himself off the couch. As he grabbed a bottle of water out of the fridge, it all came crashing back. The cause of his synesthesia episode was Mitch fucking Landrum. He was dating Addie.

With shaking hands, he lifted the bottle to his lips. The

colors were starting to blend. Even though it was silent in the loft, his thoughts were noisy, and that was enough. A soft buzzing sound that *wasn't* his phone began to settle in. He'd better pull it together, or he was on his way out again. He breathed deeply and concentrated on emptying his mind. A therapist had shown him how to do it—he focused on eliminating one color at a time until he had a blissfully blank slate.

The brain buzz dissipated, replaced by the buzz of a text. It was Travis Moore, bassist for Big Spigot, an alternative band out of Austin.

CAN U PLAY WITH US 2NITE? PETER IS IN THE HOSPITAL & A PRODUCER IS COMING 2 THE SET.

Julian rubbed his hand across his face. He didn't relish the idea of facing Cleo anytime soon, so playing would be a nice escape. He texted back: WHERE? WHAT TIME? WHAT'S WRONG WITH PETER?

He looked out the window. Cleo's car was in the lot, but it was too quiet. She'd probably gone out with the lawyer. He knocked on the door to her flat, and when she didn't answer, he went on in. It was technically his place, so why not?

The room was empty. A few plates rested on the table, dirty, of course, and a second look confirmed they were his. A box in the corner, marked *dishes*, sat unopened. He shook his head. A pile of clean laundry covered the love seat—he could practically hear it wrinkling. A lacy pink bra rested on top. He held it up, enjoying the accompanying mental image of Cleo's ample breasts. Maybe there was a pair of matching panties to go with it. He dropped the bra and stuck a finger back into the mess. Bingo! A pink thong. Snooping was great fun.

He headed to the bed, which was an unmade mass of crinkled sheets. He brushed popcorn kernels aside before sitting. There was a slight indention in the pillow, and he leaned over and touched his face to it. A tangerine scent filled his senses, and orange bubbles popped at the edges of his peripheral vision. A sense of peace and calm enveloped him as the last echo of the buzzing completely disappeared.

Still smelling sweet citrus, he sat up and pulled the pillow onto his lap. A stack of paperbacks perched precariously on the nightstand, along with Cleo's glasses, four empty tumblers he didn't dare look into, and some balled-up dirty tissues. The open drawer called to him, and he eased it out a little farther. A brush and comb, an orthodontic appliance of some sort covered in lint, and a few photographs were all he could see.

His phone buzzed, and he jumped. It was Travis again.

APPENDICITIS. LAZY FUCKER REFUSES 2 PLAY. WE NEED U @ STUBB'S @ 9.

If he left in the next few minutes, he could make it. A photo caught his eye as he went to close the drawer. He could only see half of it, but it was Cleo's face. He pulled it out. "Bloody hell," he whispered.

The photo, cut to fit in a frame, was of Cleo and a cocky-looking Lou Michaels. And it wasn't a fan photo, either. They were on a beach somewhere, looking downright cozy. If it weren't for a car door slamming and snapping him out of his stunned stupor, he might have stared at the photo until his hair turned gray. He dropped it back in the drawer and scampered out of the flat. He'd just made it into his kitchen when Cleo came barging through the door. The wrong door, of course. *His door.* Which was a good thing or she'd have busted him sitting on her bed.

He froze.

"Hi," she said. "I was out with Josh." She tapped her cowboy boot and folded her arms across her T-shirt—a puppy wearing pink earmuffs—in a *so there* manner.

"Sorry," he said. "That couldn't have been fun."

"It was awesome, actually." She looked closely at him and knitted her brows together. "Is that my pillow?"

Shit. He was holding her stupid pillow. "Um, no. I think it's mine." He winced at the Wonder Woman pillowcase covering it.

Her smug expression changed to concern. "You don't know what you're doing, do you?" She hustled him toward the couch. "You're disoriented. Lie down while I get you some water."

How was he ever going to get out of here now?

She handed him a glass and placed her palm against his head. "Are you going to tell me what happened earlier?"

A bead of sweat broke out at his hairline as he passed her the pillow. "Nothing happened. I wasn't smelling anything." *Fuck.* "I mean doing anything."

The smelling thing was new. Tangerines. He smelled them right *now*.

Cleo motioned for him to scoot farther onto the couch so she could sit. Then she leaned over and planted her warm lips firmly where her hand had been. A flash of cleavage caught his attention. He closed his eyes and swallowed a groan when she pulled away, leaving a feathery whisper where her lips had been.

"You don't feel feverish, but you're sure as heck acting that way," she said, resting her hand on his bare chest and setting his flesh on fire. "Do you want to tell me why you freaked out earlier?"

"Oh, that." This was it. He cleared his throat. "I have some sensory integration issues—more like disorders. I'm extremely disordered, you see."

She didn't laugh. "And that makes you scream and kick amps across the room?" Her brows dived into a chastising frown. She wasn't letting him off the hook that easily.

"When I get really exhausted or become upset, I don't do such a good job of handling all the colors."

"What colors?" She brought the glass of water up to his

lips and made him take a sip.

This was the bit people thought sounded cool, and therefore, the bit they misunderstood the most. "I have synesthesia. I see sounds. Sometimes feelings and sensations, too, but mostly sounds."

The other synesthetes he'd met—many of them musicians, oddly enough—didn't experience the depth of dimension he did. Most associated a certain color with a specific musical note, perhaps. But for Julian, silent things often had colors, too. Certain words, whether spoken or written, had colors. Names and people had colors. Cleo, for example, was orange, like a juicy tangerine. Addie was royal blue. They didn't actually appear to *be* those colors, of course. But they were those colors, nonetheless. Every so often he could actually taste and smell words. Or, as he'd found out with Cleo's pillow, people. He didn't go into that with her, though; he'd revealed enough already.

"Can you see these colors with your eyes?" she asked. "Or is it in your head?"

Common question. A horn honked on the street, and he made a point of following the maroon streak shooting across the room with his eyes. "Did you hear that car honk?"

"Did you just look at it?"

"Yeah. Usually, I ignore things like that. But in answer to your question, if my eyes had been shut, I still would have seen it. So I see things with my eyes and with my mind. Supposedly I'm hallucinating."

"Wow. You see all the solid objects in the world and the things the rest of us only hear. That's a lot to see."

"Too much sometimes. I constantly work at keeping the colors separated or they blend into a brown sludge. Then I can't see anything. Or breathe, for that matter. It's awful. And stupid. Sorry."

"Why are you apologizing?"

"Because I kicked the amp across the room. I could have hurt you."

She mindlessly drummed her fingers on his chest before saying, "I don't understand what the guitarus interruptus reaction has to do with your colors blending together or not blending together."

He grinned at her invented terminology. "When everything bleeds together, I can sometimes sort it all out with a guitar. When I play, the colors go back where they belong. That's what I was doing when you walked in."

"And if the guitar doesn't work? Then what?"

"I retreat."

"Retreat where?" Her fingers had stopped their nervous rhythm on his chest and smoldered there like sizzling-hot coals. Could she feel his heart pounding?

"Into my head."

She raised her eyebrows. "Is that what you were doing on the floor when I held you? Retreating into your head?"

"You held me?"

She blushed and lowered those gorgeous green eyes. Why couldn't he remember the good stuff? "I'm afraid I'll get too comfortable in my head one day and fail to come out."

The fingers started drumming again. "You're afraid of becoming catatonic?"

He shrugged. There was no way to describe the bliss of emptiness he felt when he came close. The peace and tranquility of blankness. The rude and horrifying jolt of the electroshock therapy he'd received as a child to bring him out of it.

"Are you autistic?"

The autistic/spectrum disorder label, as well as several others, had been batted about by various quacks. Like most things in his life, though, it didn't fit. He was an oddity. A freak.

"I don't think so."

She brushed his hair out of his eyes. "You must be exhausted."

"I'm okay. I just got upset earlier today. Lost my focus—colors took over."

She lowered her eyes again. This was the awkward part. He could literally feel the invisible wall going up. Everyone erected the wall; he didn't blame them.

She raised her eyes back to his. "Are you hypersensitive to touch?" Her cheeks grew pinker. He'd revealed too much of himself and embarrassed her.

"What?"

"Are you sensitive to this?" she whispered. She trailed her fingertips down his chest to his navel, which she circled before continuing to the waistband of his jeans.

"God, yes," he gasped. His skin broke out into gooseflesh.

Big Red had chosen a bizarre time to make a move, but he didn't care. She was good at it. If she asked him to lick her cowboy boots right now, he'd gladly do it.

A door slammed—icy blue with a red tail—and the sound cut through the sexually charged atmosphere, deflating the mood like a dart piercing a balloon.

"Cleo?" Josh bellowed.

"In here," she yelled back, jumping up off the couch as if it were ablaze. Adorable. He hoped he looked half as guilty as she did.

Josh came in, scowling like a disgruntled dick. "What's taking you so long? I thought you were only picking up a few things."

"I don't know that I should come over," Cleo said. "Julian seems to be coming down with something."

"So?"

"So I should stay here and keep an eye on him."

Josh eyed Julian suspiciously as he yawned and stretched. Julian couldn't help himself—he winked. Then he stood.

"No need to watch over me, Big Red. I'm leaving for Austin."

"I hardly think so," Cleo sputtered, with her hands perched upon her hips. "You shouldn't be going anywhere, much less driving to Austin."

"Thanks for sharing your unsolicited opinion about that, sweetheart, but I have a gig, and I'm leaving." He sure as hell wasn't sticking around now that things had been so clearly muddied up.

"A gig," Josh said to Cleo with an amused snort.

Julian narrowed his eyes but then shook it off. Josh had an irritating habit of never speaking to him directly, but two could play that game, and he ignored the jab.

"You're the one who isn't going anywhere, Big Red. The Dolls are coming in for a recording session. You're babysitting a gang of naughty boys tonight."

Cleo stomped the two steps it took to get in his face. "You said you'd be here for that."

"That was before I got sick." He smiled at Josh for effect and began gathering his things: keys, wallet, and a handful of picks.

"I'm not ready to be left alone with a band." Cleo lowered her voice to a whisper. "Also," she added, "you're not wearing a shirt. And we have some things to discuss."

She was right, he wasn't. He bounded over to the closet that housed his washer and dryer and grabbed a silver bowling shirt off the rod. But then he changed his mind. He was wearing jeans. Better go with the black martini shirt with the white piping.

Cleo was wrong. They had nothing to discuss. He slipped the shirt on while she wrung her hands and chewed on her bottom lip. He could practically hear her gears spinning.

"I'll stay here and help you," Josh said.

"Cleo," Julian said as he slung his guitar over his back,

"please make sure there are no extra people milling about getting in everyone's way."

"Is he saying I can't stay here with you? Like that's his business?" Josh asked Cleo.

Julian stopped at the door with Cleo on his heels. "When I said you need to make sure there aren't any extra people milling about at the session in the recording studio I own and where I provide you with employment, I meant, for example, if Josh were to ask if he could stay, the answer would be no."

Cleo rolled her eyes.

He leaned over, getting eye to eye. "You'll be fine. I have complete confidence in you."

"Julian," she whispered, "I don't know what came over me earlier."

"People respond to weirdness with weirdness, that's all. No worries." Nothing else explained it.

"So it was weird then?" She looked worried.

"In a good way," he replied. Because he'd enjoyed the fuck out of it. Then, with a quick glance at Josh, he leaned over and kissed her. It was short, sweet, and relatively innocent. But it lit him up all the way to the tips of his toes.

Cleo stood with mouth agape and eyes wide, completely silent, which was a rare occurrence. He took advantage and made a hasty exit. He licked his lips as the door shut behind him. *Tangerines.*

• • •

Cleo sat behind the desk in the studio's foyer. The place sizzled with energy, and none of it was good. The sound engineer had shown up in a drug-induced euphoria and the Dolls were idiots. To top it off, her mind was mush. What had that crazy kiss meant? She'd told Josh it was a British *ta-ta for now* kind of thing. He hadn't bought it, and she didn't know what the kiss meant or why it had happened. Apparently, neither she nor Julian would know an appropriate response to an awkward situation if it walked up and bit them on the ass.

The sound engineer was laid out on a futon, too fucked-up to work, as Hero, the band's singer, put it. Hero, a pierced ex-wrestler with anger management issues and a Mohawk, was as empathetic as a louse and would undoubtedly put a hole through the wall if Cleo didn't get a handle on the situation.

She called Julian, and he gave her the names and numbers of three other engineers.

"What do I do with the one who's here?" she asked. "He just threw up in the lounge."

"Tell the boys to keep an eye on him while you try to find a replacement. I'll call his brother to come and get him. Get the band to start setting up. They're going to want to stand around and bitch, but make them start on the drums. And I strongly suggest you send any nonessential guys home. They'll be lucky to get the drum track laid tonight, and it'll go smoother if you can get rid of some of them."

"Who are the nonessential guys?"

"Anyone who's standing around bitching instead of setting up."

An hour later, Cleo wondered if she should call it quits. No engineers had called back, and the high one hadn't been picked up.

"This is the last time we ever record in Julian's studio," Hero said. "And it figures his engineer's a junkie. Some things never change."

Her blood boiled. Soundbox was the best studio in town, especially for analog recordings, which in the digital age were an art form in and of themselves. "Well, good luck finding another studio to cut a demo for what Julian's charging you." She narrowed her eyes at Hero, knowing Julian was doing it on credit and didn't even expect to get paid.

Hero glared but didn't challenge her. Maybe she should reschedule the session. She didn't know how much more of Hero she could take.

The door buzzed, and her phone rang. She dealt with the door first. "Who is it?" she said into the intercom.

"It's Kyle, man. I'm here to haul off my brother."

Good. She let him in.

She grabbed the ringing phone next. It was Ian McConleigh, the first engineer on Julian's list. Was it possible things were looking up?

"So he needs me in a pinch," Ian said. "He should have called me first, but he had to give that addict another chance. Didn't work out for him, did it?"

What could she say? Obviously, it hadn't worked out.

"Look, I've never done this by myself," she said. "Julian left me to go save the world for what is probably another group of idiots. There's a big guy with a tattooed face yelling at me. I just cleaned up vomit. I need to pee, but I'm afraid to leave the room. Also, I am not above crying at this point."

"Are you threatening me with girl tears?" asked Ian.

"It's not a threat."

"In that case, I'll be there in an hour. Can you survive that long?"

"I'll try." After a few more details were exchanged, she hung up, relieved to know help was on the way.

Meanwhile, the guy she had buzzed in stood at the desk, glowering. He seemed to think it was her fault his brother was a mess. "Well? Where is he?"

She gave him the evil eye.

"I'm sorry," he added, softening his tone. "It's just that this gets old for me, you know? It's frustrating. And Julian will never call him again, so he's blown his last chance."

"I'm sure he'll give him another shot," she said.

Kyle looked at her like she was crazy. "No," he said. "You can't show up here if you're on drugs. Julian is hard-core about that."

At a loss for words, she merely pointed to the lounge.

Her phone chimed with a text.

DID IAN CALL?

She was about to text back when Hero barked at her. "Well? You gonna sit there and text all night? What the fuck is going on?"

She'd had her fill of foul-mouthed musicians. "Another engineer is on his way. In the meantime, you can help set up, as I've already suggested. Better yet, help Kyle get his brother out of here."

To her surprise, Hero did just that. When she buzzed him back in, he was on his phone, laughing.

"She just let me in. No, man, you know me. I won't give her a hard time. Thanks, bro."

Cleo crossed her arms and stood in front of the desk. Hero put his phone in his pocket, smiling. "That was Julian," he said.

"What did he want?"

"He told me to do what you say and nobody will get hurt." He snorted. "He didn't think you were gonna let me back in the studio."

"I probably shouldn't have. Now make yourself useful while we wait for Ian to get here."

"Ian McConleigh? Seriously? I hate that dude. He's a stupid shit," Hero said.

"Well, he doesn't like you, either. At least, I'm assuming that's what he meant when he called you a dickhead." The room erupted in laughter as Hero headed toward the drum set, shaking his head.

When Ian arrived, he had a teenage boy with him. "This is my cousin Collin," he said.

Collin didn't say anything. He just looked around, wide-eyed and starstruck to be in a real recording studio with an actual band.

Ian and Hero briefly exchanged insults, then got down to work. Collin looked at all the guitars lining the walls. "Where's the famous one?"

"The famous what?" she asked.

"His guitar," Collin said.

"He doesn't keep that thing down here, you goof," Ian hollered from the board. "I'm sure it's behind lock and key."

Cleo frowned.

"He's talking about the Les Paul," Ian said. "You know, Julian's guitar."

"Julian has approximately twenty bazillion guitars," she said. "And more than one Les Paul."

"He means the white one. Do you think Collin can see it? He's so disappointed Julian's not here. It would be great if he could at least see the guitar."

She thought she knew which one he meant, a nasty old thing Julian dragged out a lot. It was one of his three main squeezes.

"Is it kind of banged up?" she asked.

"Yeah, that's the one. Do you mind letting him see it?"

She thought for a moment. She wasn't comfortable letting this Collin kid up in Julian's loft. But she could bring the guitar down. "I don't see what it'll hurt, but you have to promise not to touch it, okay?"

The kid grinned from ear to ear. "I promise," he said.

Cleo brought the guitar down and set it in front of Collin. It didn't look like anything special to her. In fact, she wanted to take a rag to it. But Collin was tickled to death.

"Can you get a picture of me with it?" he asked.

"Sure. Squat down."

Collin handed her his phone and knelt next to the guitar

as if he were in church. Then he smoothed his hair back and smiled for the photo. Cleo was sure as hell going to ask Julian about the guitar when he got home. This kid acted like it had belonged to Kurt Cobain.

With more reverence than she'd brought it down with, Cleo hauled Julian's white Les Paul back up to the loft. And although she'd found it on his bed, she decided to put it in his walk-in closet for safekeeping.

She stepped into the spacious, cedar-lined room and quashed a brief wave of closet envy. It smelled like cedar and that special scent that was pure Julian. She inhaled deeply, clutching the guitar to her chest. Did Josh have a scent? She'd never noticed anything beyond his cologne, which was a tad heavy.

Holding the guitar, she snooped through Julian's clothes. He had snazzy rags and plenty of them. Plaid shirts, western shirts, and dress shirts hung on one rod, long-sleeved together, short-sleeved together, sorted by color. Tons of T-shirts folded neatly in celled blocks lined an entire wall. She squinted at the shelves. Good grief, they were labeled. It was like the Dewey decimal system for T-shirts.

She picked the nearest shelf, marked *F Concerts*, and pulled out a Flaming Lips T-shirt, followed by Flock of Seagulls and Foo Fighters. She laughed out loud. Nobody could accuse Julian of having limited musical tastes.

Her fingers trailed over his vintage jackets and blazers, feeling wool, polyester, and silk. She wrinkled her nose at a seersucker jacket and dropped her jaw when she came across rhinestones. With a roll of her eyes and a shake of her head, she pushed aside a row of perfectly creased slacks in order to rest the guitar in a corner. An old *Rock 'n' Spin* cover leaned against the wall. It was framed and enlarged and featured the guitarist from the band Slice. One just like it had hung in the *Rock 'n' Spin* lobby.

She squinted to get a better look, then her eyes flew open wide, and the spacious closet seemed to shrink until she couldn't breathe. She steadied herself, dragged the poster out, and plopped it on the bed for a better look. He was younger and looked completely different—long, matted hair and pale, thin face—but it was Julian!

She was such an idiot. Did everybody know but her? Did everybody know that Julian Wheaton was actually Julian *Lazros* of Slice?

He must be having a good laugh at her expense. She'd worked at *Rock 'n' Spin*—the hub of the rock-and-roll world—and hadn't recognized a guitar legend when she was freaking living with him. She smacked her hand over her eyes and threw herself on the bed next to the poster. He and Addie shared the same last name but had different fathers. That was a clue that had flown right past her. Along with a million others.

Had this been a game to see how long it took for her to figure it out? Or was she just that insignificant to him?

She sat up and looked at the poster again, pressing her fingers against the cool glass. No tattoos adorned his outstretched arms. *His arms.* The rumor was the magazine had airbrushed over the track marks. Julian Lazros had been a heroin addict. She shivered.

Maybe this was a weird coincidence. She looked closer. Nope. Low on his hips hung that nasty guitar, the same banged-up Les Paul she'd just placed in the closet.

She hadn't been a Slice fan, but everyone had heard of Julian. He'd been a tabloid favorite, a young English virtuoso who'd rocketed an American band to the top of the charts, and a hellion to boot. There'd been fights, arrests, and infamous court-ordered stints in rehab before the band finally kicked him out for good.

She'd never once wondered what happened to Julian Lazros.

After quickly checking on Ian, she sat at the studio's desk and got online. The live concert video of "Trap Me" was the first one she watched. Julian would have been sixteen, a child compared to his bandmates. Fans screamed, cried, and chanted his name. He was drenched in sweat, wailing on the Les Paul while Mitch Landrum competed for volume with a rough, jagged voice. Mitch Landrum—she'd mentioned meeting him, and Julian had said nothing!

She spent the rest of the evening babysitting the Dolls, watching Slice videos, and digging up dirt on the ghost of a boy she didn't know. In some performances, he was a brilliant young musician; in others, he was staggering, incoherent, and obscene. She watched and read some things that made her blush and some that made her laugh. But one piece in the *L.A. Times* made her cry.

"…*was found by his sister, Adelaide Wheaton, with wrists slit…twenty years old…*"

On top of the shock, she felt a tremendous amount of guilt, as if she'd read his diary. Her stomach grumbled and lurched, its usual reaction to stress and turmoil. She leaned over the desk and rested her head on her arms.

"Cleo," Ian said as he came out of the studio. "You feeling okay?"

"Not really, no."

"We're almost done. Why don't you go on upstairs? I'll buzz the intercom if we need you, but the guys are about to start packing up."

It was almost three o'clock in the morning, and Julian should be back from Austin soon. Her stomach flip-flopped at the thought.

"If you're sure you don't mind?"

"Not at all. Collin gave up the fight about an hour ago—he's asleep in the lounge. Thanks for getting that guitar down for him."

"He's a big Slice fan?"

She hoped Ian would be confused and say, *Slice? Julian was never in Slice.*

"He sure is. He thinks it's classic rock. Makes me feel old," Ian said with a shake of his head.

Chapter Nine

Cleo awoke to the smell of coffee and the realization she'd never made it to her own bed. She'd fallen asleep on Julian's couch, listening for the guys to buzz her. They hadn't, and she'd slept like the dead, or like someone in shock after finding out a friend wasn't who he claimed to be. A soft blanket covered her, although she had no recollection of Julian coming home, much less tucking her in.

Someone clanked around in the kitchen. She really wanted some coffee, but she'd slept in her clothes, her breath was horrid, and that was a stranger in there. Not the Julian Wheaton she'd thought she knew.

Sitting up, she peered over the back of the couch. He stood at the stove with his back to her, cracking eggs into a bowl. His hair was caught up in a short, stubby ponytail, but a good bit of it had escaped the hair band and bounced against his neck as he worked.

"I feel someone staring at me," he said. He turned and tossed her a smile too dazzling for anybody who'd come in so late the previous night.

Now that she knew, she couldn't miss it. *He was Julian Lazros.*

And he was shirtless. Her eyes drifted to his white linen pajama bottoms, the ones with the elastic waistband so worn and tired it was rendered practically useless.

"Late night, right?" he said. "Sorry about that. I was trying to help out a friend—shouldn't have. But at least Ian rode in to rescue my damsel in distress."

Blushing, she stood and pulled her attention from his slipping waistband. Avoiding his eyes, she homed in on the coffeepot. Julian followed her gaze and reached behind to grab a mug off the counter.

"I'm making you an omelet to express my gratitude," he said. "I'm talking eggs, cheese, and other animal-based contaminants from your side of the fridge." He held out the mug. "I touched it with my bare fingers." He shivered dramatically, and Cleo almost laughed as she padded toward him.

"Did something happen?" he asked, as she took the mug and filled it. "I mean, the guys didn't hurt your feelings or anything, did they? You're being awful quiet."

"No, nothing happened. I'm just tired."

Julian hesitated, as if he were about to say something and then thought better of it. He went back to work, whisking the eggs with a fork. The muscles in his tattooed arms and upper back flexed, and his pajama bottoms slipped lower with every whisk.

"You want to tell me what you were doing in my closet?"

She burned her mouth and throat with a huge swallow of coffee. "Huh?"

He lifted and rotated the pan, coating it with eggs before placing it back on the burner, and turned down the flame. "I mean, not that I care all that much," he said, turning to face her, "but you messed up my T-shirts. And you left a poster on my bed. One of the reasons I like things where they belong is so I don't sit on them in the dark and break them with my ass. I have glass shards embedded in my skin."

She set her mug down. "Sorry. I was putting your guitar away and—"

"What were you doing with my guitar?"

"A kid wanted to see it, and—"

"A kid wanted to see my guitar? Which guitar? Where is it now?"

"Good grief, Julian! The ugly white one, but that's hardly the point. The point is—"

"Hardly the point? You think you can just blatantly walk around getting into my shit and hauling it out for kids to look at? And then you don't even put it back where it belongs?"

"I'm sorry. I didn't know it was that special to you. It looks like any other guitar—worse, actually—and you have plenty."

His jaw clenched, and she knew she'd said something terribly wrong. "That ugly guitar was the only thing that kept me alive once. It means everything to me."

Was that how this was going to go? He was going to be pissy over a stupid guitar and pretend she hadn't made the biggest discovery of a lifetime? "I didn't even know who you were," she yelled.

"What are you talking about?" he yelled back.

"Oh my God, are you kidding me? The poster? Hello! You're Julian Lazros."

"Oh, that." He turned back around. "Fuck. Your stupid omelet is ruined."

"That's all you have to say? You can't possibly tell me it's not a big deal that you're not who you've been pretending to be. You can't possibly tell me your precious guitar being looked at, and, *oh my God*, touched, and, *oh, dear*, not put back in its proper place, is a bigger deal than me being intentionally misled and lied to."

He spun back so quickly she flinched. "It's my favorite guitar!"

His pajama bottoms had fallen alarmingly low, exposing the delicious *V* that led straight to the goods. It made it hard to concentrate.

"Got nothing to say for yourself, have you?"

She forced herself back on track. "How would you feel if I had been lying to you about who I was?"

"My God, Cleo. We're talking about more than a decade ago. I have no idea who you were or what you were doing fifteen years ago. Nor do I care…oh, wait a minute." He held a finger up and looked into the distance as if he were thinking. "Actually, fifteen years ago, you were a teenage girl trying to fuck rock stars." He reached behind him and grabbed the skillet, tossing it into the sink with a horrible clatter. "So, I guess you haven't changed all that much."

It was like a punch to the stomach. All the air escaped her lungs, and no matter how hard she tried, she couldn't get it back. He walked past her, adding, "As your mum would say, close your mouth, dear. It's unattractive."

•••

Julian plugged in a guitar and sat on his bed. If he didn't play, he would burst into a million pieces. He'd been a total shit for talking to Cleo like that, but she didn't seem to care or understand how important his guitar was to him. And he didn't like having his past thrown in his face. It was none of her business. He *had* kind of deceived her, or at least kept quiet about his past, and she had every right to be surprised. But to be so hysterical about it? And so seemingly *hurt* by it? Women were fucking insane.

He'd opened up to her in ways he never had with anyone else. And yet, the depth of their friendship was measured by how much of his lame-ass rock star past he'd revealed or not revealed. She was hurt? *He* was hurt.

He tried to play a few licks but couldn't focus. The perfect storm was brewing. He'd had little sleep, and he'd experienced more emotional upset in the past twenty-four hours than he'd suffered in the previous six months. He sat on the bed and held his head.

The buzzing began.

Shit. Could it happen twice in as many days? The colors quickly ran together, forming a wall of brown sludge. The sense of dread he always associated with a synesthesia episode washed over him.

The sludge would drown him. It would pour down his throat, into his lungs, and he'd die.

Logically, he knew it wasn't possible. But logic didn't play into this. He held his breath. If only he could call Addie. She always kept him from sliding into the darkest depths of it. But she'd chosen Mitch over him.

He took a breath and choked.

This was all Cleo's fault. Cleo and her snooping and silky hair and soft breasts. He took another breath...and smelled tangerines. *At just the thought of her.* The colors separated like a drop of water hitting the surface of an oily puddle.

He grabbed his phone and texted: HELP ME.

Cleo burst into the room less than a minute later. "What's wrong?"

The sound of her voice was orange—angry, so it had red hues, but still a brilliant orange. He focused on it, letting all the other colors fade into the background. He could breathe when he did that. He held out a shaking hand. "Come here."

"You're scaring me," she said.

"Hold me."

"I don't understand."

"Please," he whispered. "I need you."

She climbed on the bed and wrapped her arms around him.

"Now sing," he said. "Or hum."

"I'm not going to do that."

"I need your voice."

She started a childish tune…*this old man, he played one…* and Julian clung to the color of it for all he was worth.

Minutes later, Julian sipped water while Cleo bitched. She'd pulled him out so easily. And she had no idea what she'd done.

"And for your information," she rattled on, "I didn't even know you *were* a rock star, which is what we were fighting about."

"We were fighting over you carelessly dragging my guitar around," he reminded her. He tried to hide his smile as her curls trembled with a wave of rage.

"As I was saying," she continued, barely moving her luscious lips and glaring at him. "I didn't even know you were a rock star, so it was completely stupid of you to say I'm just out to"—she glanced away, and her cheeks flushed brilliantly—"pardon me, *fuck rock stars.*"

Ah. It killed her to say the word "fuck." He loved it. "I wasn't talking about me," he said, grinning.

"Then who?"

"Lou Michaels."

"Lou?" she stammered. "What are you talking about?"

"Please, love. I saw the picture."

It was a huge mistake, and he knew it as soon as he'd said it.

"Are you talking about the one in my nightstand drawer?"

Her eyebrows were arched to ridiculous heights. He tried changing the subject. "I'm feeling better now. I'd like to take a nap."

"I don't think so, buddy. You were rummaging in my drawer."

"It was more like poking. I was poking in your drawer." He was tempted to tell her to shut her mouth again but figured he'd better not risk it.

She made several idiotic attempts at speech before sputtering, "Do you know what I think?"

He had no clue, so he shook his head.

"I think we're even. At least, we should be in your twisted mind. I was in your closet, and you were in my nightstand drawer. So, let's put that part of this to rest. But the other part…"

"Look, Red," he said. "I wasn't keeping anything from you that I felt was important. That's the truth." Taking her hands in his, he looked into her eyes. "I've shared everything with you. Don't tell me you don't know who I am because of a dumb poster that represents the smallest, worst parts of me. I've trusted you with who I am."

Nobody had ever been able to hold on to him the way she'd done. She'd reached into the deepest part of him, grabbed a handful of his soul, and saved him. She knew him better than anyone ever had.

She turned his hands over and ran her fingers across the tattoos at his wrists. He knew what she was searching for, and her breath caught when she found it. A lump rose in his throat when she lowered her head and delivered a soft kiss on the raised scars across each wrist.

When her eyes met his again, they were filled with tears. "Why?"

He pulled his hands gently away and tried to shrug. He'd bared enough already. "Shall I have another go at that omelet?"

Julian knocked softly on Cleo's door. She might be napping, and if that was the case, he didn't want to wake her. The Dolls were coming back in a couple of hours to finish their session. It would probably be another late night.

"Come in," she said.

She was curled up on her love seat, hair damp from a shower.

"I've brought someone for you to meet," he said.

Cleo stood and crossed her arms in front of her breasts. "Wait, I'm not dressed—"

"We don't mind," he said, casually strolling in. She looked ready to make a run for it. "Hold on, it's just me and my guitar."

She rolled her eyes and plopped back down. "You had me in fight-or-flight mode."

"I know," he said, smiling. "That was my intention." He set a small amp on the floor next to the love seat. "Scoot."

Cleo moved over to make room, and he sat. She leaned back, not the least bit uncomfortable with him seeing her in a worn pair of pajama shorts and a camisole top so thin you could almost see through it. Actually, you *could* see through it. He cleared his throat and tried to appear as if he weren't staring at her breasts, which was hard, because he was.

"You're ridiculous," she said. "And so is that guitar."

He forced his eyes away from the outline of a nipple back to her face. "No need to be jealous, Lava Locks. It's not a woman. If I had to guess, I'd say it's distinctly male."

"Of course it is. It's a phallic symbol with strings. Does it have a name?"

He laughed. "No name. Our relationship transcends the need for such things."

She rolled her eyes, but they were keenly alert. He knew she was interested in hearing the story. It was a tough one to tell, but in light of her recent frustration over not knowing every single detail of his past, he'd decided to tell it.

She pulled up her legs and settled back against the armrest as if awaiting a bedtime story.

"My dad—well, actually Addie's dad, Paul Wheaton— bought this guitar for me when I was eight years old. It was a consolation prize for taking Addie away from me. He'd remarried, and Addie was going to live with him. He offered to take me, too, but Mum wouldn't let him. I was garnering attention with the violin, and she loved it. She also loved gin and vodka, but that's another story."

Cleo's mouth opened briefly, but she shut it. She furrowed those brows, though, and crossed her arms in front of her chest.

"And I changed my name to Wheaton, with Paul's blessing, in my midtwenties. So, I never lied to you about my name. Julian Andrew Wheaton is my legal name. I've only met my birth father two times, didn't see the need to keep his name."

"I'm sorry," she said. "It doesn't sound like you had much going on in the parenting department."

"It wasn't that bad. At least I had my guitar when Addie left. For a long time, it was the only friend I had. And for a short while, it was the only possession I had. Because when I was twenty-two, a couple of years after I'd been kicked out of the band, I sold everything I owned, except for this"—he held up the guitar—"in order to buy drugs."

"You don't have to talk about this with me. You're right. Who you were isn't who you are now. I don't need to know everything."

He suppressed a grin. If he walked out right now, she'd pop an aneurysm. "Shut up, Big Red. You're dying for the details."

She frowned but didn't deny it.

"My years in Slice were hell. I wasn't mature enough for the stress of being in a band, much less a successful one. The constant touring, the ego wars…it exhausted the shit out of me. Playing guitar helps the synesthesia because I can control the colors, but doing it in front of tens of thousands of people is another story. One guitar can't cancel out the roar of a crowd, and I barely held it together on stage. I began having more and more debilitating episodes, so many the band was crippled with cancellations. But then I found a magic cure."

"You did?" She looked up at him, her eyes full of hope.

"Heroin."

Her face fell. "Sorry. I'm stupid."

"You're just innocent. Anyway, heroin stopped the episodes cold."

He longed to tell her that her voice, or lately, even the thought of her, had the same miraculous effect. But instead, he continued his tale. "Soon, I not only loved heroin, I needed it. I went from being a functioning junkie to a nonfunctioning junkie pretty quickly, and Mitch—he was all heart, you see—kicked me out. It was especially shitty of him, since he was the one who turned me onto it in the first place."

Cleo gasped.

"Not you, too," he said. "What is it with women thinking Mitch is an angel?"

"I'm just surprised, is all." She reached out and laced her fingers through his. Warmth descended like honey, settling in his groin.

"Nobody helped you? Where was Addie?"

He gently removed his hand from hers so he could concentrate on his story. "Addie tried to help, believe me. But I wouldn't let her because accepting help meant giving up the drugs. I had a ton of money and wasn't ready to do that. The money, by the way, was completely gone in months."

"Yikes."

"Habits are expensive. Anyway, soon I'd sold everything, all my other guitars and instruments. Every piece of furniture, the gold records on my walls, the Grammys on the mantle, the toaster, the fish aquarium—you get the idea. All gone. Eventually, I was evicted, so I walked the streets with this guitar strapped to my back, looking for my next score. Sometimes, I played on the corner, with no amp, mind you, and people tossed me money out of pity."

Her hand moved toward his again. Pretending not to notice, he shoved his fingers in his pocket. "So, one evening I was walking down the street, freshly released from rehab and already scheming on my next fix and how to get it."

"Rehab didn't help you?"

"You have to want to get better, and what I wanted…" He stopped. What he'd wanted was to die, and he'd been pissed that he hadn't managed to pull it off.

Too intuitive for her own good, Cleo gently pried his hand from his pocket and ran her fingers over the raised scar at his wrist. He wasn't ready to reopen that wound, and he pulled his hand away.

Cleo got the message. She leaned back, digging her bare toes into the couch cushion beneath his thigh. Thus anchored, she looked deeply at him through shiny green eyes and waited for him to continue.

"The only thing I had left was slung across my back. There was a dealer on the corner. Knowing desperation when he saw it, he lit up at the sight of me. He was about to give me a twenty-five-dollar rock—um, that's crack, by the way—for a four-thousand-dollar guitar."

From the shocked look on her face, he doubted any of Cleo's previous or current friends or acquaintances had ever bought crack. "I had one hand on the rock and one hand on my guitar, and I just froze. I couldn't let go of it." He ran his fingers along the body of the Les Paul.

"Now, the kid had his heart set on the deal, and he wasn't going to let me off so easily. About fifteen minutes after

I walked off, he and some pals jumped me and damn near killed me. I woke up with a smashed-in face, a broken arm, and no guitar."

Cleo made a small, strangled sound, as if she was trying very hard not to cry and was losing the battle. He didn't do well with crying women. "Hush, sweetheart. You're stealing my thunder."

She pulled it together, and he reached out and touched her cheek. "This might be a spoiler, but I promise you I lived happily ever after." He tucked a strand of hair behind her ear and continued. "By some miracle, I still had all my teeth, but no guitar."

"How'd you get it back?" she asked.

"I was in hospital because of my injuries. The day I got out, I was walking down Sunset, thinking about how things really hadn't changed for me all that much, and already eyeing the street corners.

"I walked past a pawnshop window, and there it was— my Les Paul. I fell to my knees on the sidewalk. The shop owner recognized me and came out. I made quite the scene, if I remember correctly. People were gathering around, starting to enjoy the show, you know? Then this homeless guy reaches in his pocket and pulls out a dollar. He handed it to the shop owner, and then everybody started pulling out money. It was crazy. Before I knew it, the guitar was in my hands, and I took that shit as a sign. I checked back into rehab, worked my ass off to get clean, and I've been clean ever since. And I rarely let this guitar out of my sight."

"Oh, Julian, I'm sorry. I didn't mean to be so careless with it."

She got it. And he wanted to kiss her. Like, he *really* wanted to kiss her. "You didn't know. I was a prick. I'm the one who should be sorry."

"Are you going to play it for me or what?" she asked

between sniffles.

He stood and strummed the first chord. The music entered through his chest like a fist. He played it back out, sending it into Cleo in deep reds and browns, warm and smoky, like the hues of Eric Clapton.

Her eyes drifted shut with a sigh. He smiled at how easily she was swept away.

He built the intensity slowly through rhythm and volume, putting a knee on the love seat and lowering himself gradually until he sat. Cleo pulled her feet in to give him more room as he held out a warm note, and he watched her sink beneath its weight.

He dropped the notes lower on the scale and picked out an intricate melody that floated down and hovered in the air above her head, misty swirls of purple and red. As the notes drifted lower on the scale, his eyes drifted lower on Cleo.

Her hard nipples poked through her camisole. Instinctively, he tickled the strings with the tips of his fingers, watching in unbelievable awe as the perfect nubs beneath the thin blue fabric became even harder. Licking his lips, he played a pink note, wondering if those delicate delights stretching the fabric of the camisole were the color of cotton candy, or slightly lower on the subtle chromatic scale, like the juicy flesh of ripe peaches. His mouth watered.

He played down even lower, noticing the rise and fall of her chest as she breathed. Her knees parted a little, then a little more, as she leaned one leg against the back of the couch. With the neck of his guitar, he gently applied pressure to the inside of the other knee. Meeting no resistance, he pushed harder, and her legs opened wider. Her eyes were still closed, like she was in a hypnotic trance. The jewel-colored tones poured out of the Les Paul and surrounded her, shimmering and trembling like an orgasmic aura. Could she *feel* what he was seeing? He strummed faster, blurring the lines between making music and making love, and dropped the neck of the guitar so that it slid up the inside of her thigh. The back of his hand brushed her skin.

A low note seeped out of the guitar, becoming one with a soft moan that came from Cleo's lips. He shook the neck slightly, producing an aching vibrato. Cleo shone with a light sheen of sweat, and her cheeks were flushed. He brushed his knuckles across the sweet spot between her legs and watched in wonder as she arched her back, letting her head fall over the armrest of the love seat. He couldn't believe it. One more note and she was going over the edge. He *wanted* to send her over the edge. "Come on, baby—"

At the sound of his voice, everything came to a crashing halt. Cleo's eyes flew open, and her legs snapped shut.

He quit playing, and silence filled the room. Why had he opened his stupid mouth? She sat up and glared at him with the outrage of a woman who'd just had her ass pinched in a bar. Not exactly the climax he'd hoped for.

"What's wrong?" he asked, feigning innocence and trying not to look postcoital.

"What the hell was that?"

"What?"

"What you just did. What were you doing?"

"I was playing guitar is all."

"Ha!"

"Well, actually I *thought* I was playing guitar, but baby"— he smiled and added in a low voice—"I think the guitar played you."

Cleo didn't fall for it. She stood and pointed to the door. "I don't get played," she said. "Not by a guy and not by a stupid guitar."

He stood, picked up his amp, and headed out. But before Cleo could kick the door shut behind him, he replied, "Oh, but I think you just did, Big Red. And I think you liked it."

Chapter Ten

Julian appeared completely relaxed. He wore an easy smile, his ankles were crossed as he leaned against the counter, and he flirted mindlessly with the hotel clerk. But Cleo noticed his fingers in his pocket, fiddling with those picks. He wasn't as relaxed as he appeared.

The desk clerk clicked away on her keyboard as if she were writing a dissertation rather than checking for vacancies. "I'm sorry, Mr. Wheaton, but there are no other rooms available."

"Are you sure?" he asked. "Don't you have some sort of presidential suite you could upgrade us to? I don't care how much it costs."

Cleo rolled her eyes. Money was no object when it came to getting away from her.

"No, sir, all of our suites are booked. I'm so sorry, but Utopia Records only requested one room." Glancing at Cleo, she lowered her voice. "Would you like us to send up a rollaway?"

"By all means," Cleo interjected. "I don't want to be responsible for the deflowering of Mr. Wheaton here."

"No, we can't have that," Julian said, smiling. "I'm as pure as the newly driven snow."

The clerk gave Julian an inviting gaze that was anything but pure and probably against hotel policy. Good grief. Cleo stomped off to the elevators, arriving in time to squeeze in with a family wearing mouse ears. Julian came around the corner just as the doors slid shut.

He was being such a baby about the room. They'd shared a bed before without incident. But ever since he'd played that stupid Les Paul for her, he seemed convinced she'd have an orgasm if he so much as looked at her. And she had *not* had an orgasm when he'd played. Maybe she had felt a small pre-orgasmic twitch when his hand brushed her, but luckily, she'd snapped out of it just in time.

She shivered a little. Because it was chilly.

"What floor?"

"What?" Everyone in the elevator stared at her, especially the guy in the corner with his finger poised over the button panel. "Three, I guess."

She had no idea where their room was or what floor it was on. That explained the stupid smile she'd seen on Julian's face as the elevator doors closed.

Cleo got off a few seconds later and plopped down in a comfy chair by a window. Her odds of saving face were slim.

Outside the window, the California palm trees swayed in the breeze. Houses terraced a hillside in the distance, dotting the landscape with orange and red terra-cotta rectangles. She put her fingertips on the glass. It looked sunny and hot, just like home. But the radio in the shuttle had said it was a cool and refreshing sixty-six degrees. San Antonio was still pushing upward of ninety-five, and she preferred the Los Angeles version of October.

According to the clock above the elevator, it was time to get ready for the Dead Ringer release party. Julian hadn't wanted to come, but he had. And she knew it was only to keep an eye on her.

Having learned her rock star lessons the hard way, she didn't need Julian to watch out for her. The only idiot with a guitar she was falling for was him. And he wasn't like the other idiots. This was a different deal. For one thing, he wasn't a rock star. He was an artist, a musician, and a studio owner, but he was not an egotistical, maniacal, posing faker of a rock star. He was *real*. And her feelings for him went way beyond her usual obsessive crushes. For the first time in her life, she thought she really might be falling in love.

Her phone rang, startling her out of her thoughts. "Hello, love," Julian said. "Are you enjoying yourself?"

"I'm exploring the hotel."

"Lovely, isn't it? You should see the room. Wait, you can't. You don't know where it is."

"You're a hoot."

"We're in 512. Don't be intimidated by the king-size bed. They're bringing up a rollaway for you."

"I'm sleeping in the bed. You can have the rollaway if you're that scared of me."

"I'm fucking terrified of you, but since the room is in my name, I get the bed. You're technically my guest."

"I received my own invitation to this affair, so if I'm anybody's guest, it's Cory Maxwell's. Maybe I should see what kind of bed he has in his room."

Julian stuttered a little before saying, "Fine. You get the bed. And stay away from Maxwell."

"Maybe I will, and maybe I won't."

She hung up, feeling smug. She had no interest in Cory. But she didn't mind Julian thinking she might. Because instinct told her if he suspected how she felt about *him*, he'd jump right over the rollaway and hurl himself out the window.

•••

The familiar Los Angeles landscape rushed by. Julian hated limos and hadn't expected Utopia Records to send one to the hotel. He'd have sent the ridiculous thing back, but Cleo would have been devastated. She was messing with the sunroof controls, as thrilled as a teenager heading to her prom.

He took a deep, cleansing breath. He didn't like going to large studio parties and never would have attended this one were it not for the redhead bouncing on the seat next to him. She'd made it clear she was going, with or without him. And after the picture he'd seen in her nightstand, and the incident with his guitar, there was no way in hell he was letting her walk into a nest of guitar-wielding demons unprotected. Some women were crazy for rock stars, and Cleo was one of them.

She fidgeted next to him. "What time is your appointment tomorrow?"

That was the other thing he was nervous about. "It's at ten, and you can come if you want, although it won't be fun. I'm going to be hooked up to electrodes and EEG machines all morning. And probably for nothing."

"Won't it be wonderful if it works?"

It would, but he couldn't let himself think about it for fear of disappointment. Over the years, he'd taken countless medications, some of which had helped him control his synesthesia to a certain extent, but all of which had taken dire tolls. He always had to give something up—his creativity, his libido—it was never an equal trade. He'd quit trying new ones several years ago. But last week, a psychologist he'd worked with in the past called him about a biofeedback program. It sounded like New Age mumbo jumbo, but the clinic was in Los Angeles and so was he. He had nothing to lose.

"I haven't been in a limo since my uncle's funeral," Cleo said. "And it wasn't this nice." She reached over and turned up the music.

"Really? No disco ball in the funeral limo?"

She made a weak attempt at kicking him with a chocolate-brown lace-up boot. When she'd asked what people wore to big studio release parties, he'd replied they wore a little of everything. So, she'd thrown on a little of everything.

A cinnamon-colored, silky, strapless dress was cinched at her waist by a western-style belt with a silver and turquoise buckle. The color was pretty on her, and the style showed off her curves. Turquoise also dotted her ears, neck, and fingers. Somehow, she'd managed to look incredibly L.A. chic without even trying. That was good. Because she sometimes seemed to dress herself by spinning through her closet like a tornado and going with whatever stuck.

He threw his arm across the back of the seat, catching some of her hair. She'd ironed it straight. It was sexy as hell, but he missed the curls. "Sorry," he said, raising his arm and gently lifting the glossy auburn curtain to drape across her shoulder. It slipped heavily through his fingers like liquid fire. "We'll be there soon," he said, resettling his arm on the back of the seat.

Cleo's outfit had dictated what he wore, and it had been a no-brainer. He'd chosen a 1968 western suit snagged from Threadbare Vintage. It was coffee brown with black piping along the collar and a fancy yoke on the back. The pants were slim and snug, a nice fit. He'd paired the suit with a black silk shirt and bolo tie that almost perfectly matched Cleo's belt buckle. His hair was pulled back with a leather strap, and silver loops dangled from his ears. If he and Cleo had their picture snapped, they would make a striking pair. He'd mentioned that to her, and she'd squealed with delight. The idea of being identified as his gal pal apparently held infinite appeal for her.

"I'm excited about meeting Cory Maxwell," she said, cutting into his thoughts. "I hope I don't make a fool out of myself. Sometimes I get a bit starstruck."

"Cory Maxwell," he said. The name left a bitter taste on his tongue. He couldn't let Cleo get caught up in Cory's clutches tonight. "Try not to have an orgasm when you see him, and you should be fine."

Cleo's mouth fell open. "You were waiting for the perfect time to bring that up, weren't you?"

"I have no idea what you're talking about."

"Right. You set me up with that stupid guitar. And for your information, I did not have an orgasm. You'd have to work a lot harder than that, buddy." She scooted away, crossed her arms over her chest, and took to huffing and puffing.

"It was an expression, love. No need to get excited and build this to a climax."

The pain of her elbow in his ribs put an immediate end to his teasing. Harassing her was fun. She turned interesting colors when she was embarrassed or furious, and usually, those two emotions rolled out together.

"You give me chills when you play guitar," she said, turning suddenly serious and thoughtful.

"Come again?" He couldn't resist.

She sighed, and he feared another elbow jab. "You heard me," she said. She looked out the window, and her voice grew softer. "Sometimes, when I watch you play, I lose you for a moment, like you disappear in the music. You *become* the music. But then you look at me or flip your hair out of your eyes, and I see you again. I love it when that happens." She rubbed her hands up and down on her arms as if she had goose bumps.

What could he say? The woman was nuts for a guy with a guitar. Luckily, he had several. "I really like you, too," he blurted.

He cringed. He'd managed to sound like a six-year-old boy talking to a little girl on the playground. She laughed at the awkward sentiment. "Of course you like me. I'm extremely likable."

The driver announced they were almost there, and their B-list status was confirmed when he offered to let them out on the curb. They were still half a block from their destination.

"Let's go, Big Red," he said, taking her hand as she exited the vehicle like a pro. Two guys on the sidewalk did an immediate double take as she straightened her dress.

"Are you sure I look all right?"

"You'll do," he said, grinning like a fox.

...

They were swarmed by people the moment they entered the party, and although Julian did his best to keep introductions flowing, it was obvious to Cleo that he didn't know the names of half of the people clamoring for his attention. At least her concerns about standing out and drawing unwanted attention to herself were alleviated. She was, in effect, invisible. All eyes were on Julian.

"No fucking way," boomed a voice from across the room. Cleo's stomach lurched. She knew that voice.

"Julian Lazros. I don't believe it."

Lou Michaels moved toward them through the crowd. Of course Julian knew Lou. Why hadn't she seen this coming? More importantly, where could she hide?

Lou smothered Julian in a bear hug, and Cleo tried her best to disappear. But Lou spotted her. The shocked blankness on his face quickly shifted to a sneer of contempt.

"I wasn't expecting to see you here, Cleo."

"Hi," she squeaked.

"She's here with me," Julian said.

Lou faltered for a moment, but then delivered an icy kiss to her cheek. "I had no idea you two were an item."

"She works for me is all."

Lou seemed to wrap his mind around that. "I see. She used to work for me, you know."

Cleo cringed. She was certain Julian didn't miss the implication, but his face gave nothing away. He was good at impassive.

Lou looked across the room, pretending to be beckoned. With an apologetic smile, he excused himself.

"Wee bit awkward," Julian said, grinning as he watched him go.

Someone tapped her shoulder. "Cleo?"

It was Zachary Sims, the guitarist for Stalemate. She'd met him through Lou, and they'd had a whirlwind rebound romance for about two months before she'd realized there were three other women going around the whirlwind with them.

"Hey, Zachary," she said. "It's so good to see you."

That was a lie. He was an ass. To prove it, his eyes took the creepy scenic route over her body, and the gleam in them left no doubt that he remembered every curve of the road in detail. "You look hot."

Julian cleared his throat. Zachary looked up, and his jaw dropped. "Are you—I mean—are you who I think you are?"

"I'm Julian." He held out his hand, and Zachary pumped it furiously.

"Oh, fuck. Dude, you're, like, my idol." He let go of Julian's hand and began a flurry of not-worthy bows.

Julian shook his head and took a step back, as if mortified. He looked at Cleo. *Get me out of here.*

"Oh, look," Cleo said. "There's Slash."

"Where?" Zachary asked, eyes frantically scanning the room.

Cleo pointed to the left. "He went thataway."

She giggled as Zachary took off like a preteen girl in

pursuit of the latest boy band.

"Slash isn't here," Julian said.

"I know." Cleo grabbed Julian's arm and headed in the other direction. "But looking for him will keep Zachary occupied for a while. He's a Slash fanatic. No offense, big shot, but during the time we dated he never mentioned you."

Julian froze in his tracks. "You dated him, too?"

"Unfortunately."

"You should stay away from rock stars."

"Even you?" she teased.

"Especially me."

She smiled and waved a hand in the direction where Lou and Zachary had disappeared. "You're not in their league, believe me. You're way too—"

"Gotta go," he said. "I promised publicity photos." Without so much as a good-bye, he turned and headed toward the flashes.

That was weird. And she hadn't even gotten to finish complimenting him. Abandoned in a crowded room, she initiated her emergency plan and made a beeline for the bar, where people were stacked three deep. Standing on her toes, she waved her hand in the air to get the bartender's attention, but to no avail. He was probably too mesmerized by the endless Silicone Valley of boobs to notice her. Just as she was about to give up, a warm hand pressed against the small of her back. She turned and came face-to-face with Cory Maxwell.

"You must be the fabulous Cleo," he said.

She stared into those famous blue eyes, or at least the one that wasn't covered by a splash of blond hair, and couldn't think of a single thing to say. The silence grew like a gigantic helium balloon, and that only led to one thing: a gushing of hot air.

"Wow! You're Cory. I knew that immediately. I'm Cleo, but you already knew that. How did you know that, by the way?" She held out her hand, but as he was about to take it, she jerked it back and wiped it on her dress, in case it was sweaty. Then she held it out again. "That was weird. Sorry."

Cory stared at her like she was a performance artist. She dropped her hand, but he quickly reached out and brought it to his lips. "It's a pleasure, Cleo."

"Seriously, how did you know who I was?"

"I saw you walk in with Julian, drew some conclusions," he said with a smile. "Can I get you a drink?"

"Sure, that would be great." With relief, she stepped back from the throng at the bar. People made way for Cory, who caught the attention of the bartender with an almost imperceptible gesture.

Soon, he headed her way with a tray laden with colorful martini glasses. The sleeves of his black shirt were rolled up to the elbows in what was probably a calculated effort to appear casual. His expensive jeans were faded and stressed in all the right places. His dirty-blond hair was coiffed to bed-head perfection, the bleached bangs gelled flat across his forehead and hanging down the right side of his face, covering the outside corner of his eye. Every strand was exactly where it should be. In contrast, the back of his head resembled a feather duster, with tufts of hair sticking up every which way.

"I don't know what you like, so I brought a variety," he said. "We have appletinis, berrytinis, even a bananatini, and, of course, the highly coveted chocotini. I've heard it gives women orgasms." He winked.

"Oh! I'll be careful with that one."

"Let's find a place to sit and get to know each other," Cory said, leading her to a high table surrounded by stools.

With one last look at Julian, who seemed to have forgotten all about her, Cleo followed Cory.

•••

Julian hadn't seen Cleo for at least an hour. He didn't recall when she'd wandered off; things were hectic. But wander off she had, and he was pissed. Ignoring the hands that tapped him on the shoulder or pulled on his sleeves and the random "Julian, over here!" he moved through the crowd, scanning it for the telltale flash of red.

He had stupidly assumed she'd feel insecure in the glitzy surroundings and cling to him like a trembling fawn. But the last time he'd seen her she was playing footsies with Cory Maxwell, and that was after brushing off two Grammy-winning former boyfriends who, she'd casually stated, were out of his league.

She was right, of course. Lou was an icon, Zachary was a rising star, and Julian was a freak who'd made it halfway up the mountain before sliding pathetically back down on his ass.

He didn't know Cory well. He'd spent a few weeks with him and the rest of the band while working on their album. But Cory was a singer, and all singers had insatiable egos they fed with women. They preferred ones they could bedazzle and impress easily, and no woman was more bedazzled by rock stars than Cleo. Her obvious attraction to Julian was proof of that. He closed his eyes and balled up his fists. Where was she?

"Hey, kid, you okay?"

It was Lou. "Just a headache, man." *And I've misplaced a redhead.*

"It's a madhouse in here, and you've been mobbed the entire time."

He avoided eye contact and continued scanning the crowd. Maybe Lou would take the hint that Julian wasn't in the mood for chitchat.

"How long have you been seeing Cleo?"

So much for hints. "I told you. She works for me. We're not seeing each other."

Lou dismissed that with a snort. "You'd better have some good tricks up your sleeve if you're going to keep her," he said.

"What do you mean by that?"

"Don't be fooled, man. If you're making a splash, she's at your side. But she swims away at the first sign of a bigger fish. That's her modus operandi."

"You're always the bigger fish, Lou. Why would she swim away from you if that's all she wanted?" He didn't need this conversation. "You're an icon, and I'm a studio musician," he added.

Lou let out a belly laugh. "I'm washed-up, man. I'm more of a businessman now. And you're easily the most brilliant musician in this room. Don't let her know you put your pants on one leg at a time like everyone else, or she'll be gone quicker than you can say has-been."

"Yes, well, it was lovely chatting with you, but I've got to go find her now."

"Look for the shiniest star, that's where she'll be," Lou said. Then he slapped Julian on the back and sauntered off.

Shiniest star? Where the bloody hell was Cory Maxwell? Before he could take a step toward finding him, he was stopped again. He wanted to scream in frustration. This time it was Dave Gutierrez, the guitarist for Dead Ringer.

"Here's the belle of the ball," Dave said.

He'd gotten to know Dave while working on *Just a Little Sting*. He liked him all right. "Hey, Dave, how's it going?"

"Decent, I guess. You're getting a lot of attention tonight. Not that I mind. Your guest appearance on *Just a Little Sting* is going to sell a shitload of records. And that's what it's about, right? Making money? Selling records? So it's a comeback for you and money for us. Win-win situation."

A comeback? What the hell? And unless he was mistaken, Dave was drunk.

"An artistic collaborative effort is how it was explained to me," Dave slurred. "I just don't remember being included in the collaboration. I remember walking into the studio to find you wailing on that butt-ugly Les Paul while everyone said how awesome it sounded, and before I knew it, you'd stolen my solo."

Christ. This shit had to go down right now? "Did you just insult my guitar? Listen, you guys asked me to write a song. I did. You guys — "

"Our fucking management asked you write a song, Lazros. Let's get that straight."

"Whatever. I was asked to play in the studio sessions. I can't help it if — "

A pregnant girl walked up and grabbed Dave's arm. "C'mon," she said in a soothing tone. "Let's get this night over with. I need to put my feet up."

She seemed to take all the wind out of Dave's sails. He leaned over and kissed her on the forehead.

"Look, man," Julian said. "I don't know what to say. I don't want your job. I'm not looking for a comeback or anything like that."

The girlfriend glared at Dave, and he shrugged sheepishly. "He's drunk," she said to Julian. "I'm Marcie. And I'm the reason he's falling apart, so I apologize."

"What do you mean by that?" Dave asked.

Marcie pointed at her protruding belly.

Dave sighed loudly. "Baby, don't start with that. You know I'm happy."

"Doesn't he look happy?" Marcie asked.

This was interesting in a car accident sort of way, but Julian needed to find Cory. "Have you seen Maxwell?" he asked.

"Yeah, he's holding court in there with a redhead," Dave said, nodding in the direction of the room set up for dancing and mingling.

"That's *my* bloody redhead," Julian muttered, turning to head that way.

"Wait a minute," the girl called. "Would you mind signing my belly?"

Julian looked at Dave, who effectively relinquished his balls at that point. "Go ahead," he said with a sad shake of his head.

Julian obliged and signed the girl's stomach. He'd signed his share of tits over the years, but this was his first pregnant belly.

A moment later, he came upon Cory and Cleo. Cleo was surrounded by empty martini glasses as she jabbered and waved her hands all about. Her eyes were shiny as hell, and her movements were clumsy. Cory had gotten her wasted.

Cory spotted him. "Lazros! Dude, come have a seat. Cleo's telling me about the first recording session she managed by herself. Never a dull moment, huh?"

Julian tried not to sneer as he sat.

"Look," Cleo said. "My tongue is blue."

She stuck her tongue out, and Cory laughed. "Tastes like blueberries," he said.

Maybe it tasted like blueberries—Julian tried not to think about how Cory would know—but the dick gazed at Cleo as if she was a succulent chunk of lobster dripping butter.

"Can I have a word with you, love? In private?"

"Sure," Cleo said, reaching for a martini glass full of chocolate milk. "As soon as I have an orgasm."

Julian frowned.

"What?" she asked. "You didn't think it was only nasty white guitars, did you?"

Julian stood. "That's it. Time to go."

"Chill out, Lazros. We're only having some fun," Cory said, likewise standing.

"Fun's over. Get up, Cleo."

"Settle down, man," Cory said. "I'm not comfortable with you bossing her around like this. And we were just talking. I'm not trying to steal your girl."

"Bloody hell, for the last fucking time, she's not mine." The music was loud, so only the people at the surrounding tables stared. He smashed his fists into his eyes, hoping it would quell the colors bleeding together—the dark purple bass beat threatened to explode in his head.

"Julian, calm down," Cleo said. Essence of tangerine filled his nasal passages. The purple pulses and blinding lights vanished.

More forcefully than he intended, he grabbed Cleo's arm. He wanted out of there before he fell apart.

"Shit, dude," Cory whined. "Don't make me fight you. It took two hours for the stylist to get my hair like this."

"Well," Cleo cut in, yanking her arm out of Julian's grasp, "it took Julian two hours to get the seams of his pants lined up perfectly. I'm sure a fight between you two would be a thrilling display of blood and guts, but we're calling it a night." Reversing their roles, she grabbed Julian's arm and yanked. "Come on. I'm taking you out of here."

Julian knew he should feel humiliated, but he was too relieved by how the colors acquiesced at the sound of Cleo's voice. He inhaled deeply, letting the scent of tangerines saturate his body.

"Great," he heard Cleo mumble. "He's freaking out."

•••

Cleo fumed like a cartoon character with smoke coming out its ears. She crossed her arms across her chest and stared out the window. Julian had attempted to drag her from the party like a sixteen-year-old girl caught sneaking out. She didn't understand it at all. If it hadn't been for Cory, she'd have stood alone like a wallflower all evening.

"What are you so upset about?" she asked as the limo pulled away from the curb. He'd obviously come close to having a full-blown synesthesia episode, but he seemed more pissed than shaken. The man had some major nerve.

"I'm not upset," he said through clenched teeth.

"I am. I've never been so embarrassed in my life."

"So sorry," Julian hissed. "That's what happens when you hang out with a freak. I told you I didn't want to come to this stupid thing."

"You being a freak has nothing to do with why I'm embarrassed."

That came out wrong. Julian wasn't a freak.

"Speaking of embarrassed, it felt great to have the girl I came with glue herself to Cory Maxwell. I turned my back for one fucking minute—"

"Is that what you call ignoring me for the entire evening so you could entertain groupies? Turning your back for a minute?"

"You're mental. I spent most of the night looking for you. And sweetheart, you were the only groupie I saw tonight."

She gasped. "What are you talking about?"

"Nobody else was swapping spit with rock stars."

"Cory knew my tongue tasted like blueberries because he had a sip of my martini. Not that it's any of your business."

Julian pouted with his arms crossed. He jutted his jaw out and turned his head. Then it hit her.

"You were jealous!"

"I was trying to keep you from making a fool out of yourself."

He'd lost his hair band. He ran his hands through the inky waves and went back to staring out the window, scooting over as far away from her as he could and sulking like a pro. The sight of him simmering like that caused her heart to beat in an erratic pattern.

Erratic seemed to be the theme of the evening.

Before she could chicken out, she scuttled across the seat, grabbed his gorgeous face, and kissed him. He was unreceptive, with stone-cold lips. Having successfully made a fool out of herself, she let go, and they stared at each other in silence.

"This is a huge mistake," Julian finally said. He slipped a hand behind her head and pulled her in for a kiss. His tongue wasted no time, and she was startled by the silver stud. Then she was thrilled by it. Everything was soft and warm except for the cold metal ball brushing her sensitive tongue and lips.

Julian groaned into her mouth and broke the kiss. "Jesus," he said, running his hands through his hair. "We need to stop. You're going to wake up sober in the morning and hate me."

"I could never hate you."

"Never say never. Listen, this was a bad idea."

"No, it's not." She clambered awkwardly onto his lap. "Don't change your mind," she pleaded.

"I already have. Get down, Big Red."

"You want me down? As in you want me to *go* down?" Good grief. She really was drunk. And she had every intention of making the most of it.

He rolled his eyes. "Enough groupie play," he said, grabbing her hips to lift her off. "I'm calling this game over."

"That would work if you were calling the shots. But you're not." She wrenched his hands off her hips. He'd been steaming hot three seconds ago, and he could damn well heat back up. She kissed his neck and felt him shiver. He was sweet and salty, like a margarita, and she greatly preferred him to a martini.

"Off," he panted. "I need to think."

She stayed on his lap and pulled her phone out of her

purse. "While you're overexerting yourself with that, I'm going to call someone who knows how to have fun." She pretended to scroll through her contacts. "Aha! Here's Cory."

"Give me that." Julian ripped the phone out of her hand. "You don't know what you want. Thanks to Cory, you're wasted."

She was. And suddenly she felt silly. So silly she wanted to cry. So she did…a little.

"What is this?" Julian asked. "Are you *crying*?" He closed his eyes and rested his head on the back of the seat. "You've passed through the euphoric, horny phase into the depressed, crying phase with record speed. And the depressed, crying phase is my least favorite of the drunk girl life cycle."

"I was trying to be sexy, but I'm just drunk and disgusting."

He cupped her cheeks. "You're not disgusting. But you are a bit blasted. And shouldn't you save the sexy stuff for Josh?"

"I'm not seeing Josh anymore," she whispered. "I don't think he really liked me all that much. I think we both wanted to like each other, but things don't always work out that way."

"When did this happen?"

"After the guitar sex."

He smiled. "Not to disappoint you, Lava Locks, but I suspect my guitar is better at sex than I am."

"Let me be the judge of that." She kissed him on one cheek, then the other.

He talked a good game, but he couldn't play it. Surrender shone in his eyes. When she kissed him again, he kissed her back. She sensed he was perfectly willing to be taken down if she was woman enough to do it.

The limo pulled to a stop. "We're here," he said weakly. "I think we should take a few minutes to think about this."

She'd had enough. "My God, will you shut up? You've got stamina, I'll give you that. Let's hope it isn't limited to whining. Now, listen to me. You're going to get out of this car, and you're going to follow obediently, do you understand? And when we get to the room, you're going to continue that obedience, and do whatever I say."

She leaned into him, pushing her breasts against his chest. He seemed to lose his train of thought, and his endless objections with it, as he stared down at her cleavage.

"You ready to get out of the car now?" she asked.

"Yes," he said.

"Yes, what?" she asked as she smoothed his hair.

"Yes, ma'am."

Cleo led Julian through the lobby, into the elevator, and down the hall to their room. She sobered up with every step, and by the time they reached the room, her stomach was heaving like a California quake. "Listen," she said, "you were right earlier. We should think about this."

"No. I was definitely wrong. You were right." He pulled her close. "God, you've got great tits."

Nobody had ever said that to her before. Not that she didn't have fairly nice breasts, because she kind of thought she did, but nobody had ever actually said *God, you've got great tits*. "Do you want to see them?"

"Very much." Julian brushed his fingers along the edge of her strapless dress. She shivered and swallowed, her head floating in a haze of lust. The moment stretched out until she could barely breathe. She forced herself to inhale just as Julian crooked his finger inside the top. With a devilish grin, he pulled it down slowly, stretching it over her breast until her nipple popped out.

Without thinking, Cleo covered herself, but Julian gently pulled her hand away, clucking his tongue. "No, no, no," he said, staring at her exposed breast. "You're the one who wanted to get down to business. We can do this the civilized way, or"—his eyes darkened dangerously, and his nostrils flared—"I can rip this dress to shreds."

Nobody had ever threatened to rip her dress to shreds before, either. Josh would have insisted on hanging it in the closet. Her knees weakened at Julian's forceful tone. But if she melted into the carpet, she'd never regain the upper hand.

"I'm giving the orders here," she said, loudly enough to chase the tremors from her voice.

Julian raised an eyebrow and let go of her hand. "Going to punish me?" His mouth twitched as he fought off a grin—a battle he didn't quite win—and he took a small step back. "I think I might like that. What did you have in mind?"

He lowered his head and clasped his hands behind his back in a classic submissive stance.

Was he for real? The smirk told her no, not entirely. She had no idea what to do with him. She pulled her dress back up and readjusted things.

"That was brutal," Julian said, pouting. "But if you want to punish me some more, that belt of yours looks wicked."

She gasped. "I'm not going to lash you with a belt."

"Too bad. How about I drop my trousers for an old-fashioned spanking with your bare hand then?"

He was obviously teasing, but there was heat there, too. Cleo had the unnerving feeling she'd bitten off more than she could chew.

"Come here." She pointed to a spot between the bed and the rollaway. "Take off your jacket." She wasn't consciously thinking about what she was doing. It was as if she was on autopilot, and the autopilot had a secret hankering to be a dominatrix.

Julian slowly walked toward her while removing his jacket. "Shall I toss it on the bed, mistress?" he asked. His eyes taunted her, daring her to continue the game.

She yanked the jacket out of his hand and threw it across the room, watching in horror as it landed on a lamp, briefly knocking the shade helter-skelter before pulling the whole thing over on its side with a crash.

"Ooh," said Julian. "It's been a long time since I've trashed a hotel room. Can I throw something, too?" He laughed.

"You think this is funny?"

"A little."

"We'll see who's laughing later."

She ran her hands over his chest. The black silk shirt felt cool and slippery, and her fingernail gently scraped across a nipple, catching on the small ring.

"Watch it," he said, no doubt remembering the night they'd met.

Tentatively, she stuck her tongue out and traced the shape of the ring, feeling the hard nub at the top. Her efforts left a wet spot on his shirt. With trembling fingers, she loosened the bolo tie and began working on the buttons. When every last one had been dealt with, she stepped back to survey the fruits of her labor.

He was perfection. Sculpted chest, ripped stomach, dark tattoos on pale skin. His slacks rode low with a snug fit, and she could see he was enjoying himself. He reached for the cuff of his right sleeve.

"Don't do that," she said, breathlessly. "Turn around." She had an idea. A perfectly nasty, drunken idea.

He hesitated, but then, bless his heart, he turned slowly. She glided up behind him and pulled the shirt down past his shoulders, his biceps, his elbows…revealing inch by lovely inch of the masterpiece. She left the bolo tie hanging loosely around his neck.

He tilted his head, and his hair slid down his back. "What are you doing back there?"

"Give me your wrists," she ordered.

He glanced at her over his shoulder again but then shoved his wrists behind his back.

"I'm going to bind them with your shirt."

"Well, well. Somebody's been reading dirty books."

Maybe so, but they weren't exactly how-to manuals, and she struggled until she ended up with an unsightly ball of fabric anyone could work his way out of in about two seconds.

"What in God's name are you doing?"

"Why can't you just shut up? You're bound, okay? You're tied up and completely helpless. You're at my mercy. I can do whatever I want to you. Got it?"

The sloppy knot came undone. But Julian's hands were effectively trapped in his sleeves, which were now inside out. He turned to face her, clearly wanting to laugh. "I have actual cuffs at home, although I prefer silk ties. As for tonight, I'm fine with vanilla sex if you are."

"Vanilla sex is for sober people."

She drank him in with her eyes. Even though he was grinning and holding his hands behind his back in an obvious attempt at appearing bound and helpless, he took her breath away.

"Take my bolo tie off. I feel like the dude ranch version of a Chippendales dancer."

"I like it and it's staying. Now be quiet." Time to wipe the stupid grin off his face.

She stood close enough to feel the heat rising off his chest. She delivered a feathery-soft kiss to his warm skin and slipped her tongue out for a taste. He shivered, and she smiled with satisfaction. "Get on the bed," she said.

Julian looked at the bed. "Someone dumped all her shit on the bed. There's no room for a bound man in a bolo tie."

He was right. The bed was covered with her stuff. "Drop to your knees then."

"Seriously?"

With her fingertips, she gave a small tug on a nipple ring.

"I'm dropping." He knelt in front of her, hands still behind him, and looked up. "Anything you say," he whispered. "I'm yours."

If only that were true. This was a game, and it was one she'd never played before.

Perhaps sensing her loss of command, Julian picked up the slack. "Kiss me."

His smirk was gone, and his eyes smoldered. She grabbed a fistful of hair and gently pulled back.

"You can yank it if you want to," he said. "You know, *hard*."

He held perfectly, submissively still.

Did she want to? The idea of giving his hair a small yank sent a thrill through her. She tightened her fist and heard his breath catch. The look on his face—eyes closed, lips parted, anticipation of pain oozing from every pore—was delightfully dirty. She pulled his hair, harder than she'd intended, and he jerked his head. It threw her off-kilter. At first, she thought she might recover. But no...she was going down.

She fell against Julian and knocked him over. His head smashed into the leg of the writing desk before slamming into the carpeted floor. She was right behind him, and her forehead delivered the final blow with a double whammy to his face.

Julian let out a howl. "I think you busted my lip!"

She sat up and looked at his face. Blood dripped down his chin, and the sight made her light-headed.

Julian's eyes widened. "Holy fuck, put your head between your knees before you pass out."

She did, and was grateful for the opportunity it provided to properly hang her head in shame. There would never be a more embarrassing moment in her life. It wasn't possible. "Are you okay?" she asked from between her knees.

His voice was gentle. "I'm okay. Are you?"

She lifted her head a little and peeked out through strands of hair. "I'm so sorry."

"It's nothing, love. Let's get on with what we were doing." He pulled his arm out and wiped his lip on his sleeve. "Oops." He quickly put it behind his back again. "I forgot I was tied up and helpless."

Her forehead ached. The collision had sobered her up completely. Which was unfortunate. "Did you ever send for that rollaway? Because I'd like to get a head start on pretending this never happened."

Julian looked disappointed—and entirely silly—sitting on the floor with his hands trapped in his shirtsleeves. She might be able to pretend, but she'd *never* forget this had happened.

"Come on, Red. You've roughed me up a little. What's next?"

"Shame and humiliation topped off by a hangover."

"I'm not into humiliation. But I'm not above begging. Do you want me to beg for it?"

"Cut it out. Let's get ready for bed."

"Please," he whispered.

"Please what?"

"Please *fuck me*. Before I die right here."

Was he pretending to beg to save her pride? Or was he actually begging? She couldn't tell what was real and what wasn't. "I'm such an idiot. This is so stupid." She started to get up.

"Okay," he muttered. "Begging didn't work."

She stood. "You want some ice for that lip?"

"*Cleo!*" he barked.

She jumped, hand to her heart. Julian's mouth was set in a straight line. His nostrils were flared, and Cleo could see his pulse pounding at the base of his throat. He had her full attention.

"Get your ass back down here." He spoke quietly, but it was with authority. Cleo dropped to her knees.

"That's better. Now listen carefully. You're going to dominate me if it kills me, which it very well might." He leaned forward until they were nose to nose. "Kiss me."

He was ordering her to dominate him? She looked into his sexy, hooded eyes. There was only one thing to do, and that was take orders. So, she kissed him. His lips were warm and full—*that's from the swelling*—and he groaned into her mouth—*that's from the pain*—and she didn't care. It was so delicious that she didn't even mind the slight metallic taste of blood. His hands were still behind his back, so she gently held his head in place. The role-playing was forgotten. Kissing Julian—under any circumstances—was enough. It was everything, and she could do it forever.

He broke the kiss. "I'll do whatever you want," he said breathlessly. "Anything at all."

"No, Julian. Stop playing. We don't have to do it this way. Let's just be real—"

"I'm not playing." He edged forward and kissed her. She slid her hands up his chest. *So warm.* He leaned back to lie flat on the floor. His hips were raised due to his bound hands—a sexy bondage bonus—drawing attention to the large, hard piece of rock star straining his zipper. She licked her lips. *Okay. Maybe we will keep playing after all.*

She crawled on top of him, kissing his neck and running her fingers through his hair, just like she'd done in her dreams every night. Julian writhed beneath her but left his hands where they were.

"Take your clothes off," he said.

"You're horribly bossy," she replied, sitting up. "And your clothes are coming off first."

"Right. Whatever. Just hurry."

"You'd better hush," she said, placing her finger over his

lips.

At the light contact, he closed his eyes. She ran her finger down his chin, over his throat, and across his chest and belly. He shivered and lifted his shoulders, letting his head fall back. Wow. What would he do if she let her finger follow that trail of hair that led inside his waistband? Or better yet, her tongue?

She leaned over to kiss his hard, flat stomach, and he groaned before she'd even touched him. She licked and kissed her way down, taking nips and bites, losing herself in the sensations of his warm skin on her lips and tongue.

The bulge in his pants forced the low waistband up just enough to allow a peek. Either he wasn't wearing underwear or it couldn't contain him, because she could see the tip of his penis. She extended her tongue and gave it a feathery lick.

He moaned. "Stop teasing me."

She rested her cheek against the source of his suffering and felt it straining against the zipper.

"Please," he begged.

She delivered a soft kiss and slowly pulled down the zipper, releasing the subject of all the fuss.

"Holy cow!" she said as it sprang out.

"What?"

She was astonished. "I thought it was an urban legend."

"Don't worry. I'll be gentle."

"I'm talking about the tattoo, you dork." She stared at the tribal band encircling the base of his penis. "And," she added, "I have no intention of being gentle with you."

His eyes darkened. He liked that.

"You've got five seconds to look, Big Red. One…"

"Didn't it hurt?" she asked. "I mean, did they have to hold you down? How long did it take? And why would you do something like this?"

"The opiates I was on at the time helped with the pain. But, yes, they held me down. And it took fucking forever. As for the reason, I already mentioned the opiates. Now, can we talk about my youthful indiscretion later and get on with this current one? Please?"

Shaking her head in disbelief, she took the work of art in hand and inspected it properly. And the more she handled it, the more impressive it became. "I like it," she finally declared. "I like it a lot."

"Dirty girl," he said with a grin. "Of course you do. Show me how much."

She leaned down, letting her hair fall across his stomach. She wanted to make him insane with pleasure, but he'd probably had countless backstage blow jobs, and she was hardly a pro.

She tossed her hair over her shoulder, and the room spun a little. Not too much. Nothing she couldn't handle. It settled back down, and she cleared her throat, lowered her head, and *whoa!* It was like a Tilt-a-Whirl. She grabbed the leg of the desk with one hand and squeezed tightly what she already held in the other, holding on for dear life because she was most definitely in danger of falling off the floor.

Julian gasped. "Don't squeeze it. *Shit.*"

"Sorry. I just, um, I need to…"

He attempted to sit up. "What? What's wrong?"

"I think I'm going to be sick."

"Cleo, don't you dare—"

What happened next was nothing a groupie would want to write home about.

Chapter Eleven

The subdivision north of Austin wasn't what Julian expected. He double-checked the address.

He could kick himself for letting things get so out of hand after the release party. It was a good thing Cleo had gotten sick. He didn't have sex with drunk women. It was completely against the rules. How had he come so close? And under such ridiculous circumstances! He wouldn't blame her if she was mad.

He hadn't actually talked to her since the Fifty Shades of Embarrassment at the hotel room. Cleo had been asleep—or faking it—when he'd left the next morning for his clinic appointment. Then they'd been occupied with hauling ass to the airport. On the plane, they'd had no privacy to discuss it. Now, two days later, it was too late. Too awkward. They'd both sunk into silence. Cleo didn't even know how well the clinic appointment had gone, and that's what he hated most about what had happened between them. He was left with nobody to talk to.

He got out of his car and looked around. It was a fucking

suburban neighborhood. Not the neighborhood he'd thought would appeal to Mitch, but then again, Mitch had always been full of surprises.

Patches of green cedar dotted the limestone hillsides that rose above the rooftops, and a lake shimmered in the distance below. The houses were set closely together, and the winding driveways were littered with big plastic toys.

He looked down the sloped driveway of 277 Lantana, squinting through his sunglasses. He hadn't seen Addie since he'd punched Mitch in the face. He'd fully expected her to start calling and harassing him, desperate to make amends. But she hadn't. In short, she'd written him off. Landrum had a history of stealing the important people in his life. And now Addie was one of them.

Julian marched down the driveway to the front door. Yanking his sunglasses off and hooking them in his collar, he rang the bell. A pretty young girl answered. He'd expected a maid or servant, and she was obviously neither. Her blue eyes, outlined in thick liner, stared at him with blatant curiosity.

Shit, but she was young.

"Mitch here?" he asked.

"Um, just a minute. I'll go get him." She hesitated, unsure of whether or not to invite him in.

"I'll wait outside," he said.

Seconds later, the door swung open, and there stood Mitch. He didn't look all that surprised to see him. "Hello, Julian."

A piss-yellow cloud floated above Mitch's head. *That fucking voice.*

"Mitch."

Mitch raised an eyebrow at his swollen lip. "I see you've already been in one fight recently. You sure you're up for another? Or should I just invite you in for tea and crumpets?"

"Tea and crumpets sound lovely," he said, shoving Mitch

aside and stepping through the door.

Mitch followed him into the foyer and called out, "Darlin', why don't you put some water on to boil for our English gentleman here?"

They walked into a living room, which, again, was a surprise. No lavish chandeliers hanging from the ceiling, no obnoxious posters of Mitch or framed gold records lining the walls. It was a plain old living room with some lived-in furniture and a television.

"My, how the mighty have fallen," Julian mumbled.

"What'd you say there, pal?"

"Nothing. And I'm not your pal."

"Have a seat," Mitch said, pointing to a worn beige couch.

A disgusting mass of hair with four legs thought Mitch was talking to it and jumped on the couch before Julian had a chance to sit. Mitch frowned. "Scoot over, Costello. We have a guest."

Costello didn't budge, and Julian sat next to it, trying to take up as little space as possible. The mutt let out a moan and stretched, shoving Julian's thigh with its hind legs.

Mitch sat in a chair and ignored the dog's ill manners. Wearing an orange University of Texas sweatshirt and gray sweatpants, he was a man at ease. Not a worry in the world.

"I reckon you came with a couple of messages for me, Lazros. First and foremost, you want me to stay away from your sister. And second, I'm betting you're about to tell me that this state isn't big enough for the both of us. But honestly, brother, we both know I was here first."

Bloody hell, he hated how Mitch exaggerated that ridiculous drawl. "You're not hiding a six-shooter beneath that dreadful sweatshirt, are you, Mitch? I feel like I'm at the O.K. Corral."

Mitch laughed. "Who got the better of you?"

"What?"

Mitch pointed to his eye and lip. "Who beat you up? A boyfriend, a husband, or a dealer?"

Julian gingerly touched his swollen eye, where Cleo's forehead had made contact, and ran his tongue over his healing lip. "Believe it or not, I was tied up and beaten senseless by a woman."

Mitch laughed heartily. "What'd you do to deserve that?"

"We're off the subject, Landrum. You were right, of course. I want you to stay away from Addie."

The girl came in carrying a small box. "All I could find was chai. Is that okay?"

"That's fine, darlin'," Mitch said, grinning stupidly as the girl walked back to the kitchen. *What a pervert.*

"A little young, I'd say. Even for you."

The grin slipped from Mitch's face. He'd hit a nerve.

"That's my daughter, you sorry asshole. She's barely sixteen."

The piss-yellow cloud disappeared. Mitch's voice had turned into a darkening thunderstorm of black and gray. He stood, and Julian, too stunned to defend himself, waited for a fist. But it never came. Mitch just stood there, waiting for what? An apology?

"Sorry, I didn't know you had a daughter."

The girl came back in the room, trying not to spill the two cups of tea she carried. Mitch's face melted back into its former pleasant expression.

"Rachel, this is Julian Lazros. Julian, this is my daughter." His emphasis on the word "daughter" was unnecessary. Julian already felt like slime.

"Nice to meet you," he said. The girl flashed a shy smile as Mitch took the cups. Her neck had developed telltale red splotches. Mitch, recognizing the signs of a teenage girl falling under the influence of a rock star, sighed and guided her back to the kitchen.

Mitch was a father? He hadn't had a kid when Julian knew him. Now he had a sixteen-year-old?

Mitch ambled back into the room. "So where was your daughter back when I knew you? I don't remember any toddlers running amok in your dressing room."

"Not that it's any of your business," Mitch said, frantically dipping his horrible American tea bag in his cup, "but I adopted her when I married her mother."

So, he'd gotten married. "You're quite the guy. I guess you're divorced, then? I only ask because you're shagging my sister."

Mitch set his mug down on the coffee table and massaged his temples. "No, I'm not divorced."

"Brilliant. You've seen the last of Addie, then. And me. This was fun, but I can see myself out." He headed for the door with Mitch on his heels.

"Would you believe I was actually happy to see you?" Mitch said. "I thought we could hash some things out, talk like men. But you're deranged, as usual. Just as crazy as you ever were."

"Maybe I'm crazy, but you're disgusting. I feel sorry for your wife and kid."

"For your information, my wife is dead. Now get out of my house before I blacken your other eye, you stupid prick."

Julian stood at the pump, wrinkling his nose at the gas fumes—snot green—and trying to sort through his feelings. How was he supposed to have known Mitch was a widower? Now he felt like a real prick, which only increased his aggravation.

The pump handle clicked off. Julian pulled it out of his tank and replaced the gas cap. This had been a miserable fucking day, and he couldn't wait to get home—although he wasn't looking forward to a run-in with Cleo. Maybe he'd head to Rooster's for a mindless jam session instead.

He settled into the El Camino and started it up, already thinking of a backup plan in case Rooster was busy. The Dolls had a gig tonight. He could probably sit in with them. Just as he was about to pull onto IH-35 and head south toward San Antonio, a little blue coupe that looked suspiciously like Addie's darted past—heading north—*toward Austin*. Well, bloody hell. He was going to put an end to this once and for all. He turned right instead of left and took off after his sister.

Addie darted in and out of traffic, but Julian managed to keep her in sight. The exit for Mitch's neighborhood was coming up on the right, and sure enough, she took it. Julian followed her through the winding hills, back to Mitch's house. By the time he climbed out of his car, Addie waited for him, leaning against her trunk.

"I saw you in my rearview mirror," she said.

"We need to talk."

"No, actually, we don't. I'm an adult, and I'm in a relationship. I'm sorry if it upsets you, but it is what it is. If you'd like to come in and behave like a civilized human, I'm certain Mitch would be happy to have you."

"I've already had a chat with Mitch this morning, and I don't think he'd be happy to have me."

Addie's mouth dropped open. "Is that what happened to your face?"

Mitch's voice came out of nowhere. "He mistook my daughter for a groupie and made some crude accusations that are par for the course with him, but I assure you I didn't hit the little fucker." He walked barefoot toward them across the driveway.

Julian rolled his eyes. "Addie, you think you know this man, but you don't. He doesn't love you—he loves making me miserable. And he has a history of destroying the lives of young, innocent girls in order to do so."

"God, Julian," Addie said. "Everything is not always about you, no matter how hard you work at it. And I am not a young, innocent girl. Stop confusing this situation with whatever crazy idea you have in your head about Mitch and Gina."

Seriously? She'd brought up Gina? Well, since she had…

"Who was the last person to see Gina alive? Ask Mitch that! And for that matter, who was the last person to see his wife alive?"

Addie gasped and covered her mouth. Mitch took a step toward him but then stopped. "Are you under the care of a shrink right now, dude? Because you are batshit crazy."

"Don't say that, Mitch," Addie snapped.

"Listen to him and tell me he doesn't sound crazy. And if we're going to continue with the murder accusations, I'd prefer we do it inside. I've got a nice thing going with most of the neighbors, and I'd like to keep it that way."

"Where are the kids?" Addie asked.

"In the house," Mitch said, never taking his eyes off Julian.

Mitch had more than one kid? Bloody hell. Julian had a definite image of Mitch, and it would be lovely if he'd try to fit it better.

"Addie," Mitch added, "why don't you go inside and check on Emily? She was running a fever this morning."

"She's not staying here long enough to check on your sick kid," Julian said. "Come on, Addie, let's go." He reached for her hand, but she yanked it away and walked up the driveway.

As soon as she was out of earshot, Mitch got straight to the point. "I never slept with Gina, much less killed her, you stupid, *stupid* shit. She was a minor, and no matter what you believe, I'm not a sick fuck."

"So sorry," Julian said. "Rock stars never have sex with underage girls. How silly of me."

"Lazros, I've about had my fill. You know I stayed away from the young ones. Shit, I sent them to you."

If this was Landrum's idea of an apology, it was fucked-up. "Thanks for the castoffs," he said. "But if it was wet, you stuck your dick in it. I don't remember you being all that discriminating."

"How do you remember anything at all from those years? You were a pathetic junkie. If anyone was breaking any laws with minors or otherwise, it was you."

"*I* was a fucking minor."

When Julian had joined Slice, he'd worshipped Mitch, just like everyone else. And Mitch had wasted no time in taking him under his wing, introducing him to every vice the industry had to offer, including drugs and women.

The skirts that had followed Slice across the country and beyond worshipped and served two gods: Mitch, who had the predictable singer's black hole for an ego, and Julian, his newly acquired protégé. But unlike Mitch, Julian hadn't wanted the attention of the fans. He'd wanted the approval of Mitch, who he'd freakishly decided was a father figure.

As if Landrum could read his mind, he said, "You were just a kid. A punk who deserved someone way better than me as a role model. I regret the part I played in your life, and I'm sincerely sorry for it. But you gotta let it go, pardner."

"Save it." Julian started walking. Time to get his sister.

"I don't know everything that happened that night with Gina," Mitch called after him, "but I can tell you what I remember."

Julian stopped in his tracks and turned to face Landrum, his pulse pounding in his head. "I know what happened. Gina and I had a fight—she wanted me to stop drugging—which of course, I couldn't." He gave a sarcastic salute to Mitch and added, "Thanks for that, by the way. So I took off for a couple of hours to cool down, and when I came back, Gina was gone.

Ran straight to you, didn't she? And you took her in."

"I hardly set her up in the guest room. She showed up at my party, and I told her to leave. She was too young, and I didn't feel like keeping an eye on her."

"Fuck you, Mitch. It was right after 'Walk You Home,' wasn't it? You and your overinflated ego were full of envy. And you want to hear the pathetic truth? I hated that stupid song. It wasn't even good—granted, you wrote it, so that was a given—and I have no idea how it went to the top of the charts. It sucked, and I never would have been the one to sing it if Lance hadn't made me."

"It went to the top *because* of you, buddy. And you're right, I hated your guts," Mitch said. "I'd worked my ass off in that band for years, and nobody noticed us until you showed up. I should have been grateful, and I should have looked out for you. But I wasn't capable of either of those things. I felt old and washed-up, and I blamed it on you, but Julian, I never thought of getting back at you through that little girl."

Mitch's voice was like a chameleon. It just kept sliding up and down the color spectrum, changing from word to word. Could he trust anything Mitch was saying?

"I'd say you most certainly got back at me through that little girl."

"I tried to save her. Do you want to hear the whole story or not?"

Part of him wanted to hear the story of what happened the night Gina died. But the other bit, the bit that fed on rage to keep the self-loathing away, wanted to hear nothing more about it. But that bit was paralyzed with fear and unable to speak.

Mitch started talking. "She made a spoiled rich girl scene when I told her to go home, but I thought she'd left. I really did."

"She was not a spoiled rich girl. You don't know the first

thing about her."

"You're right," Mitch said. "I'm sorry."

Gina had been a tragic little waif, although Julian hadn't known it because he'd been a tragic little waif, too. Her dad was rich and absent. Her mom spent her days shopping on Rodeo Drive. And Gina spent her days trying to catch somebody's attention. She'd caught his at an L.A. show at the Roxy.

Hair spiked up in punk style, eyeliner as thick as her sullen expression, but behind it all was a quiet desperation Julian's heart recognized immediately. He'd kept his eye on Gina all through the show and nodded in her direction when he exited the stage. The roadie knew what to do.

He couldn't claim her right away. There was a pecking order, and nobody grabbed a girl until Mitch had chosen his own entertainment for the evening. Gina, along with all the other girls, followed Mitch around while he took his sweet time. Julian hated to admit it, but Mitch didn't ever party with the young ones. He'd known Mitch would pass her up, and she'd be his.

As the band boarded the bus that would take them from Los Angeles to Pasadena, a handful of groupies got on with them. The ones who hadn't been chosen by Mitch stood outside, hoping to appeal to one of the other band members, road crew, or the backup band, anyone who could get them on the bus. Gina was among them, and Julian held out his hand. She'd hesitated, but then she'd grabbed it and followed him up the steps.

On board, the party had been in full swing. Cocaine and pills were laid out like candy on Halloween. Two women were making out while Mitch watched, and Lenny, the bassist, was well on his way to receiving a blow job right there in the middle of the bus. Gina had looked around with huge eyes before grabbing Julian's arm and plastering herself against him. He'd felt her trembling. "Where are we going?" she asked.

"Pasadena."

She'd looked truly alarmed. "I have school tomorrow."

Julian had extolled the virtues of playing hooky in pursuit of other passions, but when her eyes filled with tears, he arranged for the driver to drop her off at the nearest gas station. Afraid to leave her there, he'd stayed while she waited for a cab. Then he'd gone home with her.

The two teens had made love surrounded by stuffed animals and posters of Mitch, as if Julian needed any reminders that he was a consolation prize. Then he'd sneaked off before dawn, hitching a ride to meet up with his furious bandmates in Pasadena—just in time for a live on-air interview.

As soon as the short tour was over and Julian was back in L.A., they became inseparable. Gina was his first and only girlfriend, and he'd been truly and horrifically in love. But he'd had another love then as well.

Heroin had started out as a seductive temptress, but once it caught him, it had turned into a mean, jealous bitch that wanted to own him completely.

He walked back to Mitch and leaned against his car, overwhelmed by memories and remorse. "Tell me how it happened," he whispered.

He'd never heard the details. He only knew she'd overdosed, although he still couldn't believe it. She'd hated drugs.

"I'd sent her packing and gone back to partying. I figured she'd call you, y'all would make up, and that would be it. I wasn't worried about her doing anything crazy—I didn't think she used. My worry had been that she'd try to make you jealous by hitting on the wrong asshole, and things would go too far. I watched her stomping across my front lawn and thought that was the end of it."

"But it wasn't," Julian said.

"No, unfortunately, it wasn't." Mitch ran a hand over his

face and sighed. He took a step closer to Julian, until they were almost toe to toe. "An hour or so later, I heard a commotion in the billiards room. As I headed down the hall, I about got knocked over by scumbags fleeing the scene. I knew it meant one of two things: either the cops were raiding the party or someone had gone blue. I ran smack into that dealer, Doug Addison. He and his crowd of losers used to crash our parties."

Julian nodded. He remembered. But he hadn't known Doug had been there that night.

"He looked scared shitless," Mitch said. "Told me somebody was sick and then ran. I hurried into the room and couldn't believe it was Gina. I tried to tell myself she'd fainted, but there was no mistaking what I saw. I knelt down; I was going to sit her up and try to get her walking, but then I saw she still had a fucking needle in her arm. A *needle*. I hit her in the chest—"

"That's enough," Julian said. "I can't hear any more."

Mitch hesitated. "I never stopped trying to save her. I kept it up until the paramedics got there."

"I said shut up." Julian didn't want any more details. "Fuck, it was such a waste," he mumbled.

He wanted to keep hating Mitch, an asshole who'd stood at the crossroads of every wrong turn he'd ever taken, pointing the way each time. He looked at him, ready to pounce, but all he saw was a man in a stained sweatshirt, wiping at tears on his cheeks.

"Fucking Doug," Mitch said, dabbing at his dripping nose. "He should have known better than to push that China shit on her. She was just a little girl."

Julian's knees quivered, and he leaned harder against his car so they wouldn't give out entirely. "Are you saying it was Doug's stuff? How do you know that?"

"Everybody knew it. He was arrested for it."

Julian hadn't known. After that night, he'd begun a three-year spiral into the depths of self-destruction that finally ended in a bathtub full of bloody water. He'd never paid his respects to her family or talked to any of their friends. He didn't even know where she was buried. He'd spent all these years hating Mitch because it made it easier to avoid the elephant in the room—the question of where Gina had gotten the heroin.

"Bud," Mitch said, "did you think that stuff was yours? Have you thought that all this time?"

Yes, he had. Where else would she have gotten it? His head swam, and he reached behind him to grab the El Camino's handle. But before he could yank on it, Mitch grabbed him and pulled him away from the car.

This was good. They were going to fight. He wanted to fight. He took a swing, a bad one, and Mitch pulled him in, squeezing him tightly. Julian was taller, but Mitch was heavier, and he held him easily.

"Julian," Mitch said. "You didn't kill that girl. Do you hear me? It wasn't you."

Julian choked back a sob. Maybe the drugs weren't his, but if Gina hadn't hooked up with him, she'd probably be alive. Mitch seemed to think he could forget about it, as if life had moved on peacefully and they'd left no path of destruction in their wakes. No strung-out kids, no broken hearts, and no dead girls.

"The last thing I said to Gina was, 'Stop being a crazy bitch,'" Julian said.

Mitch didn't say anything at first. Kids' voices floated on the breeze. Someone started a lawn mower somewhere. "You were young and stupid. You didn't know you'd never see her again. Believe me, I know how that works."

Julian pulled away and wiped his face. Fuck. He sniffed loudly and spat a manly loogie. Mitch did the same.

"When did your wife die?" Julian asked. It sounded horribly conversational.

Mitch adjusted his baseball cap, even grabbed his crotch briefly before replying, "Three years ago. A guy ran a stop sign. Emily was six months old and in the car seat. She barely had a scratch on her, thank God. But Meg caught it on the driver's side. She died two days later. The last thing she heard me say was, 'Get the right kind of cereal this time.'"

"Sorry," Julian mumbled. That must have been awful.

Mitch cleared his throat before adding, "My three girls have kept me going."

"Three? The biggest horndog of all time is raising three daughters?"

Mitch laughed. "Karma, man."

"No shit."

"Meg already had Rachel when we met, and we added two more to the mix. We talked about having another one, but, well, anyway." He sniffed. "I sure as shit didn't deserve her. Or the woman I've got now, for that matter."

The woman I've got now. Julian narrowed his eyes and glared at Mitch, who smiled that stupid Mitch smile and said, "Listen, about that. Addie and I have something to tell you."

"Daddy!"

Julian winced and turned toward the source of the hot pink spear that had stabbed him between the shoulder blades. Addie walked down the driveway carrying a blue bundle. "I throwed up," it shouted.

"Congratulations," Mitch said, holding out his arms. Wispy blond hair poked out of the blue blanket. "Let me take her, Addie."

Two chubby arms emerged from the blanket and wrapped around Addie's neck. "No. Addie said she'd hold me all day 'cause I'm sick."

The blanket fell away, revealing feverish blue eyes set in a cherubic face. "Who are you?" she asked Julian.

"Emily, this is my brother, Julian."

Emily put a chubby hand on each cheek and emitted a squeal that was painfully fuchsia, tinted with the scents of bubble gum and vomit. It had been a while since anyone had been so thrilled to meet him. "Uncle Julian!"

"No, no," said Julian. "I'm not your uncle."

"Brothers are uncles, and sisters are aunts," the little girl said. "Laura told me."

It wasn't smart to argue with someone of her stature, but he couldn't help it. "I'm Addie's brother, not your daddy's. You're not related to me."

The child clearly didn't believe him and turned to Addie. "But when we have the princess wedding, and you're my mommy, he'll be my uncle then, right?"

All of the color drained out of Addie's face. She glanced up at Julian. "We were waiting for the right time to tell you."

Jesus. How many shocks could he handle in one day? "There is no right time."

"That seemed to be the problem we were experiencing, pal," Mitch said.

The sounds, the smells, the unearthed emotions about Gina…Julian's legs buckled.

"Julian," Addie said, "don't start."

Like he could fucking help it. He took a deep breath, but he was still suffocating. He sat down on the driveway and covered his ears.

"Don't you start that," Addie warned, handing Emily to Mitch. "You cannot pull this right now, do you hear me? It won't make a bit of difference. We're getting married."

A slight buzzing sound set in. "Motherfucker," he said.

"Uncle Julian said a bad, bad word," Emily yelled. The pink lightning bolt almost split his head in two, and then a tidal wave of colored sludge, consisting of every sound within a twelve-mile radius, descended. The distant traffic noise, the hum of the power lines, birds, dogs, kids—it all blended in a painful collision with Addie's news, Gina's memory, and Cleo's absence.

Cleo. The scent of tangerines surrounded him, and he breathed in deeply again. This time it helped. The sludge began to lift.

"Don't go nutters," Addie said. "Come inside."

"We'll have tea," Emily shrieked. He covered his ears with his hands and put his head between his knees. Some rocking would help. Then he'd get in his car and drive home, find Cleo, everything would be fine. If he could just get to Cleo…

"He's rude," Emily whispered. It was an earsplitting sound.

"Oh, dear," said Addie. "Mitch, do something."

"Do you want me to pick him up and carry him into the house?" Mitch asked.

"He's not a child. And you couldn't pick him up. Goodness, Mitch."

"I've done it, before, sweetheart. Of course I was younger, then." He touched Julian on the shoulder. "Come on, buddy. Let's go inside."

"Is he sick?" Emily asked.

"Yes," Addie said.

"Is he gonna throw up?"

"He's not sick, darlin'," Mitch said. "He's just weirder than shit."

"Bad word," screamed Emily.

"Mitch," Addie snapped. "What's the matter with you?"

"Addie, he's a thirty-three-year-old man, rocking back and forth on my driveway with his hands over his ears. How do you explain it?"

Julian couldn't take any more. While they bickered about how fucked-up he was, he pulled himself to his feet and yanked on the handle of his car door. Before they could stop him, he'd climbed in, started it up, and taken off down the road, concentrating on the scent of tangerines and, most of all, Cleo.

•••

The studio's mail formed a nice, round pile on Cleo's love seat. She'd been trying to sort and re-sort it, but she couldn't keep track of what was what. Where the heck was Julian?

The morning after had been awful. Julian had sneaked out, leaving her to wake alone. Three hours later, he'd torn back into the room, grabbing things and throwing them into suitcases—muttering about missing their flight.

By the time they'd gotten home, it was late, and, without a word to each other, they had both fallen into their own beds. She'd woken up this morning—dying of curiosity about the results of his clinic appointment—only to find he'd left again.

Abandoning the stack of mail, she flipped on the television, leaned back into the purple velour cushions of the love seat, and closed her eyes.

A slamming car door woke her a short time later. In a sleepy haze, she stumbled to her door. Did she want to close it and give Julian a taste of his own medicine? A nice whopping dose of the silent treatment? Or did she want to sit him down and force him to talk?

He came barreling into the loft before she could decide. "Cleo!"

"Is everything okay?" she asked. He was drenched in sweat.

"Now it is." He grabbed her, pulling her close. She stood stiffly, arms at her sides, doing her best impression of a startled manikin.

Did he just sniff her hair? "Baby, you smell so good."

Did he just call her *baby*? And what was that pressing into her belly? Julian moved his hips and—*oh*. He was very happy to see her. What had brought about this change in temperament?

Tremors passed through his body into hers. "Hold me," he whispered.

She put her arms around him with a sense of déjà vu. This was a synesthesia episode. Was it ever possible for both of them to be in their right minds at the same time? She lifted her face to his. Eyes slightly unfocused. Yep. The boy was going down. What could she do to help him?

He sniffed her hair again—weird—and his lips curved into a small smile. Maybe it was that easy. "Feeling better?"

"Mmm," he moaned. "Please, Cleo, I want some more."

He was like a heavily tattooed Oliver Twist, but he wasn't asking for gruel. "More of what?"

"Of you." Her heart pounded like a bass drum. He lifted her chin with his fingertips, bent his head, and kissed her. And he was just as good at it as he was the last time. She parted her lips in invitation, he accepted, and her knees went weak; it was a good thing he held her so tightly.

He walked her backward through her apartment, straight to the unmade bed, and pushed her down gently. "Cleo," he gasped. "I need you."

Needed her to do what? "Listen, you're a little off. Or a lot, actually. *Muy loco* at the moment. The kissing was fun, but we should probably stop now."

He pulled his shirt over his head, and Cleo lost her conviction. Good grief, she'd memorized every angle, plane, and tattoo on his beautiful chest, but she still couldn't stop staring. She reached up to touch him, and he brought her hand to his lips. His tongue traced the lines of her palm, eyes searching hers, asking what she was willing to give.

Everything. God, she was willing to give him everything. But first, he had to be brought back to the surface. She wanted him mind, body, and soul—and all three were not currently available.

He crawled onto the bed with her. The window was open, and a car drove by with its stereo blaring. Julian flinched, then buried his head against her breast.

She started the trick that had worked before. "This old man, he played one…"

He clung less tightly with each verse. The shivering stopped. For some stupid reason, her singing a nursery rhyme pulled him out of it. Crazy.

"This old man, he played eight…"

Julian's hand ran up under her T-shirt, straight to her breast. He squeezed it gently and pulled the cup of her bra down, his fingers nimbly finding the nipple.

"He played knick-knack on my gate…"

His mouth went to her breast. He sucked gently before flicking the silver stud in his tongue across her nipple. She couldn't have come up with a *knick-knack paddywhack, give a dog a bone* if her life depended on it.

"Feeling better?" she asked, breathlessly.

"Mmm-hmm," he said, lifting his face from her breast. His eyes were perfectly clear, fully focused, and bright. "That's a horrid nursery rhyme. You couldn't sing a bit of the Cure, maybe? It has to be *give a dog a bone* with you?"

He was back. "Sorry. It's weird, isn't it? But that's what comes out when I'm…" She searched for a word to describe how she felt.

"Horny?"

No point in denying it.

"You just invited me to play knick-knack on your gate," he said with a devilish grin. "You'll have to open it for me, though."

He kissed her again, and she let her thighs fall open.

"What do you say, Cleo? Can this old man come rolling home?"

"Yes," she said. "We're both in possession of our full faculties, right?" She was on fire. And only Julian's touch could put it out.

"I don't know that our faculties are anything to brag about. And I need to give you something to do with your mouth. Otherwise, the two remaining paddywhacks might slip out and spoil the mood."

Like she could possibly sing right now.

"Here, baby. Suck on this." He slipped a finger between her lips, slowly working it in and out. "That's better," he said.

He went back to her breast with his mouth, and she used her tongue to caress his finger. It was strangely erotic, sucking on a finger, and when he offered another, she hungrily accepted. Just as she got used to having a full mouth, Julian's fingers on his other hand trailed down to her shorts. He rubbed her gently, and she moaned, opening her legs wider. His fingers slipped inside her shorts, pushing aside the crotch of her panties. She thrust her hips forward, and he slid a single finger in.

"Cleo," he whispered, removing his fingers from her mouth. "I want to make love to you."

Okay, he hadn't said, *Alice, I want to make love to you.* He'd said Cleo, and he knew what he was doing and whom he was doing it with. She'd wanted him so desperately and for so long, she only hesitated a second before saying, "Okay. But we need a condom."

He groaned with frustration.

"I think I have one," she said.

"Hurry."

Cleo scooted off the bed and scurried the two or three feet to her tiny bathroom, where she scrounged around urgently. The corner of a foil pack poked out from behind a tube of antibacterial ointment. She snatched it up and bounded back to the bed, where Julian lay, stripped down to nothing. The bed was also stripped.

"There were cookie crumbs," Julian explained. "Sorry." He grabbed her and pulled her onto the mattress, now covered only by the soft fleece pad she liked to spread beneath her sheets. It felt good against her skin, soft and fuzzy and *ooh!* Something hard ran up the inside of her thigh.

"Oh, Julian." She sighed.

He rose to his knees and fumbled with the foil packet before using his teeth to rip it open. He swiftly rolled the condom on, and with an impressive martial arts type of a move, had her ankles up over his shoulders.

Her shorts were still on. Julian finally realized it, and he ran a finger under the seamed crotch and effortlessly ripped it apart. Cleo yelped in surprise, then the tiny side seam of her panties received the same treatment. He held her legs open and took a good, long look.

She blushed under his intense gaze, waiting for the usual comment about her being a natural redhead. But all he said was, "Beautiful."

Cleo tensed for a forceful entry. But Julian was surprisingly gentle, pouring himself into her. He groaned and leaned in, causing her legs to part and her heels to slip off his shoulders, sliding slowly down his arms until her knees were crooked at his elbows. She was at his mercy.

He drove a strong, hard rhythm with a measured cadence. Cleo's body responded hungrily, seeking friction in that perfect spot. The fleece pad beneath her was soft, and the unrelenting man on top of her was hard. "You okay?" he asked, gazing down at her through strands of hair.

"God, yes," she whispered. "Don't stop. Don't you dare stop."

She was lost in the sensations. Gone was the mental self-talk that usually plagued her during sex, the endless internal ramblings and assessments as to her partner's or her own peculiarities, the constant estimations of timeliness or ponderings over the likelihood of orgasm. She was immersed in the act of loving. This was making love. They were creating something. Could Julian actually *see* it?

Liquid warmth radiated from the center of her body. Cleo arched her back and let her legs fall open, tingling to the tips of her fingers and toes. Usually she needed more direct stimulation than intercourse to achieve an orgasm, but Julian had her out of her mind with pleasure. He knew what he was doing—no doubt about it—but it wasn't his skill at pushing her buttons that had her about to come undone. It was the idea that it was *him* taking her over the top of the crest. It was Julian.

"Oh, fuck, baby. It's so good," he gasped. He moved faster, and Cleo's heart sped up accordingly. Lifting her hips, she opened her legs as wide as she could, and her orgasm slammed into her like a tidal wave. It was so intense she cried out, bucking and writhing as a million bursts of lights and colors exploded in her head.

Julian's eyes were wide open, taking it all in.

An instant later, he lost his rhythm, the muscles in his arms trembled and shook, and finally, he sank into her one final time before shuddering and collapsing on top of her.

He breathed raggedly into the pillow, skin slick with sweat, hair damp against her cheek. She wrapped her legs around him and melted into the fleece pad, feeling warm and sleepy. He stilled and rolled gently off her. Then he dropped his head to her breast, and she held him tightly.

She knew she shouldn't do it, but she whispered, "I love you."

Would he answer? She held her breath.

All was silent.

• • •

Julian stirred, coming slowly out of a dream. He looked around the room, waiting for the puzzle pieces to fall into place and hoping they'd do it quickly.

"My God," Cleo said. She grabbed a pillow and covered herself with it. "You don't remember a thing."

Naked, alarmed, and angry-looking women were not among his favorite things. And this one looked as if she might kill him.

"Don't freak. It takes me a minute," he said. There was still some buzzing going on in his head. He'd been a mess, very upset about something… *What was it?* It smashed into him like a baby grand falling out of a window. Addie. Goddamn.

"My sister's marrying Mitch Landrum."

"Okay, so we had sex. I was kind of hoping that's the part you would remember," Cleo said. "And there's no way Addie's getting married. You're delusional."

Of course, he knew they'd had sex. He couldn't remember the details at the moment, but he knew they'd had sex, like he knew his hair was brown and his name was Julian. He closed his eyes and silently counted…*one, two, three*…that's all it took.

When he opened his eyes, Cleo was staring at his cock, which was rock hard.

"Oh, my. I do believe you just remembered." She wore a little half smile, and her cheeks were pink.

He smiled back. "Oh, I remember all right. Every last detail." *Even the bit where you said you love me.* He'd tingled with joy, but also with panic. She *thought* she loved him, but for how long? He wasn't a big deal like Lou. He was nothing but a freak with a guitar. As for his feelings for her, what if he was only confusing the relief she brought him with something deeper? What if he was just…*using her*? He swallowed down that ugly thought.

"Every last detail?" Her blush deepened.

"I remember a certain someone repeatedly saying, 'please don't stop, don't you dare stop, I'll kill you if you stop,' and a few other things that brought a blush to my delicate cheeks."

"You must have been delirious. I don't recall uttering anything even close."

"Well, some of it was hard to understand. Because of the screaming and moaning and crying."

"I know," Cleo said, with feigned sincerity. "You were very noisy."

He wasn't going to win a jest of wits with Cleo.

"I meant what I said. Addie is marrying Mitch Landrum."

Cleo shook her head. "That's crazy. She admitted to having a boyfriend. But Mitch Landrum? She'd have said something to me or Sherry."

"I just came from Mitch's house in Austin. And they're definitely getting married." He tugged at the pillow. "Now let's have a peek, Big Red."

Cleo clung tightly. Her brows furrowed. "That's so weird. Why would she keep it a secret?"

"Because of me. She thought I'd freak out."

"She was right. You had an impressive fit. I didn't know what to do."

"Really? I'd have guessed you were certified in sexual resuscitation," he said. "And did you just refer to my lovemaking as some sort of frothing-at-the-mouth fit?"

She smiled at him and dropped the pillow. Then she pulled his face down to hers. "Your lovemaking, Mr. Wheaton, gave *me* all sorts of fits. And if you're up to it"—she pointedly dropped her gaze to the area of his body that indicated he was—"I wouldn't mind a few more."

"Nothing would make me happier," Julian said, brushing a stray curl away from her eye. "And this time, we'll take it nice and slow. I want to savor every inch of you."

...

Cleo hurried across the lawn of the Guenther House to get to the restaurant. Normally, she might take her time, walk down the sloping green lawn to the San Antonio River, or browse through some of the rooms of the historic 1860 mansion. But not today. She was a woman on a mission. There was scoop to be had. Addie—the little devil—was coming clean.

She shot right past the hostess on the patio with a dismissive wave. Sherry would be seated outside at their usual table. White linen tablecloths, pink linen napkins, fresh flowers, blue-haired old ladies, and tourists…Guenther House on a Sunday.

Sherry and Cleo had been coming to what they called First Sunday Brunch Day since the seventh grade. On the first Sunday of every month, their mothers dressed them up and dragged them to the Guenther House for a main course of southern belle etiquette. *This is what a lady does…this is what a lady doesn't.* Their moms had given up somewhere around eleventh grade, but Sherry and Cleo had continued with their own version, replacing the freshly squeezed orange juice with mimosas. Lots and lots of mimosas.

She spotted Sherry, waving unnecessarily, and hurried to her. "She's not here yet?" Cleo asked, pulling out a chair.

"Nope. Bitch better show up."

"She will."

The waitress poured Cleo a cup of coffee without asking, put a menu in her hands, and walked off.

"I cannot believe she didn't tell us," Sherry said. "I mean, that's weird, right?"

"She didn't want Julian to find out."

"We didn't know about Julian, either! Addie keeps her secrets under wraps."

"Well, this one is out of the bag," said Cleo. "Which is

excellent for us. I mean, Mitch Landrum!" Just saying his name made Cleo want to break out the eyeliner and fishnets.

"Cleo, you're sleeping with Julian Lazros—and I wasn't a bit surprised when you told me, by the way—so stop being impressed by other women's rock stars."

A mimosa appeared. Cleo took a sip and sighed in delight.

"Are we still waiting on someone?" the waitress asked.

"Yes, but we can go ahead and order for her. She always gets the same thing," Sherry said.

Cleo always ordered the same thing, too. Two huge buttermilk biscuits split down the center, slathered in sausage gravy, with a side of grits drenched in butter. Her mouth watered just thinking about it.

"Julian Wheaton," Cleo said, after the waitress had scurried off.

"What?"

"I'm not sleeping with Julian Lazros. I'm sleeping with Julian Wheaton."

"Same thing."

"No, it's not. And it's not just sex. I'm in—"

"Once a groupie, always a groupie, right?"

Cleo gasped even though she didn't exactly hate the label, misguided as it was. "Julian isn't just another guy I have a crush on. And I am not a groupie!"

"You're kind of a mediocre groupie. Anyway—not surprised by you, but Addie? Prim and proper, my arse! No way is she having regular old missionary-style sex with Mitch Landrum. He was one of the *baddest* boys of rock and roll." She jumped out of her seat. "Oh, there she is!"

Cleo set aside her irritation with Sherry and watched Addie zigzag through the tables, dodging waitresses and scattering pigeons.

Sherry pulled out a chair and waved down a waitress. "Another mimosa!" Then she turned to Addie, who had just sat down. "Start talking."

"Wait a minute," Cleo said. She raised an eyebrow and held up her napkin.

"Oh, right." Sherry picked up her napkin, and Addie, having a few First Sunday Brunch Days under her belt, did likewise.

They recited together, "A lady always places her napkin in her lap."

Daintily, they unfolded their napkins and laid them across their laps.

"Okay," Sherry said. "I read a groupie autobiography that had an entire chapter devoted to Mitch. I hear he's…ahem…a big boy who's into toys and likes three-ways."

Addie made what Sherry referred to as big eyes and blushed furiously.

"Gosh, Sherry. Give her time to catch her breath before you start talking about dildos."

Addie's eyes became even bigger.

"She's been keeping a secret," Sherry said. "Time to fess up."

Addie straightened the knife next to her plate. "Er, well, I've never had a three-way, and the only toys I've seen in his house are all over the floor and belong to his children."

Cleo and Sherry smiled at the obvious omission, which increased Addie's blush a full shade.

"That's all true," said a low, rumbling voice. "You ladies have room for a fella at this table?"

Cleo looked up to see the startling blue eyes of Mitch Landrum looking back. Her mouth was fully engaged in the fly-catching position, but she couldn't will it shut.

As usual, Sherry recovered first. "Of course we have room," she said.

Mitch's famous blond mane had been cut and styled. No eyeliner. No visible piercings. No *fuck the world* face.

Just brilliant blue eyes, chiseled jaw, dirty-blond hair, and a cheerful, relaxed expression. Leather pants and chains were replaced by jeans, a black T-shirt, and a brown corduroy jacket. Cleo managed to close her mouth.

"Mitch, this is Sherry and Cleo."

"Nice to meet you both." He smiled, and Cleo swore she heard honest-to-god church bells ring in the distance. Was there even a church nearby? Or had the gates of heaven just opened up? While she and Sherry watched, Mitch kissed Addie and then sat back and cooked her with a gaze so hot it gave the Texas sun some sizzling competition. "You look sexy."

Addie, wearing linen slacks and a silk blouse buttoned up to her chin, covered a grin with her hand. There was a distinct possibility she would spontaneously combust if the attention weren't directed elsewhere. "So how did the two of you meet?" Cleo asked.

Mitch and Addie gave each other the universal raised eyebrow of *do you want to tell it, or should I?* Mitch nodded at Addie. "An art show in Fort Worth," she said. "My tapestries were up for silent auction. I was busy trying to blend into them when I saw a man wandering around with a glass of champagne filled to the brim and an overburdened plate of tapas."

"I didn't spill a single crumb," Mitch said, taking a sip of coffee.

"Oh, do you like art?" Sherry asked.

"About as much as the next guy," Mitch said with a shrug. "Anyway, my band was playing a little hole-in-the-wall across the street, and I had some time to kill before the gig started. Figured I'd look around a little."

"And load up on free food," Addie said dryly.

"Which Addie ripped from my hands and dumped in the trash," Mitch said, with an easy grin. "God, she was so pissed and hot as hell. I knew then she must be the artist, so I bought a big swirly thing—"

"The Oceanscape piece," Addie said.

Mitch tapped his head and winked. "I'm a smart man. Arrangements had to be made for the pickup. And it was an excellent pickup, if I do say so myself."

Addie swatted him on the shoulder. "Stop it, Mitch."

Cleo couldn't help falling into old habits. "So, you're in a band?"

He grinned. "We're just a bunch of old guys playing pool halls and barbecue joints. We sure have a good enough time, though."

"They're the Roustabouts, and they're wonderful," Addie said. "You should hear them."

"We'd love to!" Cleo said. "Maybe Julian could join in."

Mitch did a spit take with his coffee, dribbling some on his T-shirt. "I just got the man to where he could stand to be in the same room with me. A pool hall stage might be a bit too small."

"All things in time," Addie said. "And you'll both get to hear the Roustabouts play at our wedding. It's not until next summer. Julian will come around. A lot can happen between now and then."

Chapter Twelve

The Los Angeles office of Dr. Frederick Hamilton was small and stuffy. Julian had already endured a long morning with his head hooked up to electrodes, and he was anxious for the psychologist to come in and tell him what it all meant.

Cleo put her head on his shoulder and yawned. Such a simple act, and yet the familiarity of it gave him a lump in his throat and increased his resolve to make the biofeedback work.

"I'm hungry," she said, and her stomach growled to back up the claim.

"We'll hit the Farmers Market on Fairfax for lunch. Can you wait?"

"Do I have a choice?"

"Not really."

Sitting in doctors' offices frustrated him. He'd done plenty of it throughout his life, and it hadn't ever resulted in anything positive. But this time might be different. For one thing, there was more at stake.

He thought about the appointment scheduled with Dead

Ringer's label, Utopia Records, later in the day, doing his best to snuff out the sense of unease. Signing the contract was a good decision. It had to be. But he wouldn't be able to fulfill his end of the deal if he couldn't get a handle on his synesthesia.

Yesterday, he'd watched Cleo interview Andy Snipes, Vaughn Gilbert, and Bruce Taylor, also known as Jump Six. Ever since the Sylvie Sandstone article, she'd been interviewing bands left and right. She was good at it, but part of her shtick was shameless flirting. It relaxed and distracted the guys so they'd answer extremely personal questions. Julian understood, but in light of Lou's comments at the release party— *You'd better have some tricks up your sleeve if you want to keep her*—it bothered the hell out of him. These guys were young, talented, and on their way up. He was thirty-three, quite possibly clinically insane, and a fucking has-been session musician. *Believe me*, Cleo had said at the release party, *you're not in their league.*

The Utopia offer couldn't have come at a better time.

The door behind them opened, and Dr. Hamilton loped in, wearing his expression of perpetual surprise—magnified eyes behind thick frames and raised eyebrows. *Ah…saved by the dork.*

Julian had been twelve years old the first time he'd met Dr. Hamilton. He'd come to Los Angeles from London for a concerto competition and, much to his mother's dismay, had ended up in a psych ward. Dr. Hamilton had been the doctor on call. He was the first person to say Julian was anything other than crazy, so Julian had a soft spot for him. Over the years, he'd let Hamilton try various things on him, but so far, none had ever helped.

Pushing his glasses up on his nose, Dr. Hamilton sat at his desk and got right to the point. "Julian, the test results are very favorable. As I told you last month when we ran the preliminaries, you are an excellent candidate for biofeedback therapy. The trials we did this morning helped us personalize the program for you, and it should be ready"—he stopped to look at his watch—"by about two o'clock."

Good. Plenty of time to get over to Utopia.

"If it works, how will things change for him?" Cleo asked.

Dr. Hamilton looked at Cleo as if he'd just noticed she was in the room. "He'll still see and experience his environment as he does now, which is important to him. But the biofeedback program, if done regularly, will train his mind to sort and process stimuli with less conscious effort. He'll have fewer episodes."

"In other words, Big Red, you'll be able to take me out in public."

"I can take you out in public just fine now," Cleo said.

"I hope it works. I believe it will," Dr. Hamilton said.

"We've got time for some lunch," Julian said, standing. "We'll see you back here at two o' clock then?"

"Yes, of course," Dr. Hamilton said. "But before you go, let's do a scent test with some of the essential oils. It shouldn't take long."

Julian sat back down. He'd been told he was unusually receptive to aromatherapy. Hamilton said the right scent could act like smelling salts for him; one pass under the nose when he felt a spell coming on could ward off disaster, or at least postpone it until he got himself somewhere he could fall apart safely.

The psychologist set a tray of small bottles in front of them. Julian faked a yawn, trying to appear casual because he was embarrassed by how excited he was. Cleo had no such concerns, and she squeezed his hand tightly. It was no big deal, just a squeeze, but it rocked through him like an earthquake. He immediately got a hard-on, as if a certain part of his psyche responded to sentimentality by saying, *What? When did we get so sappy? Go fuck this girl!*

Dr. Hamilton unstopped the first bottle. "Okay," he said. "Put on the earphones."

Julian let go of Cleo's hand and positioned the headset over his ears.

"Ready?" Dr. Hamilton asked.

Julian nodded, and his ears were immediately accosted by a barrage of beeps, bleeps, and tones.

"Don't try to control anything," Dr. Hamilton said. "I know it's hard, but you have to let it go until you're almost buzzing." This was one of the reasons Julian knew he was in the proper hands. Hamilton understood the buzzing.

He did as he was told, and in seconds his vision filled with sparks, streaks, and blotches. He unclenched his jaw, loosened his grip on the armrests of the chair, and let the colors take over. He didn't try to separate them, and they bled together, turning into a wall of brown sludge, and the familiar panic started setting in. The sickening sense of dread came next. God, he hated this. He crammed his right hand into the pocket of his jeans, seeking out his picks, just as the buzz began from somewhere deep inside him.

"Inhale," Dr. Hamilton said crisply.

Julian inhaled through his nose. *Tangerines.* What a fucking relief. All the colors immediately separated and went back where they belonged.

"Did that work?" Dr. Hamilton asked, sounding surprised.

"Yeah, it did," Julian said, happily. He started to take off the earphones, officially putting an end to the freak show.

"Let's try it with a few more. It's unusual to hit it with the first one."

Disappointed, Julian prepared to do it again. He hated getting so close to the edge. He exhaled fully, relaxed his mind, and allowed it to all start over. Just as he began to anxiously fiddle with the picks, he was told to inhale. *Tangerines.* The colors separated.

"Did that one work, too?" Dr. Hamilton asked, sounding incredulous.

"Sure did," Julian said.

"Usually, there's just one signature scent, and it often isn't even on this tray. I was prepared to go through all five trays to find one that had a small effect, then we'd use that as a starting place to perfect a scent that could lead to separation or even dispersion."

"The colors dispersed," Julian said. "It knocked it out. Can we go to lunch now?" He began to remove the headphones.

"Wait a minute," Dr. Hamilton said. "Leave those on. Let's try this with the rest of the bottles."

Julian sighed anxiously. The procedure was repeated with the remaining ten bottles, and like the first two, they all worked. "I don't understand it," Dr. Hamilton said.

"Maybe you should try mixing it up some," Julian said. "Those bottles all smell like tangerines."

Dr. Hamilton furrowed his brow. Then he lifted the tray, looking at the labels on the bottles. "Actually," he said. "Only one of these is labeled citrus. The rest are completely different scents." He popped the cap off a bottle and sniffed. "Eucalyptus," he said. He took a whiff of another. "Cinnamon." He put them up to Cleo's nose, and she concurred.

"Ridiculous," Julian said. "I know oranges when I smell them."

"And when is it, exactly, that you smell them?"

Julian felt himself blushing. "Um…well," he said. "I tend to associate the scent of tangerines or oranges with Cleo here."

Cleo grinned and raised her eyebrows. "You do?"

Dr. Hamilton smiled as if everything made perfect sense. "Miss Compton," he said, "would you mind stepping out of the room?"

"You have a smell for me, Julian?" she said. "That's so sweet! And it's tangerines?" She clapped her hands. "I love it. Can you smell me all the time? Like, do you smell me right now?"

"Apparently," Julian said, pointing at the tray. "Now, get out, Lava Locks."

She kissed him on top of his head and walked out, showering him in tangerine droplets and looking extremely pleased with herself.

"You've never told her she's a shield for you?" Dr. Hamilton asked.

"It isn't like I spend every waking moment describing my oddities to her. And…" He paused, trying to figure out exactly what it was that made him uncomfortable sharing the effect Cleo had on him. "Well, I didn't want her to think I was using her."

"So, tell me," Dr. Hamilton said. "Has she always shielded you?"

"No, of course not. Not when I first met her. But it was soon after that I first noticed it. It's gotten stronger recently."

Dr. Hamilton smiled. "That's the way it works, Julian. The feelings come first, then the sensory representations of those feelings. Not the other way around. I'm assuming she has a color, too?"

"Also orange," he answered. "I'm afraid I'm not so creative."

"Well, none of this suggests an unimaginative subconscious," Dr. Hamilton said. "And you're not taking advantage of Miss Compton, if that is a concern. If your feelings for her stop, she'll stop shielding you. It's simple."

That meant it was real. He was in love with Cleo.

"Let's see if we can find the perfect citrus scent for you. We'll think of it as Miss Compton in a bottle." Dr. Hamilton smiled as he riffled through the bottles. "She certainly made this easier."

Dr. Hamilton pulled the stopper out of a green bottle and passed it beneath Julian's nose, causing him to grimace. "That's not citrus."

"You're right. It's sandalwood. Funny how you can smell it now that Ms. Compton is out of the room." He fiddled with more bottles, grinning to himself. "You're a perfect specimen of a love-struck synesthete," he said. "I mean, no offense, Julian, but you've got it bad."

• • •

Cleo sat at the metal patio table and clutched her sweater, wishing there'd been a spot in the sun. Julian stood in line nearby, waiting to buy her the gyro she'd finally settled on. She glanced around, enjoying the opportunity to people watch.

The Farmers Market at Fairfax was Los Angeles in all its glory. Hipsters, movers, and shakers milled about, sipping their green smoothies or lattes. Industry types sat beneath canopies, conspicuously holding court and conducting business. And they all did a double take when they saw Julian.

Ever since the Dead Ringer album, he'd been besieged by offers. Agents wanted to represent him, labels wanted to sign him, and bands wanted to play with him. *Just a Little Sting* had gone platinum, and the single by the same name was at the top of the charts. Dead Ringer was raking it in because of Julian. The latest release even featured a photo of him on the inside sleeve.

She couldn't wait until things settled down. All she wanted was to retreat into their cozy studio where nobody wanted a piece of Julian.

"Here you go," he said, setting a tray in front of her. "It's lamb. Because grown-up animal meat isn't quite sad enough."

"That's right. The younger they are, the better they taste."

"Now you're talking like a rock star," he said.

She took a huge bite of her gyro and made all kinds of satisfying moans and groans. "This is good. You should try some."

"No, thanks. It was recently a baby. And you look atrocious. Like a Viking. Care for a goblet of grog with that?" He sat and began poking at his food.

"I see there's hummus among us for the people who think they're better than everyone else."

He didn't respond to her jab. Instead, he picked up his pita, looked at it, and set it down again. His right hand went toward his pocket.

"What's wrong?" she asked.

"Nothing's wrong. Why?"

She laughed. "Something's wrong, Guitar Boy. Spill it."

"No, really. Nothing's wrong. But I do have some exciting news."

She put her gyro down. "Oh?"

"Remember Dave Gutierrez?"

"Of course. He's the guitarist for Dead Ringer."

"Right. Well, his girlfriend had their baby."

"Good!" She remembered Marcie from the release party. She'd looked like she was about to pop. "A boy or girl?"

"A boy. So listen—"

"What's his name?"

"What?"

"The baby. What did they name him?"

Julian furrowed his brow. "Um, his name is Jocy. Joey Ramone Gutierrez, if you can believe it."

"You're kidding. Joey Ramone? That's hilarious. If we ever have kids, don't you even think about a little Johnny Rotten—"

She slapped her hand over her mouth. Why didn't she just set his hair on fire and direct him to the nearest exit?

"Anyway," he continued, ignoring her momentary lapse in sanity. "Dave doesn't want to tour. The North American leg starts in January, and he's refusing to go. Or I should say, Marcie won't let him go. There's no way Dave would back out on his own, Joey Ramone or no Joey Ramone."

"I don't know, Julian. Babies do strange things to people." She dipped her gyro in yogurt, wondering what any of this had to do with them.

"Not that strange. Are you kidding me?"

"Well, it isn't as if he were going to miss the first months of his child's life so he could go to war. We're talking a stupid tour."

A glass of water was halfway to Julian's mouth when he froze. "A stupid tour? You have no idea what you're talking about." He put his glass back on the table without taking a sip, then added, "And a baby wouldn't hold me back. Not that I ever intend to have children."

"Smooth."

"What?"

"Nothing. Let's change the subject. I don't care if Dave goes on tour or not." She pushed her plate of food away. Why was this conversation irritating her so?

"Actually, you might care a little. The concert promoter said the only way Dave would be relieved of his contract is if I agreed to take his place, at least for the first part of the tour."

"I bet Dave was thrilled," she said with sarcasm. Dave was already delusional about Julian wanting his job.

"Actually, he begged me to do it, and I said yes."

"What? You said yes?" She waited for him to say he was joking, but he looked totally serious.

"Well, what do you think? It's exciting, right? I mean, this is a huge tour. Dead Ringer is on top right now." He stuffed half a pita in his mouth like a little kid. "All I did was write a song and play on their record for one track, and now I'm a part of one of the world's hottest bands."

Both cheeks were bulging, and Cleo could hardly understand him. Mindlessly, she reached over and wiped his mouth with a napkin. He swallowed. "I mean, I know it's temporary, but professionally speaking, this couldn't have happened at a better time. My career is going to take off."

"I thought your career was with Soundbox, Julian. What's going to happen to the studio?"

"You can take care of it," he said dismissively. "I'm just wasting away there, really."

Cleo stood, feeling light-headed. "I need to find the restroom. I'll be back in a minute."

She wormed her way through the crowds to find the ladies' room, where she splashed water on her face and tried not to cry. How could he do this? The last time he'd been in a band he'd damn near died from it. Was he insane?

She patted her face with a rough paper towel and looked in the mirror. What on earth had Dead Ringer offered him? What could he find enticing enough to make him leave the studio? And her?

She tossed the paper towel in the trash. This wasn't going to happen. Not if she could help it. Storming out the door, she headed back to their table with a single thought in her head: *me or the band, buddy*.

She stopped short on her way back to the table. A small group had gathered around Julian. Someone had figured out who he was, and even here, where people were used to seeing celebrities, he drew attention. He signed autographs, posed for a picture with a middle-aged woman, and chatted easily. He looked relaxed. And happy.

It was as if the world had somehow begun spinning in the opposite direction, and she was the only one who'd noticed. Was it possible that this was what he wanted? The crowd grew around their table. Julian was one of the most talented guitarists of all time. Had he been wasting away at Soundbox, waiting for something like Dr. Hamilton's biofeedback program to make stardom possible again?

Suddenly, the idea of presenting him with an ultimatum seemed selfish. And risky. She plastered a fake smile on her face. If this was what Julian wanted, she'd just have to fake enthusiasm and support. And hope for the best.

Chapter Thirteen

The big buses sat in the middle of the parking lot, serving as bustling, wheeled hubs of activity. People ran around loading up equipment, instruments, and luggage while others seemed to simply run around. Cleo, for her part, tried to stay out of everybody's way.

Her stomach was in its usual turmoil. The flight to Los Angeles, the origination point of the Just a Little Sting tour, had been miserable—way too early after a sleepless night. And if Julian's tossing and turning were indications, he hadn't slept, either.

The going-away dinner she'd thrown for him had ended horribly, with his and Addie's bickering exploding into a full-blown sibling spat. Addie hadn't accepted Julian's tour plans well. Actually, that was an understatement. She'd been beside herself when he'd broken the news. And Mitch had stupidly tossed in his two cents, sending Julian into an impressive, profanity-laden tirade. Mitch had gotten the last word in, though, and what he'd said left Cleo with a gigantic, smoldering lump of foreboding right in her midsection. *I think going on tour with this particular band at this particular time is a bad idea for you, Julian. And I think you're gonna regret it.*

Julian looked up from where he stood with the road crew, waved, and headed her way. He continuously jaunted to her side to touch base with a kiss or hug before heading back into the fray. This time, he stayed to nuzzle his nose into her hair.

"Tangerines?" she asked. She wanted to keep him with her for a while.

He grinned. "Yes. What do I smell like?"

That caught her off guard. She wasn't sure how to answer. "I don't have a good way of describing it. I like it, though." She gave him her best hubba-hubba eyes.

"But what is it?" he asked. "I mean, you smell me, then what? What do you see?"

"Nothing. It's just a smell, and I only experience it with my nose. Although"—she leaned in and inhaled his unmistakable, delicious scent—"it is often accompanied by warm, tingly sensations in my nether regions."

He raised his eyebrows. "Your nether regions? You're quite wanton," he said, before getting right back to the point. "But when you're with me it's just blank? Like, there's no thing or color or anything to go along with me?"

She laughed at the unbelievable way he couldn't fathom there was no *thing* to go along with him. No colors, numbers, scents, or shapes. "No, you goof. It's just you."

"I must be boring."

"Oh, you're anything but," she replied, pulling him close for a steamy kiss.

"Sweetheart," he said, after breaking the kiss. "Why are you so worried?"

So it showed. *Because you're leaving me, because you won't tell me you love me, because you'll face temptations I'm not sure you'll resist.* "Just going to miss you," she finally said. "Why couldn't you be a plumber or an accountant?"

"I can't see you with a plumber or an accountant."

She frowned. "Are you serious? As long as it was you I wouldn't—"

"Hey, dude," Cory interrupted, coming from behind and slapping Julian on the back. "How's it going, man?"

Cory's eyes were bloodshot, and his hair was genuinely messy instead of the arranged, coiffed messy he usually wore.

"You look awful," she said.

"Ouch! You kill me, gorgeous."

"She lacks social skills," Julian said. "But you do look like shit. My guess is you haven't been to bed yet?"

"We've got nothing to do but sleep today, right?"

"Speaking of sleep, I haven't claimed a bunk yet. I'm going to go do that," Julian said. "Keep your nasty hands off my woman." Without another word, he took off across the parking lot, leaving her alone with Cory.

"Okay," she said under her breath. "I'll stay here then."

"Don't worry, Cleo," Cory said. "He's not marching off to the firing squad. Just the bus."

He put his thumb right over the bridge of her nose, between her eyes, and tried to rub the scowl away.

"I know," she said, swatting his hand. "But I also know what happens on buses."

"You've got nothing to worry about with Julian. Everyone knows he's completely whipped, poor bastard." Cory laughed but then stopped and looked her right in the eye. "He's no Lou Michaels, Cleo."

"How did you know about that?"

"Everybody knows about that. But Lou's a dick. If I had someone like you, well…I wouldn't fuck it up." He brushed a strand of hair out of her eyes.

"Anyway," he continued, "Julian isn't stupid. He's surly as hell and full of himself with that guitar, but he's a good guy. And believe it or not, I'm a decent judge of character."

Although she had no reason to believe anything Cory said, much less trust his judgment, the tension she carried in her neck and shoulders eased. It was an immeasurable amount of relief.

"And speaking of character," Cory said, glancing over Cleo's shoulder with a frown, "here comes trouble. I'm out of here." Following a quick peck on the cheek, he sprinted off.

"You must be Cleo," said a young, bubbly voice.

Two women came toward her. The pretty blond one held out her hand. *Perky.* As a rule, Cleo despised perky, but she did her best to smile. The blonde smiled back, revealing perfectly straight and capped teeth that were too white for their own good.

"I'm Tanya, and this is Melissa," she chirped.

Melissa didn't look nearly as fresh as Tanya, or as happy. She had dark circles under her eyes, and her face bore the kind of wrinkles that resulted from two packs a day and perpetual frowning. Her dark brown hair was pulled up with a clip. She nodded at Cleo.

"We're with Gus and Dean," Tanya explained. Gus was the band's drummer. Dean played bass.

Melissa snorted. "She's *with* Gus," she said. "I'm *married* to Dean."

Tanya lowered her gaze and scrunched her shoulders like a submissive puppy. Having properly chastised her friend, Melissa moved on to assessing Cleo's status. "You're *with* Julian Lazros?"

Cleo crossed her arms and remained mum. She didn't need to define her relationship for this woman. After an appropriate amount of awkward silence passed, Tanya cleared her throat and piped up again.

"You're the writer, right? Gus told me all about you. You've done great publicity for Dead Ringer."

"Thanks," Cleo said. All she'd done at *Rock 'n' Spin* was

make coffee. But thanks to Julian and his connections, *Rock 'n' Spin* now paid for her articles. She smiled. It had to be killing Lou.

"We need your number so we can keep in touch during the tour," Melissa said, while whipping out her phone. "Are you on Facebook?"

Cleo was not certain she wanted to exchange phone numbers or begin a flurry of friending with these two.

"We need to work our schedules so that we're not all at the same shows," Melissa continued. "No sense in that. And so tell me, Chloe…"

"It's Cleo."

Melissa shrugged. "So tell me, are you going to want to know about groupies, drugs, or both? Or are you one of those women who don't want to know anything? I wish I was that type, but I'm not."

What nerve. But Cleo had to admit, this topic was the burning chunk of lead in the pit of her stomach. She wasn't naive. Thanks to Lou.

She'd flown in to surprise Lou on tour. The road manager, who absolutely hated Lou, had been unusually cooperative in providing a key to his room, to help with the *surprise*. She should have known.

The familiar grunting and moaning that Lou did during certain activities had immediately clued her in. He was in the bed, and he wasn't alone. The bobbing motion beneath the sheets had left no doubt as to what his friend had been doing. And even worse, there'd been a second woman in the shower.

Lou had begun apologizing and making excuses before even getting out of bed, and the dumb woman beneath the sheets hadn't even bothered to stop her activity. When the apologies and excuses didn't yield the results he wanted, Lou had launched into a full verbal assault on Cleo, screaming that she'd set him up with her surprise visit. He'd told her to get out, that they were through, and that she didn't have what it took to be a rock star's girlfriend.

She'd fled in tears, and within a week or two, Lou had taken to spreading the word that she'd been a gold digger. And the saddest thing was, he seemed to believe it. Learning about her brief fling with Zachary had added fuel to his fire. Zachary had been no better than Lou. She'd learned the hard way that the world of rock and roll she'd grown up dreaming about was a cold and cruel place.

And she was back in it.

Tanya picked up where Melissa had left off. "We're each other's eyes and ears," she said. "But we need to know what you consider an infraction. Everybody's different, you know? Like, I don't care if Gus gets a little groupie action, but I'll go insane if he starts with the cocaine and drinking again. And Melissa here doesn't care if Dean does a little blow, but if he does a little blonde she flips. So, how about you?"

The last thing Cleo wanted was either of these women spying on Julian.

"Well, this looks cozy," Julian said, startling them. "You girls making big plans over here?"

"Hi, Julian," the two said together. Coyly.

"Ladies," Julian replied, wearing a smirk that indicated he'd overheard at least some of the conversation. "Big Red, why don't you come spend some quality time in my bunk?"

She knew exactly what constituted quality time for Julian, and if he was expecting a bus tryst, he was in for a disappointment. What did he think she was? A groupie? Regardless, she was eager to escape Melissa and Tanya. "It was nice meeting you both."

"Same here," Tanya said. "Have fun on the bus." She winked.

Good grief.

Julian tugged gently on Cleo's arm. "Come on, love."

She felt two sets of eyes boring holes into her back as she and Julian walked away. "Thanks for rescuing me. They are something else."

"You'd best not get involved in any of their games. They're hard-core. Within five minutes of getting me alone, the blonde would offer me a blow job, and the ugly one would try to sell me some blow. They're not your friends."

"Figured that out all by myself," Cleo said. "And if you think we're going to have sex on a stinky band bus, you're mistaken."

"It doesn't stink yet, and I'm not mistaken."

Julian seemed pretty sure of himself, and a thrill shot up her spine, although she had no intention of giving in. She wasn't a twenty-two-year-old groupie. She was a thirty-year-old college English professor, and they didn't crawl into bunks on buses and have sex.

A gigantic monster of a bus rose before them. It was sleek, black, and sexy as hell. She was dying for a peek.

"Ladies first," Julian said.

She lifted her foot to take the first step, and Julian pulled her back against him. His breath tickled her ear. "I'm about to fuck your brains out," he whispered.

Her breath caught, and a shiver moved through her body in a massive wave. Julian snorted—he'd felt it—and nudged her up the steps. When they got to the top, he grabbed her elbow firmly as if to say, *you're not getting away*.

Her shaky legs couldn't have carried her away even if she'd wanted them to. Which she didn't. And it wasn't like she was *still* a college English professor. She hadn't been in a classroom in well over a year. She was now a freelance journalist/studio manager and the girlfriend of Julian Wheaton—no, make that Julian *Lazros*—and maybe sex on a bus was perfectly acceptable behavior under the circumstances. The fact that she was still thirty years old, no matter what her profession, didn't dampen her enthusiasm. Which was spreading to very specific areas of her body.

The bus was ridiculously over-the-top. There was a lot to gawk at—a plasma TV and a full-sized bar—but Cleo stumbled past it all. There were people everywhere, moving out of the way, bumping into each other, jostling to and fro. And all the while, Julian kept a tight grip on her, steering her toward the back of the bus with obvious intention.

They went up a few steps—the thing actually had two levels—to the bunks. Julian opened a small door and they squeezed into the tiny space, which resembled a private sleeping car on a train, only more cramped. It was outfitted with a television/computer monitor, wifi, and a full gaming console.

"Not too terrible," Julian said.

"Not bad at all," Cleo replied, looking around. She couldn't fathom the two of them fitting in that tiny bed, smashed up against each other, hot and sweaty... She squeezed her thighs together.

"I can do the biofeedback in here easily," he said. "And I'm looking forward to some filthy, X-rated Skyping, of course." His eyes darkened, and Cleo's cheeks flushed beneath his heated gaze.

A small shelf sat beneath the window. Julian rummaged in his bag and pulled out a framed photo. "This will fit here," he said.

"Good grief, that's a horrible picture," Cleo said. She grimaced. Every wrinkle, freckle, and blemish on her face was lit up by the light that had been streaming in through the window above Julian's bed. Rod Stewart's voice rang through her head, singing about the morning sun showing her age...

On the road, Julian would be surrounded by young, willing girls eager to show off the latest improvements in cosmetic surgery. She swallowed.

"It's a gorgeous picture," Julian said, staring at it as if it were the *Mona Lisa*. "Although," he added, waggling his brows, "I passed up some of the more interesting shots." His eyes made a languid sweep down the length of her body.

"You said you'd delete those."

"I did, don't worry," he assured her. "Don't worry about anything, okay?" The rest of the world faded away as he looked into her eyes. "It's you, Cleo. You're all I want."

"And?" she asked. *Say you love me.*

His eyes twinkled. "Let's fuck."

Her disappointment only lasted a second, because Julian peeled off his shirt. The space was so small, she could feel the heat rising off his chest and smell the soap he used, the detergent lingering on his clothes, and his *desire*.

Her back was pressed up against the wall; there wasn't even an inch to spare. Julian bent and kissed her neck. People yelled at each other outside the bus, and voices hummed inside, as well. "We don't have any privacy."

Julian kissed the sweet spot right behind her ear. "That's true," he whispered. "Anybody could walk in." The bus shook as things were loaded into the storage wells.

"Excuse me," someone said, just outside the door. "Hey, has anybody seen Lazros?"

Julian put his hand over Cleo's mouth. "Shh…"

He unbuckled his belt, and she heard his zipper go down.

"I'm in my bunk," he said to the door. "What do you want?"

Oh, God. He was actually going to carry on a conversation with someone just a few steps away while he…*what would he do next?*

His knee went between her legs, forcing them apart. *Oh.*

"Wayne wants to know if you'll be keeping your Les Paul with you or if you want him to take care of it." The voice was so close. *Right outside the door!*

"I'll keep it," Julian answered. Then he slipped his fingers between her thighs, inside her panties, and she closed her eyes and tried not to whimper.

Julian's voice was right at her ear. "Oh, Cleo," he whispered. "Somebody is a naughty girl." She totally was.

He pulled his hand away and stepped back. Cleo thought she'd fall, but somehow her legs held her up.

"Onto the bunk, baby," Julian said softly. "Spread your legs."

She looked over his shoulder at the small door. "What if someone tries to come in?" Her pulse sped up.

Julian grinned. "They'll hit my ass with the door." He gently pulled on her hand until she sat on the bunk. His fly was already open, and he was *very* ready to go. He pressed her shoulder until she leaned back. Keeping a nervous eye on the tiny, uninsulated door that led to the narrow corridor, Cleo pressed her knees tightly together. But only because she wanted to hear him beg. Or demand. Or anything, really.

"Uh-uh, little girl," he said. "Spread those legs. And give me the knickers—they're going on tour."

She was wearing a western swing dress with her signature cowboy boots, but for the life of her, she couldn't remember what panties she had on. Hopefully they weren't what Julian referred to as her granny panties—white cotton underwear all frayed at the legs. She started to pull them down but stopped when another voice yelled outside the door.

"Keep going," Julian urged.

She finished pulling off her panties—they were respectable polka-dot bikinis—and handed them over. Without taking his eyes from her, Julian stuffed them in his pocket.

"Now, open up."

Slowly, she did. And his face went from lust to pure, molten desire. His eyes darkened, his nostrils flared, and a drop of perspiration appeared at his temple. She loved making him crazy that way. He ran his fingers all the way up her thighs as people loitered just a few feet away. The bus shook, and someone whistled shrilly. She could hear her own heart pounding. It was like being at the top of the drop on the world's highest roller coaster. *Julian was a thrill ride.*

But the ride stopped when a guy banged on the door. Cleo tried to sit up, but Julian held her down. "Go away," he shouted.

"We set sail in five minutes. No stowaways," the guy shouted back. The bus shook as he walked off.

"I swear this bus better not take off with me on it, Julian."

"I'll be quick," he said with a grin. "Embarrassingly so, I'm afraid." He climbed in and squeezed above her. The ride was back on. The small space excited her, and the idea that they might be heard—or seen—made her thighs tingle and her belly clench.

He pulled her dress up and peeled back the cups of her bra. "Hello, darlings," he said. Her nipples stood at attention. "You know I'd love to spend some time with each of you, but I'm afraid I can't spare it. So just look pretty for me. A little jiggling would be lovely." He kissed each one before pulling a condom out of his pocket.

"You keep condoms in your pockets now?"

"I've got to be ready for groupies at all times," he said with a wink. "And besides, I was hoping for a bus bang with my girlfriend."

He slipped on the condom and got into position. "Ready?"

She was, but she couldn't speak. He took that as a go and pushed inside with a loud groan that mortified her—and excited her. Surely, someone had heard that. He started moving, and soon she couldn't tell if the bus shook from all the people, equipment, and baggage going in and out—or from Julian doing the same.

She lost herself in the pleasure of being taken. It would

be the last time for a while, and she wanted to make the most of it. The concern over people hearing them dissipated as her pleasure rose. The familiar warmth began to spread, and she shamelessly pressed her feet against the low ceiling above Julian, tilting her pelvis so he could go deeper. God, she wanted him deeper. His sweat dripped onto her face and breasts.

A strangled moan worked its way up from her belly, and she turned her head into the pillow. She couldn't make too much noise. *Holy cow!* Forcing herself to be quiet was turning her on even more. Julian moved the pillow away from her face and firmly clamped his hand over her mouth. It panicked her at first, but she breathed deeply through her nose and then realized she liked it. A lot.

"Does that turn you on, baby?"

She couldn't say anything, but Julian saw the answer in her eyes and smiled. *Yes, she was naughty.* The only sounds were their bodies slamming together, the idling bus engine, and people talking. She couldn't cry out, but small mewling sounds escaped through Julian's fingers. He slammed into her even harder, shooting her up the crest until she broke over the top. She rode it, shaking all over and grabbing handfuls of Julian's hair.

"Oh, God, sweet baby," Julian said. "It's too good." He buried himself deep inside her, stilled, and then groaned loudly, calling out her name. Twice. Maybe three times. The last exclamation was closer to a sob of release, it was hard to tell.

"Good grief, Julian. So much for being discreet." She waited for her face to burn with its usual intensity, but it never lit up. If anything, she felt a bit…smug. And satisfied. She'd just had Julian Lazros on a bus. And it was dang good.

A few moments later, they stepped into the narrow corridor for the walk of shame. Cleo kept her eyes stuck to her boots and followed Julian out. If there were any obnoxious glances or knowing smiles, she didn't see them. And Julian didn't stop to collect accolades. They went down the steps, and she emerged from the bus sans panties and freshly fucked by a rock star. *Groupie fantasy fulfilled.*

The five-minute warning they'd been issued by the road manager had been optimistic. It was closer to an hour before the band was finally ready to board, and most of the people who'd come to see them off had left.

"Let's go!" the huge, bald road manager finally barked. "Our British stud over there has loudly christened this bus Cleo, so let's get the show on the road."

Applause broke out among the crew, along with whistles and catcalls, and Cleo's face exploded in flames—apparently a delayed reaction. Julian wouldn't look her in the eye until the commotion died down.

"Sorry," he said, with a sheepish grin and a small shrug of his shoulders. She looked, but no cartoonish halo popped up over his head. *More like horns.*

People started boarding the bus, but Julian hung back, turning to Cleo and taking her hands in his. "You be a good girl while I'm gone."

"I'll miss you," she said, blinking furiously. Because if the first tear managed to escape, the rest would follow in a torrential downpour.

He kissed her on the nose. "I'll miss you, too."

"Don't forget to do your biofeedback program."

"I won't." He cupped her face with his hands. "Good-bye, sweetheart. I'll call you every night." He bent to kiss her.

"I wish you didn't have to go."

Julian hesitated briefly, and uncertainty flashed in his eyes. Did he not believe her? "I'll be back before you know it," he said. Then his lips brushed hers, and he was gone.

...

The lights shone in Julian's eyes. He'd just finished a sonata and was braced for the applause with his violin resting on his shoulder. He fought the urge to hide behind Klaus Vanderburg, his accompanist. It would be lovely to crawl beneath the piano and squeeze himself right between Klaus's feet.

The applause hit him hard, like a barrage of golden arrows chinking away at his protective armor. Soon, he couldn't see anything for the arrows.

"Bow, Julian," Klaus said. So he did, quickly, then fled the thunderous sound. He hoped to find a small place in which to hide backstage, but his teacher caught him by the sleeve.

"Go back out, you silly boy. They love you. Go back out!" He peeked around the curtain and saw his mum in the front row. She clapped furiously. He took a couple of timid steps before his teacher's hand shoved him harshly onto the stage.

"Mummy loves you," she called. "Bravo, Julian!"

"Julian. Dude, wake up, man." Julian opened his eyes, not to an adoring crowd, but to Cory. "We've stopped. Want to get out and stretch your legs?"

Disoriented, Julian glanced at the drool stain he'd left on the lounge chair. "Stop poking me, you moron. I don't want off."

"Suit yourself. We've been on the road over twelve hours. Thought you might want to get some junk food. You want me to bring you something?"

Julian shook his head. Why was Cory always trying to get chummy? And why was he on this bus anyway? He had one all to himself, but he insisted on riding with the rest of the band for the first day. Idiot singers. Everyone had to love them, or they couldn't be happy.

Cory shrugged and walked off. Julian peered through the window at his bandmates milling about outside. He could already see the various situations brewing. Dean and Gus were sneaky bastards, and it would be a week—two, tops—before they'd be making everyone miserable with drug- and media-related problems. Cory, of course, was a typical front man, an egotistical attention hog who expected special treatment, which he was already getting. On top of that, Sheik, the professional linebacker turned road manager, seemed to hate his guts for no reason at all and had taken to calling him Princess. Since Sheik outweighed Julian by well over a hundred pounds, Julian wasn't in a position to complain about it.

He sighed and rolled away from the window and pulled his beanie over his face. At least he had the bunk sex with Cleo to play over and over in his mind. He closed his eyes and grinned. *She loved being a bad girl. So fucking cute.*

$$\bullet \ \bullet \ \bullet$$

Cleo dabbed concealer beneath her eyes and held the mirror as far away as possible. If she did that while squinting, she didn't look so bad. Late-night recording sessions combined with writing assignments and interviews made for a very sleep-deprived girl.

"Oh my God, would you stop?" Addie drained the last of the fancy mango margarita Cleo had made for their girls' night in. "You look fine. And it's just Julian, anyway."

"She looks awful," Sherry said. "Keep piling it on, Cleo."

"Thanks," Cleo said. "And you're one to talk, Addie. You iron your underwear before you see Mitch."

"You're just going to Skype with him. He won't even be able to tell if you're wearing makeup. Or underwear."

Sherry dribbled a bit of guacamole on a nacho and topped it off with a slice of pickled jalapeno. "I'm sure they only talk about the weather. And the webcams never drift below the neck."

"Stop it," Addie said. "Let's change the subject to how he's doing with his biofeedback."

Cleo applied some powder to her nose and sneezed. "Dang," she said. A peek in the mirror confirmed she'd smashed mascara tracks into her eyelids and upper cheeks. She rubbed, smearing the whole mess.

Sherry handed her a tissue. "That's a great look for you. Kind of sexy."

Cleo peeled her eyelids apart. Should she clean it all off and start over? Or just smear on some more concealer?

"You're now officially beyond concealer," Sherry said, reading her mind.

Cleo sighed and grabbed the bottle of makeup remover. She still hadn't answered Addie's question. "You know what? He's doing amazingly well. The biofeedback has really helped. Four weeks on the road, and no episodes at all."

Addie smiled and shook her head. "What a relief." Her brow furrowed though. "I still don't understand why he's on the road with Dead Ringer in the first place. He hates the spotlight. And he loves Soundbox. It's so weird how he suddenly decided to be a performer again."

Cleo didn't get it, either. "I know. But he seems happy. Maybe he only hated performing because of the synesthesia episodes. He's a natural star, after all." But the loft was lonely—an entire month without him—and the studio was missing the special spark only he could bring to recording sessions.

She finished cleaning her face. Julian would be calling any minute. No time to begin another attempt at makeup. Well, maybe some light blush… She grabbed a brush. "The concert should be over by now," she said.

"Bus or hotel tonight?" Addie asked.

"Bus. They have another show tomorrow."

Sherry stood and collected food and dishes off the coffee table. "We can take a hint. Nobody wants to be here for your cybersex session."

In the mirror, Cleo watched her cheeks turn pink. It made it hard to apply blush. "We're not going to have cybersex. Good grief, where do you come up with this stuff?"

They were totally going to have cybersex, and her two buddies needed to head on down the road. She zipped up her small makeup bag.

Addie helped put the dirty dishes in the sink. "Don't tell him we ate food on his couch. He'll blow a gasket."

Cleo laughed. "Believe it or not, he's loosened up a little. Living with me will do that to a person."

"He probably hasn't loosened up, he's just given up," Sherry said, glancing around the loft. "Do you keep any of your shoes in the closet?"

The laptop chimed. *Call coming in.*

Without being told, Sherry and Addie headed out the door. "Tell him I love him," Addie said. "And make sure he's doing all right."

"Okay, okay, okay," Cleo said, closing the door. She ran to her laptop and answered the call. Julian's face filled her screen. He smiled immediately.

"Hi, gorgeous."

Ha! Hardly. "Your screen must be dirty."

"No, it's not. But speaking of dirty, I've been thinking about you all day."

He was in his tiny bunk on the bus, lying down, and it looked like the laptop was resting on his chest. "I can see up your nostrils."

"And this is why we agreed to leave the dirty talking to

me, remember?"

She laughed. "No after-party tonight?"

"No, thank God. We'll be driving all night."

"Have you done your biofeedback?"

"Twice today. And I'll do it again before I go to sleep. It's working great. Gets easier and easier each time. What are you wearing under that T-shirt?"

"Your favorite."

"The lacy pink one?"

She frowned. "That's your favorite? I'm wearing the black one."

"They're all my favorite. Take off your shirt."

He was always so worked up after concerts. The performing really seemed to turn him on.

"Lots of girls at tonight's show?"

"The usual, I guess. Now come on, love." He grinned, winked, and edged even closer to the screen. "Show me your tits."

"Don't rock stars ever get tired of saying that?"

"That's Cory's line, not mine. And it takes all my concentration to play guitar and handle the noise. Yours will be the first pair I've drooled over tonight. I promise."

According to online buzz about Dead Ringer's concert tour, Julian and Cory were the band's crowd-pleasers as far as the fans were concerned. But no incriminating photos had popped up of Julian. She couldn't say the same for Cory—not that she'd been searching specifically for that type of thing. Much. "You're going to drool?"

"Stop stalling."

"What are you going to show me in return?"

"You've been leering up my nostrils for five solid minutes. How about a belly button next? Or my big toe?"

"If you can get your big toe in front of the camera in that bunk, then we seriously have some new positions to try when you get home."

He laughed, and his nostrils quivered like a rabbit's. Not exactly a turn-on, but still adorable. Her heart melted. The screen was so inadequate. She wanted to hold him and smell him and…heck, anything. And everything. She missed eating together, working together, hanging out in all their favorite haunts together.

Julian stopped laughing and sighed. "I don't know when I'll be home next. The schedule is being rearranged a little. In the meantime, why don't you come see me?"

That sounded awesome. She'd never seen Julian strut his stuff live, and a trip would be fun. "I'll have to look at what's on the calendar for Soundbox. But after this month, I think things are pretty clear. I'll see what I can arrange and let you know."

"Baby, you know you can surprise me, right? I love surprises. I mean, what I'm saying is, I don't need any kind of advance notice." He stared directly into the screen. No mention of Lou Michaels was necessary. Message received, loud and clear. And the fact that she knew he *hated* surprises of any kind made it all the sweeter.

"Do you know what I'd do if I was on the front row watching you wail on that nasty Les Paul right now?"

"No. What?"

"This."

The shirt came off.

• • •

Julian stretched after a run through the French Quarter. Sweat dripped into his eyes, despite the bandanna he'd wrapped around his forehead. New Orleans was humid as fuck, even in the mild winter temperatures. But the run had been worth it.

He grabbed his foot and held it behind his thigh, standing

on one leg just outside the hotel's lobby. Holy hell, that felt good. His heart pounded, but everything else was cooling down. He still floated on the small high running gave him, and a melody ran like a soundtrack in his head—one he hoped to write down as soon as he finished his biofeedback. He dropped his foot and grabbed the other one. He hadn't skipped a single biofeedback session on tour. Dr. Hamilton had warned him that his brain would revert back to old habits if he failed to strengthen and reinforce the new neural pathways. The program had made a huge difference in Julian's life, and the next time he saw Dr. Hamilton he'd kiss the little fucker on the mouth.

At first, Julian hadn't been able to tell if the program did shit. But every morning and night, he dutifully stuck the headphones on, along with the gadget that tracked his eye movement, and sorted sounds and colors on the screen while performing increasingly complex mental tasks. It was frustrating. As soon as he concentrated on a mental task, the colors and sounds went to shit, and eventually he had to give up the task to get everything else back in order. But after a few weeks, he noticed he could focus on the mental tasks longer before losing control of the colors and sounds. Now he concentrated almost exclusively on the mental tasks, while the colors and sounds seemed to take care of themselves. According to Dr. Hamilton, he was sorting them subconsciously.

On his runs, he still saw sounds the way he always had, but he didn't have to *do* anything about them. The colors all stayed where they belonged like good little puppies. With his mind freed up, he ran scores through his head like a movie soundtrack. On a good run, he could write an entire song.

The concerts weren't as easy to handle as a morning run. The motherfucking noise was insane, and that meant the colors were, too. It wasn't a completely subconscious effort to keep them sorted. But he didn't fall apart. With the citrus vial he sniffed between sets, he'd managed well enough so far.

He did a few lunges, then yanked the bandanna off his head and went inside. The air-conditioning in the hotel lobby washed over him as an icy blue waterfall. He passed up the breakfast buffet and headed to Sheik's room. He'd left the biofeedback program in his bunk last night, and the band buses were locked up tight. Julian quaked at the thought of waking Sheik at seven o'clock in the morning, but he needed to get into the bus.

Bracing himself, he knocked on the door. Muffled sounds came from the other side, and then it jerked open. Sheik's hulking form, which looked no less menacing in boxers, undershirt, and socks, immediately dwarfed his in the doorway.

"Good morning, sweetheart," Julian said.

"What do you want, asshole?"

"I need to get into my bunk. Give me the bus keys."

"You don't need in there in the middle of the fucking night. Come back in a couple of hours." He started to close the door.

"Wait, wait…it's not the middle of the night, you moron. And I left my biofeedback program in there."

"Your Sensodyne game can wait until later."

"For the billionth time, Sensodyne is a fucking toothpaste, the program isn't a game, and it *can't* wait."

Like Darth Vader, Sheik mostly had one facial expression. But he sighed through his nose, flaring his nostrils like a bull about to charge, to express his irritation. "I can't just give you the keys."

Julian rolled his eyes. "Come on, man. What do you think I'm going to do? Steal the bus?"

"It wouldn't be the first time an idiot with a guitar stole a band bus." There was no point in arguing. Sheik wasn't going to hand over the keys.

"Can you go down there with me then?"

Sheik crossed his arms. "You really need to do it right now?"

"Sorry, but I really do."

"I gotta get dressed first," Sheik said.

Julian breathed a sigh of relief. "Thanks, man. Meet me downstairs?"

The door slammed in his face.

The breakfast buffet tested Julian's willpower. He held strong—oatmeal, fruit, coffee—until the beignets were brought out. How much dairy could there be in one tiny beignet? By the time he was on his fourth, because surely there couldn't be that much, Sheik came down and began loading up a plate with eggs and at least three different species of dead animal. He put his plate on the table and pulled out a chair. "You been snorting cocaine?"

Julian frowned. "What are you talking about?"

Sheik almost grinned—as close as he ever came, anyway—and tapped at his nose. "How many beignets did you eat, you stupid fake hippie?"

Oh. Julian wiped the powdered sugar off his face. "Only one."

"Liar."

"Four."

"That shit will kill you," Sheik said. Then he shoveled in a mouthful of eggs. "Have you seen Dean and Gus this morning?"

"Nope. But unfortunately, I heard them all night long. Could you make sure my room isn't next to theirs from now on?"

Sheik set his fork down and said, "Sure. I'll make that a top priority." Then he rolled his eyes in case Julian thought he meant it.

The sweet taste lingering from the beignets had turned

sour in Julian's mouth at the mention of Dean and Gus. So far, they'd lived up to his expectations by being scumbags. He'd avoided their so-called private parties, but their behavior at the after-parties was bad enough.

After-parties were boring affairs. Sitting in bars while signing autographs and acting like an idiot was tedious bullshit, and he'd never enjoyed it. Not even when he was in Slice. And he kept getting in trouble for his uncivilized behavior. Did Dean and Gus get reamed out for pouring bottles of liquor over young women and licking it off? No. That shit was encouraged. It was Julian who didn't know how to behave at a party. *Look like you want to be here. Smile. Get off your phone.* Fuckers. All he wanted to do after a show was be alone and call Cleo. A post-concert biofeedback session was great, but a call or Skype session with Cleo was even better. He'd smell tangerines for at least an hour after, and it settled every nerve in his body.

"How many girls did they have in their room last night?" he asked.

"Four. I know because I checked IDs."

It was Sheik's job to keep everyone under control so the shows could go off without a hitch. That meant keeping band members out of the jails, hospitals, and rehab centers until the tour was over.

"Were they legal?"

Sheik shook his head in disgust. "Barely."

Speaking of man whores, Cory got off the elevator. He hadn't slept solo since the tour started, but he was at least discreet about it. And Sheik never had to ask his companions for IDs. As for Julian's needs, webcams were wondrous things. He had a date with Cleo tonight, and his dick got hard just thinking about it. He made some adjustments beneath the napkin in his lap.

Three more bites and Sheik's plate was clean. "Let's go

get your Sensodyne game."

Julian and Sheik wandered down the aisle of the dark bus to Julian's small bunk room. They pushed the door open. Julian's laptop was out and open. That was odd. He always closed it up and put it in the pouch below the shelf, along with the headphones and other stuff.

"Grab it and go," Sheik said. "It's hot in here."

"Hold on," Julian said. "Something's not right."

He rubbed the touch pad, and the screen lit up. He clicked on the icon, and…*holy fuck!*

"Whoa," Sheik said. "No wonder you spend so much time hooked up to this thing."

Porn. A gigantic cock power-drilled some poor woman. "What the hell is this?" Julian yelled.

"Well, brother, if you don't know—"

"No, no, no…you don't understand. Fuck!"

"That's what it is, all right," Sheik said.

Julian checked the disk drive. Sure enough, *How the West Was Hung*. Great. He yanked the movie out and scrounged around his bunk for the disk that went along with his biofeedback program. He looked everywhere. In the pocket, on the shelf, under the linens and pillow. His hands shook as the panic built.

"Slow down," Sheik said. "Let me help."

Five minutes later, drenched in sweat, the two of them got off the bus without the disk. "I'm going to fucking kill those idiots," Julian said.

"Hold on, now. We don't even know that Dean and Gus did it."

"Who else would have done it?"

They stormed through the hotel lobby to Dean's room. Sheik pounded on the door. When it didn't open immediately, Julian pounded on it, too. Eventually, it opened. Dean stood there naked, half asleep, and probably hungover. "What the fuck?" he said.

Julian pushed the door all the way open and barged in, shoving Dean out of the way. "Where is it?" he yelled.

The room stank like stale breath, body odor, alcohol, and cheap perfume. It was dark, so Julian flipped on a lamp. The huddled shapes in the beds stirred. Gus sat up, exposing the bare ass of one of the girls in bed with him. "What's going on?"

"Where's my biofeedback program?"

"What time is it?" one of the girls mumbled, rolling over.

"Time to go home," Sheik said. "Get up and get dressed."

"Hey, you can't kick them out of here," Dean said. He was still naked, and Julian tossed a dirty towel at him.

"The hell I can't," Sheik said. "Where's Julian's game?"

The four girls—and fuck, they *were* young—fumbled around for items of clothing. Julian averted his eyes, scanning other areas of the room for his disk.

"Do you mean this?" a blond girl asked. She wore a pair of skimpy panties and nothing else, but Julian's eyes went straight to the two halves of the disk she held.

"Oops," Dean said. "Someone must have slept on it."

Sheik dragged Julian out of the room and into the hallway, but Julian hardly felt it. All the concerts, all the noise—there was no way he could handle it if he backslid even a little in his progress. "What am I going to do now?" he groaned, shaking Sheik off.

"Call your doctor and get another one. It ain't rocket science," Sheik said. "Get him to overnight it."

"It's Sunday. And where are we even going to be in two days?"

"Georgia. I'll get you an address. We'll get you squared away. Why are you freaking out so much? You can skip a few days of that game. What's the worst that will happen? You see some colors, right? I've known a few guys who could do that.

Most musicians are freaks. You're not special."

Julian leaned against the wall. "Actually, I'm pretty special in regard to how I experience synesthesia. And I'm also pretty fucked. Unless you have some heroin on you?"

He meant it as a joke, but Sheik's left eye twitched and his jaw clenched. Obviously, he didn't see the humor in it.

"Not on my watch. You got that?"

If he could get a new disk overnighted on Monday, he'd miss three sessions. Four, tops. How bad could it be?

Chapter Fourteen

The plane would touch down in Minneapolis in about an hour. Cleo squirmed in her seat, anticipation bubbling in her stomach like champagne. But below the anticipation, something more akin to anxiety rumbled. Sometime around three weeks ago, their nightly Skype sessions had turned weekly, and the phone calls became shorter and less intimate. Julian was on tour, and it seemed Cleo was out of sight, out of mind. She smothered her misgivings. This was to be a happy reunion.

She hadn't made the trip a surprise, no matter what Julian had said. Was it trust? Or had she just learned how to be a "good" rock star girlfriend? No. She shut that train of thought down. Julian was not Lou Michaels.

Her ears popped as the plane began its slow descent. She settled back in her seat, jittery with excitement. Swallowing repeatedly helped the pressure in her ears, but it didn't do anything for the knot stuck in her throat.

···

Julian waited in the hotel lobby for his limo. He could have sent for any type of car, but he knew Cleo liked her rock star limos.

After tonight's show, he'd get three days off to spend with Cleo. He could use some rest. They'd done too many back-to-back shows, more than their contracts had specified, and had been plagued by illness and injury. Concerts had been rescheduled and postponed, and now they crisscrossed the country on a nonsensical and grueling schedule. As soon as Cleo left, they'd be flying to Ireland for a music festival, then right back to the U.S. for concerts on the West Coast. And nobody was getting along—no big surprise there.

Yesterday, the band's manager told him that Dave Gutierrez had called it quits for good. He wasn't coming back. And they wanted Julian to keep touring. The European leg would begin in three months, then they'd hit Asia. All he wanted to do was go home. Should he just come out with it and tell Cleo that he couldn't be what she wanted him to be? He sighed. The thought of disappointing her made him sick.

Tonight, he would finally say the three words he knew she longed to hear. He'd tried to tell her before. So many times he'd just wanted to say, "I love you." But the words wouldn't come. He needed to be someone she could love. Tonight, he'd do it from the stage, before tens of thousands of people, while he was front and center beneath a spotlight. At least for tonight—he'd be everything she wanted.

He glanced at the time and bounced his bag on his knee—fidgety as usual. Cleo's plane should be landing soon. He pulled out his phone. No text yet. The phone trembled slightly in his hand. He had the shakes. Shit.

He could pull this off. No problem.

People stared at him as he kept an eye on the parking lot. They didn't know who he was, but they looked anyway. He'd always been conspicuous. Addie would say he shouldn't have tattooed most of his body. Maybe he should cut his hair, wear a nice shirt and trousers. But the truth was, people had always stared. He was out of place. Always had been and always would be, and it had nothing to do with how he looked.

A family walked through the door, and one of the kids squealed about a big, fancy car outside. That was his ride. He gathered up the Les Paul and his duffel bag. The black stretch limo pulled up to the front of the hotel, and he went outside to meet it.

A uniformed driver held the door open. "Mr. Lazros, may I take your bags?"

"No, thanks," Julian said, offering the kid his hand for a shake. "I'll keep them with me."

"Sure thing, sir. My name's Donnie, and I'll be your driver tonight."

"Nice to meet you, Donnie. Could we get a move on? I don't want to be late." Couldn't have Cleo waiting on the curb in this weather. It was fucking freezing.

"Absolutely, sir."

Donnie closed the door, and Julian settled in. A great sound system was already rocking, but he winced at the choice of music. Dead Ringer. Without hesitating, he reached over and shut it off. A television rested beneath an open privacy divider and next to the fully stocked bar, and a bottle of champagne chilled in an ice bucket.

"Mr. Lazros, when the privacy divider is up, you can communicate with me via the intercom. We're not completely soundproofed with it closed, but near enough. And we have no security cameras in the cab."

Julian smiled. Rock star treatment. He couldn't resist the next question. "How are the shocks on this thing?"

Donnie laughed. "When the limo's a-rockin', I won't come a-knockin'."

"So, Donnie, after the airport, we'll head to the arena."

He handed a security parking pass through the screen. "Hang this on the mirror, and they'll let us right through to the unloading dock. And here," he said, reaching through with a sateen square on a lanyard. "This is your backstage pass. Feel free to come on back and enjoy the show once you've parked. Just make sure you're ready to pick us up by the time the meet and greet ends. I'm going to want out of there fast, and I don't want to be held up, okay?"

The kid pulled away from the curb, muttering, "Fucking awesome."

. . .

Cleo waited for the other passengers to begin exiting the plane. No point in being one of the first ones to jump up and stand in the aisle while everyone scrounged through the overhead bins. She called Julian. He answered on the first ring.

"Hey, Big Red, we're just now taking the airport exit. Have you landed?"

Every muscle in her body relaxed at the sound of his voice. Well, not *every* muscle. Some parts of her body tingled and clenched.

"Yeah, I'm still on the plane, though."

"Okay, good," he said. "I'll give you a ring when we're curbside." He paused, then added, "I can't wait to touch you, hold you, smell you…"

Her heart melted and pooled at her feet. She'd been worried about nothing.

A few minutes later, Cleo walked through the terminal doors, and a blast of freezing air hit her, blowing up her skirt— her pathetically inadequate cotton skirt. And the thigh-high crocheted tights, with their pattern of peekaboo holes, did little to protect her legs. Funny, they'd looked Eskimo warm on the Etsy shop website.

People jostled and bumped her as they hurried to their rides. She scanned the line of taxis and shuttles. A black stretch limo sat conspicuously in the long line. Surely that wasn't...

The door opened slowly, and Cleo held her breath. His hair brushed his shoulders, and it had been a few days since he'd shaved. *Sexy overload.* Before she could catcall to get his attention, he saw her, and a smile lit up his face. She ran toward him as best she could, weighed down by her bag and her stupid suede platform boots.

He met her halfway, catching her in his arms. He inhaled her hair, and a shiver traveled through him—one she knew wasn't from the cold. *She* did that to him. She wasn't ready to let go when he loosened his embrace, so she squeezed him extra tightly.

"Okay, love. Let's get in the big rock star car now. It has a heater." He peeled her off and held her at arm's length. "Let me look at you." With a smile, he took her in. "Nice boots. I guess it's only the knees to the waist that are chilly?" He narrowed his eyes and growled like an animal. "I'm going to enjoy warming that up."

She pulled her short ski jacket around her, hopping from one foot to the other. "Since my teeth are chattering, that sounds like heaven."

Julian laughed and kissed her, snorting as her teeth rattled against his. "Poor darling. Let's get in the car." He grabbed her hand and her bag, and they darted for the limo, where a young driver waited by the door. His eyes widened when he saw her. What was he expecting? Twenty years younger and a black leather mini?

"This is Donnie," Julian said.

Donnie took off his hat. "Step right in," he said with a grand gesture.

Too cold for small talk. Cleo put a foot inside the car just as a sudden gust of wind whipped up her skirt. "Oops!"

She tried holding the hem down, but the blush on Donnie's face—and the grin on Julian's—confirmed that she'd just flashed her purple panties.

"As soon as she gets near a limo," Julian said, shaking his head. "It's a problem."

"I doubt that, sir," Donnie said, replacing his hat with a wink.

Julian moved his guitar over and climbed in. Donnie shut the door, and Cleo held her hands in front of the heater vent. Pins and needles replaced numbness as they thawed. A nifty privacy screen slid silently up, and slowly her chills subsided.

"I can do things that heater can't, Big Red. Get up on my lap like a good girl."

"Mmm, that sounds enticing." She straddled him with her cold thighs against his warm legs. His hands slid beneath her skirt as she leaned over and fed him a kiss.

"Have I told you I missed you?" he asked against her lips.

"Yes, but you haven't shown me."

He kissed her slowly, exploring and tasting, but then pulled away. "You're intoxicating, baby," he said. "But I've got a show to do, and I could use some alcohol." He leaned over to pick up a champagne bottle. "Get a couple of glasses, would you?"

That was abrupt, but Cleo grabbed two flutes without leaving Julian's lap. "Do you normally have to drink before a show?" She'd never seen him need alcohol to relax, and she didn't like it.

"Just a little something to settle my nerves. No big deal."

Maybe that wasn't as bad as it sounded. A lot of musicians suffered stage fright, and they had all sorts of rituals to overcome it. Julian filled the flutes without spilling a drop.

"Here's to you being back on a big stage," Cleo said, hoping she sounded sincere.

"And here's to you being in the back of a limo. Feeling

wanton yet?"

She laughed and took a sip. "I'm nervous," she whispered.

"Why?" he asked, while running his thumb over her lower lip. She went limp and spilled her champagne in his lap.

"Oh, no! I'm sorry."

He laughed. "I've missed this so much," he howled, while Cleo scanned the limo for something to soak up the mess. There was a small stack of napkins next to the bar. She grabbed a handful and handed them to him.

"Thanks for that," Julian said, wiping a tear from his eye. "Really. Way better than a cold shower, which I was going to need shortly."

He dabbed the napkins on his soaked crotch before tossing them aside. "So, you were saying?" He poured her a fresh glass of champagne.

"What?"

"Before you doused me, you were saying you were nervous."

"Oh." She took a not-so-ladylike gulp of champagne. How could she tell him what she was nervous about? She wasn't sure herself. It was as if something huge and ugly hovered just outside her peripheral vision.

"Um, well, I'm nervous about being backstage, I guess. You'll be busy, and I'll be trying to look awesomely cool, which as you know does not come naturally to me."

"While you're trying to look cool, I'll be preparing to play in front of tens of thousands of people. I hate backstage, waiting to go on, dealing with all the last-minute bullshit from the prima donnas."

"Getting tired of your friends?"

"Got tired of them a long time ago. But Cory's not that much of an asshole."

"I like him, too."

Julian narrowed his eyes. "I don't like you liking him."

"Good grief, Julian. I can't hate everyone just to make you feel better. And anyway, this tour will be over soon."

"Yeah. About that…"

Her heart nearly stopped. *Please don't say you're going on the European tour.*

"Mr. Lazros." Cleo jumped at the sound of Donnie's voice through the small speaker, and Julian immediately moved to protect his lap. "We're approaching the arena."

"Drink up, love. Almost showtime." He downed his champagne, poured himself another glass, and downed that, too.

The limo pulled into the tunnel leading to the bowels of Minneapolis's Target Center.

"What do I do with my bag?" Cleo asked.

"Leave it in the car if you don't need it. So, listen, at a certain point, I'll have someone take you to the VIP pit. Unless you'd like to stay backstage?"

"No, of course not. I want to see the show. That's what I came for." *It's not like I came all this way to make sure you're behaving yourself.*

The car came to a stop, and Julian gathered up his things. "The VIP pit is a great spot. It's on the floor, and you should be able to see well."

"Will there be other girlfriends or wives at this show?"

Donnie held the door open. Julian looked at her and said, "I don't know. But either way, mind your own business, Big Red."

He stepped out and reached for her hand.

"Why wouldn't I mind my own business?" she asked.

"Because getting into other people's business is your job. And you're good at it. But back off. The guys are on tour and playing by different rules."

Was this a warning? Was he letting her know that he, too, had been playing by different rules? Just as she stood, a huge, scowling man came barreling toward them. She remembered him from the bus parking lot. The road manager.

"Well, look at this," he barked. "The fucking princess has arrived!"

. . .

Julian turned to face the 340-pound former offensive lineman. His tattooed head was shiny and black, and he was doing that nervous jaw-clenching thing that made Julian's teeth hurt. "Hey, Sheik. How's it going, man?"

"Don't *how's it going* me, you sorry-ass motherfucker. You missed sound check."

"I told Seth I'd be late."

"I don't care about that. Do you see Seth here? No. You see me. You answer to me, Princess. And I told you to be here three hours ago. You show up here in your princess coach with your fancy princess driver who's getting in everybody's way…"

Poor Donnie shrank in size, slinking to the other side of the limo.

"He's moving the car. No worries, pal."

"Don't you *no worries* me, you pansy-assed, butt-licking shithead. You can't do whatever you please on my watch."

"Hey, Sasquatch!" Julian turned to see Cleo glowering in Sheik's shadow when she should be cowering like a smart person. He grinned. Sheik was in deep shit. "Who do you think you're talking to like that?"

Sheik looked down at Cleo. "Princess, what is this thing yapping at my heels?"

"This is Cleo, and she's attempting to take you on in defense of my honor."

Sheik looked Cleo up and down a few times and apparently decided she wasn't a threat. "Well, get rid of it,"

Sheik said, waving his hand dismissively.

"You can't talk to people like this! What's the matter with you?" Cleo demanded.

Sheik looked at Julian as if he should do something to handle his woman. Julian shrugged and made the introductions. "Cleo, this hunk of human steak is Sheik. He has a huge man crush on me and gets worried when I'm late. It makes him testy."

"I don't care who he is," Cleo said. "He's rude and he owes everyone, including poor Donnie over there, a big, fat apology."

"Well, well, well," Sheik said. "It seems the real princess has arrived." He poked Julian in the chest, making him wince. "I'm letting you off the hook because I suddenly feel sorry for your ass."

"Don't you poke him like that," Cleo said, grabbing Sheik by a meaty bicep.

Julian coughed to stifle a laugh as Sheik froze for five seconds, then slowly lifted his arm. Cleo held on, but when her feet began to leave the ground, she let go with an irritated grunt.

"Uh-huh, that's better," the giant hulk chided. "Don't be touching the Sheik, man."

Cleo glared. "Don't be touching my boyfriend," she snapped back.

Sheik raised one eyebrow at Cleo, and without taking his eyes off her, reached out and smacked Julian on the top of the head.

"Ow!" Julian wailed. "Jesus Christ, Sheik."

Cleo stood with her mouth open, and Sheik walked away, scattering people left and right. One young man wasn't fast enough, and Sheik snagged him by the collar. "Louis, escort that half bite of royal pain in the crack"—he glanced back at Cleo—"to the hospitality room."

"Does she need a pass?"

"Yeah, give her a full-access pass."

"Follow Louis, love," Julian said. "I'll be there in a minute." Cleo hesitated briefly, then spun and marched off, with Louis following on her heels. Her skirt-covered ass swung with attitude beneath her puffy jacket, and her right stocking slipped lower with each step. Julian couldn't wait to get her naked. In the meantime, he jogged over to Sheik.

"I think you scared her," he said.

Sheik snorted. "Where'd she get them boots? Hookers 'R' Us?" Then he grinned. "My, my, my."

"Holy shit," Julian said. "You're smitten, aren't you?"

"Hell, no," Sheik said, as they started up the ramp. He put his arm around Julian's shoulders. "Well, maybe a little."

Chapter Fifteen

Cleo followed Louis through the underground maze that made up the backstage area. People scurried about like ants in their tunnels, and she dodged them as best she could. Louis stopped at an open door. "This is the hospitality room," he said. "You can hang out here for a while. Julian's probably right behind us, so he'll be here in a sec. Do you need anything?"

Cleo peered into the small, crowded space. "No, I guess not."

She walked in and looked around. A couch against the wall overflowed with young women. They giggled, chatted, and sipped drinks, and all wore revealing outfits, too much eyeliner, and the same full-access pass Cleo had around her neck. *Groupies. Real ones.* There were also reporters, radio personalities, and a few crew members hanging out.

"Help yourself to anything at the refreshment table," Louis said.

One of the girls got off the couch and walked up to them. "Louis," she said, "how are the boys doing? Why can't we get into the dressing room?" She wrapped her arms around his neck and whispered something in his ear.

"Maybe later," he said, with a lascivious grin.

"I want to meet Julian," she insisted.

"Well, you're in luck. This is his girlfriend. Maybe she'll introduce you. I've got to run."

Cleo took a step back. "Thanks a lot," she muttered. The door was behind her—maybe she'd turn and make a run for it.

"Hey," the girl said. "Are you really his girlfriend?"

"Well, I'm not a thirty-year-old groupie, that's for sure," Cleo said.

"Hey, guys," the girl called out. "This is Julian's girlfriend."

No jealous glares. Instead, the women behaved as if Cleo were a celebrity. "What's he like? How did you meet?"

"Well…" She cleared her throat. Where to begin? "Julian owns a recording studio called Soundbox—"

Someone gasped, and all eyes turned to the door behind Cleo.

"Hi, girls," Julian said.

A chorus of squeals passed through the groupie throng. They waved and threw kisses, which Julian pretended to catch before grabbing Cleo's hand and pulling her through the doorway. "Come to the dressing room with me."

"You were cheeky with those girls," she said.

"You call that cheeky?" Pulling her closer, he whispered in a sexy, low growl, "I'll show you cheeky."

He didn't act like a guilty man. But still…

Cleo hesitated to respond, and Julian drew in a sharp breath. "Big Red, are you serious?"

Cleo shrugged her shoulders. Was she?

Julian grinned with a glint in his eye. "My green-eyed monster is jealous. I must say, this is a turn-on for me. I'm terribly ashamed for that."

"You should be," she muttered. The cloud of suspicion

lifted. It was hard to be suspicious of Julian when she was actually *with* him.

He crossed his arms. "You don't really suspect me of being unfaithful, do you?"

Was now the time to take this on? And *did* she suspect him of being unfaithful? The last time she'd visited a rock star on tour was still fresh in her memory. "You've been avoiding me. And I'm not naive. Don't make the mistake of assuming I am."

Julian's jaw dropped. "You're serious, aren't you?" He uncrossed his arms and ran his hands through his hair. "I haven't been avoiding you." He didn't say it with gusto, and the monster reared its ugly head again. What was he hiding?

"Angel, ask anyone on this tour. Ask the guys, ask the women following us—those women in there, they all know— ask anybody."

A middle-aged man walked up and slapped Julian on the back. He was Seth, the band's manager, and Cleo knew Julian couldn't stand him. "Hey, you made it!"

"Fuck off, Seth."

Seth's bright smile didn't falter, it simply disappeared as if it had never existed. "Okay, I see I've interrupted something, but Wayne wants your guitar when you get the chance. He needs to tune it."

He started to walk off, but Julian called him back. "Seth, have I been socializing with groupies on this tour?"

Seth straightened up, cleared his throat, and recited, "Julian hasn't been interested in any of the ladies. In fact, all the guys have been monogamous on the tour, as far as I'm aware." *Was he reading from a teleprompter?*

"Shit, Seth. Would you say it like you mean it?"

Seth looked at Cleo quickly, then turned back to Julian. Heat crept up Cleo's neck to her cheeks, and she clenched her jaw until it hurt. Humiliation had just reached new heights.

"Honestly, Julian, I've been too busy to notice who's been fucking who. Sorry. And you'd better hurry and get your guitar to Wayne."

Seth walked off, and Julian turned to Cleo. "Listen, I don't have time to do this right now. You've just fucking got to trust me, okay?"

Maybe he wasn't being unfaithful. But something was going on, and Cleo was going to get to the bottom of it. "You need to know something, Julian. There is only one thing I'd never forgive you for, and it's cheating. I don't care about the rules on the road, do you understand me?"

"Of course I do. And I promise you've got nothing to worry about. I would never, ever—"

The dressing room door opened and Dean's head poked out. "Julian, man! Glad you could make it. You took your sweet time, though."

"I had to pick up Cleo from the airport. Not that it's any of your business."

Dean took the snide comment in stride, gave a little shrug, and waved at Cleo. "Hi, Cleo. Didn't see you at first." Looking pointedly at Julian, he added, "He didn't tell us you were coming."

"Again, none of your business," Julian said, grabbing Cleo's hand and heading toward Dean and the dressing room.

A young girl stood behind the door, firmly attached to Dean's left arm. *Oh, boy.* Dean glared at Julian, who smirked in response. Melissa and Tanya might have a system worked out, but apparently, so did the guys. And Julian had bucked it. Not something she'd expect if he was cheating.

Cory stepped away from the mirror, where he'd been preening. "Here's our muse," he said, grinning from ear to ear. Faded skinny jeans, a black T-shirt, and a studded leather jacket—as if he'd stepped right off the pages of *Rock 'n' Spin*. "Julian didn't tell us you were coming." He set down his comb and came over for a hug. "This is your first show, right? Have you heard the song yet?"

Julian grunted, and Cory went silent.

"What?" Cleo asked.

"Nothing," Cory said, looking apologetically at Julian. "Enjoy the show." He went back to teasing his hair.

Cleo raised her eyebrows at Julian. He gave a blank face back. *So many secrets.*

A shrill giggle came from the corner where Dean and the girl sat petting and kissing. "Stay out of it, Big Red," Julian warned under his breath.

"Maybe I'll go over and inquire as to Melissa's health?"

"You'll do no such thing." Julian steered her by the elbow to a table loaded with food.

She glared at him, but her stomach growled. She picked up a small piece of sushi and popped it in her mouth. The crowd in the arena began to chant, and she stopped chewing to listen. *Lazros! Lazros!* She swallowed before letting her mouth drop open. "Do you hear that?"

Julian shrugged it off, but a smile tugged at the corner of his mouth.

A long-haired boy burst into the dressing room. "We killed them!" he shouted. Cory, Dean, and Gus clapped, but Julian stood silently impassive. Actually, he wasn't impassive. He crammed his hand in his pocket, clenched his jaw, and his right eye twitched.

"Opening band," he said to Cleo. "Zombie Scourge. Idiots. And shits, too. Do you know they set their bus on fire?"

"Smitty's awesome on the guitar, Julian," Dean said. "You're just a jealous prick."

"He's nothing but a fucking shredder," Julian said. "No soul and no art. You don't recognize that because you're nothing but a mediocre bassist."

"Fuck you," said Dean.

"Fuck you," said Julian.

They were *really* not getting along. "What's a shredder?" Cleo asked, hoping to stop what might prove to be an unending volley of profanity.

"Someone who plays furiously fast riffs," Julian said. "They're a dime a dozen."

He dug through his duffel bag and pulled out a pair of baggy cargo shorts and some old-school Doc Martens. She frowned as he stripped right in the middle of the room, then had to stifle a gasp. She could count all of his ribs. "How much weight have you lost?"

Dean let out a nasty laugh. "Yeah, Julian, why are you so skinny? Lost your appetite?"

"Shut up, man," Cory said, tensely.

Julian shot Dean a look that would have frozen fire before stepping into his shorts. They hung so low they were almost obscene. Only his boxers kept him from breaking laws.

"I'm fine, love. I don't eat much on tour."

Maybe so. But still. While she was here, she was going to feed the hell out of him. "I guess it's hard being vegan on the road."

Seth walked by and slipped a stinky, lit joint between Julian's lips. "This will make you hungry," he said.

Julian took a huge drag and handed it back to Seth. Cleo felt like the nerd kid at the party—she'd never seen Julian smoke pot—and tried to look cool with it. Most likely a big fail.

Holding the smoke in his lungs, Julian leaned over and laced up his boots. Then he stood, blew the smoke out with a grin, and slapped a beanie on his head. No shirt, of course. He was ready to rock.

The VIP pit wasn't a pit at all—you actually had to climb steps—and contained the best seats in the house. Donnie sat next to Cleo, having shed his chauffeur's hat and jacket, and he screamed himself hoarse.

"I could so get fired for this," he yelled in her ear. "And it would be worth it."

Cleo oscillated between being a fun-loving concertgoer and a shell-shocked Alice in Wonderland. She hadn't really known what to expect from Julian's performance. She knew Dead Ringer was a physically active band onstage, but she hadn't been sure of what that would look like for Julian.

It looked hot.

Her man had some moves, and Cleo felt every one of them. His thinner torso was still sexy as hell, and it gleamed with sweat. His hips seemed connected to his guitar, and oh, how they moved. She was flushed and embarrassed by how he made her ache, right there among hordes of people. Donnie's cheeks were flushed, too, although she assumed for entirely different reasons.

The show was almost over, and Dead Ringer still hadn't played "Just a Little Sting." Cory stood at the mic and signaled he had an announcement to make.

"You are some lucky motherfuckers tonight," he yelled. The noise level in the arena rose, indicating the crowd definitely felt they were lucky motherfuckers.

"You're about to be the first people *ever*"—he paused for effect—"to hear Julian's new song."

Julian had written a new song! Cleo cheered with the masses until her voice blended in with the communal roar. Now she understood the meaning behind raising the roof. How did Julian stand it? Was the biofeedback that effective? It must be. Otherwise the tour would have ground to a screeching halt.

Cory walked off to the side of the stage as everyone

quieted down as much as a crowd that large could. Then he sat himself on an amp, and the spotlights went crazy. They combed the entire arena, cutting out slices of mayhem here and there, before finally settling on Julian, who stood at the center mic.

Cleo's heart banged away. He was going to sing. Holding her breath, she watched him fiddle with his guitar and pedals amid the continuing roar of the crowd. He adjusted his pants, shook the hair out of his eyes, wiped his hands on his rear, messed with the guitar strap, and relocated his beanie to the back of his head.

The crowd went silent. "This is for the love of my life, the woman who holds my heart, and it's called 'Playing Cleo.'"

Cleo went numb, then she sizzled and tingled all over. Julian looked in her direction, and everybody and everything else disappeared. It was just the two of them, alone among thousands of people. She blinked back tears and held her breath as the first note rang out from the white Les Paul, soaring like an arrow to her heart. It was the song he'd played on the love seat that night. He'd fine-tuned it and turned it into a slow, soulful ballad, but it was the same song. The memory of what it had done to her made her squirm in her seat. And that was *before* he began to sing.

I'll play you, baby
You're my symphony
I'll play you, baby
Like a melody…

The crowd swayed with their arms in the air, like a giant sea anemone. The refrain came along, the melody turned catchy, and Cleo instinctively knew Julian had a hit on his hands.

I'm playing Cleo and I'm playing her fast
I'm making her wail, making it last
She's every color there ever was

Every person I've ever loved
She's every note that's ever been played
Every promise I've ever made

When it was over, the arena exploded. Julian, seemingly oblivious to all the excitement, simply waved toward the VIP pit where Cleo stood, then threw her an over-the-top *Dating Game* kiss. "I love you, baby," he yelled. In front of tens of thousands of witnesses. *He loved her.* He handed his Les Paul to the guitar tech, then strutted offstage, hair swinging back and forth.

Cleo finally got it. He was good at this. It was who he was, and who he wanted to be. How could she ever ask him to stop?

The concert wasn't over. The crowd was on its feet, stomping, clapping, and yelling. Soon a cadence emerged as they chanted, "Sting! Sting! Sting!"

Dead Ringer came back out, and Cleo screamed her throat raw with everyone else. Julian donned a guitar, a Fender this time, and turned to face Gus, who had climbed back onto his impressive throne of drums. With psychic skill and perfect synchronicity, the two of them broke instantly into the intro of "Just a Little Sting."

Julian shone like a brilliant beacon of awesomeness, and Cleo was up on her feet dancing the entire time. He wailed out an unbelievable solo, the same one a rock critic in Denver had said was "like the world's longest orgasm." Cleo agreed, and as the final note faded away, she did, too.

She came to in seconds, confused by the sea of fuzzy, nameless faces staring down at her.

"Are you okay? We're calling for help."

She sat up against protestations, and the room spun. "No,

no. Please don't do that. I'm just a little dizzy."

"You passed out," said Donnie. "Don't try to stand."

"I'd do what he says," said a gravelly voice. Cleo winced at the sound and looked over Donnie's shoulder to see Sheik barreling her way. He pushed through the small gathering of the curious and knelt beside her, staring into her eyes before announcing, "She's all right."

"Are you a doctor? Your bedside manner needs some work."

"Nah, but I know a swooner when I see one." He held out his hand. "Let's get you backstage with some cool water."

"I did not swoon."

"Then we'd better call an ambulance," he snapped.

"Okay, so I swooned." She stood—knees shaking—and clasped Sheik's meaty hand.

Come to think of it, except for the one piece of sushi she'd had backstage, she hadn't eaten anything all day. She'd meant to get something at the airport during a layover but hadn't had time.

"I'm not sure you've apologized for how you spoke to me earlier," she said, trying to gain her balance on her platform boots.

"I spoke to you earlier? I don't even remember. Now let's get your ass down these steps."

Before she knew what was happening, Sheik had picked her up and tossed her over his shoulder.

"What are you doing?"

"Swooner coming through!" he shouted to no one in particular.

Cleo resisted the desire to pound on Sheik's back. It would only draw more attention. Donnie scuttled along behind them but didn't dare initiate a confrontation with Sheik, who unceremoniously plunked Cleo down as they arrived at the stage.

"Follow me," he said. The crowd parted for him like the Red Sea, and he led Cleo backstage.

"Cleo, if you're okay, I'm going to go get the car," Donnie said.

"I'm fine," Cleo reassured him. "See you later."

Donnie glanced at Sheik, who nodded his head. "It's under control. This is my watch."

Backstage, there were even more people than before the show. Many were fans, and an air of expectation hovered, so tangible it almost crackled. "Meet and greet time," Sheik said, opening the door to the dressing room. "You'll be spending it in here."

The door opened right into Julian. People screamed his name at the sight of him, but he only had eyes for Cleo, and they were frantic.

"Are you okay? I heard you'd fainted." He looked her up and down for injuries.

"She swooned," Sheik said.

"I did not. I felt faint, that's all. Haven't really eaten today."

"She hit the floor," Sheik said. "Swooned from your guitar playin' and hip swayin'."

Cleo rolled her eyes, but Julian didn't smile. He led her to the couch as if she were an invalid, kissed her forehead, and started screaming for someone to bring her a cookie.

"How are you feeling now?" he asked.

"Fine. Honestly, I'm embarrassed. Of all the things I thought I might do to make a fool out of myself, this wasn't even on the list."

"Don't be silly," he said. "I'll sit with you until you're better."

"Oh, no, you won't, Princess," Sheik snapped. "She's not going to die. Get your fucking ass out there and schmooze with your adoring fans. I'll get Louis to take care of her."

"Sheik, under the circumstances, I think I should be excused from the meet and greet."

"That's why I call you Princess," Sheik said. "They paid good money for meet and greet passes, and we gotta give 'em what they paid for."

"Go on, Julian. Good grief, I'm fine." Spoken like a true rock star girlfriend.

Julian sighed, stood, and went to the door. He glanced back one last time before opening it, then screams rose as he stepped out.

After finishing off a couple of cookies and sitting mindlessly for fifteen minutes, Cleo couldn't stand it any longer. She stood, felt fine, and headed for the door. Bracing herself for the din, she yanked it open. But there was no more screaming, just a manageable buzz of what seemed like a million conversations. The crowd, content and patient, stood in line for turns with the band members. Cameras flashed, and mild applause and laughter rang out here and there.

Cleo nudged her way through the fans. One of the lines was longer than the others, and it was Julian's. A girl kissed him on the cheek and walked away, and another took her place. Julian exchanged a few words with her, smiled wickedly, and popped the cap off his magic marker. Then he aimed it at…*what the heck?*

The girl had yanked her shirt up! And she wasn't wearing a bra. The fans waiting in line shouted encouragement, and without the slightest reservation, Julian cupped a breast with one hand and signed it with the other. When he was done, she jiggled the other at him. But instead of signing it, he grabbed it and posed as if he were going to bite it.

"I like to leave an impression," he joked. The fans roared as if it were the most hilarious thing in the world. Cleo turned on her heel to march back to the dressing room and ran smack into a brick wall of muscle.

"Hold on there, champ," said Sheik. "No need to get your panties in a bunch. It's all part of the show. This sort of thing is expected—he's just doing his job."

"It's his job to fondle breasts?" So much for the good and brave rock star girlfriend. Bitchy and possessive felt better.

"I don't know that you could call it fondling. Chill out. You want some wine, or a soda, maybe?"

"No. What I want is for this to be over."

Sheik's granitelike brow softened. If Cleo didn't know better, she'd swear he had feelings. "Well, you're in luck," he said, turning his attention to the crowd. "Okay, folks! The meet and greet is over," he bellowed. Sounds of disappointment rang out, but nobody argued with Sheik.

Julian's face lit up as he spotted her. He hurried over. "Somebody's feeling better," he said.

"Actually, I'm not." She tried to be curt, but Julian didn't pick up on it. His eyes filled with concern as he gently placed a hand on her forehead.

"Let's get you sitting down again. Are you dizzy?"

"No, you idiot." She spun to walk away and caught Sheik miming to Julian, snapping his teeth together.

"Oh," Julian said, spinning her around to face him. His eyes twinkled. "That was nothing. Just a publicity stunt."

Unbelievable.

"Are you nuts? I do not want you looking at, touching, or biting anyone's breasts. I mean, how would you feel if I…"

Julian and Sheik waited while she failed to come up with an adequate comparison. Her face flushed. "Let's go," she said, grabbing Julian's hand. "We need to talk."

"After-party, Princess," barked Sheik. "You're not going anywhere."

Oh, God. Her eyes stung. Was she freaking going to cry? This was the last place she wanted to be…backstage at a concert, watching rock stars—one of them her *boyfriend*—be idiots. She wanted to take Julian home, back to Soundbox, where people were real, the art was what mattered, and nobody bit strangers for publicity.

But what would happen if she came out and told him? She remembered what he'd looked like on the stage, the sheer magnitude of the magic. She shifted her face away before someone saw a tear escape.

Too late. Sheik saw it and let out a groan. "What the fuck," he said to Julian. "I'll tell Seth you had an emergency. But don't think I'm going to let you skip one again."

Donnie pulled the limo away from the Target Center, and the privacy divider slid up silently.

"Why so quiet, love?" Julian brought her hand to his lips and delivered a feathery kiss. "Didn't you enjoy the show?"

"Sure," she said. The band had been amazing—the energy insane—and Julian had performed a song just for her. But it had been a lie. Just a show.

A moment or two of silence passed. "Are you going to tell me what's wrong?"

"One guess, genius."

"The biting thing?"

"Wow, you didn't even need to phone a friend. What else have you been doing on this tour that you think is totally acceptable but absolutely isn't?"

"I can't recall what that girl—or her tits—even looked like. I don't understand why you're feeling threatened."

"I am not feeling threatened!"

"Then what is it, baby?" He took her face in his hands. "Look at me. *I love you.*"

His voice didn't waver. He stared at her as if she were the only star in a dark sky. Her heart, frozen with worry, began to thaw.

"Can I kiss you?" Julian whispered.

There was nothing in the world she wanted more. He slipped his hand behind her head, and she closed her eyes, falling into him. He kissed her lightly, his lips soft and sweet.

She needed more. Too many emotions ran through her. She needed one of them to come front and center so she could focus on it. She bit Julian's bottom lip—some punishment was in order—and he gasped. She took control and invaded his mouth with her tongue. He accepted it eagerly and sucked on it in a rhythmic manner that was delightfully filthy. He broke the kiss.

"Oh," he whispered, his eyes still closed. "That was the color of rubies."

"What was?"

"That suction sound, when we kissed. Like this." He kissed her again. Little kisses over and over.

"Hear it? It's like rubies raining down."

He put his lips back on hers, then kissed his way down to her neck. She sighed in bliss.

"Emeralds," he whispered.

He ran his tongue along her collarbone, and she moaned softly. "Mmm, amethysts. Do that again, Cleo." His hand went beneath her shirt, and she had no choice but to do it again.

She began unbuttoning her blouse, anticipating where he was going to put that delicious mouth next. Predictably, he licked downward, following her fingers as they left each button.

"Let me," he said. With one quick yank, all the buttons flew off. "Sorry. It's been a while, so prepare to be ravished." He winked, but unbridled passion flashed in his chocolate-brown eyes.

Cleo squeezed her thighs together and shivered. "Bring it."

He palmed her breast and squeezed, then pulled the cup of her bra down, lifting her breast out and covering it with kisses. "I adore you," he said, before moving to the other breast. He took his time, like she was something sweet to savor.

The concert, the groupies, the fans…it all washed away so she could be fully present with this man, her real boy who happened to come with a guitar, a limo, and a hit single. He was every thrill she'd ever chased, every fantasy she'd ever dreamed, and yet, all she wanted was the man, stripped of glitter and fame, naked and real before her.

She found it hard to keep still as he continued his ministrations to her breasts. He kissed, he nibbled, he used that silver stud in all the right ways and the thrill went straight between her legs, a place he wasn't paying any attention to at all.

"Julian, please," she begged.

"Please what?" he whispered, letting his warm breath brush her nipple.

Ah, she didn't know what to say. She knew what she wanted. She knew it distinctly. His hand needed to go lower, up her skirt, and touch her. And she needed him to do it right now, before she combusted on the spot.

"Touch me," she said.

He held a breast in each hand, squeezing her nipples between his thumbs and fingers. And she squeezed her thighs together in agony.

"I am touching you," he said.

"Not there."

"Then where?"

She moved her hips and opened her legs, issuing a subtle invitation to move the action farther south.

"Julian, please." She grabbed his hand and put it on her thigh.

"I'm sorry, love, but we seem to be having a failure to communicate." He pulled his hand away and went back to her breasts.

He flicked a nipple with his tongue, then sucked on it. She was so sensitive now, it was hardly bearable.

"Please?"

He let her nipple pop out of his mouth and grinned at her, running his hand up her stockings, tickling her inner thigh. *Oh, finally!* But then he stopped.

She groaned as he went back to her breast, drawing her nipple deeply into his mouth. The fingers of his right hand continued brushing her inner thigh, but they didn't go any higher. She was going to die. She sought friction by moving her hips, trying to get his fingers where she wanted them, but it was all to no avail. "Julian," she snapped.

"Where do you want me to touch you, baby?" he whispered. His eyes darkened, and his nostrils flared. "Say it."

She did not have a limited vocabulary. She had a broad and extensive vocabulary. Several words came to mind, and not a single one seemed appropriate to the occasion. One or two of them, while technically correct, ran the risk of shutting things down completely. And the others…

She knew what he wanted her to say. His eyes bored into hers, urging her, daring her, begging her to say it. She placed her lips at his ear and whispered the dirtiest word she knew.

He growled in response, then kissed her hard. He called her his dirty girl, his little slut, and it should have upset her, infuriated her, mortified her, but it didn't. It turned her on.

She grabbed his face. "Do it."

His fingers went exactly where she needed them to go, inside her panties, inside her, and she exploded.

Julian raised his eyebrows. "You're kidding me."

She couldn't breathe enough to answer. The waves and contractions flowed through her body. Julian kept his eyes on hers, watching and feeling, and at just the right moment, he moved his finger while rubbing the magic spot with his thumb.

"Stop," she wheezed.

Julian pouted. "Really? Because you know what will happen if I don't."

She did know. She'd have another orgasm, and this one would be mind-blowing. And probably noisy. "I don't want Donnie to know what we're doing back here," she stage-whispered.

"He won't know. We're soundproofed. Mostly."

"Mostly?"

"Come on, now. Lean back, and we'll go for the double."

Sex with Julian was over-the-top—he instinctively knew what to do to give her pleasure—and he could do it forever. She leaned back on the seat and smiled, giving permission for him to do whatever he pleased.

He pulled her panties down over her boots and held them up in triumph before shoving them in his pocket. "My second pair of the tour. Got my first pair from a hot little number I did on the bus."

The bus. That had been fun. And noisy. She closed her legs.

"Donnie is literally a few feet away. We'll be at the hotel soon. Let's wait." She chewed on her thumbnail and held her knees firmly together.

Julian placed his hands on her knees and raised an eyebrow, then exerted enough force to part her legs. She tried to snap them shut.

"Are you struggling against me? I like that."

She hadn't known he liked that. The idea of putting up a fight sounded fun. She forced her knees back together and made what she hoped was a struggling type of sound.

Julian immediately dropped his hands from her knees. "Sorry," he said. "I was just playing around. We can wait."

Cleo sighed and rolled her eyes. "I was playing around, too, you goof." She winked at him and went limp. "Your turn. Pretend to overpower me."

"Oh." He grinned. "In that case…"

In a flash, he wrenched her knees apart and held them open. Just to see what would happen, Cleo tried to close them. And they didn't budge. He was strong. She tried again, adding a petite grunt with her efforts, but he held fast, growling in response.

"What are you doing?"

"I'm looking," he said. "God, I've missed you."

He ran his hands from the insides of her knees to the insides of her thighs, bringing his fingers together at her tingling flesh. He teased her there, then opened her legs wider, eliciting a sigh.

"Pink," he whispered.

"What?"

"That little sigh. Hot pink. Like your—"

"Julian!"

She tried to sound exasperated but was too turned on to swing it. If Julian kept this up, she would come undone, and everyone within a one-mile radius would know it, mostly soundproofed limo or not.

He knelt on the floor next to the seat and dropped his head between her legs. She was definitely going to come undone.

He kissed her sensitive inner thighs, rubbing his lips, nose, and bristly stubble against her skin. He ran his tongue over her exposed cheeks, gave one a kiss and the other a bite. *He'd bitten her.* But before she could complain, he nibbled elsewhere. She inhaled sharply as his tongue began licking slowly, with definite intention.

She moaned—loudly—and the sound of her own voice startled her. "Julian, I'm afraid Donnie can hear us."

He lifted his head, and she blushed at the sight of his lips glistening in the dim light. "He can't hear me. I'm being as quiet as a church mouse. You're being more…indigo, I'd say."

He extended his tongue for another soft lick. Cleo's voice betrayed her again, and she arched her back, opening her legs even wider.

"That's a good girl." He dipped his head and sucked gently on the sweet spot where all of her nerve endings currently hummed. His warm mouth covered her completely, performing a gentle, rhythmic sucking. She tried to be quiet, but another orgasm was building. She moved against him, holding her breath as he broke the suction to explore and tantalize with his tongue, alternating kisses with feathery licks. It was too good.

"Oh, God," she gasped. "Julian, I'm going to—"

Donnie's voice burst through the small speaker. "We've arrived at the hotel."

Cleo snapped her legs shut as Julian reached next to her ear and depressed a button. "We're going to be a few minutes. Just pull into a spot."

"Let's not be a few minutes," Cleo said urgently. "Let's go up to your room. He knows what we're doing."

Julian forced her knees back open. "He doesn't know exactly what we're doing. And who cares? You said I needed to eat more. That's all I'm trying to do, love."

He grinned like the devil and went right back to work. And Cleo forgot all about Donnie as she exploded in what Julian would probably call magenta.

It took Cleo a moment to settle back down to earth.

"You think you'll be able to walk within the next few minutes?" Julian asked. He seemed obnoxiously impressed with himself.

Cleo regained some clarity. "Of course I can walk. You give yourself too much credit." Her legs felt like spaghetti.

Everyone within sight would stare to see who got out of the stretch limousine. Cleo put her coat on because it was cold outside, but also because Julian had ripped all the buttons off her blouse. She smoothed down her skirt, brushed her hair with her fingers, and generally tried to make herself look presentable. Then she remembered a small detail.

She held out her hand. "Give me my panties."

Julian shrugged just as the door opened. Donnie gazed in. "Can I help you out, Cleo?"

"Careful with the exit, love," Julian said with a wink.

With one hand firmly holding down her skirt, Cleo accepted Donnie's hand with the other and carefully slid out of the limo. Julian followed, reaching into his pocket for some cash. He pulled out a wad of bills and, unfortunately, Cleo's purple panties. They fluttered toward the ground with Julian making awkward grabs, as if they weren't drawing enough attention without a rock star in hot pursuit. He snatched them up just before they hit the ground.

"Good grief," Cleo said, as Julian shoved them back into his pocket.

To his credit, Donnie maintained a pleasant poker face. "It was nice meeting you both. Cleo, I had fun with you tonight."

Cleo was about to say she'd enjoyed his company as well, since they were being so civil while she stood there commando, but then, with his tip securely in hand, Donnie added, "But not as much fun as Julian."

Chapter Sixteen

Julian startled awake in a combination of panic, pain, and colors. The sound of his own breathing was an explosion of red and black in his head, so he covered his ears. It didn't help. He shut his eyes, and that didn't help, either. The red and black merged with the murky brown sludge growing with every rustle of the sheets and thunderous beat of his heart.

This couldn't be happening. Not now. He cracked open an eye to peek at the clock. It was four o'clock in the morning. Fuck.

Maybe it would subside. He counted to twenty and took a deep breath, scooting closer to Cleo and her magic citrus elixir. But he was too far gone. No trace of oranges or tangerines. Only one thing could help him now. Luckily, Cleo was a sound sleeper.

Bile rose in his throat, and every bone in his body hurt. Julian's head pounded, his skin burned, and his teeth chattered. Silently, he slid out of the bed onto the floor, where he felt safer, and crawled to the bathroom. Nothing came up when he tried to vomit, and he ended up hanging over the toilet bowl, drooling in the dark.

He reached up and removed the lid from the tank, careful to not wake Cleo. It sounded like a machine gun going off an inch from his face, and he almost dropped it. The plastic baggie he'd taped to the edge of the tank was still there. Relief poured through him, setting off a new wave of shivers. The anticipation was both euphoric and excruciating.

The trembling wouldn't stop, and his fingers could barely hold on to the baggie. There was no way he could do what he needed without help, so he crawled back to the bed and clumsily patted down the nightstand for his phone. It hit the floor with a soft thud. Picking it up, he forced himself to stand. He needed to get to where Cleo wouldn't hear him call Sheik.

Minutes later, there was a soft knock on the door. Julian opened it. Sheik's hulking figure blocked out the light from the hallway.

"I told you, you stupid fuck."

"Shut up, Sheik," Julian whispered. "Just help me."

"Where's your woman?"

"Asleep in the other room. Stop shouting."

"I'm barely whispering, you idiot."

Maybe so, but it split Julian's head in two. "Can we go to your room?"

Sheik sighed. "Put some damn pants on first."

Luckily, his were within arm's reach on the back of a chair. He managed to get them on by himself—no way he could ask Sheik for help—and they quietly headed for Sheik's room. Once inside, Julian thrust the baggie into Sheik's hands.

"What's this?"

Julian didn't answer. It was fucking obvious what it was: a tiny balloon of heroin, a syringe, and a spoon, which wasn't a spoon at all, but the bottom of a soda can.

"Fuck. You've graduated to needles. You been doing this shit alone?"

Again, no sense in answering. He wished he was doing it alone *now*, but the synesthesia episode made it too hard. He could barely see. He couldn't even grip the syringe…

"You're lucky you're not dead. What happened to the post-concert snort? That didn't last long, did it? I told you, motherfucker. I told you this would happen."

"Must be awesome being right all the time," Julian mumbled. He could hear Sheik's voice—like a fucking avalanche—but couldn't see him because of the brown sludge. He could barely stand. But he'd take the shit Sheik was dishing if it meant he'd get some relief.

Sheik shoved Julian, and he fell onto the bed in a crash of sound and color. He rolled onto his side and listened. Episodes meant hypersensitive hearing: Sheik pouring water into the spoon, dropping in the tar, striking the lighter. In his mind, Julian watched the tar dissolve. Then he shivered in anticipation as the cotton went in, sensing when Sheik poked the needle into it and pulled out the plunger, filling the syringe with the poison. He heard Sheik's deep, rattling breath—black and bubbly like liquid heroin—as he turned to Julian.

"Okay, Princess. Let's get this over with."

"No bump," Julian whispered.

"Damn," Sheik said. "Straight into the vein, huh? What am I gonna tie off with?"

Julian didn't care. He lay with his eyes squeezed shut, wishing Sheik would hurry the fuck up.

Something went around his arm. It was tugged tight, and Julian squeezed to make a fist, to get the vein bulging. Sheik's big hand grabbed his arm roughly, and Julian heard him gasp. "How the hell have I missed these tracks? How often are you hitting it, man?"

Morning, noon, and night, asshole. Just do it.

The needle went in.

"Just a little sting," Julian said. His lame attempt at a joke.

Julian let himself into his room. He winced as the door squeaked, freezing and sucking in his breath. Was it possible Cleo didn't know he'd left? He'd been gone for almost two hours.

On tiptoes, he crept into the bedroom. The light was beginning to pour through the crack in the curtains as he took off his pants and slipped silently between the sheets.

Cleo rolled into him immediately. "Did you go somewhere?" she mumbled. "I woke up and you were gone."

Just went to shoot up. Don't you worry your pretty head about it.

"I went to get a bottle of water out of the machine."

"Oh." She sighed. Relief washed over him like a cleansing blue waterfall. He had to make things right. Cleo should not be in bed with a junkie.

After he'd gotten his shit together—thanks to a little heroin—Sheik had pleaded with him to come clean to Cleo. "That woman's no idiot," he'd said. "Look at you, man. You think she's not going to pick up on something?"

"She'll pick up on something, but she won't know what," he'd replied. "I'll tell her I'm worn-out, tired, maybe I'm getting sick. And I'm going to clean up when we get our four-week break. That's my plan."

"Nice to know you have a brilliant plan."

"Listen, I wasn't dope sick. I was fighting off a synesthesia episode, that's all. I mean, I've been off dope for two days, and I haven't gotten sick."

"Until now," Sheik had said. He'd leaned in closer to Julian, looking him square in the eyes. "In case you've forgotten, you're on dope now. Julian, you were strung out, and you know it. Fucking idiot, that's what you are."

Julian hadn't said a word in his own defense. He'd just stared at an imaginary spot on the wall. Sheik was right. Julian remembered his chattering teeth, the nausea, the aches that started in his bones and worked their way outward through his skin. Dope sick.

"I saw that your biofeedback game came in. Stop kidding yourself about cleaning up. You've made your choice, and that pretty redhead ain't it."

It had felt like a sucker punch in the gut. But only for a moment. Heroin protected him from feeling too deeply about...well, anything.

"Listen," Sheik had said. "What are you dragging her into? There's nothing but heartache ahead for that woman."

"Shut the fuck up, Sheik. You don't know what you're talking about."

"Yeah, unfortunately, I do. By the time I cleaned up, my woman was long gone. Some nice, respectable asshole was playing daddy to my kids. Still is. And they're better off for it, too. Because all junkies care about is themselves. And you know what, motherfucker? I'm always just a step away from it. And here I am with a junkie for a best friend."

Julian had caught the embarrassed expression on Sheik's face over the profession of friendship. Trying to hide his own embarrassment, he'd quickly muttered, "Stop calling me a junkie."

"You know, you're just another shitty rock star. You don't know what love is unless you're looking in the mirror."

"You think I love what I see in the mirror? I hate myself. Cleo would lose it if she knew what was going on with me. You have no idea. But I'm not going to keep this up. I can—"

"What?" Sheik interjected. "You can quit anytime you want? Is that what you're about to say?"

"I can. I can't wait to get off this junk. As soon as we hit the four-week break, I'll have time to kick it."

Even as he'd said it he'd felt panicked. The thought of getting sober gave him the chills. He was hooked again. "Cleo won't ever have to know about any of it. And it wasn't like I did this on purpose. If you'd done a better job of controlling those freaks, this wouldn't have happened."

Sheik pulled back the curtain at the window. Julian shielded his eyes as a ray of light made its way to where he sat on the bed. He wondered if it would turn him to ash.

"Well, my man," Sheik finally said. "There's one thing I learned a long time ago in a little place called rehab, on my fourth and hopefully final stint, and that is you can't blame anyone else for the shit you get yourself into. This is yours. Own it."

Those words rang in Julian's ears as he stroked Cleo's hair. Sheik was right. Still, it was hard to feel like shit about it at the moment. Fuck, he was on heroin, and he felt great.

It wouldn't be for long, though. The highs were getting shorter by the hit. But he found it hard to care. Heroin wrapped him in a warm, soothing blanket. From beneath the comfort of it, he could watch everything, but it didn't affect him. Even when a dart of panic happened to find a weak spot in the opiate armor, he just examined it quizzically. *Look*, he'd think. *I'm freaking out.* Then he would just…stop.

Cleo stirred and touched his cheek. How was he going to manage the next few days? He'd need another fix in a few hours, or he'd be sick as shit. Just thinking about the next hit thrilled him. A day and a half. That's all he had to get through before she'd be on a plane back to San Antonio. *Was he really counting down the days until she left?*

Her fingers brushed the stubble on his chin. He hadn't shaved in days. Thank God she liked him scruffy. She moved in closer and began kissing his neck. He was overcome by love and…performance anxiety. Heroin wasn't one of those drugs that made people want to fuck like rabbits. And he was still high.

He trailed his hand gently down her back. She sighed and nuzzled in closer, running her wet tongue up to his ear. He squeezed a firm ass cheek, and she put her leg up over his hip, giving him full access. "Hmm, been thinking about me, have you, love?"

His own reaction was quick and anything but wimpy. He'd be spared the embarrassment of an addict's limp dick after all.

In an instant, Cleo was on top of him. Well, he was up for it. With a laugh, he whipped off her T-shirt and filled each hand with a soft breast. She moaned and leaned in, allowing him to pull a nipple into his mouth.

A pleasant popping sound set off lemon drops in his head as he let go. Then he moved to the other breast while Cleo sighed in peach-colored waves. Her skin was warm in his mouth and sweet as honey. He got lost in it for a while, in the suckling and licking and kissing, until Cleo gently pulled his head away. How long had he been doing that? Time was a slippery thing when you were on heroin.

"Too much for you?" he asked.

"There's something Freudian in it when it goes on too long," she said, raising that eyebrow.

"There is not," he said. "Mum."

She giggled, grabbed the nearest pillow, and smacked him with it.

"Is that how you want to play, Big Red? You want to play like that?"

He yanked the pillow out of her hands and gave her a good wallop—too hard of a wallop, actually, and she rolled off the bed with a yelp.

She was beet red and madder than a wet hen when she popped back up.

"Why, you—" He took a direct hit to the face. When he opened his eyes, it was raining feathers.

Cleo wore an adorably wondrous expression, a couple of feathers, and nothing else.

"Oh, you sweet, sweet angel," he said. "Come here and let me love you." He plucked a feather out of the air. "This might come in handy."

It did. And when she was properly giggled out and adequately excited, he positioned himself to take her.

"Wait, wait…no," she said, breathless from the teasing and torture she'd endured. "I have to pee."

"You are so fucking romantic, do you know that?"

"Spontaneous morning sex," she said, "does have its pesky kinks."

"Did you say kink, Big Red?"

"Don't make me start over with the pillow." She climbed off the bed. "I'll be right back."

She walked away, red hair swaying and sweet little ass intentionally sashaying. He reached beneath the covers to appreciate his hard-on. *Just checking.*

Things were going to be fine. He was staying on track, staying focused, not thinking about heroin…shit, he was thinking about heroin.

"Julian?" Cleo shouted from the bathroom. "What happened in here?"

Sheer panic rolled through him. What had he left in there? He'd been so out of it, most of the waking up and getting to Sheik's room was a total blur.

"Why is the lid off the toilet tank?" she asked.

"What?" His voice sounded high-pitched and hysterical in his head. *Calm down and think.* "The float thing got stuck last night. I fixed it—guess I didn't put the lid back on the tank."

He'd broken out in a cold sweat, and a quick check

beneath the covers confirmed his dampened mood.

"You're such a handyman. That turns me on, you know," Cleo said, amid the clanking sounds of the tank lid being returned to its rightful place.

Julian ran his hands through his hair. Where had he left the bindles? He vaguely remembered taking the whole baggie of goodies into Sheik's room. Surely, that's what he'd done. He hadn't left anything out on the counter or something stupid like that. He resisted the urge to barge in on Cleo for a quick look around.

He heard running water, Cleo humming, and eventually, the toilet flushing. Everything was fine. But shit, he'd lost his hard-on. The door opened, and Cleo came out. She seemed okay, and she was wearing… *What was she wearing?*

"Do you like it?"

"Where did you get that? A stripper store?"

"Yeah, kind of," she said, blushing. A black fishnet dress barely covered her ass. Were those tiny black panties crotchless? God, he hoped so.

Cleo smiled shyly, glancing at him through her lashes. "I can't believe I'm wearing this," she said innocently. "Maybe I should take it off?"

"Soon enough," he said. Her breasts stretched the fishnet, pink nipples poking through the holes. Julian licked his lips. He didn't need to peek under the sheet to know he was back in business.

"Get over here."

Cleo came right up to him and stood with her legs apart, one taunting eyebrow perfectly arched. He pressed his face against her, inhaling her scent through the black panties. Then he took a nibble while running his hands up her thighs and pulled away with a smile.

"On top, baby. Come on."

She pulled the sheet back and looked at him. Her pink

cheeks said she liked what she saw. "Condom," Cleo said.

"Uh-huh," he answered. His mind was already drifting, and the desire for dope needed to be drowned by something more powerful. He wanted to fuck. With a gentle tug he pulled her on top of him—he'd get a condom in a minute, no worries.

She let out a small cry as he entered her. *Pain? Ecstasy?* Holding her hips, he gave her a couple of pumps.

"Julian!"

He crashed back into full consciousness when he opened his eyes. "Sorry, baby," he said. "I got carried away. I'll go get a condom."

"Damn straight," she mumbled.

Cleo wasn't on birth control. No way she'd let him do anything without a condom. He gave her a kiss, helped her off him, and headed to the bathroom, where he checked carefully to see if he'd left anything incriminating. An alcohol prep pad sat on the counter, but he brushed it into a drawer. There was nothing else. He was relieved…at first. Then he had an urge to keep looking.

He opened drawers, checked the cabinets under the sink, and looked in the toilet tank. A pair of jeans in the corner received a pat-down, just in case he'd left something in the pocket, but there was nothing. The shaving kit was likewise empty, and he tossed it on the counter in disgust. The relief was replaced by disappointment. A little kick would be nice.

He grabbed a condom out of the drawer, catching a glimpse of himself in the mirror as he slammed it shut. A guy who looked like shit stared back. Shiny eyes and dilated pupils—would Cleo notice? She was out there looking like every man's fantasy in fishnet, and, well, he'd rather shoot up. It was awful, but it didn't change anything. With a sigh, he headed back to the bed.

A couple of minutes later, he was beneath Cleo, letting her ride him for all she was worth. He loved watching her, kept telling himself how good it was, telling Cleo how good *she* was, but he hovered just outside the perimeter of being fully present. *When would he be able to sneak away?*

Soon, there was no connection at all. He tried to fake it. Tried to make the proper noises, say the proper words. But he was going through the motions with an anesthetized, rock-hard cock. Heroin, if it let you get it up in the first place, helped you keep it up, sometimes indefinitely.

Memories of Slice tours and going at it for mind-numbing hours with nameless girls flooded his head. Fucking on heroin was like having an out-of-body experience—you could see what you were doing, but you didn't care.

Cleo moaned his name, forcing him into the present. This wasn't some nameless girl, for Christ's sake. With renewed determination, he kissed her, just as an orgasm ripped through her body. He was still inside her, hard and dead, and she collapsed on top of him, completely spent.

It wasn't over yet, though. He pulled out and rolled on top. She wrapped her legs around him, welcoming him back.

He started moving, and it was going along well until he realized he'd lost track of time. Had it been five minutes? Fifteen? He couldn't feel anything, and he sensed Cleo becoming less enthusiastic by the minute.

"Oh, my," she finally panted. "If you keep this up for more than four hours, you're going to need medical attention, and so am I."

Julian needed to end this thing. He gazed into Cleo's eyes, he kissed her, he talked to her, he did everything he could think of to try to connect with her, but in the end, all he managed to do was fuck her. And not very well.

Finally, he climaxed. Not with a bang but a whimper.

Minutes later, he stared at the ceiling with her in the crook of his arm. "Julian, are you okay? You seem distracted."

"What? No, I'm fine. Everything's fine. I mean, sorry if

that wasn't so great. I'm tired after last night."

The bathroom beckoned. Even though he knew there was no dope in there, he wanted to check one more time, anyway.

"Don't apologize. Everything's good," she said.

He grimaced. *Yeah, everything's good except for you just having suffered the worst sex in the history of robotic fucking.*

She sat up and looked at him. He wished she'd stop that.

"Have you been doing your biofeedback? Shouldn't you have done it last night?"

"I'll do it later. I'm fine."

"But you're supposed to do it at least twice a day."

"I said I'm fine," he snapped. Cleo blinked at him.

"Sorry, baby," he said, sweetly. He kissed her. "Everything is under control. It kills me for you to worry." All junkies were good liars.

He wanted to tell her everything. But what if she ran like hell and never looked back? Also, telling her meant he'd have to quit. And, of course, he wanted to quit, and he fully intended to quit. Just not today.

•••

Cleo lay on the bed like a limp dishrag, flipping through the television channels. Julian had gone to Sheik's room to do his biofeedback. Why hadn't he just done it in here? One minute he was intimately connected to her, showering her with attention, and the next he was distant and practically ignoring her. Something was wrong. But what was it?

Maybe he was embarrassed after the anticlimactic morning sex, or possibly he was just tired and cranky. He'd slept most of the day. What if he was getting sick? It would be awful timing with back-to-back shows next week. If only she had the courage to broach the subject of him quitting the tour and coming home.

Her brooding was interrupted by a soft knock. Muting the television, she crawled off the bed and answered the door. She gasped to see Sheik taking up every square inch of the doorway.

"What are you squeaking about, Minnie Mouse?"

With her hand at her throat, she waited for the rush of adrenaline to subside. "I didn't squeak. You startled me."

"Did you answer the door by accident?"

"No, but I wasn't expecting you. And you're terrifying. Now, what do you want?"

"Don't raise that eyebrow at me. We need to talk, Cleo."

He'd never used her name before. Dread slithered up her spine. *Don't be stupid. You know what's wrong.* Only she didn't. Nothing she could put into words.

"What is it?" she whispered.

Sheik sighed, came farther into the room, and turned to face her. "You want to sit down or something?"

"Why do I need to sit down?"

Sheik shrugged and pointed to a chair. Cleo sat, barely feeling it.

"Your boy's doing heroin."

He might as well have said Julian was a hippopotamus. For a few seconds, she just sat there, trying to figure out what language Sheik was speaking. Because it didn't make sense. Was it Greek? Latin? Yiddish? *What?*

Then the first puzzle piece fell neatly into place. Her hand went to her mouth. *Oh, God.* More puzzle pieces. The room tilted as if the chair had been yanked out from under her.

"Did you hear me?" Sheik asked.

"But why?" she asked. "How did this happen?" She stood up, needing to move. "If only he hadn't come on this stupid tour! Is he still in your room?" He needed some sense slapped into him, and she was just the woman to do it.

"Listen, why don't you sit back down?" Sheik said. "We

need to chat. It's not what you think. Not that bad, really. We just need to—"

She stopped in her tracks and spun around to face him. "Not that bad? What is the matter with you? He's doing heroin!" She'd been such an idiot. What had she said to him earlier? *I'm not naive, Julian.*

"When is he doing it? I mean, how does it work? Is he on it *now*?"

Sheik's eyes were wide, but he put his hands out as if to calm her. "It's that thing, you know, that thing he does with the colors. Heroin helps with that—"

"He has a biofeedback program for that."

"There was a little problem."

Cleo paced the room like a caged animal as Sheik told her what had happened to the program. "Why didn't he just replace it? That would be the normal thing to do. Not say, *Oops, I think I'll try heroin now.*"

"Okay, you're turning all kinds of colors. I don't think it's healthy. I'm not used to white girls yelling at me. Not as white as you, anyway. Shit."

"Answer me!"

Sheik jumped. "He did order a new one, but it didn't come in fast enough. It got lost trying to keep up with the tour. Kept arriving a day late. Jesus, girl, you're going to give me a heart attack."

Very quietly, she asked, "Where did he get it?"

"Okay, that's scarier. I liked you better when you hollered. Listen, he had shows to do. He couldn't wait. I didn't believe him—that he would go crazy and shit. But man, I saw it with my own eyes."

He walked right up to her, until they were nose to chest. "I got it for him," he said softly.

His T-shirt said DEAD RINGER—JUST A LITTLE STING WORLD TOUR. Cleo's fingernails dug into the palms of her hands. She hadn't realized she'd balled them into fists. "I hate you," she said.

"I don't blame you. I wish I hadn't done it. I wish I'd just called an ambulance, but he said they'd put him in a psych ward, and he was…" His voice caught, and he cleared it. "He was so scared."

"You felt helpless." And he couldn't very well use the same methods she did to bring Julian out of it.

"He said a little sniff of heroin would clear it all up. And it did, too. But by the time his game came in, he was hooked. The fucker hasn't even opened the package."

"Hooked? He's addicted?" She knew it was a stupid question. Heroin wasn't like a Saturday night martini.

"Yeah, 'fraid so. Turns out he's been shooting up alone."

"Oh my God, oh my God, oh my God…" She began to pace again. "People die that way!" A list flashed through her mind—famous names—and she shivered. Julian was not going to be on that list. "We have to get him to rehab."

"Listen, we've got a big break coming up, and I'm going to help him kick it then."

"Um, no, you're not. We're going to get him help right now, this very minute."

"We've got a lot of shows coming up," Sheik said. He averted his eyes. "I can get him through until then."

Cleo punched him on the arm. "Listen to what you're saying," she said.

Sheik didn't budge. He didn't wince, he didn't rub his arm. But his eyes slowly found hers. "Let's go get him, then," he said.

They walked the short way down the hall. "He's going to lie to you. It's what junkies do, and he thinks you'll run if you know the truth."

The word "junkie" had just been used in relation to her boyfriend. There really was a first for everything.

The room was dark and quiet except for the humming of the air conditioner. Julian was on the bed, facing away, as if he were taking a nap. Sheik flipped on a lamp, and Julian stirred briefly, then became still again.

"Get up, asshole," Sheik said.

Julian rolled over, then sat up with a start. "Hey, guys," he said. He smiled, only there was no hint of wickedness, glee, or mischief. This was a mindlessly happy smile. A drugged smile.

"Big Red," he said. "Where'd you find this girl, Sheik?"

"Are you finished with your biofeedback?" she asked.

"Huh?"

"You left me in the other room to come in here to do your biofeedback."

The lightbulb turned on behind his stoned eyes.

"I'm done." He kept smiling and leaned back slowly, lowering his head to the pillow.

Everything was on the nightstand. A syringe, cotton, other things Cleo didn't recognize. She walked to the side of the bed and stared down at him, arms crossed. He smiled absently, but then realization began to travel across his face. She could see the battle going on behind his eyes as he fought the good fight to stay in his happy place, but he lost and sat up quickly, eyes darting back and forth between her and Sheik. "Sheik, you stupid fuck. What have you done?"

"I'm helping you, man."

"Cleo, listen—" Julian began.

"Pack your bags. You're going to rehab," she said.

Julian fell back against the pillows and laughed. "No fucking way," he said. "Sheik's going to help me kick it in a weekend, right, Sheik?"

"We're going to do whatever works, Princess."

"Well, I'm not going to rehab," Julian said.

Amy Winehouse came to Cleo's mind. They'd wanted her to go to rehab, she'd said no, no, no, and now she was dead.

"Sheik, pack his things."

"Hold on a minute. You don't know where to take him. Let's wait until he comes down a little, and we'll discuss this some more."

Julian sighed. "Thanks to you two, I'm coming down *now*." He pouted. Then he seemed to forget all about them and began drifting to sleep or something close to it.

"Julian!" Cleo shook him.

"Hey," he said, jerking his arm as if she'd startled him. His brow furrowed like he was trying to place her. Then he said, "Stop being a crazy bitch."

...

Cleo's gasp was like a slap across Julian's cheek. What had he just said to her? *Stop being a crazy bitch.* Those were the last words he'd said to Gina.

"Don't you care that this hurts me?" Cleo cried.

He cared. He cared a lot. He didn't want to hurt her at all. He loved her.

"How would you feel if I did this to you?" she asked.

"Did what?" This was all so confusing. And he'd been having a lovely time a few minutes ago.

"Used heroin," Cleo yelled. "How would you feel if I did that?"

He went rigid. Stone-cold rigid. Every good tingle and blissful, euphoric feeling dissipated, and he came back into himself with painful clarity. He wasn't any good for anyone.

He reached out to touch Cleo. Her green eyes shone, her curls were trembling…and she backed away from him.

"Don't you dare touch me. Not when you're like this."

"You're right," he whispered. "I wish I'd never touched you at all."

His life force drained out and drifted away. What had he

done to her? This was the last place in the world she should be—standing in a hotel room thousands of miles from home, watching a junkie come down.

He thought of sweet Gina, dead because of him.

"Go home, Cleo."

"I'm not leaving without you," she said. It shattered him.

"Sheik, get her to the airport."

"No," Cleo cried. "You're coming with me."

"No, I'm not!" He screamed so loudly it hurt his throat. "I don't want to come home with you. Don't you understand? I never wanted you to come here. I want you to get the fuck out so I can do whatever the bloody hell I want. And do you know what I want to do, Cleo?" He pointed at the nightstand. "This."

"We'll get you help," she stammered.

What did he have to say to make her leave? He took a deep breath. "I don't want help. I love shooting up, and I don't want to be tied down to you. I've been cheating on you, love. I've fucked so many women in the past few weeks I've lost count. You're ruining everything by being here, so just go home."

He expected her to burst into tears and flee. But she didn't. Her delicate hands clenched into fists, and her eyebrows knit into a ferocious frown above her blazing green eyes.

"Well, I hope you fucked them better than you fucked me."

Ouch. Good girl. Get mad, baby. Let me have it.

"And if you've given me an STD," she continued, "I'm suing you."

He wasn't prepared for that one. "What the fuck are you talking about?"

"For your information, Mr. Rock Star, you were ambitious in your purchase of the large condoms. There's nothing sexier than having a man fuck you like it's a chore, and when he's finally done, leaving a condom stuck to the inside of your thigh. You came right out of that thing. It was pathetic."

"Get out of here, Cleo, before I throw you out on your ass." He stood and made a move for her. He knew he looked terrifying.

"I wish I'd never met you," she screamed, dodging him. Then she fled, pushing past Sheik and slamming the door so hard it flew back open.

"I wish you'd never met me, too, baby," Julian whispered. "Sheik, make sure she gets to the airport."

"Maybe you're making a mistake, pal."

"Hurry, go help her," he said, urgently. Then he reached for the syringe.

Chapter Seventeen

Cleo sat cross-legged on the floor and watched Addie and Sherry tape up the last few boxes from the loft. She'd been staying at Sherry's for the past couple of months and had only taken her clothes and personal belongings. Dishes, linens, small appliances, and furniture had all been abandoned since she hadn't needed them. But now the building was for sale. She had to get her stuff out.

"I can't believe he's closed the studio," Addie said.

"Me, either," Cleo said. She'd been coming in faithfully every day, scheduling bands and sessions, making sure the engineers showed up, and staying on top of the bills. She'd assumed Julian—or Sheik—would hire a new person to take over. But instead, Sheik had shown up last week to officially shut it down.

"I think that's the last of it," Addie said, stacking a box next to the door.

Cleo looked around the room. "My life in boxes," she said. "It sounds like a one-woman show. I should hit the road with it. It could start out with a scene called Rock Star Implosion in a Hotel Room—the Sequel."

"Nobody would pay to see it," Sherry said. "Too predictable."

Addie frowned. Sherry's irreverence obviously bothered Addie. But Sherry cared. She just had a different way of showing it. Opening her home to Cleo—no questions asked and expecting nothing in return—was one of the ways she conveyed her love and concern. You just had to ignore what came out of her mouth.

Cleo cleared her throat. *Sound casual.*

"So, Addie, have you heard from him?"

"Not much," Addie answered apologetically. "I don't imagine you've spoken to him?"

Cleo snorted and pulled her knees into her chest. "Of course not. I've talked to his hulking minion, but only about closing Soundbox." She slid up the wall to stand. "God, I cannot get over it. He's closing this studio. He was so happy here. It makes no sense that he even joined Dead Ringer in the first place. Why? What was he thinking?"

Addie wrung her hands. "I've asked myself a thousand times how this all happened."

Sherry dropped a box on top of the one Addie had set by the door. "Did he go to rehab?"

"Yes," Addie said. "He's clean now."

"And he still doesn't want to be with me," Cleo said, wiping the dust off her butt.

"Oh my God. Cleo," Sherry said. "The man cheated on you. He cheated on you *lots*. Like, *big-time*. Do you really want to be with him?"

"I still find that hard to believe," Addie said.

Sherry grabbed a wastebasket and began stuffing cleaning supplies in it. "Oh, please," she said. "I know he's your brother, but get real."

Cleo swallowed. Were they—she and Addie—just

stupidly naive? "I find it hard to believe, too." she said. "He was so loyal to everyone he knew—"

Sherry turned to face her. "How can you defend these guys? Do you remember Lou? And that other guy whose name I can't even remember? Cleo, rock stars *cheat*. All of them—"

"I resent that," Addie said.

"I shouldn't have said that." Sherry leaned over and picked up a couple of Magic Markers off the floor. "I'm sorry." She crammed the markers in her pocket.

"Well," Addie said, "I haven't seen him enough to sort it out. I don't know why he did anything. He disappears when he's disappointed people. In the past, I'd be tearing my hair out. But now I just can't. I have other people depending on me, people who aren't intentionally screwing up their lives at every turn. Cleo, I feel so responsible for drawing you into this. I wish I hadn't introduced you."

"Don't be silly. You're not responsible for me. And you're not responsible for Julian, either. You're a grown woman, and you don't deserve to spend your life trying to raise a grown man."

Addie smiled and squeezed her hand. "Cleo," she said hesitantly, "it's unlikely he'll show for the wedding, so I hope you'll reconsider."

Cleo wanted to go to Addie's wedding. But what if Julian was there? She couldn't risk seeing him. She'd played the scenario in her head a thousand times—each with a different ending. None of them were good. "I'll think about it. In the meantime, can we see the dress again?"

Addie went along with the change of topic cheerfully. She smiled and pulled out her phone. "Let's see," she said, navigating through the screens. "Here we go!"

A bateau neckline, a fitted bodice that flowed into a trumpet skirt—a beautifully classic and traditional gown.

Until you realized the silk was dyed in iridescent pinks and greens. They were subtle—there one minute and gone the next—but mesmerizing. They'd be stunning on Addie.

Both Cleo and Sherry made all the right noises. "You did such a fabulous dye job on that," Sherry said.

"Thanks. Wait until you see my princess of a flower girl." Up popped a picture of cherubic Emily. Her princess dress, dyed pink, made her look like a confectionary delight. Or cotton candy.

"I could eat that little girl up," Cleo said. "*Your* little girl, Addie."

Addie appeared to melt. Emily was hers as surely as if she had come from her womb.

"These are all my girls," Addie said proudly, pulling up the portrait Mitch had taken of her with Rachel, Laura, and Emily.

"A perfect family," Sherry said. "No doubt about it." She looked at Cleo. "Cleo, you know…"

"What?"

"Nothing. Never mind."

"What?"

"It's just, you knew Julian wasn't ever headed for that, right? For a family? It was totally outside the realm of possibility. He was never a real boy, remember?"

"The same thing could have been said of Mitch once," Addie said. "People change." She put her phone back in her purse.

Addie was right. Mitch *had* changed. But Julian didn't want to.

"Listen," Addie said, clapping her hands together suddenly. "This has been a ton of fun. But I've got to get back to Austin. I have two girls who need a ride to basketball practice and a new dye studio to set up."

"Yeah," said Sherry. "Maybe next time we can do

something even more cheerful, like watch a program about childhood leukemia."

"This will all turn out fine," Addie said to Cleo. "One way or another, it will all turn out."

Cleo didn't see how.

"I'm really happy for her," Cleo said, watching Addie drive away.

"You are not." Sherry snorted.

"I'd like to be, though."

Cleo picked up the mail, glancing through it as they climbed back up to the loft.

"Isn't this a perfect ending to a fun evening?" she said, holding up a brown envelope.

"What is it?" Sherry asked, as they pushed the door open and entered the box-littered room. "Are you being audited?"

"Even better. It's a lab report. I was so freaked out after Minneapolis that I got tested for a few things."

"Oh my God, Cleo. Are you serious? Are you telling me you went and got tested for, like, the clap and AIDS or something?"

"Well, why not? I had sex with a promiscuous IV drug user."

"It isn't like he was squatting in a culvert somewhere sharing needles with street people. And it isn't like you had unprotected sex, either."

"Actually…"

"Actually what?"

"We had a condom mishap. And you know how I am about these things."

"You had a condom mishap and you're worried about *AIDS*?"

"Yes. I had a condom mishap with an *IV drug user*."

"You had a condom mishap with *Julian*, and you're damn lucky you didn't get pregnant. I mean, I'd have been more worried about that than AIDS."

"It was a couple of days before my period, so I didn't get too freaked out about it. Besides, I'm not sure when it came off—before, during, or after. It was hard to tell, and I didn't examine it for evidence."

"Ooh," Sherry grimaced. "Too much information. Still, I bet you were relieved when you started."

"Yeah," Cleo said, absentmindedly. *Please don't let me have some kind of horrible disease like syphilis.*

She ripped open the envelope and removed the single sheet of paper. As she glanced at it, she felt the oddest sensation, as if all the blood in her head had suddenly dropped to her feet. Her mouth slacked open, and she looked up at Sherry.

"Cleo? Give me that."

Sherry ripped the paper out of her hand and frantically scanned it.

"Shit. You scared me to death. It says here everything is negative. What in the world is the matter with you?"

The room spun. "I think I'm going to be ill."

"You did start, didn't you?"

Surely, she had. Cleo thought back. Had she? She'd been in such a panic over the breakup and the ensuing mess it had made of her life that, come to think of it, she couldn't remember.

"Cleo?"

"Um, sure. I'm sure I did," she said. "I just can't remember when."

"You should have had two periods since Minneapolis."

Cleo dropped the remaining mail. How could she not have thought about this? "Oh, shit," she said. "Shit, shit, shit."

She poked gently at her breasts and felt a sense of relief. "I'm about to start my period. I can tell. I have all the signs, sore breasts, cramping. Probably tonight or tomorrow in fact." She swallowed loudly. "It's the stress I've been under. I've skipped. That's all this is."

"Sore breasts and cramps are also signs of pregnancy. You need to take a test. I have one at the apartment."

"No! Jesus, I'm not pregnant. Stop being so dramatic. I'd…um…I'd like you to go home now."

"You don't live here anymore."

"What? Oh, right. Of course."

"Come on, honey. Let's get you back to my place."

Chapter Eighteen

Cleo's stomach heaved and her heart pounded. *He was here.*

She'd seen Mitch look to the back of the church. His face had paled, then he'd glanced at her, eyes wide and mouth open. It wasn't cold feet—he'd seen Julian.

She stirred in the wooden pew, hands damp and sticking to the organza of her mint-colored dress. She could *feel* him back there.

"Quit squirming. Do you have to pee again?" Sherry whispered.

"He's here," Cleo said. She didn't have to say who.

Sherry twisted in her seat.

"Nice and subtle of you," Cleo hissed.

"Well," Sherry said, turning back, "I don't see him."

"You don't?"

"Nope."

"What a relief," Cleo said, melting into the pew. "If he were to find out I'm pregnant…"

"He'd run. Don't sweat it. Also, you're just four months along. You don't even look pregnant. I keep telling you that."

Would he run? Of course he would. Oh, he might throw some money at her—he was good at that. He'd already sent her the royalties from "Playing Cleo," which had been released as a single and was topping the charts. Guilt money. Well, she didn't need it and hadn't cashed a single check.

Luckily, she'd had the brilliant idea to write an unauthorized biography about Lou. A publisher had jumped on it, and she'd received a nice advance. She didn't want any ties to Julian at all. He'd been clear about not wanting children. All he wanted was to be a stupid rock star and do stupid rock star things like be a stupid rock star cliché. She was done with clichés.

Mitch and Addie thought she should tell him about the baby. And she'd put Addie in a horribly awkward position, asking her to keep the pregnancy a secret, but it was all for the best.

The "Wedding March" began, and everyone stood, looking toward the back of church. Addie emerged, and Cleo joined the collective gasp at the sight of her. She was breathtaking—regal, really. And her face lit up as she looked down the aisle at Mitch. Even little Emily, tossing rose petals in her princess dress and tiara, couldn't quite steal the show away from the bride.

Cleo rubbed her belly. A sonogram had confirmed she was *not* carrying a tattooed fetus with a full head of hair and a guitar strapped to its back. The baby was a girl.

Addie passed, and Cleo started to turn toward the front of the church, but something large, dark, and tattooed in the back pew caught her eye. Sheik. Her heart jumped to her throat, and she frantically scanned the crowd, looking for Julian's dark waves. It didn't make any sense for Sheik to come to Addie's wedding without Julian, but Cleo didn't see him.

Everyone began to sit, but Cleo remained standing. She

looked directly to the right of Sheik—he had to be there—and *oh, shit*. He was.

Her hand went to her mouth as she spun and plopped into the pew. He'd sheared his sexy head of hair down to a buzz, and he wore sunglasses inside the church, as if the paparazzi might appear out of nowhere. Good grief, what an ego.

"What is the matter with you?" Sherry whispered.

"Julian," she said. "He's back there."

"Motherfucking sons of whores," Sherry muttered, causing the entire pew in front of them to shift and turn.

The ceremony passed in a blur of nausea after that. When Addie and Mitch finally marched back down the aisle to the cheers and applause of the guests, Julian was gone.

•••

Julian closed his eyes and leaned his head back against the headrest as Sheik ranted.

"I can't believe we missed the flight. Last one out tonight and all because you had to sit in the church parking lot and spy on Cleo. We were supposed to get in, say hello to your sister, and get out. Now we've got to spend another night in this one-horse town."

"San Antonio isn't a one-horse town. And I don't know why you won't let me drive." Sheik was a domineering dickhead, and Julian was sick of it.

"'Cause you have a death wish and I don't."

He should deny having a death wish, but it seemed more trouble than it was worth, and besides, the jury was still out on that.

"You need to clean yourself up, man," Sheik said, with a twinge of disgust.

Julian closed his eyes. "I am clean."

"You're not using. That's not the same thing. You need to

get back into life, Princess. As long as you're like this—"

"Like what? I'm the vision of health and vitality."

"You got no goals."

"I'm in the middle of recording a solo album. I'm buying a house in Los Angeles. Those are goals."

"You don't care about any of that shit."

Actually, he did care about the solo album. But mostly, Sheik was right.

"Don't worry. Just because I've got nothing to live for doesn't mean I'm going to kill myself. I failed miserably the last time, and Addie's never stopped bitching about it."

"You got something to live for. We saw her in that church."

"Thin ice, Sheik."

Seeing Cleo had almost fucking killed him. Her shiny red hair, pretty green dress, luminous skin…it had all come together to create a bombshell. No need to wonder if she'd seen him. Subtlety had never been her forte.

She hated him, of course. There had been a few text messages he could probably have her arrested for. But he was glad she was angry. It was better than what he was. *Shattered.*

Addie hadn't told him much about how Cleo was doing. She was living in Kerrville, a small town in the Texas Hill Country, and she was dishing dirt on Lou. Julian figured he'd be next.

He fingered the small citrus vial in his pocket. A tiny whiff would give him a warm shiver. A deep inhalation could prove embarrassing.

When Cleo left Minneapolis, Julian had hit the heroin hard. But only for a few weeks. Then he'd kicked it, cold turkey.

"I tell you what," Sheik said. "We get you back to L.A., get a personal trainer or some kind of shit like that, set you out in the sun, then we come back here and get the girl."

Julian knew he looked bad—pale and skinny with the

requisite black circles beneath his eyes. He didn't care, though.

"Sheik, why don't you find a real job and stop taking advantage of my generous nature? I mean, how much am I paying you, anyway? I don't need a personal assistant."

"I'm more of a goddamned nanny. And you're not paying me enough, Princess. Not nearly enough."

"Then quit. You don't owe me anything—I'd have found the dope with or without you, okay? Stop following me around like I saved your life or something. You saved mine, for Christ's sake."

"As I was saying, we'll get some meat back on those bones and—"

"I've told you a million times. I'm no good for her. Even if I cleaned up spectacularly well, I'm not what she wants. I never was, and I never will be. That's why she left me."

"She left you because you told her to, asshole. Right after you lied and said you'd been fucking everything that moved. She wanted to help you, to get you out of there, and you should have let her. You never belonged in that band."

"That's true, I didn't. And that's the problem. She was going to get me out of there and do what? Watch me play backup for garage bands in my pathetic analog studio in between hooking myself up to electrodes so she could take me out in public every now and then? How long was that going to keep her happy?"

"Probably forever, you stupid shit. She certainly doesn't seem too happy now."

"She's fine. She's interviewing stars left and right. I saw a picture of her with Cory, did I tell you that?"

"About a million times. And that woman looks seriously forlorn," Sheik muttered.

"Did you just say forlorn? Wake me when we get to the loft. We'll need to get to the airport early, so don't let me oversleep in the morning."

Julian turned his back to Sheik and pretended to curl up in the seat for a nap.

"I'm stopping at a restaurant. Some of us still like to eat. All you do is sleep and play that fucking guitar. Sorry-ass excuse for a human being, if you ask me."

Couldn't argue with that.

...

Sneaking into the loft after the wedding had probably been a bad idea. Cleo had intended to drive straight home to Kerrville, where she lived with her brother, Ben, and his spouse, Marcus. The two had recently moved back to Texas from Portland so Ben could take a position with a small orthopedic group. They had a beautiful house with plenty of room and were begging Cleo to make it a permanent arrangement. But she'd been plugging away at the Lou Michaels biography and interviewing celebrities for an online publication. She could afford her own place. It was just a matter of finding a perfect home for her and the baby. The problem was, whenever she thought of home, she thought of the loft.

She'd cruised by for a last look—it still hadn't sold—and since she had a key, she'd let herself in to look around. Somehow that had resulted in a climb up the spiral staircase to the bedroom, where the bed still remained, along with a few of Julian's clothes. Naturally, Cleo had stripped down, thrown on one of Julian's T-shirts, and crawled into bed to torture herself with his scent. According to Addie, he was on a flight back to Los Angeles. So he'd never know and probably wouldn't care—beyond thinking it bizarre, which it was.

It was dark in the room, except for the light coming in through the window. Cleo listened to the band playing across the street at Sunset Station. The partygoers were whooping it up, despite the threatening thunderclouds. She wasn't going to get any sleep, but that was typical. Insomnia had become her normal nocturnal state.

She snuggled down into the covers and watched the shadows play across the wall. If Julian were here, he'd describe the colors of the instruments and the voices of the partiers, and she'd listen and try to imagine what he saw. Instinctively, she closed her eyes. *Purple. The bass would be purple...*

They hadn't talked since their cinematic breakup, but Cleo had heard rumors. He was clean and recording an album. She didn't know what his long-term plans were beyond selling the studio and loft. Was he doing his biofeedback? Did the vial marked *citrus* still clear the colors out of his head? A steady rain began to fall. A clap of thunder shook the loft, and Cleo pulled the comforter up under her nose.

A storm rolled in out of nowhere. Just like the first night she'd spent in the loft.

...

Julian strained his eyes to see through the downpour. "That's her car, all right," he said to Sheik. "What the bloody hell is she doing at my loft?"

"Let's go in and find out, cream puff. You won't melt in the rain."

"I'm not going in there. Let's go to a hotel."

Sheik grunted and opened his door. Julian felt for the lock on his, but wasn't fast enough, and Sheik came around and yanked it open. A wall of cold water poured in, and Sheik grabbed him by the collar and pulled him into the deluge.

"Hey, let go of me!"

"I don't think so, you scrawny mutt," Sheik yelled. "You can either walk in there on your own, or I'll carry you in over my shoulder."

Well, fuck. Julian smacked Sheik's arm away and made a

run for the door. Sheik was right beside him, and they arrived under the eave drenched and looking like drowned rats. Julian struggled to dig the keys out of his pocket, dribbling guitar picks at his feet.

Once inside, they proceeded through the darkened studio to the stairwell leading to the loft. Their shoes made squishing sounds on the wood floors. The place felt desolate and empty. Julian entered the code to the loft, then they padded up the stairwell. The sconces flickered as thunder shook the building.

"She has no right to be here," Julian muttered. "It's my place."

"Shut up, you big baby. She is here, and I'd take advantage of that if I were you."

Julian opened the door at the top of the stairs, and the lights flickered. Then they went out completely. Cleo was probably terrified. She didn't do storms.

"Stay down here, Sheik."

Julian felt his way to the spiral staircase and climbed it in the dark. He opened the bedroom door just as a flash of lightning struck, revealing a lump of trembling blankets and linens in the center of the bed. *Hello, Goldilocks.*

He walked to the side of the bed and stood there for a moment, strategizing. Should he shake her? Clear his throat? Whatever he did, she was going to freak the fuck out. He braced himself and poked her.

The blankets and linens exploded, and like a girl popping out of a cake, Cleo shot from the bed wearing one of his T-shirts. Only instead of singing, she screamed and threw punches. Charming. Predictably, one connected with his jaw.

"Jesus Christ," he said, grabbing her wrists and holding them. "It's me, calm down!"

"Julian?"

"Who else?"

"Oh my God," she said, yanking her wrists free and

smacking him one more time for good measure. "What the hell are you doing here?"

"This is my loft. What the bloody hell are *you* doing here?"

She looked so completely perfect in his bed that it seemed a silly question. She was there because she *belonged* there. He shook his head to clear it of the orange bubbles. They made it hard to think.

"I don't really know what I'm doing here." Cleo sighed and moved toward the edge of the bed. "I'll leave. I'm sorry."

The loft shook with a rumble of thunder, followed by the machine-gun rat-a-tats of hail pelting the roof. Cleo grabbed Julian's neck, burying his nose in her hair. *Tangerines.*

"I've got you," he said, wrapping his arms around her waist. "It's just a storm."

He was home, in his loft. And Cleo was in his arms. He squeezed her tightly, willing the rest of the world to disappear, until there was nothing left but the two of them.

His clothes were wet, but Cleo was the one shivering. Her red hair cascaded down her back, and he ran his fingers through it. They came to rest above the swell of her ass. He swallowed as the shirt rode up to reveal bare cheeks and a thong. And now a wet T-shirt, thanks to him. His jaw clenched as his cock grew hard. How was he ever going to let her go?

Her fingers brushed his jaw. He tensed. Did she still hate him? Her hand moved to his head, and she ran it softly across the bristly stubble of his scalp.

"Why did you shave your head?"

He swallowed, trying to find his voice. "I don't know. I guess I wanted to be different."

"Are you?" she whispered.

How could he answer that? He was better, and he was worse. Better, because he was off heroin. Worse, because he was without Cleo. "I'm sorry I made such a mess of things," he finally said.

There was a long pause before she answered. "Why? Why did you do it? Why did you have to join that band?"

Was it really not obvious? He pulled away just enough so that he could look at her. "I wanted you to love me."

Her mouth opened as if to speak. Her brows rose in question, then furrowed in confusion and something akin to anger. Finally, she said, "I did love you."

No. She just thought she did, after she'd discovered he was Julian Lazros. Only he hadn't really *been* Julian Lazros. And never would be.

"You don't understand. I don't want to be a rock star. I'm just a studio musician—and I *like* being a studio musician. You needed more than—"

"How dare you tell me what I needed?"

Was she serious? It was obvious what she needed. She loved the thrill of being around famous performers. Her romantic relationships had been with rock stars. She'd been obsessed with rock stars since childhood. And now she'd made it her fucking *job* to be with rock stars. "But—"

Cleo's lips were drawn in a tight line, and she trembled, but not from the cold. He'd obviously pissed her off. She hastily wiped a tear away. "Because of some childish obsessions in my past, you believe I'm nothing more than a *groupie*. That at my very core, I'm capable of nothing deeper than a *crush*. That I was willing to give my heart and soul to you because of a *guitar*. How could you claim to have loved me while thinking so poorly of me?"

"Cleo, even my own *mum* couldn't love me if I wasn't on a stage."

He covered his mouth with his hand. Where the fuck had that come from? It wasn't even true and…*yes, it was*. He lowered his eyes and pulled away a bit more. This was all stupid. What was he doing here?

Cleo lifted his chin. "Look at me."

He didn't want to. He knew his eyes were filled with shame and embarrassment, and the only thing worse than him knowing it would be Cleo knowing it, too.

"Why did you cheat on me?"

His eyes snapped up to hers. "*What?*"

Cleo raised an eyebrow. "You *did* cheat on me, didn't you?"

"No, of course not. I just wanted to get rid of you. For your own good, because I'm toxic to people I love."

"Oh, Julian. You don't have to be. And I need to tell you something—"

He crushed her mouth in a kiss. He simply couldn't wait any longer. He hadn't been with a woman since their breakup—hadn't even considered it—but now the pent-up longing came crashing through, and he just wanted to kiss her, love her, and *fuck* her.

Soon, their lips and tongues found familiar patterns, and Cleo made a sweet, helpless sound in her throat. She wanted him. She fucking *loved* him. Julian felt a rush of euphoria—it set him on fire and lit him up more than heroin ever could. He wanted to pounce on her like a hungry puma on a skittish rabbit.

They fell onto the bed.

He kissed her neck, and she sighed in surrender, then giggled a turquoise stream as his fingers trailed across her ribs. He dragged the tip of his tongue across her collarbone and lifted her shirt to find what he desperately craved. With his head cradled in her arms, they sank blissfully into the sanctity of him at her breast.

"You're so voluptuous," he whispered. Her breasts were warm and soft—a place he could lose himself—but there were other places to explore. His hands paused at the small curve of tummy above her pubic bone. Voluptuous, indeed.

Someone had been hitting the cookie dough ice cream.

He didn't dare comment on her sexier, fuller curves, but he loved every bit of them. The sweet swell of her belly begged for a kiss, and an inexplicable knot rose in his throat as he delivered it. Cleo squirmed, and he knew what she wanted.

Her panties slipped off easily. "Open up for me, baby," he whispered.

She did, with a soft moan the color of lime sherbet, and he went straight to the soft, sweet flesh between her legs. Her lips parted for him, full and swollen like a juicy peach.

He cupped her bottom in his hands, tilted her, and began the rhythmic sucking and licking he knew she loved. And then he touched her with the tip of his tongue, right at the perfect spot. She exploded in purple shock waves that rolled over him, caressing his skin like velvet gloves.

He covered her with his mouth, holding on with gentle suction, until the rolling waves of her ecstasy faded.

It wasn't this way with other women. He didn't know what they wanted or how to give it to them. But with Cleo, he knew what to do, as if her body were an extension of his own. With trembling lips, he kissed her one last time before laying his head to rest on her thigh, cherishing the beauty of what she'd given.

After a moment, Cleo pulled him to her. She gripped his hips, restlessly moving against him. "Let's make love. I want you."

He wanted it, too. So bad that it hurt. But he remembered a small detail. "I don't have a condom, baby. I wasn't expecting to get laid at my sister's wedding."

She didn't laugh. "I can't get pregnant. It's okay."

A thrill coursed through him. Problem solved. But then… why was she on birth control? His heart sank. She'd been with someone. But could he blame her for that? He'd left her, told her he cheated on her…

"Please," she said. "I want you." Her eyes were filled with desire. Need. And what she needed and desired was *him*. Just as he was.

Her flesh yielded instantly. He groaned with pleasure and sought a rhythm. He kept his eyes open to look at her, and she looked back, glassy-eyed with pleasure.

Since getting off heroin, everything was more intense. Sex, it turned out, was no exception. Their bodies moved together—faster and faster—creating a symphony of colors, scents, and sounds that nearly overwhelmed him. But nothing blended. He was with Cleo, and he was safe.

Every nerve came alive before the final thrust. He lingered for a moment, on the precipice, letting the tangerine droplets drizzle over him, bringing him closer to the edge than he thought possible. Then he drove in deeply, one last time, screaming until he was hoarse as white lights exploded around them. He collapsed on top of Cleo, gasping into the pillow as her flesh gently squeezed him.

He nuzzled her neck before kissing his way down to her breast. And all was right with the world.

The early morning light poured in through the stained-glass window above the bed and splashed kaleidoscope jewels across the white comforter. This was Julian's favorite time of day—it was silent and there were no other colors bouncing off the walls or careening through his head.

He yawned and stretched, then inhaled deeply. Cleo had made coffee. Maybe he'd sink back into the pillow for just a few minutes.

His eyes snapped open. *He was in the loft, and Cleo had made coffee.*

Springing up like a jack-in-the-box, he grabbed his

trousers and ran for the door, jumping into each leg between strides. By the time he hit the stairs, he was at a full run, zipping up as he went.

He burst into the room, but all he saw was a big, ugly, bald guy.

"Calm down, Princess. I'm assuming she's the one running the shower." Sheik was perched on a bar stool, a steaming mug of coffee in his hand.

Julian exhaled in relief and grabbed the stool next to Sheik.

"Well?" Sheik barked.

"Well, what?"

"From the racket I heard last night, you two are back together. You gonna cancel that offer on the L.A. house and stick around here like a man?"

"That will be up to Cleo. But that's what I'm hoping."

He was invincible. Fucking great. There was absolutely nothing standing between him and the rest of his glorious life.

He looked toward the stairs and ran a hand over his head to straighten his hair, only to discover he still had none. He wished he'd at least brushed his teeth. Sheik splashed some dubious black goo into a mug and slid it over to him.

A phone rang, and Julian jerked, spilling coffee onto the bar. He was wound a little tightly.

"This must be the redhead's," Sheik said, picking up the phone at his elbow. "She's got a text," he said, squinting, "from some guy named Marcus."

A flash of alarm went off in Julian's head, a literal red alert. "A guy named Marcus?" He yanked the phone out of Sheik's hand. *Don't look at it. It's just a text. It's just a text from a guy named Marcus.*

He looked at it.

DARLING, GLAD YOU STAYED IN SAN ANTONIO AND DIDN'T TRY TO DRIVE HOME IN THE STORM. I HAVE A BIG SURPRISE WAITING

FOR YOU. AND I DO MEAN BIG.

Followed by two obnoxious hearts and a cartoon dog holding a bouquet of roses.

What the fuck? Julian slammed the phone down.

"What is it? What's wrong?" Sheik asked.

God, he'd been so stupid. So fucking stupid thinking everything could work out. Things didn't go that way for him. He ran a hand over his head, wishing he had hair to grab. How could she do this to him? How could she tell him she loved him—wait—she'd said she *had* loved him. And she'd said she *wanted* him. Not the same thing. And she was on birth control because she had a motherfucking boyfriend named Marcus.

The red began to deepen... *Don't let it turn brown, don't let it turn brown...* He covered his eyes with his fists and gulped deep breaths.

"Oh, shit," Sheik said. "Where's your little happy vial?"

He felt Sheik digging around in his pocket. Then the scent of tangerines floated under his nose. The colors dispersed, and his head cleared. He still loved Cleo, loved her with all his heart, or the vial wouldn't work that way. But she didn't love him. She'd moved on. *It's better that she has. You're a freak, and you're no good for anybody.* "Let's go. I need out of here."

"Wait a minute. Aren't you even going to tell Cleo good-bye?"

"No." He grabbed his keys off the counter. "She's got a boyfriend, Sheik."

With Sheik barreling after him, Julian ran for the door.

Chapter Nineteen

Cleo's throat felt like sandpaper. She looked in the cup on her nightstand—empty. She sighed in disgust and rolled her eight-months-pregnant self out of bed to get some water. She'd retired early, hoping to be unconscious when *The Big Talk Show with Andy Harris* came on. Julian was scheduled to be a guest. Instead, she'd woken up in time for it to start.

Ben and Marcus wouldn't resist tuning in, even though they'd promised not to. But Cleo was not going to watch. She'd go down to the kitchen, and if the television happened to be on, after murdering Ben and Marcus, she might glance in its general direction.

She hadn't seen Julian since the night after Addie's wedding a whopping four months ago. *Wham bam.* What had she expected? He was a rock star who'd found a girl in his bed. So he'd done what rock stars did in that situation. He'd fucked her. Oh, he'd been all *wah, wah, I want you to love me*. But in the morning? He'd fled the scene.

She was glad she hadn't blabbed about the baby. She'd almost done it. What had she thought? That he'd fall to his knees, cry tears of joy, and profess a fetish for pregnant women?

Maybe she'd write an unauthorized biography about him like she was doing about Lou. She gulped her water and slammed the glass down on the counter. Okay, so she'd never do that. He was the sperm donor for her child.

She glanced at the living room, where, sure enough, the television was on. She waddled toward the sound of canned laughter, ready to rip the two tittering Benedict Arnolds apart. They jumped when she entered the room.

"What are you doing?" she asked icily.

"It was his idea," her brother said, pointing at Marcus, whose glasses and bald head reflected the glow of the television.

"Throw me under the bus, why don't you? You wanted to watch, too."

Ben ignored Marcus and held his arms open to Cleo. He was tall, dark, and handsome. With the exception of the green eyes, he didn't resemble her in the slightest. "Don't be mad," he said.

Cleo didn't take a step toward his open arms, and he lowered them. "Has he come on yet?"

"Shh," Marcus hissed. "Right now. It's time, and you're right. I want to watch." He pushed his glasses up on his nose and scooted over, giddy as a schoolgirl, patting the cushion for Cleo to sit.

She sat and propped her feet up on the coffee table.

Ben sat next to her. "You up for this?"

She didn't answer, just stared at the television, where Andy Harris smiled into the camera.

"Our next guest is in the midst of a huge musical comeback," he said to an already cheering audience. "We knew him as the teenage bad boy of Slice, and more recently as the bad boy of Dead Ringer. But now he's gone bad boy solo. Please give a warm welcome to Mr. Julian Lazros!"

The crowd cheered, and the studio band played a version of the old Slice song "Walk You Home."

Julian hated that song.

"Sweet baby Jesus," said Marcus, fanning himself as Julian walked out. "He's so hot."

Ben reached behind Cleo to thump Marcus on the back of his head.

Cleo's heart pounded away. Julian was dressed in jeans, a vintage western suit jacket with rhinestones that she knew had once belonged to Glen Campbell, and black cowboy boots. He smiled shyly at the audience and shook hands with Andy. He ran a hand through his short waves—they'd grown back—and flashed a grin at the camera before taking his seat.

Cleo wanted to touch him. Her fingers tingled with the desire to comb through his hair. What was wrong with her? Why couldn't she shake him after everything he'd put her through?

Andy delved into Julian's comeback, mentioning his work with Dead Ringer and the *Just a Little Sting* single that had brought him into the spotlight. Julian acknowledged his contribution to the album, and the next topic was the tour and how he'd brought it to a grinding halt.

"You were drawing them in like crazy," Andy said. "Then you, uh, had a little trouble?"

Andy made a ridiculous face, indicating he knew very well that Julian had more than a little trouble. Dean had done an interview with *Hot Gossip*, leaking the news of Julian's heroin relapse to the world.

"You could say that," Julian said, seemingly unaffected.

"Do you think the band will regroup?"

"I have no idea. I wish them the best of luck, though. They didn't deserve what I put them through. I'm not good in a band—it's well documented that I don't play well with others." The audience laughed at the understatement.

"Aren't you in a band now?"

"Yeah, but it's different. No manager, no major label. It's just me and my friends making music together."

"So, you're in a garage band, is that what you're saying?" Andy tapped his pencil on his useless, oversize desk.

Julian laughed. "Pretty much. We don't tour. We're not out to produce record after record. In fact, I don't know that we'll ever make another one. The other guitarist is Dave Gutierrez, also formerly of Dead Ringer."

"Dave is a new father, right?"

"Yeah, he's back in the green room with the baby right now, probably trying to breastfeed."

"He's one of those dads, huh? Does he wear the kid in a pouch and change its diapers?"

"Yeah, he does all that," Julian said with a grin.

"You'll never see me in that situation," Andy said, sticking out his chest and pounding on it. "I'm a father like my father was a father. I yell at the kids, tell them they'll never amount to anything, and hand them off to the nanny."

Julian laughed. *Asshole.*

"So, do you have any kids? I mean, that you know of?" Andy asked.

Julian shook his head. "Parenthood is not in my past, present, or future," he stated. "I look at poor Dave covered in spit-up, and Joey Ramone is cute and chubby and all that, but really, I'd rather hand my balls over on a silver platter."

"Nice," Cleo said, just as the baby gave a rib-splitting kick. The poor thing probably heard it.

"He didn't mean that," Marcus said.

Her heart, currently scrunched up against her windpipe with the rest of her organs, deflated like a sad balloon. "I'm pretty sure he did," she answered.

Meanwhile, Andy blabbed to the camera. "The new

album is called *Lazros: Mayhem in Memoriam*," he said. "And the single on it, 'Playing Cleo,' is topping the charts."

"Seventy percent of the profits go to a charity dedicated to addiction outreach programs," Julian stated. The audience applauded.

"It seems as if he's gotten his life on track," Ben said.

"Don't you dare start."

"I think it's wrong not to tell him, that's all."

"Nobody asked you. And we all just heard what he thinks about parenthood. He said it's not in his *past, present, or future*. Now shut up so Marcus can hear." Cleo wiped angrily at a tear as it slipped down her cheek.

"A lot of people say they don't want kids before they actually have them," Ben said. "You know that."

No way. She couldn't let a sliver of hope that Julian would ever want the baby feed some sort of fantasy that he'd also want *her*.

"A baby deserves a father," Ben said, just under his breath. "You'll never know what Julian wants if you don't tell him."

Cleo stared at the television.

"Before you play," Andy said, striking a serious tone, "I'd like to give you an opportunity to confirm or dispel a rather persistent rumor."

Julian stuffed his hand in his pocket, seeking his picks. He was nervous—and obviously didn't know what Andy was going to ask. Cleo's stomach, located just beneath her deflated heart, twisted into a knot. The baby had probably given it a spinning roundhouse kick. She crossed her arms and sank farther into the couch. Why should she care if Julian felt uncomfortable or made a fool out of himself?

"The rumor is—" Andy paused, intentionally building the suspense. "The rumor is that you have a very distinctive tattoo."

Relief flooded Julian's face as Andy continued. "It's

supposedly in a very delicate place." He winced.

Julian gazed at the camera through his thick lashes. "I'll confirm it." The audience cheered and catcalled.

"Good grief," Cleo said.

"It's just a tribal band," Julian continued, nonchalantly. He stood and reached for the button on his jeans. "Care to see?"

Andy waved his hands in front of Julian. "Keep your pants on, friend!"

The audience booed. When things finally settled down, Julian removed his jacket and pulled up his sleeve. "It's like the one I've got on my arm, only a wee smaller."

"Dude, that had to hurt."

"I was illegally anesthetized at the time. Really, you don't end up with ink on your dick unless you're on drugs." Julian looked into the camera. "Don't do drugs, children, or you'll end up discussing indelicate matters on late-night telly."

"And with that public service announcement, we'll go to a commercial," Andy said. The audience cheered, and the studio band began to play.

What an embarrassing spectacle. "Yeah," Cleo said to nobody in particular. "That's my baby's daddy up there talking about his penis tattoo on national television."

"Oh, my," Marcus finally said, looking at Cleo with wide owl eyes. "Have you seen it?"

Cleo patted her tummy. "Ya think?"

"That's probably not an exclusive club," Ben said. "You could Google it right now and see it for yourself. Although I'd rather you didn't."

Marcus feigned offense with a gaping mouth and a hand to his heart. Ben raised his eyebrow, in true Compton fashion, and nodded in the direction of the kitchen. "You want to put some water on to boil? Maybe make Cleo some tea?"

Marcus sniffed and left the room.

Cleo leaned her head on her brother's shoulder. "I hate that he's looking like a shallow idiot."

"He can't help it. It's the way he's made," Ben said. "And I just can't quit him."

"I'm talking about Julian, you goof."

"Oh. Well, he's not looking so bad, Cleo. It's to be expected on a show like that. He's supposed to entertain people, and people find this shit entertaining. That was all scripted, you know. You're sensitive because you love him."

Her stomach dropped—to where she didn't know, but it definitely dropped. "I do not love him. I had a crush on him the same stupid way I had a crush on Lou Michaels and a million other rock stars. It's just that he's an artistic genius, a virtuoso guitarist and violinist, and people are laughing at him."

She could acknowledge his talent without *loving him*. And if tears welled up, it was strictly hormones. She'd cried over a tractor commercial earlier.

"Cleo, you have to tell him," Ben said. "You know you do. It's his baby."

The baby drop-kicked her stomach back under her chin. Little traitor. She'd better not be choosing Team Julian along with everyone else. *Tell him, tell him, tell him.* Addie and Mitch harped on it constantly, as did her parents, and as of late, even Sherry had jumped on the bandwagon.

She'd seen Sheik last month. He'd needed to get some items she'd moved out of the studio. He'd gawked like an idiot when he saw her massive form, but he hadn't asked any questions. Surely, he'd told Julian.

"Sheik knows," she said quietly.

"What?"

"You heard me."

"Well, what did he say?" Ben asked.

"Nothing."

"Did you tell him it was Julian's?"

"I didn't tell him anything. We both acted like I wasn't as big as a house. But I wouldn't have to tell him. Who else's would it be?"

"You need to tell Julian yourself. You're leaving way too much to chance."

She couldn't bear it if Julian rejected her and the baby *to her face*. Why couldn't anybody understand that? "I don't want to talk about this anymore. He is not good daddy material in any way, shape, or form, and I'm not introducing him as a character into this fun little family film. So zip it."

They sat in uncomfortable silence, watching car commercials and listening to Marcus putter about in the kitchen.

"Would you paint my toenails? I can't reach them."

"Marcus will do it. I'm not that kind of gay."

"What did I miss?" Marcus asked, hustling back into the room with a plate of cookies and a cup of tea.

"Nothing," she said. "Look, he's back."

Julian was on guitar with the Big Talk Show Band. They played a crappy tune, but he sounded great. When the band finished the song, Julian headed to center stage, where Dave stood with his guitar. Cleo didn't recognize the drummer or bassist—they certainly weren't Dean or Gus.

Andy met Julian at the mic and held up the new album. "'Playing Cleo'?" he asked.

The crowd went nuts as Julian nodded.

"So, is there a Cleo?" Andy asked.

Julian slipped his Les Paul over his shoulder. "There certainly is," he said. Then he turned and looked directly into the camera, blew a kiss, and silently mouthed, "I love you."

Marcus gasped. "That was for you!"

How could that possibly be true? Her pulse pounded in her head. If she could reach him, she'd slap him. Then she'd kiss him. God, she hated him.

"Why don't you call him?" Ben asked. "You know, feel him out."

"No." Cleo stood up. Her heart beat in an erratic rhythm of uncertainty, and the baby gave her a kick to the kidneys. "I need to get over him, not drag myself back into his ridiculous dramas."

Ben stood, too. "So you want a clean break? Is that what you're saying? Never look back sort of thing?"

Finally. Jesus, had she gotten through to someone? "Yes, I need a clean break. No more Julian Wheaton. Or Lazros, or whatever the hell his name is. I do not want to see or hear or smell any semblance of him in my midst ever again. *Comprende?*" Even as she said it, she couldn't comprehend *ever again.*

"Which is why you're trying to buy his building and live in it? Sis, you're saying one thing and doing another. If you wait until it's too late, well, then it's too late."

"Actually, *I'm* going to buy the building," Marcus chimed in.

That was technically true. Cleo didn't want her name to appear on any of the paperwork, so Marcus would buy it, and she'd buy it from Marcus. And she'd reopen Soundbox if she could.

"That loft is no place to raise a baby," Marcus said. "*This* is a place to raise a baby. We have a nice house, a huge backyard, and good schools."

They'd moved on to favorite topic number two: Cleo's Big Residential Mistake. She breathed a sigh of relief.

• • •

Julian sunned himself in the garden of what had some-how become the band's L.A. house. He'd just finished his biofeedback session, and the small and stinky Joey Ramone Gutierrez squirmed in his lap. Dave practiced some guitar riffs on an acoustic while Marcie made dinner, so that left Julian playing nanny.

"This kid has shit in his nappy, and I'm not going to do anything about it," he yelled for the second time.

"I'll get it," Dave said. "In just a minute…"

"You've been saying that for twenty minutes," Marcie said from the patio, where she reigned over the grill. "Put down your guitar and change Joey Ramone's diaper."

Dave sighed and set the guitar in the grass, then reached for the little shit factory, who let out a scarlet wail before cramming his fist in his mouth. "Go with Daddy," Julian said. "You stink."

Dave and Marcie talked often of moving out, but Julian wasn't in any hurry for them to leave. All of Dave's money was tied up in legal battles with concert promoters and record labels, and it was a ridiculously big house, so why not share? He'd bought the place four months ago, and he still felt like a guest. But the loft had had a few offers. It would sell soon, so he'd better get used to it.

He picked up Dave's guitar and began strumming. Before he knew it, "Playing Cleo" floated out like orange feathers in the breeze.

Annoying.

He stopped, took a deep breath, and began playing something else. When it, too, turned into "Playing Cleo," he set the guitar down in defeat.

He still couldn't believe Cleo had made love to him that night in the loft. She wasn't the kind of woman who cheated on a boyfriend. So many things didn't add up. His stomach clenched, thinking about how she must have felt when she found him gone. Boyfriend or no boyfriend, after the night they'd shared, he shouldn't have left like that. He'd been an ass.

He jerked in his chair. He'd been an ass. He'd never apologized for that, and Cleo deserved an apology, no matter who she was dating. It was impulsive, but he had nothing to do that afternoon. His heart pounded as his mind hummed with possibilities. What if she wasn't even with the heart-texting jerk anymore? What if she was completely unattached and available and he was sitting here in L.A., wallowing in self-pity?

He raced through the house and began a frantic search for his keys. Thanks to Joey Ramone, there was always a frantic search going on for something. Dropping to all fours, he ran a hand beneath the couch. He pulled out three teething toys and a little book about a mouse that, judging from the teeth marks, also served as a teething toy.

The front door slammed, and he peeked over the back of the couch to see Sheik. "Hey, man. You here for dinner?"

"What else? It sure ain't the company. What are you doing down there?"

"Looking for my keys. I hope they're not in the fucking toilet." He stood and scanned the living room.

"Where are you going?"

Julian yanked up a couch cushion. "Aha!" He stuffed his keys in his pocket. "I'm going to the airport," he said, heading for the door. "Hold down the fort."

"The airport? Why?"

"I'm going to see Cleo."

Sheik's eyes almost popped out of his head. He looked stupidly alarmed. "Listen, you need to let her go, remember? We talked about this already."

Julian kept walking. "That was before," he said. "I've changed my mind."

By the time he got to his car, he was trailed by Sheik, Dave, Marcie, and Joey Ramone.

"Listen to me," Sheik said, as Julian climbed into the El Camino. "She's got a boyfriend, remember? Leave her alone."

Julian looked at Sheik towering over his car. "First you told me to leave her alone because she didn't need a junkie. Then you told me to stop being a junkie and go get her—pestered me for months about it—and now you're telling me to leave her alone again. What gives?"

"Julian, please don't go. You'll regret it."

He raised his eyebrows. First of all, Sheik never begged anyone to do anything. Second, he never said please. And third, he'd called him Julian, instead of You Pansy-Assed Motherfucker. Something was up, but Julian didn't care. He had to try.

He rolled down the window. Sheik bent over and stuck his huge face through it, but before he could say anything, Marcie pulled him out of the way.

"Go, Julian," she said.

Julian sat in the rental car in front of the Guenther House in San Antonio's King William Historic District. It was a gorgeous summer day, and under different circumstances, he might be tempted to stroll the manicured grounds that sloped down to the San Antonio River. But he couldn't afford to take his eyes off the restaurant's entrance. His stomach churned and growled like the worst case of stage fright.

There was a good chance Cleo would show. It was the first Sunday of September. He checked the time—almost ten. If she was coming, she'd be here soon.

Car after car pulled into the small lot, expelling women with gift bags. Someone was having a baby shower.

Just as the parking lot's security guard seemed to be taking a special interest in him, Cleo's red car zipped into a space not too far away.

His heart pounded. He clutched the wheel with one hand and grabbed the door handle with the other…then he froze. His brain had yet to choose between staying or going.

Cleo got out of her car and plopped her purse on top of the roof. Her curly hair had been straightened and shone in the morning sun. Her pink cheeks glowed beneath a pair of big, sexy sunglasses. Every cell in Julian's body reacted to her magnetic pull, and he opened his door reflexively. He began to stand as she came around the front of her Honda and… *what the hell?* He hurriedly folded himself back into the rental. *She's pregnant?*

He shook his head and rubbed his eyes. Was he mistaken? He crouched low as she passed in front of his car. *Bloody hell.* She wore a tight blue dress that clung to her very round belly.

Silent hysteria took over—a kaleidoscope of colors that, miraculously, didn't blend together—as he remembered the night in the loft with no condom. But that had been four months ago. And Cleo looked much farther along than that. Julian leaned forward and touched his forehead to the steering wheel. It all made sense now. The rounder figure, the fuller breasts.

Nausea rolled through him. Indecisiveness tormented his gut. Should he run after her? Of course not. She hadn't gotten herself pregnant. He slammed his fist into the steering wheel. *Marcus.* He wished he knew what the fucker looked like so he could enjoy the fantasy of smashing his face in.

Julian started his car and drove off in a daze. Thanks to the biofeedback and mind-training program, the colors stayed where they belonged. He was falling apart, but at least he could see where he was going. He finally stopped in front of a seedy bar on the wrong side of town—one he knew by reputation only. All he had to do was walk through the door, and he'd have everything he needed to dull the pain within minutes.

He sat in the car for over an hour. Eventually, the door to the bar opened, and a guy poked his head out to stare him down. Parking in front of a drug dealer's lair, then sitting there watching it, was not a smart thing to do. He pulled his shit together and left.

Minutes later, he was in front of the loft. He wanted to go inside—he wanted to go *home*—but it wasn't his. Not for long, anyway. There'd recently been an offer. And just in time, too, because it had already attracted a homeless guy to its back steps. The man looked up at the sound of the car. Not a homeless guy. Julian's head fell back against the headrest as Sheik walked to the car.

"Yo," Sheik said, climbing in and staring straight ahead. "Did you see her?"

"You knew."

"Yeah. She met me when you sent me down here for those things from the studio. It was hard to miss."

"Nice to see where your allegiance lies."

"I didn't want you to be hurt. That's for real."

No air moved in the car, but Julian didn't have the energy to roll down a window. He would never recover from this.

As if Sheik read his mind, he said, "I believe in you, Julian. You'll get through this."

"I don't see how I can."

"You're not gonna go find a dealer, are you?" Sheik asked.

"No."

"Or head to the nearest liquor store?"

"No."

"You gonna cry like a girl?"

Julian just swallowed.

"Well, hell. Get it over with, then."

Chapter Twenty

A decent offer had finally been made on the loft. Julian was awash in relief—he was ready to close this chapter of his life—but he was also overwhelmed with an almost debilitating feeling of sadness. He was changing a lightbulb atop a tall, teetering ladder in the L.A. house when Sheik came to tell him about the closing date.

"Look at those pretty-boy legs shaking." Sheik laughed, watching Julian balance.

"Shut up, man. I hate this fucking house. How are we supposed to change out these lightbulbs all the way up here?"

"You're in Los Angeles, asshole. You're supposed to hire someone to change your lightbulbs."

"Whatever. Do I have to fly to San Antonio for the closing?" He finished screwing in the lightbulb and sat on the top of the ladder.

"I don't think so," Sheik answered.

"Who's buying it?"

Sheik looked at the paperwork. "Some guy named Marcus Porter."

The guy buying his loft had the same first name as Cleo's boyfriend? A small tingle worked its way up Julian's spine. "Where's he from?"

"Some place called Kerrville."

"No way." Julian tried to stand, then quickly sat back down, with Sheik holding onto the ladder and looking at him like he was insane. "Are you kidding me? That's where Cleo lives."

Exercising a little more caution, he delicately came down the ladder steps and ripped the paper out of Sheik's hands.

"What?" Sheik asked. "What's wrong with you now?"

"Cleo lives in Kerrville with a guy named Marcus, you idiot."

"Stop calling me an *idjit*. And I'm sure there's more than one Marcus in that town."

Julian skimmed the documents. Nowhere on them did it say, *This is Cleo's stupid motherfucking boyfriend*. But it was too much of a coincidence. Cleo loved the loft, and the guy was buying it for her.

There was no need for him to fly to San Antonio and hand over the keys to his loft personally. But he felt he had to. Maybe seeing Cleo and knowing she was happy with this Marcus fellow was necessary, like going to a funeral in order to believe someone had really died. Although a funeral would probably be less painful.

• • •

Two weeks later, Julian stared at the parking lot through the loft's dirty window. His stomach felt like it might rebel against the coffee he'd tried to drink earlier. Waiting was the worst.

He heard Sheik and the Realtor at the top of the stairs. Sheik was making small talk about property values, but with his gravelly voice, it sounded threatening. The Realtor was probably scared to death.

"Mr. Wheaton?" the real estate agent said, entering the room. "I've left some papers back at the office. Would you please tell the buyers I'll be back as soon as I can? Then we'll head to the bank."

"Sure," Julian said. One less person to witness his humiliation.

As soon as the Realtor left, a black Prius pulled in beneath the pecan tree. The driver's side door opened, and a long arm emerged, followed by a leg in khaki trousers. Both were attached to a tall man with dark hair. He was trim and fit, kind of buff, actually, and extremely handsome in a wholesome all-American way. Julian's blood boiled, but instead of red, it was green. *Jealous.*

Cleo climbed out of the car and held her flyaway hair out of her face as she looked up at the loft. She wore cream-colored leggings and a chocolate-brown sweater, which she filled out beautifully. Full breasts, round hips, and a fertility goddess belly. His pulse sped up, and it took everything he had not to fly down the stairs and take her in his arms. But she wasn't his. Marcus closed the door and leaned over, planting a kiss on her forehead. Then they shared a long, leisurely hug that made Julian's stomach heave.

"Sheik, go down and let them in, okay?"

Where should he stand? In the living room? The kitchen? Should he greet them by opening the door at the top of the stairs? Since he was frozen where he stood, the dilemma was pointless. He stared helplessly at the door.

Sheik entered first, followed by Marcus, who stopped cold when he saw Julian. Cleo came around and gasped. She actually swayed on her feet, and Julian reached for her. But Marcus grabbed her first and held on tightly.

"We were told you wouldn't be here," Cleo finally said.

"Surprise!" Julian said. He tried to smile, but it felt

like a grimace. "And congratulations on the loft and…er, everything." He glanced at her stomach. "I mean, wow. *Wow.* You're pregnant, right? Unless you've swallowed a basketball. Which is extremely unlikely."

Sheik startled him with a slow clap. "Good job there, blabbermouth."

Cleo rolled her eyes at Sheik, then went back to frowning at Julian. Marcus merely looked Julian over with interest, like he was a curious specimen in a laboratory. Julian looked back, hoping he appeared more relaxed than he felt. Marcus smirked—*smug bastard*—and his intensely green eyes sparkled with amusement.

"I'll, uh, I'll be back in a minute," Cleo said. Then she waddled around the room, as if looking for a place to sit. There was no furniture downstairs.

"There's a folding chair in the closet upstairs," Julian said. "Let me go grab it for you."

Cleo looked at the stairs as if they led to a secret escape hatch. "No, it's all right. I'll go have a look around up there… I'll find it."

"I don't think that's a good idea," Julian said. "I mean, can you even make it up the stairs?"

Cleo raised an eyebrow slowly. "I can manage. I promise the baby won't just fall out as I lumber up."

Julian knew that. But he was worried about her. She looked ready to explode. And he didn't know how she balanced with the…protrusion. "I just don't want you to hurt yourself," he said, feebly.

"I'll go with her," Sheik said.

"What?" Julian didn't want to be left alone with Marcus. He glanced at Cleo as she lifted her foot for the first step. If she fell from the top, she'd roll brilliantly back down the stairs like a hedgehog. "Okay. Yes, please go with her."

"Good idea," said Marcus. There was something

unnervingly familiar about him. He clasped his hands behind his back and rolled onto the balls of his feet, then back onto his heels. He raised an eyebrow.

Julian thrust his hand out, forcing the fucker into a shake. "Marcus, I'm Julian Wheaton. It's very nice to meet you. And, again, congratulations."

Marcus gave his hand a firm squeeze. "Nice to meet you, too. I've heard a lot about you. And I'm not Marcus," he said casually. "I'm Ben."

Julian stood there like an idiot, with his mouth open, holding the guy's hand.

So, first there had been a fucking Marcus, and now there was a fucking Ben? Cleo, it seemed, had quite possibly been doing a lot of fucking, and Julian didn't like it. He wrenched his hand away and jammed it in his pocket.

Ben laughed. "She said you do that when you get nervous."

Cleo had been talking about him to this jerk? He finally understood the term "stabbed in the back." Because that's what he felt like. A knife, right between the shoulder blades. Before he could respond, things became more confusing when a gigantic stuffed panda burst into the room. Beneath it was a pair of hairy human legs.

"That's Marcus," Ben said, pointing at the bear. "Marcus, this is Julian."

The bear slowly slid down, revealing a bald head and a pair of curious eyes that stared through the thick lenses of hipster glasses. The panda dropped with a thud.

Marcus said hello and indicated the bear was for Cleo. "Well, for the baby, I mean. It's kind of a welcome-home bear." Marcus threw out his arms and struck a ridiculous pose.

"Forgive me," Julian said, "but I don't know who to congratulate. I mean…"

The four of them—Julian, Marcus, Ben, and the panda— wore identical wide-eyed expressions of confusion. Finally,

Julian said, "So, Marcus, you're buying the loft. Do you have any questions for me? It can be moody. The plumbing is shit. There are two water heaters, but only one works. I guess Cleo can fill you in on all that."

"I'm not going to live here," said Marcus. He pushed his glasses higher on his nose. "I thought maybe you guys had talked and you knew. Cleo's buying the loft. She's doing it under my name because she didn't want…" Marcus's voice petered out, and his unfinished sentence hung in the air.

Ben cleared his throat. "Because she didn't want you to know she was buying it."

None of this made a bit of sense. "I'm confused, so I'm going to be blunt, okay?" Julian said. "Which of you is with Cleo?"

"We both are," Marcus said.

It wasn't often that Julian felt like a prude, but holy shit, really?

Ben smirked and raised that eyebrow again. Julian's hand clenched into a fist. "Let's see if I can clear things up for you, Julian. I'm Cleo's brother."

Julian froze—mentally and physically—with his mouth hanging open. It took a few seconds for his mental train to switch tracks. He knew Cleo had a brother named Ben, but they'd never met. He chuckled with relief. "Oh, man, I didn't connect the dots. I mean, I did connect the dots, but it was a weird and twisted picture."

Ben didn't laugh. Just raised his eyebrow again. How had he not recognized that eyebrow lift? "I thought you lived in Portland. Nice to meet you. Again. I mean, I already met you, but I didn't know who you were. I do now. So, hi. Shit. Sorry, I'm talking stupid."

"It's okay," said Marcus. "He's used to it."

Julian looked curiously at Marcus, who was suspiciously splotchy faced and grinning like a love-struck teenager.

Oh.

"And Marcus is with me," Ben said, looking Julian straight in the eye, with a tight-lipped mouth. He was a bit more possessive than was necessary. Something was still unexplained, though.

"Then who's the baby's father?" Julian asked.

Ben came closer. "All right, I'm going to say this real slow, so see if you can keep up."

Julian didn't like his tone.

"The baby is due in two weeks," he continued. "Do the math." Then he grabbed Marcus and headed for the door.

Marcus turned. "The gestation period for a baby is nine months."

"I'm sure he knows that."

"He seems kind of slow," Marcus whispered, as the door closed behind them.

Julian did the math. Cleo had gotten pregnant while he was still on tour, but they'd been together then, so that made no sense. No sense at all, unless she'd cheated on him, and he immediately dismissed that idea. But then another popped into his head.

Minneapolis.

The room spun. He needed something to lean against, but he didn't think he could make it to the nearest wall. He leaned over and put his hands on his thighs as a solid hand clamped down on his shoulder.

"Settle down."

Julian turned his head and looked at Sheik. "I think that baby might be mine," he whispered. Then a thought struck him, and he straightened. "Did you know?"

"Nah, man. Are you serious? I thought she had a boyfriend, just like you. Figured it was his."

Julian reached into his pocket and pulled out the citrus vial.

Sheik smacked the vial out of his hand. "The real thing is upstairs, stupid."

"I need to get a grip. Give that back."

"Listen, stud muffin, the time to get a grip is over. There's a woman up there who doesn't think you've got the balls to climb the stairs, much less be a father."

"Well, she's wrong," Julian said. He headed for the staircase but then stopped. "She wasn't even going to tell me. No way she's going to let me back into her life."

Sheik nodded at the stairs. "No doubt you got some explainin' to do. You best get started. And don't worry about the real estate lady. I'll get rid of her. I have a feeling this loft is about to become community property."

Julian threw the bedroom door open. Cleo sat on the folding chair, so pale and vulnerable it almost broke his heart. He went straight to her.

"This is my baby?"

She nodded.

Emotions he didn't even have a name for poured through him, along with every fucking color on the spectrum. He focused on scarlet red. It probably wasn't the smartest thing to do, but it felt good. "I am so angry with you, Cleo. I've never been this angry with anyone in my life."

Cleo shot up out of the chair. Wow. Julian wouldn't have bet she could do that. It defied the laws of physics. Her small hands clenched into fists, and her face went bright red—the same shade that filled his head—and she said, "It's not like I did this to myself."

"I know that," Julian said in exasperation. "But you didn't fucking tell me. I wasn't going to know about my own baby? And shit, Big Red, you were going to do this by yourself?" He reached for her, but she took a step back. His heart plummeted. She was so close, and he couldn't even touch her. What if she really wasn't going to let him back in? He swallowed the lump in his throat. *What about his child?*

Words like "visitation" flashed through his mind, sickening his stomach.

"I'm doing fine by myself," Cleo said. "I don't need you."

He didn't doubt that for a minute. "You don't want me? Fine. But you are not keeping that baby away from me, do you understand?"

The anger on Cleo's face shattered like a mask. It looked as if she might smile—or cry—or something. She seemed confused. Had he not been clear? Should he spell it out?

"That is my child—"

"You don't even want children!" Cleo blurted. "And you certainly don't want me."

He almost laughed at the absurdity. "I never thought I'd be in a position to even have children. How would I know what I wanted in that regard? As for wanting you…" He couldn't even finish the sentence. Every muscle and bone in his body ached with the need to touch her.

"You can't even stick around for the morning after, much less potty training and homework."

What was it Sheik had said? *You have some explainin' to do.*

His heart broke as her lower lip trembled. "Why did you leave?" she whispered. "I was going to tell you, but you left."

"Because I'm an idiot." He'd assumed the worst of her even though she'd never given him any reason to do so. "I saw the text from Marcus," he stuttered. "I thought you had a boyfriend."

Cleo looked at the ceiling, holding her hands up, as if appealing to a higher power for patience. "What text?"

"The morning after we were together. You were in the shower, and Marcus sent you a text about having a big surprise for you when you got home. I drew the most logical conclusion." He didn't say that last bit with much conviction.

Cleo stopped looking to the heavens and glared at him, instead. He wished she'd go back to praying. "Logical conclusion? *Logical conclusion?* Surely, there's more to this than you getting pissed off about a swing set?"

"He said it was really big," Julian said. "And he put hearts after it—and a dog holding flowers." He lowered his eyes to the floor and fixated on a spot.

Cleo began a hysterical fit of laughter. Julian looked up. She was bent over double, hands across her belly. His head filled with orange bubbles, and his nose filled with the scent of tangerines. He stared blankly, then laughter bubbled unexpectedly from his own lips.

When Cleo heard it, she stopped laughing. Julian's laughter petered out, replaced by the slow burn of unease. Cleo took a step toward him, and even though he wanted to flinch, he held out his arms instead. Which was a stupid move, because it opened him up to Cleo's usual method of attack. She reached out and twisted his nipple. Hard.

"Ow," he howled, rubbing his chest. "Why do you fucking do that?"

"After everything I was willing to go through with you? You left me over a text?"

When she said it like that, it sounded even worse than it was, and it was pretty bad to begin with. But it wasn't true. "I left because I was scared," he whispered.

"Of what?" Cleo's brows were no longer bunched in a scowl.

"Of hearing that it was too late. That you loved someone else. Because"—he swallowed—"how could you ever love me?"

Cleo moved closer. Warmth radiated from her skin. How long could he keep his hands off her? He *needed* to touch her, to be lost in her.

She stroked his face with a single finger, trailing it down

his cheek. "I've never loved anybody but you."

Was it possible? He searched her eyes, and what he saw blew him away. There was no hiding from Cleo. She looked into him—*deeply* into him—and saw everything. He wasn't hiding behind a guitar or shrouded in fame. It was just him. Real. Flawed. Terrified.

And she loved him.

"Can you ever forgive me?"

She didn't answer with words but put her arms around his waist and squeezed. Her round belly was solid and warm. How could something so new and unexpected feel so perfectly right?

He ran his hands up under her sweater, feeling her taut skin. "Does it hurt?" he whispered.

"Sometimes it's uncomfortable. But mostly, I love it." She smiled, and his eyes stung with tears. He dropped to his knees and left warm, breathy kisses across her skin, then pulled her waistband down so he could feel her entire round belly.

"This must be shocking," she said. "I'm huge and, um, striped. Those are stretch marks."

"You're gorgeous. And I have a huge hard-on." He rubbed small circles on her tummy.

She laughed. "You're starting up some activity down there."

"Good," he said. He definitely wanted to start up some activity down there.

"No, I mean here."

Cleo placed his hand firmly on a spot on the underside of her belly. He felt a tiny poke through her skin. Gasping in delight, he quickly kissed the spot.

"Poke her. She'll poke back."

She? He hadn't even thought to wonder about that. "It's a girl?"

Cleo nodded. He firmly pushed on a little bump beneath

his palm, and it pushed back. Enthralled, he played that game for a while, chasing the flutters with his lips and fingers. Then he stopped and traced the dark line that ran down the center of Cleo's tummy. "I want to see you. All of you."

Cleo looked alarmed. "Oh, no, no, no, Julian. Not now. Not here." She glanced at the window. "And not in direct sunlight."

"The more light the better," he said, rising. He kissed her and lifted her sweater, pulling it over her head. She gave little resistance, so he unclasped her bra, releasing her breasts. They were big, ripe, and heavy with large, dark nipples.

"Pregnant boobs," she said apologetically. "This is what they look like."

"God, they're perfect," he whispered.

He brushed a red nipple with his fingertip, watched it pucker, then leaned over and covered it with his mouth. He groaned with pleasure and suckled gently, wondering what breast milk tasted like. He had every intention of finding out.

"Unless you want me to have the baby right now, you should stop that," Cleo rasped.

He looked up at her. "Really?"

"Nipple stimulation can bring on contractions at this stage."

Holy shit. He didn't want to do that. In fact, he broke out in a light sweat just thinking about it. "Okay, well, there are other things I'd like to play with. Lie down, Big Red. Time for the full pregnant lady exam."

"Julian!" she said. Her cheeks flamed red.

He sat on the floor and gently pulled her down next to him. "A quick look, love," he said.

"There's not even a blanket in here," she protested, modestly covering her breasts with her arms. Julian took his T-shirt off and laid it on the ground.

"Sorry, but this will have to do." He knew she was going

to do it; he could tell by the look on her face. It was the same embarrassed yet excited expression she'd worn on the band bus and in the back of the limo after the concert. It was her *I'm about to do something naughty* face, and he adored it. He helped her lie down.

"Lift up," he said firmly. She raised her hips, and he slipped her pants off. Then he gently pushed her knees apart.

"You're a goddess," he said. And he began to worship.

Chapter Twenty-One

The magazine, open on the bed, failed to hold Cleo's attention. She'd been tucked into bed early by Marcus and Julian, but she was restless. The nesting instinct had kicked in with vigor, and she wanted to get back into the loft. But it was too late in the pregnancy to begin a move.

She'd been achy all day, and it was difficult to find a comfortable position in bed. Her feet were swollen lumps, and when she tried to lean forward to stuff a pillow under them, she was met with the obstacle of her tummy.

Should she text Julian? He was strumming her dad's old Martin guitar on the porch. She hated to give him another scare. Every time she moved, he freaked out and ran to her side, pretty much terrified.

She poked her tummy, hoping the baby would kick. There hadn't been much movement all day. But the doctor had said this would happen as she approached her due date, a mere three days away. She needed Julian.

Bracing for the overreaction, she texted him. She heard the chime of his phone through the window and then laughed as she heard him bolt into the house.

He burst through the door about three seconds later. "Are you okay?"

"I'm fine. But would you lie down with me?"

Julian's face melted in relief. He pulled his T-shirt over his head. "You scared me."

The sight of his naked, tattooed chest stirred up some wicked delight. But she curbed her enthusiasm. She didn't know if it was the visit to the obstetrician's office he'd suffered through earlier in the week, or if it was her Shamu-esque appearance, but Julian had done a good job of keeping it in his pants.

He sat on the bed as a Braxton-Hicks contraction hit her. Perfectly normal—the doctor said they were small contractions preparing the uterus for labor. They didn't alarm her, but dang, they were starting to hurt. Today had been one gut-squeezing Braxton-Hicks after another.

Julian snuggled up close and spooned, putting his hand on her belly. "Shit, Cleo, it's so hard."

She placed her hand on his. "They're kind of beginning to squeeze the air out of me."

"Are you sure you're not in labor? You've been down with these all day."

Marcus breezed officiously past their door. "It's just a Braxton-Hicks contraction," he called out in his nurse voice. "No need to worry ourselves."

Julian jumped off the bed and kicked the door shut. Marcus and his infinite spouting of pregnancy facts hadn't played well with him. He was definitely at a disadvantage in that area, as Marcus was a registered nurse.

"Want to mess around?" she asked, rolling over and grunting like a sea lion.

"Nah. I'm really tired," Julian said.

"That's too bad. After the baby comes, there will be no

sex for at least six weeks. That's what the doctor said." It was mean but, well, a girl had to do what a girl had to do.

"Really?" he said. "Six weeks?"

"Or longer."

Julian groaned and plopped back down on the bed. "I want to, but the doctor said it could bring on labor. And I'm not ready."

She hoisted herself into a sitting position. "I don't feel ready, either. But we're about to become parents, anyway. And I've missed you so much." She blinked to keep the tears from forming. He was right here in front of her, and yet she couldn't have him.

She ran her fingers over his bare chest and kissed a tattoo. "I've missed this." She kissed another one. "And this…" She slipped her tongue under a nipple ring.

"Shit, I love it when you do that," he said.

So she did it some more.

"You, um…want me to get up and lock the door to keep Nurse Nellie out?" he asked.

Before she could say yes, a Braxton-Hicks squeezed the air out of her. She produced a strangled moan, which Julian obviously misinterpreted. He jumped up and locked the door, saying, "The last thing we want is a three-way with Marcus."

Cleo curled up in a ball as the fake contraction did a good imitation of a real one. Either that or she had an elephant sitting on her stomach.

Julian sprinted back to the bed. "Don't hold your breath, baby. Let it pass." He extended a hand toward her.

"I swear to God, if you touch me, I'll kill you," she wheezed. And she meant it. She couldn't stand anything touching her. In fact, she needed to get her pajama bottoms off. They felt like a tourniquet. She struggled with them, then stopped to pull her socks off, because her feet were hot. She had to have some air. *Dang!* She couldn't breathe again.

"I don't know how we're supposed to do this if I can't touch you," Julian said.

"Are you stupid?" Cleo said, once she got her breath back. "You think we're going to have *sex*? While my pants are trying to kill me?"

She blew a tuft of hair out of her face, an act that took everything she had, and a look of pure terror crept into Julian's eyes. *That's right, Guitar Boy. Be afraid. Be very afraid.*

"Never mind," he said quickly. "You know, about the sex."

He swallowed loudly, and the sound of his fear made her happy. In fact, if she could breathe, she'd unleash a wicked laugh, maybe even levitate. *She was either possessed or…she was in labor.*

"Cleo?"

"Are you still talking?" she wheezed. "Here, help me get my pants off. I'm hot. Are you hot? Where's Marcus?"

She managed to get her pants down to her knees and one arm out of her shirt, while Julian did nothing but stare at her, even though she'd clearly asked for assistance.

"Oh, God." She was hit by a contraction so strong all she could do was grunt.

"Marcus," Julian screamed. "Get up here!"

Marcus's footsteps pounded up the stairs, followed by a loud smack as he hit the locked door.

"Oops," Julian said, bounding to the door.

"What are you doing to her?" Marcus asked, peering into the room.

"Nothing," said Julian. "She's ripping off her clothes and acting crazy."

The contraction dissipated. Muscle by muscle, she relaxed and began breathing. "Whew," she said. "That one was bad. Get me a nightie, would you, Marcus? My pajamas are constricting."

"Is she in labor?" Julian asked.

Marcus, digging through Cleo's drawers, said, "Sometimes the Braxton-Hicks contractions are strong. She hasn't lost her mucus plug." He sighed as if Julian were the most exasperating person in the world and gently tossed a nightgown to Cleo.

"What the fuck is a mucus plug?"

"I'm pretty sure I lost it this morning," Cleo said, noting the disgusted look on Julian's face.

"Why didn't you call me in to look at it?" Marcus asked.

Julian paled. "Why the hell would you want to look at it? What's wrong with you? And if the plug's fallen out, what's keeping the baby in?"

"Good lord, it's not like a bathtub plug. The baby doesn't just swoosh out," Marcus said.

Cleo was a mess. "Help me, would you?" Her head was somehow stuck in the nightgown. Through the gauzy fabric, she saw Marcus push Julian aside to get to her.

"Here, sweetie," he said. "Let me help you with that."

Julian grabbed Marcus. "Get away from my practically naked girlfriend."

Cleo struggled to pull her head through.

"I'm a nurse," Marcus said indignantly.

"So?"

"I'm a gay nurse!"

Cleo finally pulled the gown over her head, but it was through the armhole. And it had taken such effort. "Leave him alone, Julian. And would you please help me?"

Julian looked at her and laughed, easing the tension. "Let's get the right parts in the right holes, shall we?"

"I love it when you talk dirty."

"I guess I'll just leave you two alone." Marcus sniffed. He turned to leave, but when he did, Cleo had the air knocked out of her again.

"Ooh," she gasped.

Marcus ran to her side. "Are you all right?"

Again with the elephant. She couldn't speak.

Julian sure was pale. The contraction eased, and Cleo said, "I need my socks back on. My feet are cold. And my teeth are chattering."

"Honey," said Marcus, "maybe I should check and see if you're dilated?"

"Bloody hell, Marcus," Julian said. "Put that finger away."

Cleo gasped, then inhaled. *Oh, yeah, that's how that works.* She was in labor. Where was her brother?

"Cleo, you're making me a little nervous." Julian said. "Because these are coming close together, and we're a good drive from a hospital."

"I'm making myself a little nervous," she said.

"I think we should start timing," Marcus suggested.

"So, you think she's in labor? For real?" Julian's voice was high and shrill.

"Yes, I'm in labor, you idiots," she said. "And here comes another one…oh, no…"

Marcus started timing. Cleo tried to breathe through the contraction. And she needed the freaking light turned off. It hurt her eyes. She grunted, and oh, it felt great.

"Are you pushing?" Julian asked. "Because I don't think you should be, and you look like you are."

"Shut up," she grunted.

A door slammed downstairs. "That's Ben," Julian said. "Thank God. We've got a doctor in the house now." He shot out of the room. In a few seconds, he returned with Ben and Sheik.

"How often?" Ben asked.

"This one came on in under a minute," Marcus said. "But it's the only one we've timed, and her water hasn't broken."

"I'm going to take a look, sis."

"Should I call the doctor and get her things in the car?" Marcus asked.

"Yeah, that would probably be a good idea," said Ben, lifting her nightgown. Sheik turned and rushed after Marcus.

The pain had lessened considerably, and Cleo felt drowsy.

Ben peeked under the gown. "With the next contraction, give me a tiny push and let's see what happens."

Cleo grunted, and a gush of warm fluid rushed out. "And there's the water breaking," Ben said.

A thudding sound shook the second story of the house.

"And there's Sheik fainting." Marcus sighed as he came back into the room. "Is there no limit to the number of morons we can fit in this house?"

"See to him," said Ben.

"What? We don't have time for that. We need to get Cleo to the hospital."

"Actually," said Ben, "that's the one thing we don't have time for."

...

Julian couldn't believe what was happening. Cleo was in active labor, the pushing stage. Ben was calmly between her legs, like this was all no big deal, and Marcus had done a hurdle jump over what was apparently Sheik's prone body blocking the doorway. "Call an ambulance," Julian yelled.

"Bring me my bag," shouted Ben.

"Do you think the ambulance will make it in time?" Julian asked.

"Nope. But it'll be here for after, and we'll get them both to the hospital to be checked out."

Shit. He had to hold it together for Cleo. She was red in the face, panting and crying. And he was sitting here panic-stricken, which was exactly what he'd been afraid would happen when push came to shove, so to speak.

Blue, green, and gray—*oh, no, not gray*—swirled around

in his peripheral vision. Cleo's moans and sobs didn't provide any hint of the orange her voice usually carried. There was nothing to focus on but his own fear. He closed his eyes, but the swirling colors—they looked like a fucking hurricane— became even more brilliant in his mind. He shook his head, trying to clear it. A tremor began to move through him, the precursor to the buzzing that would soon take over and render him useless. Biofeedback could get him through concerts, but apparently not through childbirth.

Someone called his name. It was Ben.

Julian opened his eyes. Ben stared at him, brows furrowed and lips drawn into a straight line.

"I said get behind her. Help her scoot to the edge of the bed."

Julian did as he was asked, and Cleo leaned against him, her hair tickling his nose. He inhaled. *Tangerines. Thank God.* The swirling colors separated and floated away.

Cleo turned her pretty face up to his. "Are you okay?" she asked.

That moment of sweetness nearly killed him. "I'm fine," he said. "Let's have a baby."

He knelt in the spot where her water had broken, dampening the knees of his jeans. Ben asked him to reach forward and bring up Cleo's knees, but she shook her head. "No. Not like that."

Marcus came in with Ben's bag. "Yikes," he said. "Don't make her lie on her back with her legs up. That's what got her into this mess."

"Jesus, Marc." Ben sighed.

"Well," he said, "she needs to be on all fours or squatting. That's what they said in the hippie childbirth classes."

"Here comes one," Cleo whined.

"Get her up," Marcus snapped.

Marcus was the one who'd been there for Cleo these many

months. He was the one who attended childbirth classes. Not Julian. "Marcus?" he said. "Should you be doing this?"

"Don't be silly. Just do what I say," Marcus said.

With Marcus instructing him, Julian helped Cleo into a squatting position and wrapped his arms across her chest.

"Makes more sense, doesn't it, Mr. Fancy-Pants Know-It-All Bone Doctor?" Marcus said to Ben.

"That's Dr. Fancy-Pants," Ben said. "And yes, it makes more sense. Push with the next contraction, Cleo. You're doing great."

A contraction came, and Cleo bore down. A rush of power surged through them both as she pressed against him. When it ebbed, she melted into his arms, and he hummed softly, until her body tensed with the next contraction.

"I love you," he said in her ear. He squeezed his eyes shut and prayed, holding her through another hard push before she collapsed against him.

"I'm so proud of you right now I could burst," he whispered.

"I'm the one who's bursting." Cleo panted. Then she was back up for another push.

"Whoa! That was good, Cleo," Ben said when it was over. "This is not going to take long at all."

Julian patted Cleo's damp forehead with the corner of the sheet. Maybe the next contraction wouldn't catch her too soon. Marcus pulled out a sterile, waterproof pad and placed it gently beneath her. Then he placed another pad on the floor next to Ben and meticulously laid out instruments. None of them looked good.

"Don't worry," Marcus said. "Ben's only going to need the scissors to cut the cord." He also placed a couple of towels on the bed, although it seemed a bit late for that. Mostly, Marcus seemed to be trying to busy himself.

"Marcus," Julian choked out.

"Hmm?"

He wanted to apologize for being a jealous shit, but his throat was swollen shut. Marcus smiled briefly, nodded his head, and said, "Okay, Cleo, another push."

"What's going on in there?" Sheik yelled from the hallway.

"We're having a baby," Ben hollered, laughing like a kid. Then he got serious. "Okay, Cleo, lean back a minute. Julian, change places with Marcus so you can see your daughter being born."

Julian moved next to Ben, peeked at the action, and felt light-headed. He inhaled deeply, searching for the scent of tangerines. He found it, and a sense of peace poured over him like a warm waterfall.

"I think this one's gonna do it," Ben said. "Push!"

Cleo pushed. And the top of their daughter's head emerged before slipping back into the birth canal. "Cleo," Julian said. "Red hair, love. She has red hair! One more push, okay?"

Cleo sobbed and laughed when the next contraction came. Seconds later, Julian stared into his daughter's scrunched-up face. She opened her eyes and quickly shut them, her tiny eyebrows knitting together in a familiar way that sent an arrow straight to Julian's heart. Then she opened her mouth and belted out an impressive first wail. *Sweet pipes.*

"Cleo," Julian said. "She's like the sun."

Epilogue

Cleo gazed at the dreaming baby in her arms. The teakettle whistled downstairs, and the little one furrowed her tiny brows.

"There, there, it's just a teakettle," she soothed. "Get used to it. It's all Daddy knows to do at times like these." The baby produced a milky grin, melting Cleo's heart.

Padded footsteps squeaked their way up the stairs, accompanied by the sounds of a clattering tea tray. Cleo looked up to see Julian pausing at the door, gazing at her as if she were the most beautiful creature in the world instead of a postpartum wreck of a woman.

"Want some tea, love?" he asked. "I have anise and fennel…milk production and all that."

"If I produce any more milk, I'll be able to feed a third-world country."

Julian smiled and set the tea tray down on the cedar chest that overflowed with diapers and baby blankets.

"Time to baby-gaze," he said, climbing onto the bed. He snuggled against Cleo's breast, where the baby nursed, and leaned in to kiss a tiny cheek. He sniffed the baby's fuzzy head, and Cleo felt him shiver.

"The ocean?" she asked.

Julian nodded and smiled in a state of dreamy intoxication. The only sounds were the baby's suckling and the soft buzzing of an amp in the corner.

A downstairs door slammed, and Julian flinched. "Mommy," a high-pitched voice screamed. "Uncle Sheik has to put five dollars in the F-word jar!"

Julian stood and faced the door—a shield between the baby and what was about to burst into the room. Goldie was first, with Ruby hot on her heels. With no trouble at all, they dodged their father and jumped onto the bed.

"Don't wake the baby," Goldie screamed at her sister. The baby began to wail. "I told you. I told you you'd wake the baby. Mommy, Ruby woke the baby."

Cleo didn't bother pointing out that two-year-old Ruby, with her thumb firmly embedded in her mouth, hadn't produced a peep. Goldie, on the other hand, was a five-year-old human foghorn.

Ruby pulled her thumb out of her mouth. "My kiss bebe Asher?"

"It's Azure, Ruby," Goldie screamed, standing on the bed. "Like zha zha zha *boom*." She swung her hips and plopped down hard, bouncing the baby in Cleo's arms. "It means blue. Because she cries blue sounds, right, Daddy? Ruby keeps saying Asher but that's wrong. She still has baby talk."

Ruby leaned over and planted a sloppy kiss on the crying baby's head, while Goldie continued her running monologue. "Azure means blue, and Ruby means red, and Goldie means yellow, but not because I have yellow hair, right, Daddy? I have red hair. And Ruby has brown hair. Isn't that funny, Daddy? We don't have the right hair, any of us. Because you named us for our colors that only you can see."

"That's right, angel," Julian said. "Ruby cried jewels, and you were like the rays of the sun." He tousled her hair affectionately. "And now you're like glass in a blender," he murmured, just loudly enough for Cleo to hear.

"And Azure sounds blue and smells like the ocean," Goldie continued. "But to me she just smells like poop."

"Who wants to take a nap?" Julian asked, and Cleo recognized the tone of forced enthusiasm.

"Not me, Daddy," Goldie said. "Because I'm not even a little bit sleepy."

"Of course you're not." Julian sighed. "But Ruby is. And Mummy is. And you need to be rested for when Joey Ramone comes over later."

"I'm gonna marry Joey Ramone," said Goldie, decidedly.

"You most definitely are not," said Julian.

"Am, too. I like how he plays guitar."

"Oh, dear," Cleo said.

"He sucks," Julian grumbled.

"*Julian.* Good grief, he's six."

"He still sucks," Julian replied as everyone settled in. Goldie snuggled up against Cleo, and Ruby settled into her favorite spot, the crook of Julian's arm. Without dislodging her, he reached over and grabbed the old Martin acoustic.

He strummed a chord, and Cleo waited for the usual naptime set, "Ruby Red Kisses" and "Golden Was the Day." But something new floated out instead. Something dreamy and sweet and...*blue.*

"What's this?" she asked.

"'Azure Skies, Midnight Cries,'" Julian whispered. "It's a work in progress."

"I like it."

"I was thinking about dusting off the Les Paul later. I think you might like that better," he said.

"Really?" She raised an eyebrow. "What did you have in

mind, Guitar Boy?"

"The usual," he said, running his fingers over the strings and switching seamlessly to "Playing Cleo."

Her heart skipped a beat at the melody.

"We'll start out with something nice and slow," Julian said. "Then we'll work our way up to something a little faster... and *dirtier*." He grinned, causing her skipping heart to thud instead.

"And?" she asked. "Then what?"

"Then," Julian purred, "we'll stop in the middle when the baby cries."

Cleo laughed. That was their song, all right. And she couldn't wait to play it again.

Acknowledgments

I'd like to say I wrote this book all by myself, but that's hardly the case. Many people contributed to what finally became *Color Me Crazy,* and some of them are even still speaking to me.

First and foremost, thank you to Jessica Snyder for saving this story from the publisher's slush pile. In my mind, she emerged from the dark depths covered in slush (whatever that is) and waving the manuscript victoriously above her head. Sometimes, depending on my mood, she's wearing a cape. And thank you to Kerri-Leigh Grady for passing the *Crazy* torch to Karen Grove, who fanned the flame into an inferno. That might be an exaggeration. She turned this story into a novel while treating me like a delicate flower. (She also saved Julian from plaid pants.)

Thanks to my pep squad for their amazing stamina. Author Amy Bearce is the best friend a girl could have. She was the first person to read the original manuscript, and she read every version after, giving each one the same earnest consideration. Most importantly, she was always ready for an emergency trip to the coffee shop. Author Alison Bliss never got tired of waving her Texas-size pompoms (all the way from Indiana). Actually, she probably got really tired of it, but was too polite to say so. Author Samantha Bohrman kept me laughing and from quitting, usually by telling me to shut up and quit, already. I hate that I fell for reverse psychology.

I'd also like to note the contributions and support of Jeannine Hanscom, Claudia Corrozza, Roselle Kaes, Kasey Corbit, and Louise Gornall—awesome ladies, each and every one.

A big high five goes to my street team for promoting this book and keeping me saturated in BuzzFeed quizzes and pictures of Alex Minsky.

And last, but not least, I need to thank my sisterwives: Ann, Cat, Dee, Heidi, Julie, Pamela, Sara, and especially Cynthia, who tried her hardest to stick around.

About the Author

Carol Pavliska began her writing career as a family humor columnist and blogger, a pursuit she abandoned when her children grew old enough to realize they were being exploited. To save them from further embarrassment, she turned to writing fiction. Her debut novel is a steamy contemporary romance so, unfortunately, the children are still embarrassed.

Carol and her husband, both diehard Red Hot Chili Peppers fans, raise their vegan brood of mortified offspring on a cattle ranch in south Texas. No lie.

To learn more about Carol Pavliska and keep up with her latest news, go to carolpavliskabooks.com or connect with her on social media. She'd love to hear from you!

***Check out more titles from Entangled Select
Contemporary…***

THREE SIMPLE WORDS
a *Kingston Ale House* novel by A. J. Pine

Blogger and bookstore owner Annie Denning believes in happily ever after. She just finds it in romance novels rather than in real life. When best-selling author Wes Hartley, whose female readers find him as hot as his hero, offers to do a signing at her bookstore, she's ecstatic—even if she hated his book. But Wes has been struggling with words that just won't come, and as the deadline for book two rapidly approaches, he fears he may be a one-book wonder. Until he connects with Annie and discovers his muse; but Annie wants her own happily ever after, and Wes just doesn't believe those exist.

12 STEPS TO MR. RIGHT
a novel by Cindi Madsen

Savannah Gamble might be a dating coach, but that doesn't mean she's got her own love life figured out. When her former best friend, Lincoln Wells—the same guy who broke her heart after an unforgettable one-night stand—reenters her life, all her rules point to the fact he's not her Mr. Right and she should stay far, far away. But rules can't always compete with chemistry.

Bound to the Bounty Hunter
a *Bound* novel by Hayson Manning

Harlan Franco lives by his own rules: be in control, be detached, and never mix business with pleasure. These rules are tested when he's being paid to secretly guard the sexy, unpredictable, pain in the butt, Sophie Callaghan—a woman determined to stay away from him. Sophie is on a mission. What she doesn't need is hot, broody, and controlling Harlan barging into her life. After a night where both live out their darkest desires, Sophie tries to fight the explosive chemistry between them. But the ties that bind her heart to this bounty hunter are tight and tangled.

Stolen Away
a *Hearts of Montana* novel by Jennie Marts

Cash Walker is a tough-as-nails cowboy, except when it comes to the shy woman who shows up at his farm with a goat riding shotgun in her passenger seat. Recently divorced from an abusive husband, Emma Frank has come home to Broken Falls, Montana where she strikes up a friendship with a handsome cowboy who helps her find her own courage. There's a darkness in Cash's past that's kept him from ever letting anyone get too close, but he can't seem to stay away from Emma.